GRACE IN THE SHADOWS

Book One in the Journey of Grace Series

KARON RUIZ

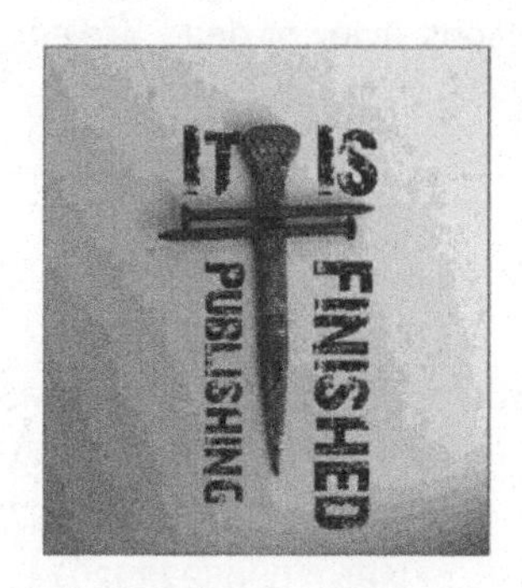

GRACE IN THE SHADOWS

Cover Design by Jake Grotelueschen
Editing by Carrie Padgett
Author Photo by Bethany Paige
Formatting by Karon Ruiz
www.karonruiz.com

3rd Kindle Book Edition created April, 2022
3rd Print Edition created April, 2022

Karon Ruiz

Printed in the United States of America

Paperback Second Printing: May 2020
It Is Finished Publishing
ISBN-13: 978-0692892978
ISBN-10: 0692892974

Thank You Jesus, for teaching me that *what is bruised and bent You will not break; You will not blow out a smoldering candle. Isaiah 42:3*. Not only did You come to heal the broken-hearted, You came to heal the broken.

Until we emerge from the shadows of self-performance, we will never understand the light of scandalous grace.

Jesus invites us all ....

"Are you tired? Worn out? Burned out on religion? Come to me. Get away with me and you'll recover your life. I'll show you how to take a real rest. Walk with me and work with me—watch how I do it. Learn the unforced rhythms of grace. I won't lay anything heavy or ill-fitting on you. Keep company with me and you'll learn to live freely and lightly." Matthew 11:28-30
The Message Bible

Map of McCormick, Arizona

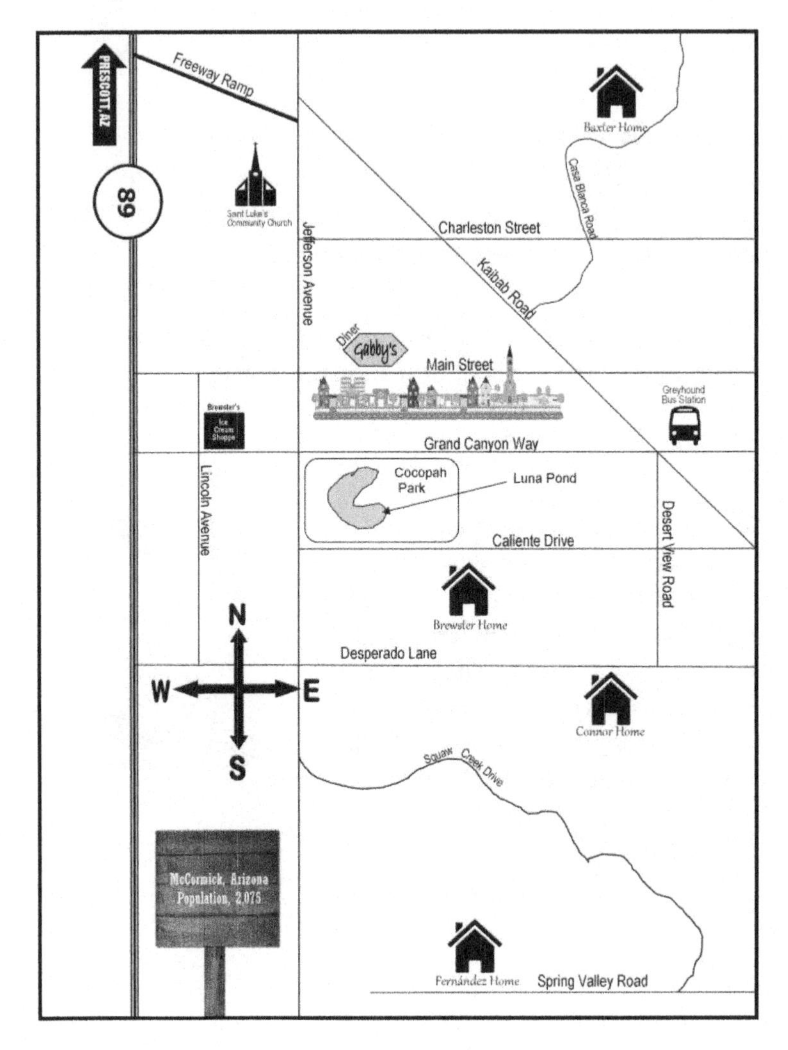

Chapter One

THE WHITE LINE OF POWDER sang its siren song and Dalton Baxter surrendered. He closed his eyes, anticipating the heady rush, the gush of confidence, the elation. He licked his lips and picked up his straw. Crimson light passed through a high window staining his trembling hands. He steadied his fingers and sucked the crushed Oxy through his nose. Gritty particles warmed his sinuses, a welcome contrast to the ice crystals he'd inhaled that horrible day on Agassiz Mountain.

He leaned back in his chair, waiting for the expected relief to arrive, welcome as a warm quilt on a snowy day. Not that McCormick, in Arizona's high desert, saw much snow. He spun his chair to look out the window at the dusty parking lot. Make that welcome as walking into an air-conditioned room on an August afternoon.

Dalton jumped at the sound of knocking metal. The refrigeration unit above his office came on, confronting the morning heat with a motor that shimmied and shook so hard, Dalton thought it might fall off the roof.

His brow furrowed. The machine's days were numbered. He had to do something about it.

And he would. Soon.

He turned back to his desk. A Power Point presentation glowered from his monitor creating colored patterns across the smooth cherry-wood top. He watched the reflections and counted the seconds until the tension in his neck and shoulders eased.

Finally.

Euphoria clutched him in its usual grip and surreal contentment quieted an inner ache. Moments ticked by. The drug performed its miracle. He sat up and straightened his shoulders.

Dalton wiped powder residue from his desk, licked stray specks from his fingers, placed his grinder and pliers inside a metal lock box. He grabbed the prescription bottle, counted six pills remaining, then refastened the lid.

He slammed down the bottle, scowled and rubbed his temples. He needed more.

This afternoon.

The shadow of the job interview loomed over him. Four days. In four days, people would expect him to have his act together. To be a functioning member of society. He shoved a stack of books off the desk, sending them flying against the wall.

What's wrong with me? Why don't I think ahead?

Meds. He needed his meds. He couldn't pull off such a critical meeting without his meds. Why had he waited so long?

The doorknob rattled. "Dalton?" Sammy's sweet, concerned voice.

"Just a—a minute." He winced as he stood, the familiar pain below his kneecap, though now a whisper, lanced up his leg. The bottle of painkillers—not enough, not nearly enough for the interview—sat on the corner of his desk, mocking him, waiting to be filled. He grabbed the worn Bible next to his printer, opened it and tented it over the box.

Somewhere above him, God was surely tsk-tsking the irony of covering a sin with the Word.

He unlocked the door, kept it mostly shut and wedged his face through the narrow opening. Sammy took a step back. Suspicion darkened her eyes.

"Sorry ..." He softened his voice. "I'm not finished."

"It's nearly eight-thirty." Her voiced clipped. She placed her hands on her hips. "You asked me to remind you."

"Already?" His eyes pleaded. "Can you cover for me?"

Sammy hesitated as if she wanted to say something. Instead she turned and walked away, the angry clacking of her heels keeping time with her trim hips as they swished under a swirly blue dress.

Dalton closed the door and collapsed into his swivel chair, then turned over the Bible. A streak of yellow caught his eye and the highlighted words seemed to leap from the onion skin.

I cried out to God for help; I cried out to God to hear me ...

The verse kindled so many memories. Mom had a Scripture reference for everything from a skinned knee to a so-called friend's treachery to Dad's temper.

When I was in distress, I sought the Lord ...

He refused to read anymore but her voice wound through his thoughts. He glanced at her old photo on the credenza. "I'm doing the best I can." He gently closed her favorite book and traced the name imprinted in the black leather cover.

Sarah Grace Baxter

He missed her.

He slid the Bible to the end of his desk, then jammed the metal box behind some files in his cabinet. He slammed the drawer shut, knocking over the cane in the corner. He picked it up, the burnished maple glistened in his hands. Keeping the staff close reminded him how far he'd come since the accident. If he could just get off the meds—he leaned the cane against the wall—everything would go back to normal.

Dalton returned to the Power Point slide on the monitor. At last, his elusive focus arrived.

He'd have to hurry.

An expectant congregation would arrive soon and lately his preaching seemed to model his life. Scattered. Insipid. Uninspiring.

That would change today. It had to.

"The fifty bucks I shelled out for this sermon better work," he muttered. Today's message must be a game-changer. His future depended on it.

ജ

Sunday, 8:25 a.m.
Saint Luke's Community Church
McCormick, Arizona

Outside the building, Samantha Baxter rested against hundred-year-old clapboard, staring at the graveled parking area. A handful of Sunday school teacher's cars populated the almost vacant lot.

A hot breeze teased her face, gifting miniscule relief from the morning humidity. Not fooled by the cloudless blue sky, she knew a storm brewed behind the horizon. In the high desert, things were not often what they seemed. She'd grown up in Arizona and could sense a monsoon well in advance.

She wiped her brow, dragged in a ragged breath, and tried to steady her emotions.

Impending temperamental weather lost its hold on her attention. Something else overshadowed the thoughts spiraling through her mind.

Dalton's odd behavior.

His mysterious trips out of town.

The frequent withdrawals from their savings account.

His lack-luster performance in the pulpit these past few months.

The sum of her fears equaled trouble. She fingered a strip of paint threatening to peel away from the clapboard.

Was there another woman?

He always seemed to have an excuse. "Got to get that water cooler in the annex fixed," he told her when she asked about a five-hundred dollar withdrawal. "Don't worry. Once the council approves it, I'll get reimbursed." She had yet to see either their bank balance head north or a noticeable improvement in the fountain's flow. It still dribbled like a third-world shower.

She'd been concerned when he'd abandoned the old hymns for contemporary music. "We need to modernize," Dalton said one morning after the congregation had left. He paced through the empty nave, waving a hymnal in her face, then lobbing it to the floor like a discarded shoe.

"Why don't you mix in a few modern praise songs?" she asked. "Keep some hymns for the older folks."

Dalton shook his head. "We need a complete makeover. These downer hymns about God's wrath aren't working anymore."

Sammy glanced at a bank of ceiling-high stained glass windows, populated with intricate craftsmanship, each depicting one of the twelve apostles. The lead-encased ancients guarded the sanctuary, scrutinizing the modern world. Examining their stoic faces etched into glass, she grimaced. Did it have to be all or nothing? Tradition mattered, too. Why couldn't her husband compromise? For the sake of the seniors.

"I'll talk to the musicians. We'll switch things up next week, make them into a praise team," he said. "An upbeat worship service will improve attendance."

At least this time, Dalton listened to reason. The seniors were the more faithful givers. She pointed out they couldn't afford to offend them. Dalton had agreed and decided hymns could be sung if combined with an upbeat tempo.

Samantha brushed away from paint flecks and stared at Dalton's precious BMW that sparkled in the parking lot. Its glossy black hood shimmered under the sun, bright and flashy, defiant. Two years ago he'd driven it home, and switched his clerical garb to Brooks Brothers suits. She'd rescued his white collars from a Phoenix seminary thrift store, bringing them home, stuffing them behind rows of socks in her dresser. Maybe Dalton had grown tired of the collar, a beacon for the down and out who would swarm him like bees to sweet honey.

The sports car, with its ding-less doors and shark-mouth grill, scowled under narrowed-eyed halo lights, mocking McCormick's mediocrity.

Perhaps people were leaving Saint Luke's because Dalton had changed? In ways besides leaving his collar in the drawer? Lately indifference seemed his Sunday morning MO. This was the fourth Sunday in a row he'd left her alone to greet arrivals. She could have tolerated that if it hadn't been for the locked door. How dare he bar her from entering the office they shared?

Samantha ground her teeth, balling fists at her sides, wanting to hit the side of the building. Before another sun set over her small town of McCormick, she'd learn his secrets.

Even if they broke her heart.

ᘓᘐ

Dalton's anxiety mounted as time ticked by. He'd glanced at another slide of *Why Tithing Will Change Your Life*, and pushed away from his desk with a frustrated jab. The whole thing had been a waste of money—money he could use right now. If it wasn't inspiring him, how would it loosen the wallets of the pew sitters?

He drummed his fingers and scanned the books on his desk, desperate for a fresh idea. Sammy's photo caught his attention. He'd taken it a few years ago when the whole family had gone to the Grand Canyon. She looked beautiful, straddling an old mule as they descended the gorge. Gordy and Grace had laughed uproariously at the tour guide's jokes about his "stubborn ass."

Those were happier days ... before his accident.

If looks could kill, today hers would have done him in. The scowl on her face earlier reminded him of her testy question a few weeks ago. It seemed laden with accusation. "Why are you constantly leaving town?"

"A minister's job is demanding, honey. You know that."

Her eyes filled with hurt. "So demanding that you disappear for hours—sometimes all day—without telling me where you're going or why?"

He made up some story but wasn't sure she believed him. Remorse at his lies filled him, but he didn't have a choice, not if he wanted any peace. Not if they were ever going to get out of this hick town and back to the big time. Besides, Sammy had a high pain threshold and he didn't. She wouldn't understand why he still needed his medicine. No one did. Especially his doctor.

He picked up the prescription bottle. His name, faded, the r in Baxter, almost gone. Yet the words, OxyContin 40mg, still distinct. Near the bottom, large bold letters seemed to shout:

NO REFILLS AFTER MARCH 1

March had come and gone as had Dr. Donaldson's refills.

"Your knee's mended, Dalton," his orthopedic surgeon told him. "You might have a little discomfort. Take Tylenol. And Dalton ... my advice ... no more back country ski trips."

He couldn't recall much more of the doctor's yammering that day. Only that his pleas for more drugs were refused. So he'd found someone to give him pills, not lectures.

He tossed the prescription container in a bottom drawer behind some office supplies. Once he got out of this dreary town, he'd learn to cope without them. Then he'd give Sammy the life she deserved.

CHAPTER TWO

8:45 a.m.

SAMANTHA FACED THE NAVE, GRIPPING the back of a pew, coated with generations of varnish. She stared at Dalton's closed door. She'd excused his mood swings and erratic behavior because of his skiing accident last Christmas. But no more. The lump crowding her throat affirmed that something much greater than a torn-up knee possessed her husband.

But what? Or worse, who?

The view of the cavernous church refused to console her. Its mahogany vaulted ceiling felt like a protective shelter on most mornings. But today it, along with the creamy glows from natural lighting, failed to assuage. Shudders and hollow sounds from the creaking building magnified an inner ache.

She stared longingly at the large stained glass window above the baptismal. Jesus carried a baby lamb over His shoulders.

"Help me," she prayed.

She bit her lip and dabbed the corners of her eyes with a tissue from her pocket.

Get it together, Samantha. God's people are coming.

She headed toward the ladies' room, aging planks groaning with each step. Inside, she stared at her face in a walled mirror behind a bank of sinks. She frowned at her reflection, then wiped away a smudge of mascara. She reapplied lipstick, stared for a minute at herself in the mirror, then left the bathroom. A musty scent drifted by as Samantha waited in the vestibule. A familiar odor from oiled wood and aging fabric failed to lift her mood.

Is Dalton in trouble, Lord?

Her hands trembled. She caught her breath.

Is he cheating?

ꙮ

Dalton grumbled at the Power Point. He tapped his fingers. The drug-induced rush and excitement of the past few minutes waned when he clicked through the slides.

Whatever made him buy this? The word, "boring" should have been listed in the online description.

The benefits of tithing and why it would change your life seemed uninspiring and definitely overdone. He needed something fresh to grab their attention. Persuading congregants to give a little extra had always been easy but today ... today he couldn't take any chances.

He rocked in his chair, staring at the monitor until the images blurred and his breathing evened. When his chin touched his chest, he shook himself awake, then sipped ice water.

Hearing a kick drum, anxiety saturated his body. The worship team arrived. He was running out of time. Thirty minutes had been shaved to fifteen.

Bold lettering from a book on his shelf caught his eye. *A Happy Life Is Possible.* Written by a mega-pastor from Alabama. Dalton pulled it down and studied the glossy photo on the back cover. Joshua Johnson, trim-fitted in black Calvin Klein, leaned against a desk holding a pen like an unlit cigarette. His wide toothy grin reminded Dalton of the used car salesman who'd sold him his BMW two years ago. Dalton sniffed the crisp, clean pages. If only he could deliver motivating messages like this man.

He skimmed the first chapter. Hmm. He tapped his lips. It could work. If he did this right, even the clock-watchers would sit up and take notice. A dynamic sermon meant more money in the collection plates. More money in the plates meant more available for borrowing. Enough for a couple of months of medication would be all that he would need for a new start in Phoenix. Then he could get off the pills and redirect his journey. The Associate Pastor position at New Generations Church might be the bottom rung, but at least he'd be climbing, earning a decent wage.

The only thing he'd need for the new position would be his passion. The unrelenting fervor that had once driven him to preach had gotten buried, unreachable, deep within himself like his body, entombed by last winter's avalanche. He'd dug himself out of death then, beating all the odds. Surely, he could reclaim his zeal. If not, why even be a pastor?

What if my calling's gone? A chill prickled his skin and he rubbed his arms. He glanced up at the ceiling tiles.

Have You taken it, Lord?

He didn't wait for an answer, but pushed the thought away. Once he got settled in Phoenix, things would be different.

"Someday, I'll be someone," he whispered to the smooth white pages. He lingered, inhaling the smell of fresh ink, hoping to gain the book's potent power of persuasion. He set the book next to his computer and staccato-struck keys, pin-pointing the major tips from the first paragraphs. He hit the print button as confidence swirled. He straightened his shoulders and smiled. This would work.

He retrieved a small yellow notepad from his desk and flipped to the back where he kept a running total of the money he'd borrowed. He recorded today's date and drew a black line. He'd fill in the amount once the offering was counted.

A noise from the roof sounded and Dalton cringed. Was the swamp cooler finally giving up its ghost? He lifted his face and begged. "Hang in there, will ya?" At least until church is over.

Spread out near a stack of theology books, a utility bill caught his eye, screaming a reminder with threatening red ink. Stamped at the top, the words FINAL NOTICE, niggled at his gut. If he didn't pay it soon, there'd be a lot more problems than a non-working cooling unit to deal with. He shoved it aside and returned to the notebook. He wiped his brow and studied his chicken-scratch, tallying the money he borrowed. The power company's approaching deadline dictated he loan himself the bare minimum this time. Parishioners shouldn't have to suffer in the pews during a heat wave. Not if he could help it.

If they'd come through with an extra large offering, his troubles would be over.

ഇഗ

Two mammoth front doors split open with a loud clunk. Hot air assaulted Samantha's face. She put on the best pastor's-wife-expression she could manage along with a welcoming smile. Helen and Emmet Crawford, looped at the elbows, stood in the entrance of Saint Luke's Community Church.

"Good morning." Samantha offered a cheerful tone, looking at the old man.

Carved furrows bracketed his mouth, his eyes arched, conveying concern. "We'd like to speak with the pastor. Where is he?"

"He's been delayed. Is there something I can help you with?"

"It's that boy your husband sent to help with yard work ... Tyler ... uh ... what's his last name, Mother?"

"Benson," Helen said.

"Some of my tools ain't there," the old man continued.

Helen leaned close and lowered her voice to a whisper. "I told Emmet that we should talk to the pastor first. He wants to call the police."

"And I will if we can't handle this here," Mr. Crawford said.

Samantha breathed deep. Amanda Benson held a volunteer position as the council's treasurer. She'd be horrified if she found out her teenage son had been stealing. "You're certain it was Tyler?" she asked.

Emmet's brow knitted and his mouth twisted downward. "Some things went missin' a week ago. After he left yesterday, my weed eater wasn't there."

Samantha nodded. "We can meet with Pastor Dalton after the service if you're able to stay." She'd have to put off her demands for answers for now. This took priority.

The couple agreed and walked with purpose toward their favorite pew.

Another thing to deal with. Since Dalton's accident and therapy she carried so much of the load around here. He'd better help with this.

Each time the doors opened, attendees hurried by, offering hasty hellos before rushing to the coolness of the nave. A few of the regulars stopped to shake her hand.

Hunched with her cane, the Widow Snyder asked, "How are you dear?" Her smiling grey eyes matched her hair.

"I'm fine, Winnie. I didn't expect to see you this morning. Are you feeling better?"

"That flu bug passed, thanks to your husband's prayer."

"Pastor Dalton went to see you?" Samantha's voice cracked as she gripped the woman's hand.

"He stopped by yesterday." Winnie's eyes twinkled. "He changed two light bulbs and loaded my water bottle for me. He's a true shepherd."

Samantha's wondered as she watched Winnie walk toward a pew in the sanctuary. Dalton helped with household chores for old ladies, yet hid from her in his office? He visited shut-ins, yet took unexplained trips out of town, always vague about where he went? The man she'd loved for almost two decades cared for others, yet the stranger she lived with seemed sneaky and aloof. What's going on?

The mystery must be solved. She couldn't go around accusing Dalton of something nefarious. This might be a big misunderstanding on her part.

Minutes ticked by as people passed, scurrying to their seats. Samantha turned to go inside when she heard a familiar voice.

"Sammy, Daw ... ling ... how are you?"

She pivoted to see Deidra Storm enter the vestibule, doors clanging shut behind her. Deidra opened her arms for a hug. A Louis Vuitton handbag dangled at her side.

"Good morning, Deidra." Samantha returned the embrace while pungent perfume drifted around her nose. "I'm good ... and you?"

"Mah ...velous ... Daw ... ling." Deidra's thin smile stretched between plastic cheeks. A silky black shirt, its top two buttons undone, clung to her like fresh paint.

"Drake and I must have you and Dalton over for dinner soon. Now promise me, hon. I won't take no for an answer." Before Samantha could speak, Deidra swiveled and forged toward the front, leopard-print pants hugging her hips.

Close to nine o'clock, the trickle of congregants stopped. Samantha examined the sanctuary. Half empty today. The heat? Yes, it must be the heat. It had to be.

She started toward her usual seat but the doors parted again. Filling the threshold with her buxom self, Laney Fernández puffed heavy breaths. Their eyes met, and a wide grin drew across Laney's face, lighting the anteroom with infectious joy.

"Goodness me. Thought I was late." The older woman hunched over, gasping. "I ran all the way from the Sunday school room." She reached for Samantha's hand.

"Martin's holding a seat for you." Samantha pointed to the other seniors near the platform.

Laney glanced over, then back at her. "I'll stay for worship, but they need an extra hand in the kid's room."

"Really? Is Gordy there? I told him to wait with Grace until the teachers arrived."

"He left when Bev showed up. She's alone today so I told her I'd come back. I don't mind helping."

"Thank you, Laney. Grace loves your Bible stories."

"I adore those children. Their starry-eyed questions make me feel young again." She tossed Samantha an affectionate wink. "Guess I should be getting to my seat." She took a couple of steps then turned around, examining the empty vestibule. "You're greeting by yourself again? Is Dalton's leg bothering him?"

"He's fine." Samantha regretted her sour tone and hurried to add, "He can be a perfectionist when it comes to his sermon prep."

"How about I help you next Sunday? That way that man of yours can take his time and not feel pressured to get out here. *Híjole* ... he's barely back on his feet."

Samantha swallowed hard, her eyes welled.

"Oh, *mija*! Did I say something?"

"No, I'm okay ..." Samantha wiped an escaping tear. "Just tense. That's all."

Laney leaned near, traces of her breath brushed Samantha's ear. "That's an understatement, dear," she said. "You've carried much of the work around here for months now. And with Dalton's knee surgery, things must be piling up."

"You're right, Laney." It seemed easier to go with the older woman's take on her situation. "And my teen volunteers are still at camp."

Laney swept a hand to her cheek. "That says it all. You need help, don't you? I can come tomorrow."

"Tomorrow? What about your job?"

"Got laid off. Have lots of time on my hands."

"Lost your job?" Samantha asked. "I'm sorry to hear that. Will you and Martin be okay?" Samantha gripped Laney's elbow.

"We'll survive. I'd planned to retire in the next couple of years anyway."

"You worked at the hospital for so long, how can they do that?"

"Budget cuts." Laney shrugged. "Have to admit at first my anger got the best of me. But then I realized this might be a good thing. These past few years long hours on my feet pushed me to a breaking point. Complained about it constantly. You can ask Marty."

"I can understand that, Laney. You work very hard."

Laney scanned the sanctuary then turned to Samantha. "God must have something else for me to do. Looks like He's already leading me." The smile that began at the corners of Laney's mouth, brightened as her cheeks lifted into deep laugh lines, six decades of youth and poise shone through her smile.

"I appreciate it. If you get here around nine, there'll be plenty to do." Laney had no idea what she'd just volunteered for. Samantha's to-do list stretched from assembling crafts for the upcoming Vacation Bible School to cleaning out the leftover salad dressings and condiments in the dining hall's refrigerator to painting the nursery walls. Laney's assessment that everything had fallen on Samantha's shoulders since Dalton's accident was more accurate than she knew.

"I'll work all day if you let me to take you to lunch at Gabby's," Laney said.

"Can't let you do that. It'll be my treat." Samantha said. "Bless you, Laney."

Laney swayed side to side down the center aisle dancing to whatever song her soul heard while the a team of musicians woke up their instruments, filling the nave with off-key tones. Samantha watched and smiled. Maybe meeting Laney for lunch was a good idea. She sure could use a friend.

Seeing Dalton's empty chair on the platform deposited fresh angst in her chest. It had been weeks since she felt welcome in his life.

She shuddered. "Lord, I need to know the truth," she prayed again. "Even if he's having an ..." She didn't want to voice it, but did. "... an affair."

How could a man who prayed for the sick and offered them assistance be a man who would betray his wife and family? It didn't seem possible.

She fumed. That's what she got for bending over backwards, helping him during his recovery?

She dabbed a final tear, drank in a long breath, then smoothed her dress. With her head held high, she formed a smile, then joined the sea of familiar faces for another Sunday morning charade.

CHAPTER THREE

8:55 a.m.

THANKFULLY, THE ROOF'S TWO AGING coolers continued to rumble, earning their keep. Sunlight streamed through Dalton's window and baked cars in the gravel lot. He could hear people settling inside, waiting for the service to begin.

He cracked open his office door and scanned the sanctuary. Most of the senior citizens were in their usual spots up front. They were big givers and today he desperately needed a large offering. He ran his eyes around the room, not seeing the one man he wanted to meet with today.

The Widow Snyder noticed him and waved. Her eyes sparkled over a broad smile. He returned a wave and pulled into the shadows, then shut the door. She sure looked a lot better than she did yesterday. Had God answered his prayer? When he got to his desk, he rifled through some papers until he found it.

The pawn ticket.

Dalton located a red Sharpie then retrieved the notepad from the bottom of his drawer. He wrote in large letters at the top of the page,

Redeem kettle

Winifred Snyder would have given away anything if it meant helping the church with financial needs. Dalton grimaced, remembering her trusting smile as she rested on her sofa. Tinges of guilt penetrated his euphoric mood. Had needing his medicine so desperately brought him to this?

Dalton walked to a small mirror hanging near a bookcase. His arms and legs tingled while flecks of white powder clung to his nose. He brushed them into his hand and licked his skin clean, then re-wiped his desk a second time.

He tapped his phone and texted Matt Connor.

MEET @ 1PM 2DAY SAME PLACE

He stared at the screen, willing Matt to respond. But the phone remained silent, so he switched it to vibrate and slipped it in his pocket, grabbed his sermon notes, and tucked the book under his arm. He exited the small office and collided with his favorite chair on the platform.

Deep in the nave, the dawn's chill lingered, encouraging congregants to fill up the front rows near the kneeler's bench. Dalton pasted on a smile and nodded at familiar faces. His eyes connected with Deidra Storm and she winked.

Sheesh. That's all he needed. Drake must be out of town again.

The musicians collected their instruments and lead guitarist, Josiah Appleton, walked over. "Hi, Pastor D." His tanned face and sun-bleached hair mimicked a California surfer.

Dalton shifted to cool. "How ya' doing, Sy?"

"Great. We've got some new music today. Hope you like it." Dalton assured him he would, then scanned the congregation. Where were Matt and Carla? Why hadn't Matt returned the text? Their usual pew sat empty. Dalton forced a smile at those who were seated. Parishioners nodded a greeting.

Knots of people chatted in groups, oblivious to their children. Several youngsters hopped over pews and ran through the aisles. Why couldn't these people control their kids? *We have a Sunday school!* His soaring confidence, plummeted like a misfired missile.

The musicians began an upbeat version of *Crown Him With Many Crowns*. Congregants stopped talking and began singing. Sammy rushed down a side aisle toward her usual spot next to the deacons.

Clustered together, Charlotte Sims, Martin and Laney Fernández, and other seniors bellowed the hymn with conviction. Emmet Crawford glared.

What's the matter with him?

Dalton's vibrating phone interrupted his thoughts. He fished it from his pocket and tapped the screen.

CAN'T. C @ HOSPITAL

Matt's response stopped him. Dalton tried to find air, re-reading the text again. His heart ramped, knocking against his rib cage. He dug his fingers into the cold metal chair and frowned at the words, letting their reality sink in.

This can't be true. Not today. Not when he needed to meet Matt. The girl's condition couldn't be that bad, could it? She'd been to the hospital many times before.

He jabbed the key pad, SORRY. NEED 2DAY. WILL PAY EXTRA

He adjusted his pious expression and hoisted his tenor, rejoining the congregation's melody. Moments stretched to minutes. The earsplitting instruments coupled with the lifeless phone orchestrated a tune of turmoil in his stomach.

Seriously? Did they need to sing all the verses?

Come on, Matt! Answer the text.

The Oxy floundered, failing to quell his climbing aggravation. The initial rush had been amazing, but now ... not so much. Stress had dampened his usual high.

During the third praise song, his phone shivered.

NO

Rage surged. He stabbed the phone screen without thinking.

WHEN CAN I SPEAK 2 CARLA?

The cell went still. Too long.

Dalton tapped: HELLO?

The cell pulsed. WILL B THERE

Like warm oil, relief coursed through him. Informing Carla Connor that her husband had returned to the drug business had been a long shot. A long shot that had worked. He grabbed the glass of cold water from under his chair and took a lengthy drink. Maybe it would dilute his growing sense of shame. It didn't. He hadn't counted on Charity returning to the hospital. *Please, God, let her be okay.*

The song ended and Dalton walked to the podium. "Good morning, everyone." A chorus of nodding heads and polite smiles filled the sanctuary.

Armando Cristiano located a cordless mic and stood a few feet away, holding the church bulletin. He ran through the announcements while Dalton tried to control the tremor in his legs. He took in lengthy cleansing breaths. The meds always did this, but after months of taking them, he'd learned how to control their side effects.

Laney Fernández scooted out of her pew and down a side aisle. She's leaving now? He hadn't even started yet. Dalton resisted a scowl, watching her disappear into the vestibule.

Armando's monotone rambled to a close, then he returned to his seat. Liz Cronklin, the council secretary, got up and said the opening prayer. The musicians played a soft wordless hymn and after she said "Amen," they followed her off the platform, finding seats in the sanctuary.

Dalton leaned into the podium. His hands framed a stack of papers that covered Joshua Johnson's book.

"This morning I'm beginning a new series. Many of us forget that fundamental to our faith is that God wants us to be happy. He reminds us of this in Ecclesiastes 7:14."

Several seniors thumbed through their Bibles and his brow furrowed. Were they checking his biblical accuracy? Wouldn't be the first time. They'd surely needle him about skipping the remainder of the passage where God appoints unhappy times as well. Thank goodness most of the congregation no longer brought their Bibles.

"No matter the circumstances, we can find true fulfillment and joy by connecting with something called 'the Inner Secret.' Let me explain what this is. There's a God-planted tool inside your soul. Discovering it, using it ... will transform your life.

"The concept is simple. Avoid negativity. When pessimistic thoughts come, cast them aside. How? Locate your Inner Secret and draw strength from it as if it were a bottomless well of positive power." He paused and checked the congregation for visible responses.

Grandma Johnson fiddled with her hearing aid.

Marianne Wilkes shushed her squirming children.

Martin Fernández stared with raised eyebrows, conveying skepticism.

Were these people even listening?

Desperate for affirmation, he looked at Deidra.

She puckered and blew a kiss his way.

Dalton's train of thought derailed, spiraling into an abyss of uncertainty. He stared at what he'd written and couldn't find his place. His hands convulsed like a rabid animal, shaking against the wood, knocking the hardback off the pulpit. Sammy bounced from her seat and headed to the kneeler's bench where she picked up the book and handed it back to him. When he mouthed her a thank you, she smiled and gifted a wink. She hadn't seen Deidra's gesture. Thank God.

As he gripped the edge of the podium, rivered veins popped to the surface of his hand. He steadied his breathing, focusing on the crowd, keeping his gaze away from Deidra Storm.

He expounded another twenty minutes. "Avoid negative thinking," he said. "Push it from your mind." Despite his own admonition, Deidra's actions rattled him. He had much to learn about practicing what he preached.

"You make a mental exchange, substituting the unconstructive thought with a positive one," he explained. "It's that simple. Stop doubting. The epistle James tells us that questioning God will hinder what He wants to give us."

A few people nodded but the scripture failed to erase the suspicious looks from the old folks who sat near the front. Talk about pessimism.

He held up the hard back. "This book, *A Happy Life Is Possible*, will help you. In fact, much of what I preached today came from it. You may purchase one after the service in the annex. They should arrive by Wednesday."

A harmless lie. The online purchase he'd made minutes before the service began wouldn't arrive at the church by Wednesday, let alone by next Sunday. McCormick's distant location, miles from any large city, didn't merit any favors from online retailers. And Dalton wasn't about to fork out extra money for priority mail.

"Don't worry," he continued, "if we need more, I'll place a rush order tomorrow." People hated being left out. They'd be shoving old ladies aside to obtain books from the first batch.

"Keep your eyes on our website." He retrieved a handkerchief from his pocket and dabbed the sweat on his forehead. He jotted down four words on the back side of his notes.

Apology—UPS — late delivery

He'd post that on the website Wednesday morning, explaining why the books were late.

Dalton motioned to the clock above the piano. "I've gone a little over today. Let's prepare our hearts for the offering."

He stepped aside and sat in a chair while Armando's wife, Ana, stood to lead the prayer. Once she finished, the ushers collected four silver platters from the top of a dusty organ while Dalton returned to the pulpit. This better be good. He had already kept them five minutes late and they hadn't even sung the closing hymn. Many shifted in their seats as temperatures climbed outside. Within thirty minutes the old swamp coolers would reveal their ineffectiveness and congregants would be eager to return to their air-conditioned homes.

He must stick to the plan. He'd acted in this play before, perhaps using a different script, but the results were the same. Today's plea would be no different.

"As we consider our offering today, remember what we discussed earlier. The 'Inner Secret.' What I'm about to share could change the course of your life."

Heads leaned, wide-eyed with expectation.

Dalton lifted his brows, slightly opening his mouth, pausing his speech. He had to convince them what they were about to do would, indeed, change their lives forever.

"We made a commitment to the Yavapai Mission in Prescott this past January but unfortunately our benevolence fund is depleted."

Bodies relaxed, telegraphing disinterest with the mention of giving a nickel more than their regular tithe. People crossed their arms while polite smiles straightened into flat lines.

Who could blame them? So many were already struggling. The collateral damage from the massive recession had affected many in a small town with little to offer the outside world.

Did he need to do this? He could find the money someplace else, couldn't he?

He'd use his inheritance money if he still had it. Buying that new car and fancy suits had seemed important at the time. Now he wasn't so sure.

He surveyed the faces staring back at him. These folks weren't interested in helping a homeless shelter up north. His years in the pulpit told him one thing. These people wanted out of here. Fast.

He schooled his voice to a gentle plea. "Examine your hearts." He let the final word crack a bit. If he couldn't convince them, he'd never have a shot at the new job. "God may be speaking to you about increasing your donations. People at the mission will be put on the street if we're not generous today."

Now the hook. He raised his voice along with the book.

"Think of the positive energy you will bring into your life. Giving will produce a windfall of happiness. I guarantee it. Remember your Inner Secret." He served a generous portion of guilt. "Can we put families on the street during a heat wave?"

Now for the final four words to seal the deal.

"Think about the children."

The men pulled out their wallets and the women opened their purses as the plates were passed. Dalton smiled. Mission accomplished.

"Cash is preferable," he added. "That way the shelter won't have to process checks. I'm heading up there today to meet with the director. Your generosity will be the answer to his prayers."

From her seat in the front pew, right on cue, Samantha smiled at Dalton with her supportive-wife-look.

Good thing she decided to drop Gordy off at the bus stop after church so she wouldn't ask to go with him. Dalton returned a grin and Samantha's smile grew.

That's a switch. She'd been so touchy. Maybe his message persuaded her, too. With the collection over, four ushers took the heaping plates to an area behind the baptistery. He licked his lips. It looked like a good haul.

ഇഎ

Warm relief flooded Samantha's heart. How could she have misjudged him? Her husband wanted to help the needy.

This was the Dalton she loved.

Convincing him to talk to the Crawford couple before rushing off to Prescott shouldn't be a problem. He'd straighten things out with his typical charismatic way of bringing calm to anyone's storm.

This was the Dalton she knew.

Though she bowed her head for the closing prayer, she didn't hear a word of it. She'd join Dalton for his trip up north so they could talk. And after the mission meeting, they could go to Boondoggles for dinner. The iconic Prescott steakhouse, her favorite, showcased cowboy charm with its red-checked tablecloths and sawdust covered floors. Their happy place where they could reconnect. It had been too long.

She mentally organized her afternoon. She'd ask Elaine Ainsworth to watch her little girl for the afternoon. Grace would be going home with Elaine for her daughter Lucy's birthday party right after church. Grace could stay until evening. That way Samantha and Dalton could linger in Prescott, enjoying a long over-due romantic dinner.

CHAPTER FOUR

10:27 a.m.

DALTON HAD ONE GOAL IN mind. Get these people out of here so he could get on the road. He still needed to print the directions from his Google Earth app. Where he was headed wasn't on any conventional map and time was a commodity he could not waste.

The keyboardist began the final hymn.

Amazing Grace, how sweet the sound,
That saved a wretch like me.

He tried to sing but the words stuck in his throat like peanut butter. Hadn't he specifically asked the Worship Team to leave this one off the rotation for a while? Apparently his insistence about not singing the old hymn had been ignored.

'Twas grace that taught my heart to fear,
And grace my fears relieved ...

His seventh birthday ... A day of red splatters and crimson cheeks. His father had been the culprit of both. A tossed plate of marinara and the pounding of his flesh had fused in his brain. His mother scrubbed and scrubbed but the spaghetti sauce blemish had been impossible to remove. *Amazing Grace* always brought back the memory.

Waiving a mud-caked hammer, his father charged toward him while he quivered in a corner. His mother, tried to intervene, shouting, "Wallace, please. He didn't mean to. You promised to take him fishing, remember? He was looking for worms ..."

"Shut up!" Dad yelled as he slapped her.

She fell against the wall. "It's his birthday ... leave him alone!"

He struck her again. Harder. Dalton heard her jaw crack. She crumpled to the floor like a discarded rag doll.

Pulsing veins threaded his father's neck as he got into Dalton's face, breath reeking with whiskey. "This is an expensive hammer, boy!"

Dalton stared at it, eyes wide, lips trembling. Using its claw to dig holes near the horse stables hadn't been a good idea. Even on what should have been a happy day.

"Why are you so stupid?" his father bellowed as he knotted a fist inches from Dalton's face.

"No ... please Dad ... no!" Strikes one and two hit each side of his face.

His mother crawled and reached Dalton in time to take the third blow. That seemed to appease the old man's wrath. Dalton cowered, rubbing his face, whimpering as he watched his father storm out the front door.

He gripped his mother's hand as she led him to a rocker in his bedroom. Once Dad was gone, he spilled his emotions all over her shoulder. He sobbed for several minutes, sitting on her lap like a little kid. But he didn't care. He needed her to hold him as if he was three again. When she rocked him, his heartbeat quieted, syncing to the gentle sway of the chair. Twilight streamed through his window, amplifying the growing welt on her face. The bruises encircling her wrists from last week's beating looked like black bracelets. He felt the tips of her fingers draw tiny hearts on his cheeks as she repeated what she'd often told him. "You're always in my heart, little man." She wiped his tears, then lifted his chin and sang *Amazing Grace* as the dusk danced across his bedroom wall.

A sudden awareness of the congregation's singing yanked him into to the present. Dalton breathed deeply, straightening his back, grateful for the hymn's last familiar words.

When we've been there ten thousand years
Bright shining as the sun ...

He swallowed the lump in his throat, the hymn's words overpowering his medicine's ability to help him forget. Too many horrid memories were associated with it. He'd have to remove *Amazing Grace* from the worship team's repertoire permanently.

The song ended with a crescendo and Dalton walked to his usual place at the end of the nave. Many filed past, shaking his hand, and a few even offered compliments and appreciation. The congregant line dwindled. Deidra Storm brought up the rear. His stomach lurched, watching her approach behind Mable Hatfield.

"Thank you, Pastor, for the wonderful sermon," Mable said. "I can't wait to get my book. I don't have a computer. How can I know when to pick mine up?"

"No problem, Mable. Give the church office a call Wednesday morning. When they come in, we'll put one aside for you."

"Oh, that's wonderful ... bless you." The elderly woman grinned, revealing a row of silver-capped teeth. She squeezed his hand and exited through the vestibule.

"Paaaaas...tor!" Deidra exclaimed, her loud voice echoing off the high ceiling. She moved close, offering bursting cleavage for his view. Dalton stepped back, nearly tripping over a stack of hymnals.

"Hello, Deidra ... uh ... where's Drake today?"

"Away on business," she cooed, then winked. "I'm all by my lonesome if you want to come by."

Dalton scanned the sanctuary for his wife. Samantha was nowhere in sight. "I've got a busy week. I'll give you a call later," he lied. That incident at her home a couple of weeks ago had been a big mistake.

"Okay, Pastor." She wrapped him with spidery arms for what seemed like an eternity, then strutted through a side exit. He hurried down the aisle toward his office, his injured knee objecting at each step.

He entered the tiny room with Carlos Miñoz and Rob Winters close behind. They placed the brimming collection plates on his desk.

"Thanks, guys." An abundance of cash covered the regular tithing envelopes. People had been listening. Today of all days, paper currency was king.

"Your wife asked me to find you," Carlos said. "Mr. and Mrs. Crawford want to talk to you."

Dalton stifled a groan. He asked the men to keep the mission offering separate from the regular tithe and took a step toward the door, then swung around and grabbed his cane. Always good to have his sympathy stick with him when meeting complainers. And the Crawfords were known for grumbling about everything from how hot it was in the sanctuary to the modern worship songs.

When he emerged from his office, his eyes met Sammy's. She sat near the older couple who were knotted together like two grey socks. Emmet Crawford's face was written in disappointment.

What could be wrong now? The clock raced. At this rate he would be late for his appointment with Matt.

Dalton ambled through the aisle, leaning on the cane. When he reached Mr. Crawford, he shook the old man's hand. "Is there something I can help you with?"

"It's that boy you sent. He's been stealin' from us."

"Are you sure?"

Mr. Crawford laid out Tyler Benson's offenses.

"I suggested we have a meeting in the annex," Sammy said. "I already called Amanda on her cell phone and discussed this with Mr. and Mrs.

Crawford. Tomorrow evening at six will work for everyone. That way you and I won't have to rush home from Prescott."

Dalton's throat tightened. Sammy couldn't come with him. Not today!

"Perfect, then. Tomorrow it is," he said.

He watched the couple shuffle through the front doors, then draped an arm around Sammy's back.

"Aren't you taking Gordy to the station?" he asked.

"He decided to hang out with Bethany so he's taking a later bus. Barb offered to drop him off, so I could go with you."

"What about Grace?"

"I told you yesterday ... don't you remember? She's got that birthday party at the Ainsworth's."

"Oh, that's right." He could never remember his daughter's numerous activities.

"Elaine offered to keep her until this evening." Sammy beamed. "It'll give us a chance to have some time together, Dalton. It's been way too long ... since your accident."

Though he couldn't disagree, she couldn't go today. He'd need to make it up to her.

Mid-morning sun streamed through stained glass, creating color patches across Sammy's cheeks. Her beauty drew him like bees to honey. Of all days to leave town. They'd have a quiet house with no kids. It *had* been too long. He missed her. He yearned to hold her but urgency consumed him. If he didn't get his meds today, his shot at an opportunity to put himself back on course would be lost forever.

"Why don't you rest?" he asked. "I'll make the trip by myself."

Sammy's smile flipped to a frown. "I'm not tired, Dalton." Her tone, suddenly ice-like.

"Don't be angry. I know you've been working a lot of extra hours around here. You've been picking up a lot of slack for me." He leaned on his cane. "You need some time to yourself."

"You don't want me to come, do you?"

"It's not that, babe." This wasn't going well. "It's a quick trip, Sammy. When I get back, we'll have the evening to ourselves. Besides, you'll be bored."

"Why don't you want me to go?"

His eyes widened and his face heated. "You're over-reacting. Think of the peaceful afternoon you'll have without Grace underfoot. I'll even record the offering when I get back." She hated that job. Surely she'd be thrilled. He pulled her close to kiss her but she wriggled free.

"What's your problem?" he asked.

"*My* problem?" she snapped. "Are you serious? You're the one with all the secrets. You take off to God knows where at a moment's notice." Tears welled in her eyes but she wiped them away. "What's going on with you, Dalton?"

He blew out a sigh. If only he could tell her. But not now, not yet. He opted for a peace offering.

"Let's go to Phoenix next weekend for dinner. Make reservations at that Camelback Mountain restaurant you like so much. What's the name ...? Belford's? ... yes ... that's it. Pick out a movie and we'll make a night of it."

Her lips formed a straight line; her eyes smoldered with anger.

"How about it?" *Come on, Sammy!*

"Hmmm ... let me see, Dalton," she finally said. "Maybe we could do that ... if I'm free and if I don't need to take a trip somewhere. I'll get back to you."

She whirled around and stormed out of the church.

The hollow clanking of the church doors announced he was finally alone.

CHAPTER FIVE

Sunday, 10:57 a.m.
Camelback Children's Hospital
Phoenix, Arizona

"YOU CAN'T LEAVE NOW!" THE corridor of Camelback Children's Hospital echoed Carla Connor's voice.

Matt tightened his arms around her. "I'll be back in an hour, Car'. Charity's stable."

"You heard what Dr. Morton said. Her whites are high."

"I know, hon. My boss is driving me crazy. If I don't get that package to his desk today, I could lose my job." His daughter's climbing blood counts argued against him. "How did I know this would happen when I agreed to pick it up last week?"

"He'll understand. He knows you've got a sick child. Did you call him?"

"I left several messages," he lied. "He's not returning my calls." He lowered his tone, trying to calm her. "It shouldn't take me long. I'll run over there now and be back within the hour. Promise." Another lie.

"Matt ... something feels wrong." Her deep brown eyes pleaded. "Please don't leave."

He twisted from her arms and walked toward the elevator before she changed his mind. He hesitated at the nurse's station. Could Carla be right? Maybe Charity was worse than he'd thought.

He stepped into the elevator and punched the button, wishing it was Dalton Baxter's face. What a lying hypocrite. Why Carla worshipped the guy, he couldn't understand.

As the door glided shut, he saw Carla crumpled in a seat, crying. Anger and guilt battled in his gut. He hated to leave her. And he hated himself for being so weak.

Instead of a quick run across town to a UPS store, the trip to Prescott would take ninety minutes. He'd meet his supplier, Bulldog, on the town's outskirts before seeing the preacher at a bus station. The additional rendezvous would cost him an extra hour but it didn't matter. Even if he broke all speed limits, Matt wouldn't be back at the hospital until late afternoon. Carla would have on her fight face by then and things would get ugly.

But he had no choice. He had to do this. If Baxter told her the truth about returning to the drug trade, their marriage would be over and he couldn't take that. Their relationship had barely survived his past brushes with the law. Then Charity came out of remission and things had gotten even worse. The mounting bills on the kitchen counter and lapsed mortgage payment made his return to illegal work imperative. If he didn't get the house payment up to date, he'd have a lot more to worry about than another argument.

Baxter. What a piece of dirt. Why couldn't he wait a few lousy days ... at least until Charity stabilized?

The elevator's bells chimed and the doors opened. He walked through the lobby skirting patients in wheelchairs surrounded by Sunday visitors. A set of gigantic glass doors yawned, exchanging cool air with Phoenix heat, blasting Matt's face as he exited. Pavement steamed around his sandaled feet as he headed to their old Buick station wagon with the cracked back window. Once inside, he shut off his phone and slipped it into his pocket. Within an hour Carla's frantic calls would begin. She'd be desperate. He didn't blame her. The frequent vigils at Charity's bedside had taken their toll. Carla was about to snap.

So was he.

He'd be gone at least four hours which should give him enough time to dream up a plausible story. Carla might buy his excuse about having poor phone service but explaining why he was four hours late would be a problem.

As the car rumbled through the parking lot, the engine back-fired, giving him an idea. This piece of junk might be good for something after all. A breakdown in downtown Phoenix might be believable. At least he hoped so.

Surely Charity would be better by the time he got back. Maybe even well enough to go home. If that happened, Carla's temper would subside. He'd grab a peace offering in the hospital gift shop once he got back. Maybe they'd have her favorite yellow roses.

CHAPTER SIX

Sunday, 11:15 a.m.
Saint Luke's Community Church

SUNLIGHT SHIMMERED OFF THE CEMENT as Samantha walked to the back side of Saint Luke's Community Church. Gravel crunched underfoot as she made her way across a pointed shadow from the church's steeple. She straightened her shoulders and sucked in a deep breath, trying to get a grip. Gordy waited around the corner and he didn't need to see how upset she was.

Her son leaned against her car, a paperback tucked under his arm, his belongings stacked near his feet. Sandwiched between a green duffle, his backpack, and a computer bag was an old leather suitcase he'd found at a thrift store. Samantha knew it contained one of Gordy's most prized possessions, a high-powered telescope.

"Hey kiddo. How was youth group?" He looked more like Dalton every day, minus the peppery sideburns and slight paunch.

"Boring." Gordy shrugged.

"Ready to go?" Samantha opened the trunk.

Gordy stuffed his gear inside, then covered it with his windbreaker. He twisted around and looked at the church. "Isn't Dad coming?"

"He's going to Prescott."

"Again?"

"He's got mission business." She slammed the trunk a little too hard. "I'll drop you at your girlfriend's. Here ..." She handed him an envelope. "Your ticket's inside and I put in some extra cash."

"Girlfriend? Bee's my buddy, Mom. You know that." Gordy stuffed the envelope into his pocket.

"Sure she is, son."

"Can I drive?"

She tossed him the keys, then climbed into the passenger seat.

Gordy lobbed his book to the passenger floor, then slid behind the steering wheel. He pulled out Samantha's iPhone charger, handed it to her, inserted his into the opening and attached his Android. "Sorry ... my phone's dying."

Hers was too. She'd recharge it after dropping him off.

He adjusted the seat and mirror, then secured his seatbelt. New driver ritual out of the way, he started the engine.

Samantha picked up the dog-eared novel off the floorboard. The chunky paperback copy of Dostoevsky's *Crime and Punishment* had a folded page two thirds in. "Not done yet?" she asked.

"Nope," he sighed. "I can't believe I waited so long. My AP essay's due when I get back." The Camry's wheels sprayed stones as Gordy did a turnabout.

"You'll finish." She smiled. Deadlines were Gordy's oxygen.

"Are you sure I can't take my van? It's only a two hour trip." He rolled through the driveway. A carpet of manicured grass bordered nearby.

She shook her head. "Driving that windy road through the forest is much too dangerous. Especially in that old thing. You can use Grams' car while you're up there. I'm sure she'll have you running errands all over town."

"No kidding." He turned right on Jefferson Road. "This year's list is gigantic. I'm not complaining. I need the money."

"She'll make sure you have plenty of free time too, Gordy." Samantha studied his sculptured face. She found it hard to remember the little boy who had once resided there.

"I emailed Jerome. I haven't heard back yet."

Samantha smiled. Her son needed some down time before school started. "Just make sure you do that, Gordy. Grams isn't looking for slave labor. She wants you to have fun."

"Work comes first. I need to pay you and Dad back, remember?"

"It's okay to make smaller payments," she said. Gordy's nickname should be Mr. Responsible. His eagerness to repay the money he'd borrowed for his telescope was Exhibit One.

"Really?" He smiled. "I'll take you up on that. I'd like to buy some new filters."

"Go for it. I'll talk to Dad." Minutes ticked by as they reminisced over past family vacations in Grams' quaint town of Huckleberry, Arizona.

"I worry about Grams living so far away all alone," Gordy said. "Why doesn't she move back to McCormick?"

"Too many good memories. That cabin was my parents' sweet spot. She really misses your grandpa. Besides, our heat drives her crazy."

"I love it up there. It's great for research," he said. "The clear skies and elevation are perfect."

"To see sun spots?"

"Uh huh. Lately the solar activity is off the charts." He shot her a worried look. "Have you thought about what I told you?"

"Yes, Gordy. Good grief," she said. "But I've got other things to worry about."

"You and Dad are fighting again, aren't you?"

"We've had some arguments. All married people do. Don't worry about it."

"He keeps leaving town. What's with that?"

She gave him the company line in the calmest voice she could manage. "Yavapai Mission is in a crisis. Your father's taking an offering up there."

It didn't explain all the other trips. Even to her it sounded lame. "Remind me again about those CTMs ...?" Maybe she could steer him back to his favorite topic.

He laughed. "CMEs."

"What does that stand for again?"

"Coronal Mass Ejections. The sun spits out plasma."

"Sounds awful."

"They can be."

"And this is why you're worried?"

"We could lose power, Mom. We had a near miss last week. NASA said it was similar to what happened in 1859. Remember? I told you that."

"Oh yes. Telegraphs were exploding all over the place."

"That solar storm lasted seventeen hours. Scientists believe it had to have been an X-class mega flare. Something like that would be catastrophic today."

"Why didn't I learn about that in school?" Samantha asked.

"Other than frying some communication systems, it didn't affect many people."

Samantha mused over the information, feeling amazed by what her son knew. If this catastrophe happened, what would come of his college plans next year? The faded *M.I.T.* logo on Gordy's t-shirt signaled much more than a youthful pipe dream. His exceptional S.A.T. scores enticed several colleges but Gordy only had his eye on one. Massachusetts Institute of Technology had come courting and promised a full ride. By this time next year he'd be packing his bags and heading for the East coast on a promised father and son road trip with Dalton. With America's heartland between them, Massachusetts seemed to be his destiny.

"Do some research." Gordy interrupted her thoughts as he turned left on Caliente Drive toward the Brewster home. On the northeast corner, Cocopah Park, surrounded a crescent-shaped body of water aptly named, Luna Pond. Gordy spotted several kids jumping in and cooling off. He smiled to himself, remembering his own carefree adventures there on hot summer days just a few years ago.

"Google CARRINGTON EVENT," Gordon continued. "You and Dad should be putting away food and water. Check my data. It's in the green binder on my desk."

"So ... you think the power might go off for a long time?"

"Only if we have an EMP."

"EMP?"

"Electric magnetic pulse event. If we have a severe one, it could take down the grids. Experts say it's not if, but when."

Samantha sighed. She didn't want to think about not having air conditioning in Arizona. Especially during an August heat wave. She shook her head. "I'm sure the government has some sort of back-up plan."

"I hope so. The ejections have been much stronger than usual. The Internet is fired up with speculation."

Why on earth did a seventeen year-old ponder such gloomy thoughts? If he would get his head out of the books, perhaps he might meet a nice girl. Bethany Brewster was beautiful. Why didn't he see it? Better grab a little happiness now before he had adult-sized problems like hers. She squeezed his arm. "Research is fine, son. But having a little balance to your life is also important. You know what they say, 'all work and no play ... and all that.'"

"Studying the solar system is fun."

Yes, she conceded. To her intelligent son, she guessed it was.

ꕥ

Gordy pulled into the Brewster driveway and turned off the engine. Samantha climbed out and met him at the trunk. After he unloaded his gear, she gave him a lengthy hug and kissed his cheek.

"Here," she said, handing him a small box of motion sickness pills. "Those last few miles always get you, remember? Don't forget to take them an hour before you hit the road."

"I will. Thanks," he said, stuffing the package into his backpack.

"I've got some things to do," she told him. "Please thank Barb for taking you to the bus station. See you in two weeks." She climbed into the car as he grabbed his stuff and headed toward the front door.

He gave her a thumbs up as she backed out of the driveway.

She'd miss him. He brightened her days with laughter and sarcasm about everything from politics to the inept education he endured in a town with few options. It would be lonely around the house the next couple weeks. Especially since Dalton all but ignored her.

She paused at the stop sign down the block and tapped her fingers on the steering wheel. Her afternoon plans could alter her life forever. For half a second she considered chucking the whole idea and spending her day by the pool. But nagging worries bothered her like summertime mosquitoes. If she swatted away the thoughts, they'd only return and eventually bite into her vulnerabilities.

On impulse, she took a right on Kaibab Road. The shortcut to Saint Luke's. She pressed the accelerator, hoping to avoid a McCormick policeman with too much time on his hands.

Today she would follow her husband like a private eye.

CHAPTER SEVEN

Sunday, 11:30 a.m.
McCormick, Arizona

MARTIN IDLED THE FORD FUSION at a stop sign where Charleston intersected Kaibab Road. Laney bellowed the familiar words to the old Beatles song blaring from the stereo, her contralto voice filling the car. She winked at her husband hoping he'd join her. He'd seemed distracted all morning.

She shook an imaginary tambourine as she crooned about a hard day's night and working like a dog.

"You've got that right, Baby." Martin scowled. "You've worked way too hard to be let go like that."

Laney stopped singing and caressed his arm with her hand. "It's okay, sweetheart. We'll be fine."

"It's not the money. You deserve to be treated better than that. I think it's age discrimination. We should sue."

Laney laughed. "Sue? Marty, goodness ... I'm looking forward to doing something else. I've come to terms with this. Life is a gift. You take what you're given, no more."

Her husband smiled, drumming his fingers against the steering wheel. "I thank God everyday for you, Baby."

She flashed him a warm smile. The song ended, a commercial ensued and Laney lowered the radio. "You too, darling. But on a more serious note, I'm worried."

"You're not the only one," he agreed. "I hope we're wrong. Maybe Amanda miscalculated."

Laney shook her head. "She's gone over the books a number of times. Who would steal from a church?"

"Let's not go there, yet." The light flashed green and Martin let his foot off the brake. He eased into the intersection as a white blur barreled past. He slammed his brakes and punched the horn. "They nearly hit us!"

As the vehicle sped away, Laney spotted a familiar bumper sticker: *A family that prays together stays together.* "That looks like Samantha's car. She never drives that way. I wonder what's wrong."

"Where's she going in such a hurry?" Martin asked.

"She's heading toward the church. I hope everything's okay." The white Camry wove in and out of traffic until it disappeared in front of a large truck.

Laney's cell rang and Carla Connor's face filled the display. A Sunday call from Carla couldn't be good. Had her little girl taken a turn for the worse? Maybe Samantha was on her way to help.

ꙮ

Samantha floored the pedal and swerved around a monster truck that moved at a snail's pace in the slow lane.

She bit her lip. She ran a red light!

Aggravation surged as she recalled the conversation with Dalton.

Do the tithing entry? Who are you fooling? Dalton hated that job as much as she did.

She turned left on Jefferson and raced through the alley behind the church, stopping at a cedar fence. She jumped from the car and peered through a knot hole. Dalton's black convertible was parked near the building. Freshly washed and waxed, it glittered in the mid-morning sun.

Got the car detailed again? I swear you love that thing more than me. Did you do it for her?

Dalton appeared from a side exit clutching a hammer. His Nike exercise bag hung over his shoulder.

He never mentioned the gym. He'd kept a set of workout clothes in his office when he wanted to unwind after a long day. But on a Sunday? What happened to Prescott? Why did he have that hammer?

He climbed into the convertible and revved the engine. He peeled through the parking lot, the car's wake flinging a spray of gravel.

Samantha got into the Camry and sped through the alley. When she turned on Jefferson, she could make out Dalton's car. It ascended the north bound onramp of Highway 89 toward Prescott, Arizona.

It sure didn't appear he was going to the gym.

Samantha kept a two car-gap distance, clenching the steering wheel as she locked eyes with his bumper. Finding her way to the Yavapai Mission was easy, but if her husband made any detours, she'd lose him.

Once in Prescott National Forest, it didn't take long for the straight highway to change to S-curves. The highway threaded through the bushy landscape under a brilliant sky, its cadet color resembling an Arizona peacock. Dalton zipped in and out of traffic, creating more distance so Samantha swung into the fast lane. A big wheeler coming from behind rewarded her with a voluminous blast from its titanic horn. She waved an apology and forged ahead.

She sneaked a peek at her ringing cell phone. Laney Fernández. She let it go to voicemail and noticed the low battery warning. She scanned the car but couldn't see her charger. Samantha turned off the phone to save what was left.

She prayed the little black bug on the horizon was still Dalton's car.

She increased her speed, checking her rearview for a highway patrolman. The long glistening tarmac behind her, empty of traffic, had to be sign God was helping her. Maybe today she'd discover the truth.

CHAPTER EIGHT

11:50 a.m.
Brewster Home
McCormick, Arizona

GORDON NURSED A COKE SITTING across from Bethany Brewster on her back patio. They relaxed by a patio table feet away from a kidney shaped pool. He stared at the empty diving board.

"Gordster? What are you thinking about?"

He looked up. Brilliant white teeth crowded Bee's smile, last year's braces now absent. Her endearing smile made his stomach flutter.

"I'm sort of bummed summer's nearly over," he said. "As much as I love my classes, I'll miss having fun with you." They came from different social worlds but summers always equalized them.

"Ugh ... don't remind me. I have Crabapple for home room."

Gordon laughed. "Poor Bee. And you thought she was retiring." Mrs. Crabbner had earned the moniker with her sour manners and the gnarly fingers she'd wave in your face.

"She's horrible. I'll probably fail literature."

"You'll be fine. Teachers like you."

"Not as much as you, Gordster." She squeezed his arm. "You're smarter than most of the teachers."

Heat climbed to his cheeks. She was always saying things like that.

"I know you'll be busy with all your AP classes. Can you still come to my games?" she asked.

"Wouldn't miss them." He hated sports. But watching Bee cheer and then hanging out afterwards was always fun. She went out of her way to include him with all the popular kids.

"Do you really have to go to your grandma's? I'll be soooo bored the next two weeks."

"I promised. Besides I need to finish my research and the elevation really helps. When I get back I'll show you the sunspots I've been viewing. Lots of fireworks exploding from the surface." Excitement pricked his chest as he explained his favorite subject.

Mrs. Brewster poked her head through the kitchen door. “We leave in five minutes,” she called.

As Gordon stood he couldn’t help noticing Bee as she pushed her chair under the table. The numerous freckles that once populated her nose and cheeks had either faded or were hidden by her suntan. Tinges of green hair framed her face, a sign she’d been doing her usual backstrokes in the pool. Her dad always went a bit overboard with chlorine. Long golden hair, splintered with sunlit streaks, draped petite shoulders. Gordon found it hard to stop staring.

“What?” She shoved his arm playfully.

He snapped out of it. “Nothing.” Embarrassment heated his cheeks. Lately he’d been swatting butterflies in his stomach whenever she was near. She was like a sister, wasn’t she? These new feelings made no sense.

Gordon checked his cell. Almost noon. His bus would leave in thirty minutes.

They followed Bee’s mother to the Suburban. Gordon loaded his stuff and climbed into the back seat.

The fifteen-minute drive to the McCormick Greyhound bus stop provided ample time for Gordy’s silly jokes. He soon had Bee and her mother in stitches.

“Gordon, I think you’ve missed your calling as a stand-up comic.” Mrs. Brewster pulled into the depot driveway.

“I’ll keep that in mind if things don’t work out with NASA,” he said.

After Bee’s mom stopped in the Greyhound unloading area, Gordon jumped from the car, grabbed his gear and waved. “See you soon, Bee.”

Her beaming face was framed by the front passenger window. “Gordster ... you’re the only one who calls me that.”

He laughed. “Besides Grams, you’re the only one who calls me ‘Gordster’.”

She giggled as he watched them pull away. The hiatus between them would seem long. She’d probably be even more beautiful when he saw her again.

CHAPTER NINE

12:40 p.m.
Highway 89, Prescott National Forest

WINDING AROUND CURVES, DALTON BOUNCED his knee to the beat of Pearl Jam. When he rounded the next bend, an enormous oak tree appeared on the opposite side of the highway.

That must be it. He pulled out the satellite map he'd printed on his office computer. The tree's low hanging branches hid a secret entrance to a dirt road. When he returned this way in an hour, he'd follow a five-mile stretch to Copper Lake, a deep snow-fed reservoir near an abandoned mine. The location was miles from popular hiking trails. Avoiding people was vital. He just had one meeting to make before implementing his plans. His pulse quickened with the thought that soon he'd have enough meds to last until he could get out of McCormick.

"Quack, Quack!" His phone chirped.

He tapped it. *Deidra!*

Why didn't she get it? Hadn't he made it clear?

That visit to her home had been a disaster.

"José will only take cash," he'd told her when he dropped by to solicit money for a supposedly wounded swamp cooler on the church's roof. "He's a great repairman but is here ... well ... you know ... illegally."

"Four thousand? That's a lot," she said.

"It's about ready to croak," he told her. "I wouldn't normally ask but our building fund is very low. It's only a loan, Deidra. I'll pay you back in a month."

He sipped a second glass of Cabernet Sauvignon as they sat on cool leather couches in the white carpeted living room. Afternoon sun poured through an enormous bay window. A gigantic candelabra reflected color prisms across the walls. The whole place seemed gaudy, like some overdone Christian television studio. Too much gold and glass for his taste.

"Can you wait until Thursday? Drake will be back from Phoenix."

Dalton swirled his wine. “José needs to get started tomorrow. It will be much higher if I get a contractor.”

Dalton couldn’t wait two days. He needed the money now.

She moved close, draping an arm around his back. “I think I can help, Pastor.”

“Really, Deidra?” He scooted away. “I appreciate this.”

“Helping the church would make me feel so good.” She reclaimed the distance. Her lips, drenched in red lipstick, added in a hushed tone, “Especially if it means helping you, Dalton.” Suddenly she covered his lips with hers.

Her open mouth seemed to swallow his. Dalton wrenched away, choking on a gulp of wine. “Deidra ... please ...” He got to his feet and walked toward the front door.

“Oh, Pastor ... it’s just one little kiss. I’m so lonely.” She pouted at him. “Please ... come back. I’ll behave. I promise.”

His pockets were still empty. Maybe she meant it. He returned to the couch while she picked up their glasses and walked toward her kitchen. “Let me fill yours up.”

“That’s not necessary. Two’s my limit.”

She ignored him and left the room. After a few minutes, she returned with the wine and a plate full of cheese and crackers. They chatted another twenty minutes and she’d yet to produce any cash.

Increasing inebriation coursing through his veins failed to quell his surging guilt. “I really need to get going.” Dalton stood. “Now about that money?”

She jumped up, thrusting her bosom toward his chest. He stepped away, his back against the wall beside the couch. She threw her arms around him, her lips finding his as she unfastened the top button of his shirt.

Dalton broke free from her grip. “Stop, Deidra ... I ... uh ... need to leave.”

This wasn’t worth it. He’d find money somewhere else.

Her eyes welled, filling up like empty pools. “Please don’t go. I’m sorry,” she said, grabbing his arm.

“I came to ask for help. Not this. I love my wife.”

“I love Drake, too ... really I do. But I have needs and my husband ... well you know ... he’s much older than me ... You know what I mean, right? It’ll be our little secret ... I promise.”

So he was a gigolo now. This was crazy. He had to get out of there.

“I’m here for one thing, Deidra. I need to fix the cooler or people will suffer miserably this summer. You can choose to help me or not. It’s your decision.”

"Okay, Pastor. Whatever you say. But if you change your mind, I'll be here." She brushed his cheek with her lips, false eyelashes tickling his face, then turned and headed toward her bedroom. He jiggled his keys in his pocket, staring at the front door. This wasn't good. Not one bit. After he got that job, he was quitting those pills. Cold turkey, he promised himself.

The last time he tried, he gave in after two days. But that was different. Now he had strong motivation. Once he got the job in Phoenix, he'd try harder.

Deidra returned, wearing a hungry stare. She stuffed a wad of cash into his hand. He transferred the thick bundle to his pocket and walked to the front door. "Thanks again, Deidra," he said, not looking at her.

"Anytime, Pastor ..." She followed him through the foyer. When he reached for the doorknob, she hugged him too long.

"Please ... Deidra ..." He looked down at her and smiled, deciding to take a different approach. "You're quite beautiful. But I can't be any more than a pastor to you. This is the way it needs to be."

Her eyes misted. "But ... I ... uh ... I need you."

She wasn't listening. He'd bolted through the door then and sprinted down her walkway to his car.

What a mistake that had been, he thought as he raced around a serpent-like curve on Highway 89. He might have dodged Deidra's bullet, but every time he looked at his wife, the guilt from that day consumed him.

CHAPTER TEN

12:55 p.m.
Prescott, Arizona

SAMANTHA DIDN'T HAVE TIME TO be charmed by the trees shading Old Town Prescott's 1880's cobblestone walkways that bordered western saloons and little boutiques. Tourists meandered, seemingly enjoying their Sunday afternoon. Dalton's BMW zoomed through Montezuma Street near the old Federal courthouse. Samantha focused on his bumper.

She watched him turn right on Sheldon.

"The mission's the other way. Where's he going?"

Dalton barely missed a man on a bicycle before swerving into the bus station.

Samantha followed him into the parking lot. She wedged her car into a snug spot between a blue SUV and a tired Astrovan with a banged up bumper. Dalton sprinted through the front entrance, his Nike bag flying behind him. She crept around cars and followed him through the double glass doors. Once inside, she scanned the lobby, darting behind an artificial plant.

ꙮ

Dalton entered the men's room and the stench of old urine made him gag. His shoes stuck to the floor as he walked toward the back, using his shirttail as a mask. A grimy wall covered with gang tags held two sinks, one plugged with brown water. An empty paper towel holder, missing a screw, hung crookedly between them. He shuddered. He bent over and inspected the stalls to make sure he was alone.

"Hey," said a familiar voice.

Dalton bolted up, his head barely missing the sink's edge.

Matt Connor, standing near the door, glared at him. He wore an olive green windbreaker that looked too small. He hadn't shaved in days.

"Thought you'd beat me here," Dalton said. "Bad traffic?"

Matt's dagger sharp eyes seemed to pierce his. Dalton dropped the chit-chat and handed him a thick envelope. "It's all there. There's extra for Charity like I promised. How is she by the way?"

Matt still said nothing. He grabbed the package, entered a stall, and slammed it shut.

ഇന്ദ

Matt riffled through the bundled cash, grateful someone had taken great care in forming one hundred-dollar packs. Probably the church ushers. It was all there.

He flung open the stall door and yanked out a brown paper bag from his jacket. "Here," he said, tossing it to the man who claimed to be his pastor.

"Sorry about your girl," Baxter told him.

"Sure you are ..." Matt spat. "I'm done. Find another dealer."

The pastor's eyes formed large circles. "Come on ... Matt ... this isn't enough ..." Baxter waved the bag in his face. "I need to meet you one more time. A few weeks from now."

"Don't call me again." Matt pivoted and headed toward the door.

"Wait!"

Matt twisted around. The preacher cowered before him. His hands shook as he clutched the brown bag. That familiar hungry look filled his eyes. Baxter was a full-blown addict.

"What happened to you, man?" Matt asked. "You're pathetic."

"How dare you." Baxter's voice climbed. "You were nothing when I helped you out of the gutter."

"That's what I mean. Last year you drove me to my AA meetings. Now look at you."

"Is it the money?" Baxter shouted. "Do you need more?"

"Yeah, right. I know where you got this money. You make me sick."

The preacher grabbed his shoulders and pushed him against the wall. "You can't do this. I'll tell your Probation Officer."

And Baxter would make good his threat. Officer Jenkins, his P.O would get a kick out of hauling him off in cuffs if he knew Matt was dealing again. Never mind that Baxter was one of his clients. Jenkins would never buy that.

Matt shook himself free and yelled, "Back off!"

Baxter lunged toward him, grabbing his neck. Matt gasped for air. "You gonna kill me ... Paa ... stor?" He clawed at Baxter's fingers.

ഇന്ദ

Dalton released Matt's neck and backed away. Bile filled his mouth and he whirled around to wretch into the sink. He turned back to face his dealer. "Sorry."

Matt rubbed his throat, then pulled something from his jacket and hurled it at Dalton's head.

The bottle struck his ear. Dizziness overwhelmed him and he collapsed, hugging his head. Matt kicked him in the stomach and ran through the exit.

Dalton clutched his gut and groaned. Pain radiated while he rested his face against the filthy ground. At the back of his head, a knot formed. When got to his knees, his leg injury pulsed with agony. He used the sink edge to pull himself up.

He looked longingly at the brown paper bag before jamming it into the Nike bag.

Dalton twisted a faucet and was rewarded with a dribble. He splashed water on his face, then cursed when he reached for the empty towel holder. Dalton stared in the mirror. A crack splintered the center of the glass making him look like a side-show freak. "How did I wind up here?" He rubbed a quivering hand over his eyes. "This is not me. I've got to stop!"

After a few deep breaths, his pulse evened. He fished for his cell and tapped it awake It showed several voicemails he'd have to check later. He powered down the phone and tossed it in the gym bag, then removed a change of clothes. After pulling on a pair of shorts, he picked up Matt's bottle. Under a vintage black and gold label, a quarter cup of amber liquid lined the bottom.

Desert Durum, 92 proof. The expensive stuff.

Dalton crammed it into his duffle. A little nip might come in handy later.

ꙮ

Frozen behind a fake fern, Samantha watched Matt Connor run through the lobby, recognizing the signature pony tail bouncing off his collar. He'd just come from the men's room. Had he met Dalton in there?

Minutes ticked by. No sign of her husband. Maybe he'd left some other way. Was she wasting her time? A squeal from the door jarred her back. Dalton hurried past wearing shorts and a tank top, the Nike bag flailing over his shoulder. He burst through the front door and she ran after him. He started the BMW, then tore through the parking lot.

She rushed to her car. She couldn't lose him now.

ꙮ

Gordon knew he shouldn't have ordered the bacon cheeseburger at the last rest stop. He convinced himself that since he was older, his stomach could handle the windy road through Prescott National Forrest.

Wrong.

He fished through his backpack for the motion sickness pills his mother had given him. He'd been joking around so much with Bee and her mother, he'd forgotten to take them. Swallowing them now wouldn't help much but maybe they'd take the edge off the nausea. He downed two tablets and took a swig from his water bottle. The road's hairpins were continuous with no straight pavement in between. His vision blurred. He snapped his laptop shut and covered it with his windbreaker. If he lost his cookies at least he'd be ready.

He already missed Bee. As much as he enjoyed visiting his grandmother, lately being with his childhood friend seemed a lot more interesting. Maybe Mom was right. Maybe Bee was his girlfriend. She seemed different this summer. Had she been flirty today? Her turquoise eyes seemed to sparkle as she stared at him by the pool. It was odd. Had he misinterpreted her body language? Whoever this person was, she didn't resemble the Bethany he knew.

A new longing stirred inside but he couldn't define it. And unlike past summers, he couldn't wait to get back to McCormick. Hopefully Grams would keep him so busy time would fly.

CHAPTER ELEVEN

1:30 p.m.
Northern Arizona

DIVIDING THE DESERT LIKE AN ink ribbon, Black Canyon Freeway glistened under the afternoon sun as Matt raced toward Phoenix. Urgent voicemails convinced him to break all speeding laws. Carla yelled between desperate sobs. Charity was dying.

"Matt ... please!" Her last recording begged. "She may not make it much longer."

What if he was too late?

He tapped Carla's number. "God ... get me there in time."

She picked up after two rings.

"Where are you?" she screamed.

"I'm on my way. How's Charity?"

"Barely hanging on. Where have you been? Why didn't you answer your phone?"

"It was off." That part was true. "I'll explain when I get there. I'm an hour away."

"An hour?" Carla's tone hitched higher. "Every breath drains more life from her. I'm scared, Matt."

"Is anyone with you?"

"Laney Fernández. Her husband and some others are in the hallway praying."

Matt dragged in a deep breath, his eyes welled. "Tell Laney thank you." He couldn't have asked for anyone better to help his wife.

"We've tried reaching the pastor," Carla continued. "His phone goes to voicemail. Samantha's too."

Matt gritted his teeth. *You despicable bastard. It's a good thing you aren't there!* Baxter's earlier threats about telling Carla seemed ridiculous now.

"Did you hear me? We can't reach the pastor."

"You've got good people there, Car'. Don't bother with the Baxters. I'll be there soon, I promise."

"Promises from you mean nothing." The click and silence cut him like a razor slicing cocaine.

He tossed the cell into the passenger seat. His shoulders drooped. She was right. Knowing Charity lingered at death's door and he hadn't been there tortured him more than anything Carla would say once he admitted what he had done.

He pushed the car past eighty and barreled toward Phoenix, watching for cops who might be trolling the desert road.

ɛɔcз

Carla planted a warm kiss on Charity's forehead, then swabbed her child's cracked lips with a stick sponge. Her little girl slept. Her fever had dropped and her skin felt clammy.

"She seems so peaceful, Carla," Laney said. The older woman sat next to her, patting Carla's arm.

"She does. But her breathing ... I can't bear to hear it." Death-rattles filled the room. Would Matt make it in time?

"I know it's hard, dear. She's close to Glory now."

Charity's eyes flickered and she looked at something near the window.

"It's okay, baby. Mama's here." Carla squeezed the little girl's hand, then tucked a home-made quilt around her.

Charity muttered.

"What is it, sweetheart?" Carla leaned near the child's mouth.

"... Angel ..." Charity gasped. "... sing ... ing ..."

Carla's eyes brimmed and she looked at Laney. "She said something about an angel singing."

Laney's eyes filled. "Oh ... darlin' ... your baby is seeing the gates of heaven ..."

Charity spoke again. This time both women heard.

"He's here ... Mama ..." The girl smiled, looking at the back wall. "I ... go ... with ... Papa ..."

"Papa?" Carla asked.

Another laborious breath, then Charity drifted back to sleep.

"That's what she calls Matt." Carla patted away beads of sweat on Charity's face. "First an angel? Now her father?" She searched Laney's face. "Is she hallucinating?"

"No, honey. God walks His children through death's door when it's time." Laney wrapped an arm around her back. "You've always said Matt and she are close. Why wouldn't the Lord send an angel who looks like her daddy right now?"

"Why would God do that? Matt left Charity when she needed him most."

"Matt's a good man, Carla. Give him a chance to explain."

"I needed him to be here and he wasn't. God has forgotten me."

"Oh ... no ... dear. He's right here with us, right now."

Carla shook her head. “So many people prayed. Why won’t He heal her?” Tears streamed down her face.

“I ... uh ... don’t know ...” Laney stammered. “No one can explain why a child dies before her parents.”

“Thanks for not offering pat answers. I’m sick of those.” Carla rubbed Charity’s arm under the quilt. Phoenix sun pierced through the window blinds leaving patterns across the calicos.

“Cling to your faith, Carla. No matter what happens. Hold on to Jesus.” Laney’s generous arms squeezed love as Carla stared at her sleeping child. The girl’s agonizing pauses lengthened between raspy breaths, forecasting the inevitable.

CHAPTER TWELVE

Sunday afternoon, 2:11 p.m.
Prescott National Forest

DALTON OPENED WITH THE PAPER bag on the passenger seat, swerving into the opposite lane. A horn from an approaching SUV jarred him back. He tipped it over and a Ziploc bag toppled out. It was packed to the brim with tiny yellow pills. He removed two tablets and gulped them down with the last of his cold morning coffee.

The restlessness would pass once his medicine kicked in. It always did. He was grateful for that because he still had much to do before sunset.

The BMW scaled the mountain, eating up the breath-taking curves. Except for an old recreational vehicle lumbering along behind him, Dalton had the highway to himself. He floored the accelerator, creating distance. With a little luck, his quick exit wouldn't be noticed by the RV driver.

Racing around a curve, Dalton saw it. The oak tree he'd passed earlier. It shrouded the dirt road on the satellite map. He swung around the tree and entered the hideaway. This obscure way to Copper Lake would be perfect. No traffic meant no witnesses. The rough, dusty roadway might punish his car, but that wouldn't matter.

ꟿ

Samantha couldn't see Dalton's car. She leaned toward the dash and scanned the horizon. The large RV she'd been tail-gating offered concealment but prevented her from seeing if he made any unexpected turns.

When the camper pulled over, she passed, giving the driver a wave. Ahead, she could see a red billowy cloud near a gigantic tree by the highway. Had Dalton exited here? She had to find out.

She entered the thicket and scanned the road ahead. Dalton's BMW ascended a distant hill as rocks jarred her car from side to side, forcing her to slow down. Seeing a weathered sign a few feet ahead, she braked.

Copper Lake, 1 mile, no through traffic.

No through traffic? Where was he going? She forged ahead, then scanned the forest for a hiding place. A hiking trail, covered with brush, seemed wide enough to accommodate her car.

Samantha drove into the woods as far as she could, then stopped the car and turned off the engine. She got out, popped the trunk, and looked for her running shoes. No luck. She frowned at her feet. The classy Italian sandals she'd worn to church would have to do. She opened a case of Costco water, retrieved two bottles, stashed them in a tote bag, then shut the trunk.

When Samantha turned on her phone, it beeped, indicating its impending death. She scavenged the car for the charger. What could she have done with it? Maybe it had fallen on the Brewster driveway. She powered down the cell to save what energy was left for later, then tossed the phone into the tote, then locked the car.

Afternoon sun washed her face as she began her hike. The evergreen setting should have calmed her, but it didn't. Her sandaled feet objected to each step. Minutes later she arrived at the road and began a steep climb toward Copper Lake.

Breathless, Samantha reached the summit and sat on a rock overlooking the dark snake-like reservoir below. The indigo water slithered through a gully. It was surrounded by a craggy shoreline, lined with layers of minerals that glistened in the afternoon sun. Dalton was nowhere to be seen.

A revving engine caused Samantha to jump. She darted behind a Ponderosa pine and peeked around the trunk. Dalton sat in his car near the end of the lake. He exited the convertible, ran to the passenger side, then retrieved something. It flashed in the light. It looked like the hammer she'd seen earlier.

He crammed it inside the gym bag, then went to the back bumper of the car. It looked like he was pushing the car. The BMW moved toward the lake.

What's going on? Her mouth fell open. *He worships that car*. It took great restraint not to scream. Her eyes couldn't make sense of the scene unfolding in front of her.

The car gained speed until it broke through the lake's glassy surface. Waves spiraled outward. Water poured over leather upholstery and for a moment, the BMW floated, then dived forward, hood first, into its watery grave.

Samantha shook so hard the bark from the tree scraped her cheek.

Dalton tied his red running bandana around his forehead, then straddled the Nike bag over his shoulder. He picked up a leafy tree limb and dragged it from side to side, walking backwards uphill, eliminating the tire tracks. When he reached the summit, he hesitated, looking at the scene below. After a few moments, he tossed the branch aside, then turned and hurried down the road.

She wrapped her arms around herself, trying to hug away the shaking as she forged back through the forest. Pine needles snapped with each step toward the road. She poked her head out of the thicket and saw Dalton at the bottom of the hill. He ran, putting more distance between them.

Samantha hurried after him, loose gravel filling her sandals, rubbing her feet raw. Focused on Dalton's bobbing head, she tripped over a dead branch and fell. Ow! Her knee collided with a jagged rock.

She sat on the hard ground, panting. She located one of the water bottles in her tote and rinsed the grit from her mouth before inspecting her knee. It was scraped and stung a little but didn't look too bad. She dribbled water on the welt and patted it dry with her sleeve, then gulped down the rest of the water.

Knowing Dalton might have made it to the highway by now encouraged her to get moving. She managed some wobbly steps downhill. Had she lost Dalton for good?

CHAPTER THIRTEEN

3:16 p.m.
Camelback Children's Hospital
Phoenix, Arizona

MATT BURST INTO THE HOSPITAL room. He noticed the empty bed. His throat tightened. He gasped for air.

"Matt? We're over here," his wife called. Carla held Charity near the window. Laney Fernández sat in a chair next to her.

He could breathe again.

"Carla?" Matt's voice choked. "How is she?"

"The doctor was just here. It could be any time."

Laney stood up and gave Matt a lengthy hug. She waved him to the empty chair. "Sit darlin'," she ordered. "I'll be right outside if you need me."

"Thanks, Laney." Matt watched her leave.

He dragged the chair close to his wife and sat. He wiped sweat from Charity's forehead with his palm. Her ragged breathing added to a pot of regret that had simmered since he'd left Prescott. What kind of father would leave his wife and child during a time like this?

"I'm sorry, Carla," he managed between sobs. He wrapped his arm around Carla's back. Though she didn't speak, she seemed to offer forgiveness when she leaned her head against his chest. "Can I hold her?" he asked.

Carla released her grasp, lifting Charity to Matt. The morphine drip line made the transfer tricky. He scooped her feathery body into his arms.

Matt kissed her face and whispered, "It's Papa. Can you hear me? I love you, my little Charity Bug."

Charity's eyes flickered.

"Can you hear me, sweetheart?" he asked again.

Carla leaned near. "Charity ... Papa is here. Wake up, baby."

Her eyes opened and locked in recognition with his. Her lips came together to form a faint smile.

Matt moved close. "Mommy and I love you."

“Yes, baby, we do.” Carla chimed in.

Charity’s sunken eyes stared at him, their dim light warming his spirit. The moment ended too soon. She sucked in a raspy breath and slipped back into unresponsiveness. But a slight smile remained fixed on her face.

Matt guided Charity’s legs so they rested across Carla’s lap. Letting her go was something they’d do together.

CHAPTER FOURTEEN

3:25 p.m.
Prescott National Forest

HIGHWAY 89 SHIMMERED UNDER THE afternoon sun. Dalton stood on a pinnacle and scanned the terrain. He removed his bandana, blotted sweat from his eyes, then mopped his forehead. Despite the high temperatures, he felt invigorated.

He wadded the headband and jammed the end of it into his pocket, then descended toward a grove of chaparral trees as brush scratched his legs. He pulled back the foliage and pushed through to a shrouded area in the woods, a tiny meadow surrounded by junipers and oak trees. A melon-sized rock caught his attention. He smiled. He couldn't have asked for a more perfect place to complete his plan. Secret and hidden from view.

Dalton yanked the stone loose and rolled it over. He dug for several minutes with his hands, but barely made a dent.

He pulled out the hammer. It had been a good thing he'd stashed it in a toolbox in the church annex. Today it would serve him well. As he pummeled the ground, a smile crossed his lips. "If only my old man could see me now." Dalton couldn't imagine his father could see anything from where he was roasting and begging for sips of water right now. It gave him a sense of satisfaction knowing he pummeled the ground with the old man's hammer. He smiled, eagerly stabbing the soil.

When he had dug a wide hole, a couple of feet deep, he stopped and set the hammer aside. That should work.

Dalton sat on the boulder and rested. He burrowed through the canvas, locating the prescription container and the Ziploc bag. After unfastening the lid, he opened the plastic and poured in a generous portion of pills, filling the bottle to the rim.

He stared longingly at the yellow tablets before firmly screwing the cap on. Their unpredictable effects would be too risky if he took them too soon. He set the pill bottle aside.

Stay on track, he scolded himself. Seeing Matt's whiskey flask, he opened it and guzzled down the liquid gold. The burning brew coated his throat. The fire in his esophagus felt good.

When he stripped down to his undershirt and boxers, he noticed the short's pocket was empty. The bandana was gone. He scoured the meadow. He must have dropped it somewhere.

He leaned back into the tall grass as the sun descended over the western horizon. He craned his face upward, looking at heaven. Puffy clouds sashayed across the pristine sky as a cool breeze washed his face. Was the Almighty watching him through the billowy gaps? If God did, Dalton knew He'd be angry. It would take a lot of good deeds to rebalance the scales in Dalton's favor.

Dalton sat up and dug though his canvas bag. He pulled out the slacks he'd worn to church that morning, along with a pair of Ralph Lauren wing-tips. He opened a side pocket and found an energy bar and a container of water. He ingested both in seconds. His mood soothed by the alcohol, Dalton squared his shoulders. He was as ready as he could be.

He felt around the gym bag until he found the clerical shirt and white ecclesiastical collar he'd put inside. The impulsive idea to bring them seemed to control him right before leaving Saint Luke's. With no time to hunt through his clothes at home, he'd rushed to the church vestry hoping by happenchance, he'd stored an extra set in the closet. He had.

He flapped the black fabric and memories flooded back. It'd been years since he'd worn it. Today it would help him. At least that is what he hoped as he put it on. He fastened the neck button, then threaded in the stiff white collar. He left the shirt open over his undershirt.

He placed the pill-laden Ziploc on top of his gym clothes, then sausage-rolled them, before stuffing them into the canvas along with his keys and wallet. After putting on his pants, he used the end of the hammer to rip one of the knees, then massaged dirt into the frayed fabric. He placed his phone and prescription bottle inside his pocket. He laced up his leather shoes, jammed his sneakers into the bag, then zipped it shut.

He centered the duffle in the hole, then buried it. He used a dead branch to rake the surface, then marked the grave with the rock. He stood, gripped the hammer and breathed deeply.

The preparation was over. Time to put the play in motion.

CHAPTER FIFTEEN

4:17 p.m.
Prescott National Forest

SAMANTHA RETURNED TO THE CAMRY and started the engine. She inspected her face in the mirror. Sweat had melted off all of her makeup. She was a hot mess but she'd deal with that later.

When she reached the road, she headed toward Highway 89, scouring each side of the landscape.

No sign of Dalton.

Where could he have gone? Nearing the oak tree, she wondered which way to go. How far could he have traveled on foot?

"Lord, help me find him!"

Then she saw it. Red and familiar, flapping in the breeze, Dalton's doo rag flagged a clump of trees. He must have dropped it. She pulled over and parked.

Samantha waded through deep sage, taking cautious steps, protecting her hurt knee until she reached the bandana caught on a bush. She yanked it free, stuffed it into her tote, then stuck her head through the thicket. Dalton stood in the distance in a meadow wearing his clerical shirt. That was odd. He hadn't worn it for years. What was more puzzling was that he pressed the end of a hammer against his face. Her breath hitched. "What on earth?"

ꕥ

Dalton placed the tool's claw against his right cheek. One miscalculation would blind him. He gripped the wooden handle with both hands and extended the tool as far as it would go.

Only pure determination kept his hands still.

He stared at the hammer as if it were a judge's gavel. "If this goes wrong, I deserve it." The Almighty's punishment would be merited.

Don't do this, Dalton!

Kind, yet full of warning, he'd heard that familiar voice before. The day he'd hawked the Widow Snyder's heirloom. And again, the afternoon he'd stood in front of Deidra Storm's door, deciding whether to knock.

Don't do this, son.

Son?

The man who had brought him into the world had never endeared him with such a term.

"Bastard," often.

"Stupid," always.

But never, "son."

Dalton gripped the hammer tighter. *I am unworthy to be called Your son.*

He glanced at the sky. "I need my medicine," he whispered.

He was too far in to stop now. His car ... his beautiful car ... already water logged and beyond saving. He had to finish this or sacrificing the BMW would be for nothing.

He took some deep breaths to steady his hands. He closed his eyes and counted to three.

He struck his cheekbone as if it were a slab of concrete. The sound of shattering bone filled his head as he toppled to the ground. His vision, saturated with stars, he felt dizzy. His back slammed into the marker stone. He screamed, rolling in the dirt, pressing a shirttail against his face. Blood gushed, shrouded in black fabric.

ꟷ

Samantha screamed too. She fell to the ground, shaking and yelling. "Dear God, no!"

Why? What devil directed him?

Dalton's shrieks surrendered to moans.

She got up and pushed her face through the foliage again. Dalton struggled to stand.

Once on his feet, he tossed the hammer into some bushes. He took his shirt off and wadded it into a ball. He pressed it into his cheek. Would he pass out?

Dalton wobbled to a nearby tree and tapped in a number on his cell phone. Samantha strained to listen, but his words were inaudible.

Once he stopped talking, he slipped the phone into his pocket and left the clearing. Samantha could see him stagger downhill, out of sight. She entered the glade and found the hammer. Her gut twisted seeing the blood coated claws. She wrapped it in the bandana and crammed it into the tote bag.

A patch of freshly turned earth caught her eye. The stone where Dalton fell had been planted right in the center of the darker dirt. Samantha shoved it aside and dug. With only a few scoops of soil removed, she saw the gym bag. She tugged at the handle and yanked it free.

CHAPTER SIXTEEN

4:55 p.m.

DALTON SCANNED THE HIGHWAY FOR oncoming cars then walked to its center line. He gently pulled the shirt from his face. The wound had clotted. He pressed it with his fingers.

"Owww ...!" he howled. Blood dribbled across the asphalt. He examined the drops. Evidence. Should the CSI guys show up, his story would be substantiated.

He rubbed his palm into road grit, then held his breath. He shut his eyes and pressed sand into open flesh. He screamed. What felt like a thousand burning needles pierced his skin. Dizzy, he hobbled to the side of the road.

Dalton sat on a large granite boulder edging the highway. The worst was over.

He wadded his shirt again into a tight ball and pressed it against his wound. After several minutes, he removed it. Thank goodness the bleeding stopped. He shook out the shirt and put it back on, then inserted the ministerial collar in place. He fished his phone from his pocket and checked his voicemails. All were from Martin Fernández, each one increasing in urgency, asking him to come to Camelback Children's Hospital ASAP. Matt's kid wasn't doing well.

Thoughts swirled through his head. No wonder Matt came unglued at the bus station. His daughter had taken a turn for the worse.

Please ... God ... don't let her die.

Why hadn't he gotten his meds last week when he'd seen them getting low? Delaying the drug purchase hadn't been very smart. Sorrow coursed through him like a canoe navigating the rapids of the Colorado River.

His father was right.

Dalton *was* stupid and stupid is as stupid does.

Now his parishioners needed him and he'd failed them. He'd hope to gain their sympathy today, not their disdain. He closed his eyes against the pain, both his face and internal.

Maybe seeing his injury would deflect their anger.

And maybe Matt's girl would get better.

And then again, maybe not. Suddenly, everything felt doubtful. His plan. His brilliant plan. What if it didn't work? Then this would all—the car, the pain—be for nothing.

Charity had been sick a long time. What if her body gave up fighting this time? Then he'd stolen Matt's last few minutes with his child before she died.

He'd borrowed so much money from the church. What if someone found out and accused him of being a thief? Then he'd be arrested ... maybe even ... serve jail time?

He bent his head, away from the glaring sunlight. The swelling bulge beneath his eye couldn't disguise the growing shame inside. He pulled out the pill container from his pocket. He held it up to the light and wetted his lips. One more wouldn't hurt.

As he twisted the lid, he heard a distant siren. He quickly stuffed the bottle into his pants.

ꕤ

Samantha heard the shrilling of an ambulance. She grabbed the gym bag and stood. Dalton wasn't completely insane. At least he'd called 911. She left the glade and climbed a hill overlooking the road.

Dalton sat below. Seeing the flashing lights from the oncoming ambulance, she crouched behind a thick spray of weeds.

CHAPTER SEVENTEEN

5:40 p.m.
Highway 89

DALTON LEANED AGAINST A JEEP Cherokee. A highway patrol female officer and two male EMTs clustered around him. The medics cleaned his facial wound, then dressed it with gauze and tape. The AHP officer, wearing a Smoky Bear hat, stood by, pen in hand, looking at him.

"The bleeding's stopped, Reverend, but it could reopen," an EMT said. "Hold this against your face." He handed him an ice pack.

Dalton did as told and thanked him, then looked at the patrolwoman.

"When did this happen?" Sgt. Margaret P. O'Reilly asked. She seemed too young to be a Sergeant.

"About f-f-forty minutes ago." Dalton shuddered. He grit his teeth, glancing at the dipping sun. If they were to check out the blood splattered highway, they'd better get to it.

The officer, her hair pulled so hard to the back she almost squinted, made notations in her pinch book.

"I normally don't pick up hitch hikers," Dalton explained. "He was just a kid. I thought he was in trouble, so I pulled over."

"Can you describe the assailant?"

"Clean cut. In his twenties, I guess."

"Anything else?"

"Brown hair and wire-framed glasses. He looked desperate."

"Do you remember what he was wearing?" Her unblinking stare ruffled him.

"A light-colored Polo shirt ... sorry ... maybe it was white or light blue ..." Dalton arched his eyebrows. "I don't remember." Being too certain of details signaled a lie, he knew.

"Long pants or shorts?"

"Shorts. I think they were cargo pants. I guess I remember that because my son, Gordy, dresses like that."

After he estimated the man's height and weight, Dalton added, "I can't believe I was so stupid to let him into my car."

The officer just looked at him. Uncertainty roiled in his gut. He adjusted the white collar. She believed him, didn't she?

"He needed to get to Winslow," Dalton continued. "A friend abandoned him on the side of the road after an argument. He said his phone was dead."

She wrote something. "Then what happened?"

"I didn't want to leave him here, so I offered to take him to Prescott. I was on my way up there anyway. Once he got inside, he pulled out a hammer from his backpack. He hit me in the face. I could have been killed."

"That is very possible, Reverend Baxter."

"I played dead right over there." Dalton pointed to the center line of the stained highway. The officer nodded and continued writing. "When I heard him drive away, I got up and crawled to the side of the road. Thank goodness I still had my phone."

"Which way did he go?"

Dalton pointed in the direction of McCormick. "South."

"You mentioned four thousand dollars being stolen ... is that the exact amount?"

"Pretty close to that amount. I can call in the exact total tomorrow. It was a church offering. I was taking it to a mission in Prescott. It's recorded on the office computer."

"Do that. We'll need it for the report." She handed him a business card. "Here's my contact info." Sergeant Kelly closed the pinch book and slid it under her arm.

"Reverend Baxter we're done here ... for now. At the advice of the EMTs, I recommend you be taken to Camp Verde General. They have a trauma center."

Dalton agreed and thanked her, then shuffled toward the ambulance, leaning against the EMTs. He looked forward to getting to the hospital. Pain meds waited at an ER.

He caught himself before he licked his lips.

ꟷ

Samantha watched Dalton climb into the emergency vehicle. The patrol car circled around and headed toward Prescott. Within minutes the ambulance, lights spinning, followed.

Once they were gone, she re-focused on the Nike bag. She yanked it open and dumped out the contents in her lap. She unfurled the gym clothes and a Ziploc bag fell out. It contained hundreds of little yellow pills.

It didn't take her but a second to figure it out.

Oh, Lord! He's addicted.

She recalled an incident about five months ago. Dalton had stormed through the front door after a doctor's appointment.

"He won't give me anymore," he yelled, waving an empty bottle in her face while she stirred a pot of stew. "My knee's killing me and Doc Donaldson wants me to take Tylenol. Can you believe that?"

She thought at the time he was overreacting. Now everything made sense. The weird seclusion in his office. His manic mannerisms while he preached. The confused expressions on congregant's face. And sometimes he was outright rude to his flock.

But why would he deliberately destroy his car? And whatever possessed him to hit himself? And then why – would he put on his clerical clothes? She held up the plastic bag in the waning sunlight. Where did he get them?

Then she remembered. Matt leaving abruptly from the bus depot restroom.

Dalton, how could you?

After Matt's arrest and prosecution for dealing drugs two years ago, the Connor marriage teetered. Coupled with a previous D.U.I., it had been a miracle the judge granted probation instead of jail time. Carla agreed to stay if Matt maintained sobriety and worked an honest job. No more drug dealing. No more alcohol. Period.

Samantha remembered the day of Matt's sentencing. She and Dalton had gone to several hearings to offer support. She would never forget the day Matt stood before Judge Fairbanks, expecting the worst.

"Mr. Connor," he said. "I've decided to handle your case a little differently. You seem to have a lot of friends in the courtroom and your pastor has written a letter about you. I believe you want to make changes so I will grant a period of probation for three years."

Matt shook so badly Samantha thought he might fall. His public defender steadied his elbow and patted his back.

"I expect to never see you in my court room again, is that clear?"

"Yes, your honor," Matt answered, then made his way back to the galley. He collapsed into Carla's arms. They both wept.

"I know you can't drive right now," Dalton told him when they'd all left the courtroom. "I'll get you to your A.A. meetings, brother."

Matt and Carla's faces filled with hope. That had been a joyful day.

Samantha squinted at the horizon, seeing the flashing red in the distance. Anger knotted her stomach.

Sitting in the dirt, things became clear. When Charity came out of remission last year, the couple's debt mounted. If not for the church fundraisers several ago, their home would have gone into foreclosure.

Dalton took advantage of the situation. What a hypocrite.

Samantha shook the pills. Street drugs were expensive, where had he gotten the money? His inheritance was gone after that stupid spending spree last summer with the purchase of the BMW and those fancy suits. Samantha burned, remembering the new jet ski and upgraded golf clubs in the garage. There was nothing left. How many times had she warned him to slow down?

Certainty rose in her chest as her eyes welled.

Her husband stole the mission offering.

Dalton, I don't even know you anymore.

She stood and brushed dust from her slacks. What should she do next?

She took a deep breath. One thing at a time.

She'd pick up Grace and then get home to a quiet house where she could think. Decisions needed to be made. Decisions that could change her future.

Samantha climbed into the Camry and started the engine. Sweat circles clung to her armpits. An hour from now she'd relax in a hot tub with a glass of wine so she could get her thoughts together and figure out her future. She'd witnessed Dalton walk to the ambulance. He'd be well taken care of. A night apart from him would help her sort things out and get some perspective.

Samantha tapped her phone but it was completely dead. She hunted under both seats for the charger a second time but no luck. Easing into the dirt road, she headed toward the highway. A trail of red dust billowed behind. Once she reached the main road, she forged south toward McCormick.

ജ്ജ

7:05 p.m.
Camp Verde Medical Center
Prescott, Arizona

Dalton stared at the water-stained ceiling tiles. No matter which way he laid, the mattress poked a different part of his body. Searing pain burned from his lower back. The thin cushion didn't help. Thirty minutes had passed since he'd been left in an ER cubicle surrounded by curtains. He hadn't seen a doctor.

He gingerly touched the bulge beneath his eye. It felt like it had ballooned to twice the size. His right eye closed shut. He gritted his teeth as he maneuvered to his right side. He tapped Samantha's number.

The call went to voicemail. Again. He left another message.

"Why haven't you gotten back to me?" It was more of an accusation, not a question. "Call me, I need your help."

When Dalton pressed the end button, his phone buzzed.

A text from Martin. Again.

CALL ASAP. EMERGENCY!

He'd call him as soon as he heard from Sammy. What if things were really bad with the Connor girl? Dalton gulped and pushed that thought from his mind. She'd be okay. She had to be.

Had Sammy gone to Phoenix to help? That might not be such a bad thing. She'd taken his place before for hospital calls. Like that time a few years back when Glenn Porter's mother was dying and needed visitation. He had been praying by her bedside when he'd gotten the call about the car accident. Evan Cooper had been rushed to the ER and Sammy had stepped in then. She'd stayed with Yolanda Cooper all night keeping a prayer vigil. Evan pulled through.

Lord, please don't let Charity Connor die, he prayed. *If not for me, would you intervene for Matt and Carla?*

Yes, that had to be it. That's why she hadn't called.

He'd need to figure out how to get home if Sammy couldn't come.

He tapped his cell awake and stared at Deidra's icon. Drake was out of town. It would be an easy solution to his problem but sitting next to Deidra for ninety minutes in her Lexus was the last thing he wanted.

CHAPTER EIGHTEEN

Sunday, 7:17 p.m.

FINDING A WORKING PAY PHONE was Samantha's number one priority. Elaine might be worried having heard nothing from her all day. She snaked around curves until she reached a tiny rest stop called Desert Springs. Noticing a phone near a restaurant, she pulled over.

The town consisted of two buildings: Daisy's Diner and a deteriorating Chevron station with a couple of pumps. Behind the restaurant, a scrap yard dotted with twisted metal, dead refrigerators, and rusty cars waited to be officially declared DOA.

A public phone hung near the diner's door. Samantha scavenged through her purse for quarters but only found two.

Elaine accepted the collect call. "I was getting worried," she admitted after Samantha apologized. "I figured you and Dalton must have lost track of time. Did you have fun?"

Yep. A barrel of laughs. Samantha avoided her question. "I've got at least an hour of driving time. Can Grace eat dinner with you?"

"Already taken care of. The girls are eating pizza as we speak."

"I owe you, Elaine. Thanks." Samantha hung up. Thank goodness, her friend didn't press for more information.

ଽଓ

Sneaker clad feet scurried past Dalton's ER cubicle. No one had been to check on him since they'd taken his vitals. That was awhile ago.

Hey hospital people ... my face is killing me. I'm starving! His stomach grumbled. He hadn't had anything but that energy bar in the mountains.

His cell buzzed. He cringed, seeing who it was. Martin would need to wait.

Once he had the pain under control, he'd call Martin immediately.

Where on earth was the doctor?

He pressed the call button and minutes ticked by. An ER nurse poked her head in. With a tone loaded with impatience, she asked, "Yes?"

He pointed to the gauze that covered his face. “Can you get me something for this pain?”

Helen Schmidt, R.N. flung back the curtain and grabbed the clipboard from the back of the gurney. “As I explained earlier, Reverend Baxter, we’re very busy tonight. The physician will be here soon. I can’t offer you anything more than Tylenol.”

“I’ll wait for the doctor. I need something stronger.”

She shrugged, slapped the curtain closed, and disappeared.

Tylenol ... was she kidding? That wouldn’t help. Frustration pulsed in his chest, keeping pace with the pain throbbing in his face.

He patted the lump in his pocket. Taking his Oxy now would be risky. He’d experienced the unpredictable effects too often.

He sighed and surrendered to the pillow. He shut his eyes. Tried to think of something besides the pain.

ꟃ

Sunday, 7:55 p.m.

Paloverde trees framed the Baxter yard like a cozy desert painting. Samantha eased her car into the driveway. She opened the garage door and parked next to Dalton’s empty spot. What kind of story would he come up with to explain the BMW’s disappearance? She rolled her eyes. More lies were coming, no doubt.

She opened the side door to the kitchen, Grace trailing behind. Samantha dropped her keys and purse on the counter, then plugged in her phone.

Grace tugged at her sleeve. “Where’s Daddy?”

“He had to go to Prescott.” Samantha looked at her and smiled. “He’ll be home soon.”

Dalton was resourceful, he’d figure out how to get home. Hopefully not until tomorrow. She needed time to herself.

“I need to make some calls, sweetheart. Go get your p.j.’s on and we’ll watch a movie.”

Grace raced through the breakfast room and disappeared into the foyer, on her way upstairs to her room.

Samantha tapped her phone. A green light flashed, indicating voicemails.

The first few were from Laney. Charity Connor was in the hospital.

Samantha’s breath hitched. The messages were time-stamped hours ago.

Several were from Dalton. “Sammy, call me back,” his third one ordered. “I’m in the ER. I’m okay but I need your help. I can’t understand why you have your phone turned off. This has been a rough day for me.”

I bet it has! A smoldering wick of anger reignited.

Gordy's voicemail calmed her heart. He'd arrived safely at Grams'. Samantha already missed him.

Another message from Laney. She and Martin were at the hospital. Things didn't look good for Charity and no one could reach Matt. Could she and Dalton come to Camelback Children's Hospital as soon as possible?

She clicked off the phone, stuffed granola bars and water into her purse along with a spare phone charger, then hurried toward the stairs. Grace, wearing her pajamas, was heading toward the den. Poor thing. This would be a long night.

As she scaled the stairs, her phone buzzed. Dalton's smiling face filled the display. She frowned and slipped the cell into her pocket.

I'll deal with you later.

She washed away the grime from her face and dragged a brush through her hair. Haggard eyes peered back from the mirror as she refastened her ponytail. Brushing her teeth never felt so good. A clean shirt and jeans made all the difference in the world. She laced up her running shoes, then grabbed an iPad before heading to Grace's room for some fresh clothes for her daughter.

"You need to get dressed again." Samantha paused, carefully choosing her words. "Some people from church need our help." Grace and Charity were best friends. If the news ended up being bad, she'd tell her later.

"The movie just started," Grace whined.

"We'll stream it to my iPad."

Grace slowly tugged on her pants.

Samantha's impatience grew as the fabric inched its way up Grace's legs. She pulled her daughter close and tried to zip her pants.

"No, Mommy ... I can do it myself." Grace pushed away Samantha's hands.

"Okay, honey, hurry." Samantha forced herself to take a deep breath as she watched her seven year old methodically dress.

Grace grabbed her t-shirt and dragged it over her head.

At least the sneakers had Velcro fasteners.

Minutes later, Samantha backed out of the garage and sped through the dark neighborhood, heading toward the highway. Wild waves of anger rolled over her like a raging storm. She frowned at the window, gripping the wheel, grateful for the dark car and that Grace had been captured by a Disney film.

Dalton should be here. He should be caring for his flock. He should be praying for the Connor family. He should be offering comfort.

She drove through the empty highway toward Phoenix, making a decision. This time she'd go it alone. She could do this. She'd been on hospital visits before. If only she'd get there in time. *Lord, please be with these precious parents.* Her heart ached for Carla as she increased her speed on the empty freeway.

Within an hour she noticed the shimmering lights of Northern Scottsdale, a ritzy city that hugged the eastern side of Phoenix. Her GPS lighted her way to Camelback Children's. It wouldn't be much longer.

Animated colors reflected across the seat while Grace slept. Samantha released her daughter's fingers from the iPad and turned it off. She inserted a worship CD in her player.

Chris Tomlin crooned. The soothing words covered her with peace as it always did.

Until ....

Chris sang about surrendering his life ... at the cross ...

She hadn't surrendered Dalton into His hands.

She didn't want to.

She snapped off the stereo.

Forgive me, Lord. Not now. You can deal with him as soon as I'm finished.

CHAPTER NINETEEN

Sunday, 9:05 p.m.
Huckleberry, Arizona

GORDON STEADIED HIS TELESCOPE ON the redwood deck under a canopy of stars. He plugged its USB to the laptop's live satellite feed. He made some adjustments, then grabbed his coffee cup from the patio table. He blew on the steam and took a careful sip, then stabbed a forkful of Gram's homemade apple pie. He washed it down with another sip of brew. Both were delicious, just like he remembered.

He leaned against the railing and looked into Gram's garden. Towering Ponderosas acted like sentries, guarding the cabin at each end of a wooden fence that surrounded her vegetables. Rows of bushy cornstalks were ready to be picked. Clusters of trees, bursting with apples, surrounded the garden. He had his work cut out for him.

The lights of Huckleberry flickered below. Piccadilly Street with its one-hundred-year-old Victorian street lamps marched through the center of town. Tomorrow he'd check it out and see if anything had changed. Other than a low-budget flick at the Cochise Theatre, nothing ever did.

Gordon set down his mug and peered through the view finder, guiding the tube in its cradle until he'd locked on to both Ursas Major and Minor in the Northern sky. The constellations were brilliant in the cloudless night, showcasing the Big and Little Dippers. Polaris, the ancient North Star of biblical heroes Abraham and Job, tipped the smaller dipper.

The star's intensity captured his attention until the squeal of a screen door startled him. His head bobbed up. Grams stood in the doorway.

"It's getting late, Gordster," she said. "Shouldn't you be getting to bed?"

Gordon grinned. "I'm a little old for a bedtime, Grams. Besides, I got plenty of sleep on the bus."

She padded across the porch wearing a flannel bathrobe and floppy slippers. Long gray hair draped her shoulders as she carried a steamy mug.

"What are you looking at?" she asked.

"Ursa Major. Really hangs low this time of year. Wanna look?"

Uncertainty flickered across her face. "How do I use one of these things?"

"Lean here. Place your eye over the opening," he told her as she bent over the scope.

"Not sure what I'm staring at, Gordy."

"Do you see the Big Dipper?" he asked.

"No ... Oh ... wait a minute ... there it is." She raised her head and smiled, then looked again.

"Do you see the bear? Look down from the cup of the Dipper ... do you see it?"

After a few moments, she raised her face, looking puzzled. "I'm not sure."

Gordon Googled the constellation and pointed to his laptop screen. "See ... it looks like a bear."

She returned to the scope. "I see it, Gordy. It's amazing."

"Tomorrow, I'll give you a lesson in astronomy."

"Wonderful." She lifted her face and smiled at him.

"What time are you gonna put me to work?"

"You sleep in. After breakfast we can start the canning. If there's time, you can pick the corn."

"Would it be okay if we put off the canning?" he asked. "I'll pick the corn but was hoping to do my research in the afternoon. The forecast says no clouds."

"No problem. You'll have plenty of time to do my stuff. I can pay as you go or at the end of the week."

"Whatever works best for you," he said.

"I'd give you more if I could. I love it when you come."

"Thanks, Grams. You're contributing to a good cause."

"What are you buying this year?"

"Another solar filter. I'm checking out the sun tomorrow."

"Is that safe?"

"With a filter it is. There's nothing to worry about."

"I guess I'll hit the sack." She yawned. "It's been a long day." She gave him a long hug, then deposited a kiss on his cheek before heading toward the cabin. She pivoted around at the screen door and called out, "There are clean towels on your bed upstairs."

"Thanks, Grams. I won't be long," he told her as she disappeared inside.

Polaris, the celebrity star, dominated the black carpet of the night. Gordon took a series of photos, saving them to his Amazon cloud account. He rubbed the fatigue in his neck, then disconnected the equipment and tucked the laptop under his arm. He draped the telescope with a tarp and swallowed the last dregs of his coffee before heading inside the cabin.

A nightlight guided him up a steep, pine staircase to the first bedroom on the right, a cheerful room he'd used since childhood. He snapped on the light and noticed Grams' promised towels placed at the end of a turned down bed. A homemade quilt, folded over, invited him to sleep.

Once in his pajamas, he climbed between cool, crisp sheets, then settled on his back and studied the small room. Moonlight filtered through lace curtains, projecting eerie ghost-like images across the wall. He stared into the darkness, wondering about Bee. Two weeks would be a long time and he already missed her. His tossing and turning caused a chorus of creaks from the brass-knobbed bed. The tick, tick, tick from a wind-up alarm clock on his nightstand competed with his breathing.

Ten twenty p.m.

He shut his eyes. Sleep refused to come. His mind wandered up Moonscape Peak, the small mountain that overlooked Huckleberry. Sun viewing there would be incredible and would be worth the hike up that treacherous trail.

He'd get up early and pick Grams' corn. By the time she had pancakes on the griddle, he'd have it shucked. Then he'd head to town before hiking up Moonstone.

Minutes ticked by and Gordon fell asleep.

CHAPTER TWENTY

Sunday, 10:31 p.m.
Camelback Children's Hospital
Phoenix, Arizona

SAMANTHA PRESSED DALTON'S NUMBER AND dialed.

"Sammy ... finally ... I left you voicemails. Why didn't you call?"

She sucked in a deep breath. A cauldron of simmering anger boiled.

"I'm at Camelback Children's. Didn't you get Martin's text messages?"

"Yes. I haven't had a chance to call him back. I'm in the emergency room in Prescott. Can you come and get me?"

A satisfactory response seemed elusive. Dead air hung between them.

"Did you hear me, Sammy?" he asked. "I'm in the ER."

"Charity Connor is dying."

More silence. "Dalton, did you hear me?"

"Wait ... dying? Charity is dying. Are you sure?"

"She doesn't have much time." Samantha's eyes welled. Matt and Carla were a few feet away in their daughter's hospital room.

Even though she knew the answer, she asked anyway. "Why are you in the ER?"

"I was held up on the side of the road," Dalton began. He prattled out a rehearsed story, full of omissions. She stifled a groan. Fresh tears dribbled down her cheeks. Why would he concoct such a story? Had the drugs corrupted him so thoroughly that he deliberately injured himself to get more? Where was the Dalton she loved? Where was the Dalton who cared for addicts? Where was her Dalton?

Dalton continued. "From out of nowhere he lunged at me with a hammer. That's why I'm here. They just took x-rays."

It was out of nowhere, that was for sure. She'd had no inkling of Dalton's intent. And she knew exactly where that hammer was: in her Camry's trunk. Where it would wait until she knew what to do next.

Who was this man? Had she loved him for nineteen years and never known him?

"Sammy ... are you there?"

She fought the impulse to slam the phone against the wall and instead let out a deep sigh, pretending ... just like Dalton. “I’m here.”

“He pushed me out of the car!” Dalton’s voice pitched. “Fortunately, I had my phone or I might still be walking around that highway—bleeding. I’ve been here for over three hours and still haven’t seen a doctor.”

“I ... don’t know what to say, Dalton.”

“You don’t sound very sympathetic.”

“I ... I’m tired.” Fatigue swallowed her. She pressed a tissue to her nose, so he wouldn’t hear her sniffles. She wished she’d never followed him. Not knowing this would have been better.

“Sammy ... I hate to tell you this ... the worst part is ... the church offering ... it was stolen.”

No, Dalton, it wasn’t. Matt has it.

“I can’t come. I can’t talk anymore,” she told him, shaking. “The Connors need pastoral care.”

“I ... uh ...” he stammered, then said, “Don’t worry about me. I’ll find a way home.”

ꕥ

In a shadowy corridor, Dalton ran toward the sound of a woman’s wail.

When he reached an open door, people held candles around a bedridden girl. A woman sobbed, crumpled on the floor.

Dalton knew the child was dead. “Who is she?” he asked.

The circle of lights opened, welcoming him in.

A man pointed. “She’s healed!”

The girl’s curls looked familiar. The nose ... the round chin ...

“Graaaa ... ce! Nooooo, God, please!” Dalton screamed.

“She’s whole again, safe in God’s arms,” a lady said.

The woman on the floor glared up at him. *Sammy!*

“You did this!” she shrieked.

Someone grabbed his arms and shook him.

Dalton spun around. “There’s been a terrible mistake!”

“Mr. Baxter, wake up!”

“What ... huh?” Dalton forced his eyes open. Sleep paralysis held him in a tight grip.

“I had a hard time waking you.” A doctor hovered over him under a florescent glare. He mopped Dalton’s face with a towel. Dalton slowly moved his arms.

“I’m Dr. Adams.” He placed a cold stethoscope against his chest. Dalton jerked.

“How are you feeling?” the doctor asked.

He was confused. Then he remembered where he was.

"My face is on fire." Dalton pointed to his bandage. "The nurse could only give me Tylenol. That stuff doesn't work for me."

"Let's have a look," the doctor said.

The physician removed the dressing and examined the wound, then dabbed it with antiseptic while Dalton clenched his teeth.

"I've looked at your X-rays. The lateral surface of your zygomatic bone has multiple fractures."

"My zygo ... what?"

"Your cheekbone is cracked. Fortunately, you won't need any reconstructive surgery. I'll need to suture the lesion in case it reopens."

"Sure, Doc. Whatever you say. But what about my pain?"

"We'll give you some acetaminophen with codeine to take home." He loaded a hypodermic needle, then injected Dalton's face. "This anesthesia should numb your skin in a couple of minutes. Do you have any questions?"

"Acetaminophen? That's Tylenol, isn't it?" Dalton suppressed a groan.

The doctor smiled. "Yes, it is. Nothing gets past you, does it, Mr. Baxter? Don't worry. With the added codeine, it's much more potent than the kind you buy at your local drug store."

"Can't you prescribe something stronger? Awhile back I used a drug called ...um ... let's see if I can remember ... Oxy ... something or other?"

"Oxycotin?"

"That's it. I took it last year after a back-country skiing accident on Agassiz Mountain."

"Let me guess ... Doyle's Saddle, right?"

"Dumbest thing I ever got talked into."

"That eastern bowl is amazing. Don't tell me you attempted that without some serious training?"

"Guilty. My wife would have killed me if I hadn't almost done it myself. My buddy and I met up with an avalanche. He escaped. I tore up my knee pretty bad. Now about those meds ..."

Dalton could sense the doctor's breath as he worked on his face. The anesthesia worked well. Dalton felt only light pokes as the physician stitched.

Once the gauze and tape were reapplied, Dalton asked, "What about my medication?"

"Codeine will be less habit-forming." The doctor pulled out his prescription pad.

"My cheek feels like it's been hit by a Mack truck and I've got a job interview this Thursday. I've got to have something more effective," Dalton pleaded. "I was careful before, Doc. I can handle Oxy ... trust me."

The doctor's eyes seemed to search his. "Okay ... I'll give you a ten-day supply. But Mr. Baxter ..." He held up his pen like a nun's 12-inch ruler.

"You need to be careful. Twelve hours between each dose. Do you understand?" He wrote out the order and gave it to him.

Dalton snapped the paper. "Absolutely."

After signing release documents, the doctor looked up. "Have you arranged for a ride home?"

"I've got someone I can call."

Adams pointed to the wound. "Have that looked at by your doctor within a week." He gestured to the prescription in Dalton's hand. "We have a pharmacy near the lobby where you can fill that." He checked his wristwatch. "The nurse will be back in a few minutes with your first dose. No more pills before nine a.m. tomorrow. Is that clear?"

"Got it. Thanks, Doc."

Dalton played a few rounds of solitaire on his iPhone as he waited for the nurse. The same surly woman swung back the curtain and handed him two yellow pills and a cup of water. "Frau" Schmidt glared, folding her arms, watching him like a prison guard. Crushing the pills would be out of the question. He gulped them down and leaned his head against the pillow.

When Schmidt started to leave Dalton asked, "Were you able to get me something to eat?"

"The cafeteria's closed," she grumbled, then rummaged in her pockets. She handed him some meager rations: a package of broken crackers and some juice. "I found these in the staff lounge. Chew on your left side."

Minutes later, she returned with an orderly. They helped him into to a wheelchair while familiar warmth coursed his body. As he rolled through hallway, he felt better. For half a minute, he considered going to Phoenix tonight. Showing up at Camelback Children's, with his injury on display, Sammy and the others would realize he cared. By the time he reached the lobby, a more logical voice won the debate. Going to Phoenix wasn't a good idea. Engaging an angry father wouldn't be fun. Matt hated him. The welt behind his left ear testified to that.

The orderly wheeled him toward the pharmacy while Dalton prayed for Charity Connor.

God ... I screwed up today ... please let her be okay. The mounting debt between him and the Almighty seemed formidable. Could he ever even the scale? *I'll make things right once I get that job ... I promise.*

He'd never meant to let anyone down. Sammy's caustic tone replayed in his head. Maybe the dreadful nightmare had been a warning from God. He shuddered. If he didn't get his act together, would tragedy visit the Baxter home?

When he arrived at the pharmacy's double glass doors, he saw a line of people wrapped around a rope chain. One person manned the counter.

He patted the bulge in his pocket. The supply of pills he'd brought from the mountains would get him by. He tugged the attendant's sleeve. "I changed my mind. I'll get my meds tomorrow."

The attendant left him sitting near glass doors in the lobby and Dalton scrolled his phone contacts.

ᘓᘐ

Sunday, 11:25 p.m.

"Deidra?"

"Oh ... Dawling ... I hoped you'd call."

"Sorry I didn't get back to you. I'm still in Prescott. Would you be able to pick me up at Camp Verde Hospital? Samantha's in Phoenix helping another congregant's family. I'm in the lobby near the ER."

"ER? What happened? Are you okay?"

"I had a little accident. I'll explain once you're here."

Dalton waited over an hour, thumbing through magazines. He looked out the window, watching. When would Deidra's car appear in the hospital round-about?

How should he handle this? She'd expect something for this little "favor." Once back in McCormick, he'd remind her again that they could only be friends. No sense in upsetting her now. It might cost him a ride. Hopefully, she wouldn't try anything. Not tonight. Not with his face stitched and swollen.

He jiggled his foot, perusing the latest *Time* magazine, sucking the last of his apple juice with a straw. He'd tried eating a saltine, but even with the Oxy, burning needles exploded through his jaw so he chucked the crackers in the trash. His stomach grumbled, imagining Sammy's homemade chicken soup simmering on the stove. But she was angry and hours away. Lukewarm Campbell's would have to do.

Headlights appeared at the end of the circular drive, then a red Lexus materialized behind the glow. Deidra had made it in record time. She emerged and waved as Dalton rolled himself through the exit. He met up with the driveway attendant who pushed him to the car. Wearing white silky shorts, Deidra staccato-stepped in pointy stilettos. They met at the passenger door.

"Wow, Deidra, you got here sooner than I expected," Dalton said.

"I probably broke all the speed laws. Oh, Pastor ... hon ... You look awful."

"I've had better days." He collapsed into the creamy leather, hoping she wouldn't talk his ear off the whole way home. His eyes burned, begging for sleep but the Oxy kept him alert. Maybe a cat nap against the window?

Deidra rattled off questions while the car snaked through the encroaching darkness of Prescott National Forest. She floored the accelerator, squealing around treacherous cliffs. The way his stomach tossed, good thing it was empty. Deep dark gulches dropped down into blackness. Dalton gripped the edge of his seat. He hated being a passenger with this speed demon.

"So, you think they'll catch the guy?" she asked.

"I hope so."

"How can people do such things?" She reached over and squeezed his knee.

"Owww!" Dalton yelled.

She snapped her hand back. "I'm sorry. Was that your bad knee?"

"Yes," he lied.

"You poor man. I'll get you home as soon as I can."

Good idea. He yearned to close his burning eyes.

"Deidra, do you mind if I get some shut eye?" Pretending to be asleep would be easy. "It's been quite a day."

"Of course, Pastor. I'll play soft music to relax you."

A quick tap of a button, the stereo released classic rock and roll.

"Oh, darn. That won't do." Deidra pressed a few other buttons from jazz to easy listening. When she landed on a talk-radio station, she stopped. The host seemed to capture her attention. "Recent sun activity has authorities concerned that the planet might be hit by a geomagnetic super storm," he said. "If that happens, the power grids might be taken down. People would be wise to put away food and water ... enough for thirty days."

Dalton twisted his face toward her. "Gordy's into that. Always saying the earth could have a kill shot from the sun."

"Drake has an obsessive interest too. Drives me crazy. I don't want to think about it." Deidra tapped a button and brought Michael Bublé into the car.

"Me neither. As if we didn't have enough to worry about." Dalton turned back to the window, snuggling against the headrest. Romantic songs melded together, and he drifted in and out of sleep. The last thing he remembered was Deidra singing about feeling hot and fevered when someone kissed her. Her voice seemed to grow louder ... almost as if she sang to him..

Monday

The Lord is near to the brokenhearted and saves the crushed in spirit. Psalm 24:18

CHAPTER TWENTY-ONE

Monday, 1:55 a.m.
Connor Home
McCormick, Arizona

"THIS CAN'T BE REAL. TELL me it's a bad dream, Laney. Is Charity really gone?" Samantha stared at her child. Grace dragged in a tired breath while sleeping under the mermaid blanket on Charity Conner's bed. Samantha stroked the child's cheek while warm air bathed the tips of her fingers. They'd arrived in McCormick about thirty minutes ago and Grace had slept the entire time.

Laney's eyes filled as she huddled near the window. "I can't believe it either." Laney dabbed them with a tissue.

Martin Fernández had led the solemn caravan of cars from Phoenix while Matt and Carla huddled in the backseat of their station wagon. Close to midnight, Charity had taken her final breath and despite their objections about leaving her, Martin eventually convinced the couple to return to their desert home.

"Shouldn't we check on Matt and Carla?" Samantha asked.

"When you went to the bathroom I did. Matt would like us to leave."

"Who else is still here?"

"A few of the council members and their spouses. They're discussing arrangements."

Samantha poked her head into the hallway. Hushed voices came from the kitchen. She glanced at the Hello Kitty clock near Charity's bed. "It's almost two. Folks need to go to bed. We'll meet at the church later to make plans. I know Matt wants us to leave, but I can't. Carla's a mess."

"It'd be nice if someone was here. Martin and I will stay. You go. Dalton needs you."

"Believe me, he's fine." He had his pills, didn't he? "He's probably asleep."

Laney draped an arm around her shoulder. "Can we talk?"

Samantha's stomach twisted. "Okay." She tucked the blanket around Grace and kissed her forehead, then followed Laney to the living room.

Laney motioned her to a plaid couch by the fireplace.

When they were seated, Laney's eyes glistened with kindness. "Did you know Martin and I almost hit you yesterday morning on Kaibab Road?"

"Was that you?" Samantha gasped. "I'm sorry. I was in a hurry."

"Where were you headed?"

"To the church." Samantha's cheeks warmed. "I needed to speak to Dalton before he left." She took in a deep breath. "I ended up following him all the way to Prescott."

"You did?" Laney's brow furrowed.

"There's a lot more to this carjacking story than what I told you earlier."

"What?"

"If I reveal what I know, my whole life will change." Samantha's eyes pooled. "Nothing will ever be the same."

"Do you want things to stay the way they are?" Laney asked.

No, she didn't. She was tired of hiding in the shadows, hoping Dalton would come to his senses. Between sniffs into a wad of tissue, Samantha poured out her heart. As she unraveled the twisted tale, the knots in her stomach loosened.

"I hid behind a fern at the bus stop. Dalton was in the bathroom and I'm pretty sure I know what he was doing there."

"You do? What?"

"Buying drugs."

"You can't be serious." Laney's eyes became saucers. "How do you know that?"

"I put things together when I followed him to the mountains." She decided not to mention seeing Matt Connor exiting the bathroom door and that he was most likely Dalton's dealer. She'd spare Carla and everyone else that part of the story. Hopefully Matt would confess on his own.

She then proceeded to describe Dalton's mountain mayhem.

"He sank his car?" Laney asked.

"That's not all ..." Samantha told her about the foothill chase. "He took his father's hammer and hit himself in the face."

Laney's mouth dropped. "What on earth ...?"

"It was all part of a devious plan." Samantha's anger climbed, remembering Dalton's howls of pain, her own cries of disbelief.

"What plan?"

"Covering up a so-called robbery."

"I'm lost. What do you mean?"

"He took the mission offering and used it to buy drugs. I know this because after he left the area, I dug up the duffle bag and found the pills. They're hidden in my car."

"Oh ... mija ... how long has he been using?"

"I think since his skiing accident."

"His leg was pretty mangled after that avalanche mishap. Then with knee surgery, the recuperation had to be awful." Laney scooted close. "Dalton's hooked on opiates," she said matter of factly. "He couldn't get free if he tried. He needs help, Samantha."

Disbelief flooded Samantha's chest and she blinked. "Are you making excuses for him?"

Laney placed a hand on Samantha's clenched fist. "Of course not. He can only blame himself for the initial abuse. Once a person takes more than prescribed, an addiction is certain. Why on earth the government hasn't taken them off the market is beyond me." She squeezed Samantha's hand. "Dalton's out of control. I've worked with addicts. I know how they think."

Samantha wagged her head. "I ... uh ... don't know what to do."

Laney hugged her tight, then looked into her eyes. "It'll be okay. Your family and friends are here to help."

"I'm scared, Laney. When the council finds out, Dalton will go to jail." She ripped her tissue into shreds, afraid to meet her friend's eye. "Won't he?"

"Let's not get ahead of ourselves. Let me talk with Martin. Maybe we could handle this without involving law enforcement."

"I don't think so. He filed a police report."

Laney exhaled a deep breath. She kept silent a moment. Samantha's hopes rose like campfire smoke in the dawn. "With the right lawyer, a judge might be persuaded to sentence him to a recovery program instead of jail. I've seen that before."

Laney's words blew away the thin wisps of optimism and reality barged in. "Dalton's used all of our money. We can't pay attorney fees."

"Maybe the church's benevolence fund can help."

"After what he did?" The shredded tissue looked like snow in Samantha's lap. She gathered the pieces into a ball.

"None of this is your fault, Samantha. The congregation will want to help."

Samantha shook her head. "This is so humiliating. I'm embarrassed to ask."

"I know, honey." Laney's eyes filled. "May I pray with you?"

She shrugged as Laney took her hands. Samantha didn't know if God would even listen. The woman's kind words loosened the blanket of shame that had suffocated Samantha for the past twelve hours. Hope stirred in her heart. Having a friend beside her made all the difference in the world.

CHAPTER TWENTY-TWO

1:45 a.m.
Baxter Home

ENTERING HER DARK KITCHEN, SAMANTHA groped her way to the light. Grace's face meshed with Samantha's shoulder. She flipped on the switch near the sink. Florescent bulbs hummed above. The usually warm terra cotta walls felt joyless and cold. Dirty cereal bowls and half-drained coffee cups from Sunday reminded her of the normalcy she craved. She should be sound asleep upstairs, nothing keeping her awake. Charity Connor should be alive, maybe having a sleepover with Grace. Dalton should be strong and whole.

Grace raised her head. "Mommy?"

"Shhh ..." Samantha stroked her daughter's hair. "Let's get you to bed. You've had quite a night."

Samantha carried Grace up the stairs to her room. She tugged off her sneakers and laid her between crisp sheets. She stroked her daughter's hair until she fell back asleep, then left the room.

As she headed toward the staircase, Dalton's snores crowded the landing. She poked her head in their bedroom and stared. Slivers of moonlight streaked across his bare chest as he laid on their king size bed. White gauze shrouded his face.

He slept peacefully.

A whirlpool of anger roiled in her stomach. It wasn't fair.

Samantha padded down the stairs to the kitchen and got her keys, then hurried to the garage and popped open the Camry's trunk. After pulling out the canvas bag, she unzipped it and dumped out the contents on the garage floor. Clothes and shoes, along with the zipped baggy, tumbled out on the concrete. She dug through the tote, finding the hammer, then extended it like a dead mouse. She cringed at the sight of dried blood clinging to the claw tips.

After a careful inspection of the tote and its contents, Samantha had a plan. She crammed everything back inside the Nike and headed outside to a shed near the back of their property. Eight fifty-five gallon drums containing an emergency water supply lined one side of the storage unit. After crawling under a utility sink, she secured the duffle behind a barrel.

She returned to the kitchen, filled a kettle with water and placed it on the stove. Sipping hot tea under the starry desert sky was just what she needed to clear her head.

With a shrill whistle of steam, she drowned a chamomile bag with boiling water, then stirred in some honey. Cradling her cup, she walked to the backyard, vapor wafting heavenward.

A million stars invited her to the solace she craved. A gentle breeze played with her hair, offering mercy from the heat. Paloverdes swayed, silhouettes of their branches danced in the moonlight. The soothing tea quieted her soul.

She looked forward to crashing on the den couch. Sleep would deliver her from this horrible day and away from Dalton's incessant snoring. Better enjoy it now, mister! This was the so-called calm before the storm. Things were about to change. The peaceful town of Daltonville was about to be hit by a tornado.

With her tea almost gone, she glanced at the kitchen window. A microwave clock glared neon green through the glass.

2:22

The electronic trinity stopped her.

Father, do those numbers mean anything?

His answer came instantly inside her head. The word *"Daniel"* saturated her thoughts. The warm cadence of His voice brought comfort. *Daniel ... the Daniel in the Bible?*

She collected her cup and went back inside. After finding her Bible on the kitchen counter, she thumbed through to the Old Testament prophet.

He reveals deep and secret things; He knows what is in the darkness, and light dwells with Him. Daniel 2:22

Would God show her what the truth was? Was Dalton hiding more than a drug addiction?

Revelation dawned. God was in the darkness *with* Dalton. Didn't the Bible also say if we make our beds in Hades, even there, He is with us?

It had been a horrible day. Was there anything else Dalton hid from her?

Please show me, Lord.

A rooftop air conditioner rattled. She waited for that still, small voice but heard only the motor's hum.

"Ahem ..." A raspy cough crowded the silence in her home. Had Dalton gotten out of bed?

A throat cleared, followed by more coughing.

Samantha jumped back. Definitely not Dalton. Who was in her house at this hour? She crept to the kitchen and opened the cabinet above the stove. She found a loaded Ruger behind the *Better Homes and Gardens Family Cookbook*. She grabbed the weapon and forced herself to walk toward the den, clutching the gun, trying to steady her shaky hands.

A light came on in the den.

"Who's there?"Samantha yelled.

"It's me." It sounded like Deidra Storm. The earthy voice was unmistakable.

"Deidra?"

Looking like she'd escaped from a 'seventies sitcom, Deidra filled the entryway, wearing one of Dalton's shirts. Disheveled hair raged around her face while smudgy eyeliner added to the dark circles under golf-ball sized eyes.

"My Lord! It's me, Samantha, don't shoot!"

Samantha lowered the weapon and stared. Deidra wore her bunny slippers, the ones the kids gave her last Christmas.

"What are you doing in my house?"

"Didn't Dalton tell you? I picked him up at the hospital." Her brow furrowed. "I couldn't leave him alone in his condition so I decided to sleep on your sofa. I thought you knew, hon. I'm sorry to frighten you."

"He didn't tell me." What else was new? "I didn't see your car. How was I to know you were here?"

"I moved it. Didn't want to give the neighbors anything to gossip about. Poor thing, he had trouble walking so I helped him to bed.

I bet you did. Anger and frustration battled in Samantha's chest. She drew a deep breath and managed to speak calmly. "Look Deidra, I can handle things. We've had a rough night so I would like you to leave."

"If you insist." Deidra huffed as she brushed past Samantha and disappeared into the breakfast room.

"Don't forget to leave my slippers," Samantha called.

Moments later, Deidra reappeared and returned to the den wearing flip flops. She pressed the slippers into Samantha's hands.

"I'll return the pastor's shirt in a few days," she said before charging through the front door leaving a wake of expensive perfume.

CHAPTER TWENTY-THREE

Monday morning, 7:50 a.m.
Huckleberry, Arizona

RHYTHMIC THUMPING ROBBED SHIRLEY WESTON from her last few minutes of REM sleep. Golden fingers of morning sun crossed her sheets and arms. She sat up, rubbed her eyes. What was that noise?

Oh, yes. Gordy. He must have gotten up early. He was already shucking corn.

A chunky braided rag rug covered planks of honey-colored maple under her bed. She planted her feet on the rug's softness as she squinted at the clock without her glasses.

7:50.

She'd slept in. She had a hungry boy to fill.

Shirley climbed into her robe and grabbed a hairbrush from her bureau. The mirror didn't soften her sixty-seven years. Every line advertised heartache, worry, and loss. She dragged the brush through her unruly grays, tacking clumps of long hair at her temples with tortoise shell combs.

She picked up a framed photo of herself and her husband, Stephen. They stood outside The Love Place, a San Francisco coffee house back in the 1960s. Stephen's flaxen hair hung six inches longer than hers. They'd been so happy. Had it been over fifty years since that rainy summer day?

I miss you, my love. She kissed the picture and set it down.

Hearing a *kachunk* against the redwood decking brought her to the present. She padded through the hallway toward the back door. She pushed open the screechy screen and her grandson looked up.

"Hi, Grams." His smile always warmed her. He sat on an Adirondack chair by a plastic tub nearly filled with corn.

"You're up early, Gordster."

"I got up at five. This is my last bucket." He brushed silky strands from his arms. "I thought I'd head up to Moonscape today but changed my mind." He craned his neck at the sky. "There's an incoming storm, which makes a minuscule viewing window this afternoon."

"Are you still going to Huckleberry?"

"I'd like to. Can I use your car?"

"The keys are on the hook. I thought I had an astronomy lesson today."

"I'll be back by two. They'll be plenty to look at."

"We've got a new Dairy Queen near the hardware store."

"I'll check it out." Gordy downed a swig of coffee.

"Don't forget to take the tubs inside so I can prep the corn for the freezer."

"Sure, Grams."

"I'll make us some breakfast." Shirley went back indoors. She collected eggs, milk and flour. Flapjacks just the way Gordy liked them were on the menu. As she cracked eggs into a bowl, she looked forward to sharing a meal with one of her most favorite persons on the planet.

CHAPTER TWENTY-FOUR

9:10 a.m.
McCormick, Arizona

SAMANTHA COVERED HER EYES. LIGHT streamed through the sliding glass window, drenching her face. Pressure gripped the sides of her head. She sat up and massaged the knots in her neck.

Seated inches from the T.V., her daughter watched a cartoon.

"Grace?"

Blond curls spun around. "Mommy, I'm hungry."

"It's late. You must be starving." Samantha got to her feet. "You can eat out here, if you're careful."

Grace jumped with delight and found her favorite place at the coffee table while Samantha trudged toward the kitchen.

Minutes later, Samantha deposited a bowl of Greek yogurt with sliced strawberries in front of her daughter, then returned to the kitchen. She pulverized some espresso beans and filled a coffee press, then lit a burner under the kettle.

She drowned the coffee grounds with boiling water, then shoved in the plunger and set it aside. A thick, black ooze seeped to the surface.

Though the breakfast room was soaked with morning sunlight, it failed to cheer Samantha. Her special place in the 1950s vinyl-backed banquette did nothing to lift her spirits. Instead anger climbed as she sipped her coffee.

She slammed down her mug and headed upstairs.

ജൽ

Samantha flung open the bedroom door.

Dalton didn't budge.

She flipped on the light and jabbed his shoulder. He groaned, but his eyes remained shut.

"Wake up!"

His face looked awful. The puffy skin encircling the eye above the bandage was red and swollen. A half moon bruise hung under his good eye. She pushed him again, harder.

His eyes flickered and a frown formed. "What?"

"There's something we need to discuss."

"I've got to sleep."

"You can sleep after we talk."

He managed a sitting position and leaned into the headboard. "I'm sorry I couldn't make it to Phoenix last night. Is this about the Connors?"

"It's about you. Lately ... it's always about you."

"I had my own health emergency, didn't I?"

"Charity Connor passed away."

He shook his head and didn't say anything. For a moment she thought she saw genuine empathy in his eyes. "I'm sorry. I didn't realize it would happen so soon. I hoped ... prayed she would rebound." He lowered his tone. "This is awful." He sighed. "I'll stop by the Connors as soon as I can. But I've got to rest. Then I'll help."

He rolled over and moaned, then crunched a pillow under his neck. The purple contusion on his lower back reminded her he'd slipped on that rock in the desert.

Served him right.

She headed toward the vanity where she collected a brush and her makeup bag, then pulled out some clean underwear and clothes from the dresser before stomping downstairs.

Hearing a kid's television program on in the background, Samantha dialed Laney's number on her cell.

"Laney ... I'm so angry right now, I don't know what to do," Samantha said when Laney answered the phone.

"What's going on?" Laney asked.

Samantha covered her mouth and lowered her voice. "I'm ready to kick Dalton out," she whispered, eying the den entrance. The sound of cartoons blared.

"Did you confront him? Does he know you followed him?"

"We didn't get that far. After I told him about the Connors, he rolled over and went back to sleep. He kept saying he had his own health issues and he needed sleep. It's almost like he believes he really was car-jacked. It's like he's in denial."

"That's about to end," Laney said. "There's a council meeting today. Everyone will know."

Samantha stared at last year's Christmas photo on the wall. She and Dalton snuggled by the fireplace, wearing matching sweaters. Grace nestled on Dalton's lap while Gordy stood behind. But within a week Dalton would be under a surgeon's knife. All due to his foolhardy back-country skiing trip.

"Samantha?"

"Sorry, Laney ... there's a meeting?"

"In a few hours. Everything will be okay, mija."

"I'm not sure about that."

"I'm coming over."

The thought of company, of hostessing, filled her chest with dread. "That's not necessary. You need to rest after a long night helping that poor family."

Laney seemed to read her mind. "You're my *friend* right now, Samantha, not my pastor's wife. You don't have to get dressed, put on makeup or fix coffee."

"But ..." Laney's words threatened to unlock the dam in Samantha's throat. She swallowed. "Don't you need to sleep?"

"Martin and I got home few hours ago. He's out cold but I'm still riding last night's caffeine high. I'm here for you, Samantha. I'm on my way."

༄༄

Grace rested on the shag carpeting, watching a Disney movie. Samantha pushed aside guilt, surrendering to reality. The electronic babysitter would have to do. Laney would be here soon and Samantha needed to take a shower.

A forceful spray of water massaged knots from her neck. The pelting against her body felt good, she was tempted to linger. Instead, she turned the faucet off and grabbed a towel. After dressing, she pulled back her dripping hair into a pony tail. She applied some lipstick and stared. Haggard eyes stared back.

When she returned to the kitchen, she paused in the doorway. Laney said no hostessing. But that was like telling the IRS not to bother collecting this year. She refilled the kettle, then found two ceramic mugs. She placed cream and sugar and some boxes of herbal tea on the breakfast table. The frozen loaf of homemade banana bread thawing on the counter would have to do if Laney was hungry.

After she arranged the refreshments, she crumpled into the breakfast booth and considered her plans. As much as she loved Laney, she wasn't sure she'd listen today if it meant softening her attitude toward her husband. She fumed at Dalton and she liked it. No one could convince her not to. She draped her anger and disgust around her shoulders like a warm shawl.

She'd steer the conversation to the Connors. That would be a better topic. Helen and Emmet Crawford's six p.m. pastoral appointment would need to be rescheduled. There were funeral arrangements to be made and since Dalton was bailing on his responsibilities, she'd pick up the slack. Again.

ᘛᘚ

Hot needles pierced Dalton's face, jarring him from fitful sleep. He felt for fresh blood that might be seeping through the gauze. His fingers came away dry. He got up and went to the bathroom mirror to inspect his cheek. The crisscrossed tape easily peeled away. The doctor's stitching held. A tiny bit of dried blood was all that remained from the suture.

Dalton's hands shook as he pressed down the tape again. He rummaged under the sink for his pill bottle he'd replenished up in the mountains. He'd hidden it last night behind a package of toilet paper. He gazed at the yellow tablets.

According to Dr. Adams, it was time for a dose. With a sigh, he shoved them back into their hiding place. If only out of sight was truly out of mind.

But he'd tough it out. Taking the pills now would rob him of sleep he desperately needed. He gulped down two sleep aids from the medicine cabinet before stretching out in bed again.

He check-listed his day as he stared at the ceiling. First he'd fill Dr. Adam's prescription. It wasn't much, but it would help. Filing a claim for the BMW would be next on his list. He'd meet with the insurance guy this afternoon. He'd need new wheels so he could return to the mountains and dig up the duffle. His supply of Oxy would get him through the next few months while he adjusted to the new job, then he'd taper off his medicine. He could no longer count on Matt to provide them.

He swallowed hard. Matt. How sad he must be. With Charity's death, the man must be out of his mind with grief. Why yesterday of all days had he forced Matt to meet him? Why had he been so stupid as to not buy the pills last week? Then Matt and his family would have been together for her last few hours.

Once he got his new job in Phoenix, he'd figure out how to help that poor family. That was the least he could do.

His insomnia seemed to rule the morning. Sleeplessness was imposed by an advancing army of guilt. Images of a grieving father led the charge.

CHAPTER TWENTY-FIVE

10:15 a.m.
Baxter Home

SAMANTHA ANSWERED THE KNOCK AT her front door. Laney wore a gingham shirt with long tails that hid abundant hips. Her face, painted with makeup and pink lipstick, couldn't hide last night's hospital ordeal. She looked like Samantha felt. Exhausted.

Laney reached for her. "Samantha ... mí querida, come here." Laney offered a comforting hug as the women lingered at the threshold.

"Thanks for coming, Laney." Samantha shut the front door.

"How are you, my dear?"

Samantha steeled her emotions but her tears refused to obey "I feel awful." So much for redirecting the conversation.

"That's why I'm here, mija." Laney scanned the foyer. "Is Dalton asleep?"

"Yes. Upstairs."

"I could use a cup of tea. How 'bout you?"

"I have it ready." Samantha clutched her friend's arm as they entered the breakfast room.

"You sit." Laney motioned. "I'll get it." She headed to the kitchen, retrieved the kettle and filled up two mugs, then returned to the counter and sliced the banana bread.

"Let's talk about Dalton," Laney said once she'd sat down.

"Do we have to? I thought we could discuss Charity's service."

"I really think you need a friend to confide in. Am I right?"

Samantha sighed. She knew the moment she'd agreed to this visit, how the conversation would go. But she did need a friend. And Laney had proven her heart big, her shoulders wide, and her lips sealed.

"I feel so ashamed." Samantha drew a ragged breath. "Does the council know yet?"

"The meeting's at noon. All the members should be there. Some of the spouses."

"Will you tell them everything?" Samantha asked. "The stolen offering, the phony carjacking, the ...?" She couldn't bring herself to mention the drugs. The insurance fraud. The self-inflicted wound. She fought the urge to curl up into a ball and sob until sleep took her.

Laney laid her hand on Samantha's. "We have no choice."

She nodded and drew a deep breath. "What about the congregation?"

"We'll tell them on Sunday."

"Dalton will be arrested, won't he?"

"One thing at a time, mija." Laney squeezed her hand. "Maybe there's still some way we could handle this between ourselves as a church family."

Hope flickered like the flame from a drippy candle. "So ... maybe ... he won't go to jail?"

"We don't know what the council will vote to do."

"What does your gut tell you?"

Laney met her gaze before answering. "That charges will be filed. He committed a crime." She tore open a pink package of sweetener and sprinkled it in her mug. "I'm praying for a solution other than jail time."

"A solution?"

"Dalton needs treatment. As I suggested before, maybe we could work with a judge." Laney sipped her tea before setting the mug back on the table. "I know you believe this but it bears repeating. Trust your Father. He deeply loves you and knows what you need."

"Oh ... Laney ... I can't seem to find Him right now. He's seems so far away." Samantha grabbed a tissue and dabbed her eyes. "If He loves me, why did this happen?"

"I won't pretend I have an answer. But Carla Connor is asking the same question, dear."

Oh dear Carla! Samantha cringed. New shame blanketed her. She still had her precious baby in the next room.

For the next hour Laney listened while Samantha emptied her heart.

"I thought he was seeing another woman," Samantha told her. "He often took pills, but I thought it was aspirin." She sipped her tea. Steam beaded around her lips. "I'll never forget the day he flipped out."

"What happened?"

"The doctor refused to give him a refill. He ran through the house slamming doors. He ended up here, pounding the life out of this table with his fists. In all our years together I'd never seen him like that."

"Were you afraid?"

Samantha shook her head. "I know it seems weird, but I wasn't. Dalton would never hurt me or the kids."

"Drugs turn placid people into monsters. I saw it often at the hospital," Laney said, frowning. "He showed you yesterday what he's capable of." Laney replenished her mug with hot water, then dropped in a fresh Chai bag.

"Dalton's not a monster. That much I'm certain of. I just wish I knew what to do."

"I'd like to share a passage I was reading last night. It might give you some insight." Laney seemed to consider her words before clearing her throat. "Did you know that God is the revealer of deep and hidden things?"

"What do you mean?"

"In Daniel. I read it last night." Laney cast her gaze to the ceiling, apparently rummaging her brain for the exact quote. "It says ... 'He reveals deep and hidden things and He knows what lies in darkness ...' Don't ask me for the reference number.."

"2:22?" Samantha asked.

Laney chuckled. "I've never had a good memory, but that should have been easy."

"I got that same verse early this morning." Samantha told her about seeing the digital clock at precisely 2:22 a.m. "I asked the Lord and He told me to go to the book of Daniel. I couldn't imagine what it meant. Even now, I'm still a little unsure."

Laney chewed a generous bite of banana bread. "The second half of the verse is what catches my attention. *God is in the darkness*. The Lord may be trying to show you He's with Dalton in this awful place."

That had been her interpretation too. But it sure didn't seem fair or just. Dalton needed to feel God's wrath for what he'd done, not be rewarded with His companionship. *Let him pay, Lord!*

"God forgave people like King David for murder, Peter for denying Jesus, all kinds of people, all kinds of sin," Laney continued. "Every time I read their stories it gives me hope. He is the God of the second, third and umpteenth chances ..."

"Maybe God can forgive but I'm not sure I can." Samantha's voice pitched. "He's betrayed me. Not only me, but my children and let's not forget the people at church. They've trusted him to be their shepherd. He miserably failed them. How could he have taken that money? Many in our congregation are struggling. He has the gall to play on their emotions like some superficial T.V. preacher. It makes me sick."

Laney nodded. "I don't blame you. But no one is beyond the Lord's forgiveness. Dalton may end up in the blackest pit, but God's light can overpower any darkness." She sipped her tea again, regarding Samantha over the cup rim. "God may even be asking you to be a source of that light."

"Me?" Samantha raised a hand in reflexive protest. "I'm not sure I can ..."

"Ask the Lord for willingness. Then take a baby step as He shows you. Nothing more. That puts the ball in God's court, doesn't it?"

Willingness? Maybe she could do that. If God gave her an attitude adjustment. "I prayed a good part of the night that He would show me what to do."

"Do you have any direction?"

"I decided to attend the council meeting. Can I ride with you?"

"Sure you can, honey, but are you sure about this? It might be rough."

"These are my friends. They'll be no excuses made for Dalton. I promise you that. I need to be there. I need to have a voice." Samantha reached for her cell phone. "I'll make childcare arrangements and then we can leave."

She called Elaine Ainsworth, asked for yet another favor, then found some paper and a pen in a drawer. She scribbled a note, placed it on the table, then headed to the den. "Grace, honey, put your shoes on."

She turned back to the kitchen. Laney was gathering her purse and keys. Her eyes flicked to the note Samantha had just left.

I'm at the church for the bereavement meeting. Grace is at Elaine's. Sammy

Laney moved it to the edge of the table then met Samantha's gaze. Her face flushed.

"I'm sorry for snooping. But I'm glad you're at least communicating." She pulled her bag to her shoulder. "The devil has done his work in your family, Lord knows. But don't forget that a smoldering wick will not be snuffed out ... a bruised reed, He will not snap. He alone can reignite your love and passion for each other. Only He can bring the healing. That's what I'm praying for."

CHAPTER TWENTY-SIX

10:20 a.m.
Connor Home

MATT HAD CRIED HIMSELF TO SLEEP. The moist pillow made that obvious. He rubbed his eyes and squinted at the clock. Ten twenty. Laney's sleeping pill had worked. He'd been out for eight hours.

He collected clean clothes from his dresser and peered at the mirror. Tear tracks marked his cheeks. His face was swollen, his eyes lined with red. He stared back at himself, his gaze as barren as his soul, as empty as Charity's room down the hall.

Where was Carla? He needed her. She was his strength. His rock.

After getting cleaned up, he left the bedroom and found himself in front of Charity's door. He twisted the knob and stopped. Why go in? His baby was gone.

He forged through the family room to the kitchen. The counters and sink were spotless, thanks to the kind hands of the church ladies who'd left hours ago.

Where was Carla?

Realization dawned. He raced down the hallway.

When he opened Charity's door, Carla huddled on their child's bed, shoulders shaking with sobs. Her knees were tightly drawn to her chest and she clutched Mr. Teddy, the stuffed toy Charity slept with. Her wails had surrendered to quiet grief. Like his.

"Car'... we're going to get through this, babe." He sat and stroked her back. He ached to ease her pain.

She looked up, her eyes ringed in smudgy mascara.

"How, Matt? I don't think I can."

"We'll help each other."

She struggled to sit, then wiped her nose with the back of her hand. He offered her some tissues from the box on the nightstand.

"Let's take a trip to your mom's place ... after ..." He halted his words. He couldn't bring himself to say it.

"After we bury our baby?"

He hung his head and nodded. It was hard to know what to say.

"Did you sleep at all?" he asked.

"Not really. I took Laney's pill but it didn't help." Carla's face contorted and she bit her lip.

"What is it, sweetie?"

"I can't seem to stop worrying."

"About what?"

"Was there something else we could have done? Maybe another bone marrow transplant?"

"Don't go there, honey." He hugged her tight. "The doctors told us it wouldn't work a second time. Remember?" He stroked her face. "Can I get you anything?"

"Could you make some coffee while I take a shower?"

He agreed and helped her to her feet as she gripped the bear. She lifted it to her nose and sniffed. "I can still smell Charity." New tears trailed down his face as she placed Mr. Teddy in the center of the pillow.

Matt wiped his eyes and swallowed back the sadness. For Carla's sake, he'd hold it together. He wrapped his arm around her waist as they walked to their bedroom. When she disappeared in the bathroom, he headed back to the kitchen to put something together for breakfast. Carla needed to eat something.

He needed a plan. It was time to man up and do the hard stuff for his wife even if that meant picking out a casket without her. But where should he start?

He collapsed on a kitchen stool to collect his thoughts. Mr. Coffee gurgled at the end of the long granite counter.

Fifteen minutes later, a yellow legal pad, framed with his own nonsensical doodling, held his confusion and trauma. He tossed the pen on the tablet. He couldn't string two thoughts together. And there was so much to do.

Laney told him there'd be a bereavement meeting later this afternoon at Saint Luke's and that the church ladies would take care of most of the arrangements. No thanks. He'd handle things himself. If he ever stepped into that building again, it would be too soon. The whole place was filled with memories. Charity as Mary in the annual Christmas pageant last year. She'd worn a head covering that hid her patchy scalp. His heart ached, remembering the image of his too-thin little girl clutching the baby Jesus on a makeshift stage.

Imagining the high and mighty Dalton Baxter anywhere near his daughter's service deposited fresh rage. That creep better stay far away if he wanted to take another breath on this planet. Matt would never forgive Baxter. He'd lost precious hours with his baby, words she'd spoken he'd never hear. His face felt hot. Dalton Baxter should die an early and painful death. An overdose of OC would be too merciful.

Charity's four-year illness, like an unwanted house guest, had refused to leave. Brief remissions gave them seasons of hope but all along, deep in his gut, Matt believed the disease lurked below the surface. And then one day, just like he'd imagined, the beast woke up, only to storm through his home, stealing his most precious possession from right under his nose.

Matt stirred cream into his coffee as swirling thoughts ravaged his brain. He must tell Carla the truth about where he had been on Sunday. He had to. But not today. Maybe not this week.

He stared at the notepad. Where could he find a place to have a service? Relatives were coming and Carla's church friends would want to attend as well.

What about the pastor's wife, Samantha? Carla would insist she be invited. That might present a problem. He'd need to come up with something as to why her husband could not attend. No matter how he framed it, Carla would object unless she knew why. He'd have to be honest with her. But would she believe her pastor was an addict and one of Matt's best customers?

Not bloody likely.

ꕤ

Noon
Baxter Home

The throbbing in Dalton's temples woke him. Bright sunbeams crossed the sheets. He picked up the alarm clock and stared. He'd slept almost three hours. Well past the dosing time Dr. Adams had prescribed.

Had Sammy told him that Charity Connor had died? Maybe he'd imagined it. Maybe it was just a bad dream. Maybe God had healed her.

He rubbed his eyes and struggled to his feet. A pang in his lower back slowed his movement. He staggered to the sink and pulled out his medicine from its hiding place. With shaky hands he fumbled and opened the lid, then swallowed two caplets. That should perk him up. Fifteen minutes and he'd feel like a new man, the screams from his cheek and backside, quieted.

When he returned to the bedroom he noticed Sammy's made up side. So she hadn't slept there.

Memories flooded in all at once. He sank onto the bed's edge.

Sammy did come in. And she'd been angry at him. Charity Connor died.

His chin fell to his chest. He should have gone last night. Even in his pain. What kind of pastor was he?

His stomach grumbled, reminding him he hadn't had anything to eat since Deidra gave him a yogurt from the fridge. Chewing had been impossible. He must get something in his stomach. He stood and moved to the doorway.

"Sammy?"

No answer. The house was still.

He clung to the railing as he descended the stairs. "Sammy? Are you here?" he called out once he got to the breakfast room door. The table showed signs of recent activity. Two drained coffee mugs and some banana bread. His mouth watered. Then he saw a note.

Grace was with the Ainsworth's. Sammy was at the church bereavement meeting helping with Charity's service.

Matt must be in hell right now.

God ... I really messed up. Please help me fix this. Helping anyone right now would be impossible. Maybe he'd feel better tomorrow. Good thing Sammy was handling this.

Dalton headed to the fridge to silence his hunger.

CHAPTER TWENTY-SEVEN

1:00 p.m.
Saint Luke's Community Church

IT DIDN'T TAKE LONG FOR SAMANTHA to realize Laney had been right. Attending the council meeting turned out to be much harder than she'd imagined. Martin described the scene at Copper Lake. Wide-eyed council members straightened their backs and gawked. Samantha looked away, avoiding their eyes.

"That BMW ... he's so proud of ..." Martin continued. "He pushed it into the reservoir."

"You've got to be kidding. Why?" Brad Sanders interrupted. Samantha looked up. "First he steals the offering." Brad glowered at her. "Then he sinks his car in a lake? This is outrageous!"

Samantha returned a hard stare over a frown. She'd known having Brad on the board might be a problem. But she'd bitten her tongue and smiled when the congregation elected him. She should have known he'd be like this. So much for making amends. So much for trying to forget the past. Brad would never let her forget.

"Let me finish ..." Martin waved him silent.

"Something should be done." Brad's lips formed a thin line, his accusing eyes bearing into hers. Samantha knew something much more than Dalton's behavior had set him off.

"Hold on, Brad," Martin continued, "After burying his pills, Dalton injured himself with a hammer. That explains why he was hospitalized last night."

Harold and Betty Roark leaned their hearing aids toward Martin, hanging on every word. Betty's brows arched, her voice quivered. "Why would Pastor Dalton do such a thing?"

"To convince law enforcement he'd been carjacked. He needed to account for the missing money," Martin explained. "Sinking his car also promised him a nice insurance settlement."

Samantha fought the urge to run out of the room. These folks were her friends. She'd served them dinner at her table. But today, crowding the small vestibule, the council formed a tight circle of judgment.

Life would never be the same.

Laney squeezed her hand. Samantha's jaw clenched. She willed her tears to stay put as she returned the gesture. *I love you too, Laney*, her fingers said.

Natalie and Jeremy Andrews, the youngest couple on the council, had twin girls, Grace's age. Their families had shared picnics and barbecues. Would Grace still be welcomed in their home? The kindness in Natalie's expression seemed to say it would be okay.

Amanda Benson, one of two women in leadership, sat next to her husband, Lyle. A CPA, Amanda volunteered numerous hours as Council Treasurer, readying reports for the annual business meeting. She'd definitely be taking a closer look at the church's books. She and her husband hadn't been told yet about their son, Tyler. The council now had much bigger issues to deal with beside some missing tools.

Liz Cronklin, the council's secretary, came without her husband. Rod had to work and couldn't get away. Liz had been typing with a frenzy, taking the meeting minutes on her tablet until Martin got to the part about sinking the car. Her head suddenly bobbed up, her mouth fell open. It took her a few moments to recover and resume typing.

Brad Sanders sat across from Samantha, wearing a perpetual scowl.

"Laney and I tried to reach Dalton more than once yesterday," Martin said. "As you're aware, the Connors were in dire need." He turned to Samantha. "We're grateful you came today. After what you went through, I'm amazed at your strength. Do you know how strong you are?"

Tears filled Samantha's eyes again. She shrugged. Strong or a naïve, trusting fool? It felt the same.

"This has been very difficult for Samantha. Coming here today was her idea," Martin said. "She'll do her best to answer any questions you might have. Keep in mind, until yesterday, she knew nothing about any of this. Samantha?"

Samantha tried to swallow down a growing lump in her throat. "I am so sorry about all of this. Matt and Carla need us. Yet here we are, dealing with the unthinkable. You've all been very dear friends and I owe you the truth." She surveyed the circle. Other than Brad, each person offered her gentle smiles under eyes of grace.

But no matter what they asked, she had to keep the identity of Dalton's dealer secret. For Carla's sake.

"My husband is addicted to pain medication. That's ... uh .... no excuse for what he's done." Her tears streamed now. Laney handed her a tissue and Samantha blew her nose.

"For months, Dalton seemed isolated, as if he was keeping something from me," Samantha said. "Yesterday morning he locked me out of his office. That was the final straw. I decided to follow him to Prescott. I wondered if he was ... uh ..."

"Seeing another woman?" Amanda asked.

"Y-yes." Samantha stammered. "When I saw what he was really doing, as crazy as this sounds ... I thought an affair would have been easier. At least we wouldn't be looking at prison and public scandal." Samantha cupped her knees with both hands.

"You have nothing to be ashamed of," Laney said.

"I feel awful. I'm so embarrassed."

"Maybe you're feeling a little guilt," Brad said. He leaned back and crossed his arms over his chest.

"What are you implying?" Martin asked, his brow furrowing.

"How could she have no knowledge of this? She lives with the guy." Brad tipped his chin in Samantha's direction.

She shot him a frustrated look. "I didn't know anything about this. Like you, I trusted the offering would be sent to the mission."

"We believe you, Samantha," Betty told her.

"We do, honey," Laney chimed in.

"Couldn't get into his office, huh?" Brad's voice notched. "We need to see what's in there."

"Later, Brad," Martin said. Does anyone have any questions?

Betty raised her hand. "Until Sunday's offering, where do you think he got the money, dear?" she asked.

"There wasn't much left of his inheritance after he bought that stupid car," Samantha said. "Once that money was gone, he drained our savings. At the time, he told me he was transferring it to stock and I believed him. I'm such an idiot. Except for my small teaching pension, we have nothing left."

"Give yourself a break," Laney said. "You've always trusted people. That's one of your best qualities."

"We still need a full investigation." Brad stared at Samantha. "We can't just accept your word on this." She held his glare until he looked away.

Jeremy raised his hand. "If we place Dalton on an unpaid leave of absence, what would that mean for your family?"

"Leave of absence? Are you insane?" interrupted Brad. "He should be removed today. Then we'll press charges."

"You're out of line," Martin said. "Go home and cool off."

"Calm down, brother," Harold added.

"I'm not going anywhere." Brad shifted and glared at Samantha. "I'm as much a part of this council as anyone else and I'm not leaving."

Samantha refocused on Jeremy. "In answer to your question, we have no other source of income. I'll go to work. Thank goodness I've kept my teaching credential active."

Samantha dabbed moisture from the corners of her eyes. "Would it be possible ... for the sake of my children ... uh ... I have no right to ask but I don't know what I'm going to do ..."

Laney put an arm around Samantha's shoulders. "I think what Samantha's asking is if there is any way we could deal with Dalton without going to the police. Is that right, Samantha?"

Samantha sniffed and nodded.

"Could we?" Natalie asked. "None of this was Samantha's fault. Why should she suffer?"

"What do you all say?" Martin asked. "Do we need to involve law enforcement? Raise your hand if you think we could handle this as a church matter."

Other than Samantha and Brad, every hand went up.

"I don't agree," Brad snapped. "He needs to go to jail. After all, we reap what we sow, don't we?"

Samantha's anger burned. Dalton needed to feel the pain she'd felt past twenty four hours. But jail? Her kids would be devastated. Her daddy sentenced to years behind bars would destroy Grace. Gordon would be humiliated. Life at McCormick's only high school would become unbearable for a nerdy kid who'd already endured years of teasing by the cool kids on campus. Having his father in prison would heap embarrassment on all of them.

Liz stopped typing and frowned at Brad. "The Bible also teaches 'mercy triumphs over judgment.'"

"This money came from hard-working people, Liz," Brad growled. "Our so-called 'pastor' needs consequences."

Amanda waved her hand. "There might be a problem with us not going to law enforcement," she said. "The false police report. We know about it. That makes us legally obligated to tell the authorities."

"That might land him behind bars," added Harold, "but what else can we do?"

"Maybe he could get community service if we don't press charges," Martin offered.

Samantha raised her head. Feelings of hope surged.

"Not true," Jeremy said. "Lying to the police is one thing, but insurance fraud is a felony. He will serve time. Amanda's right. We must report this or we'll be named accessories."

Hope slid into despair. *Jesus, please help me.*

"Has Dalton filed a claim yet?" Lyle Benson asked.

"He called an hour ago and left a voicemail. He wants to use my car. He has an appointment later today with our agent."

"We've got to stop him from making this worse," Martin said. "We'll head over there now. It would be better if you didn't come."

Samantha nodded, relieved. Seeing Dalton now would be excruciating. "I'll be at the bereavement meeting in the annex. If Dalton doesn't answer the door, there's a key under the ceramic frog near the front steps."

Feeling dismissed, she folded her chair and headed toward the door.

In a matter of moments, she'd lost her place in her beloved church. She forged across the threshold as more tears streamed down her cheeks. Dalton hadn't just tanked his own life but he'd taken her down with him. She wiped her face after the doors clanked shut.

No "A" had been threaded into her clothing, but like Hester Prynne, in *The Scarlet Letter*, disgrace felt unbearable. A garment of shame barred her from the life she loved, much like the banging doors behind her.

CHAPTER TWENTY-EIGHT

1:55 p.m.
Saint Luke's Community Church

"LET'S BE CLEAR ON WHO'S DOING what," Martin said. He hugged a metal box close to his chest. After four years as the head councilman for Saint Luke's, he'd never thought he'd be conducting a meeting like this.

"I will go to the bank," Amanda said. "We'll need a second signature to make the changes." She picked up her purse and stood.

"Tell them I'll be there before they close," Martin said.

Amanda nodded and she and Lyle stacked their chairs with the others, then left the building.

Natalie Andrews got to her feet. "I'm going to the bereavement meeting." She walked toward the door. "Let me know if there's anything else I can do."

"Thanks, Natalie." Martin turned to Harold. "Could you and Betty stay here until the locksmith arrives?"

"We will."

"I have a problem with that," Liz said.

"What's wrong?"

"I'd rather wait with Betty. I feel uncomfortable around Pastor ... uh ... Dalton. Harold can take my place." She handed Martin her iPad. "I'm sure one of you fellows can take notes. The church bylaws require this be documented."

"She's right." Martin looked at the other men. "Any volunteers?"

Harold and Brad shrugged their shoulders.

"I'll do it." Jeremy took the tablet.

Brad pointed to the metal box. "Shouldn't we force that open?"

Martin sighed. Brad was testing his last nerve. "If we have to. Samantha might know the combination." Martin handed it to Liz. "Hold on to this. Everyone ready?"

The men headed out the front door to Martin's gold Fusion where they all piled in.

ꕥ

2:20 p.m.
Baxter Home

Dalton foraged through the refrigerator. He'd eaten the rest of Sammy's yogurt an hour ago and was still hungry. Warm scrambled eggs would be easy on the jaw. The Oxy had waned and an ache reclaimed his cheek.

After eating, he inspected his face in the hallway mirror. A red fissure of swollen skin revealed a tiny glint from his right eye. He'd be a sight to see at the insurance office. Sammy never returned his call so he'd be stuck with Gordy's van.

A familiar tremble took over his fingers. His brow furrowed as he studied his hand. It had only been a few hours since his last dose. Did Matt scam him? Had the pills been cut with fillers? But that didn't make sense. He'd felt invincible yesterday. Today, stopping the jitters was imperative.

He had to convince his agent, Mike Klaussner, he'd been a victim of a crime and needed a loaner car until his claim was settled. If he appeared confused or shaky, the agent might be suspicious. It could be weeks until he got his money. A loaner would be better than driving that 1966 hippie van anywhere, let alone to his interview on Thursday.

He fished another Oxy from his pocket and swallowed it.

He retrieved Gordy's keys from a hook and headed toward the front door.

The bell chimed.

His gut twisted. He didn't have time for this. Maybe he could get out the back.

The doorbell rang again, followed by a heavy knock.

"Coming!" He charged to the door and yanked it open. Somber-faced Martin Fernández and most of the council members congregated on his steps, all wearing dour faces.

What did *they* want?

Martin stared. His eyes widened. "We need to speak with you."

"My God, look at his face!" Brad said.

Dalton nodded. "I took quite a beating," he said. "I can't meet with you now. I have an appointment downtown."

"We're here on important church business," Martin said. "You'll need to reschedule. May we come in?" Martin didn't wait for an answer but charged past, the men following in line like an army unit on patrol. When they reached the end of the foyer, Martin turned around. "Are you coming? We'll be in the den."

What were they doing? He needed to leave.

He opened his mouth to protest their presumptuousness. Then he followed more slowly. When he reached the den, the men had distributed themselves on the couch. Only Martin remained standing.

"Look Martin, I told you, I need to leave. I'm meeting my insurance agent. Is this about the Connors? You're welcome to wait here. We can discuss the funeral arrangements when I get back."

"Matt and Carla are well-taken care of. We're here on another matter," Martin said.

Dalton waved at the clock on the mantle. "Later. Got to go."

"It's not happening that way." Martin's steel-like stare made the hairs on the back of Dalton's neck stand up.

"We know everything," Brad said. "The car. The drugs. You hitting yourself with that hammer. The false police report. All of it."

Martin glared at Brad. "I told you I would handle this."

"Whaaaa ... ?" Dalton's voice cracked. "What are you saying?"

"Do I have to say it again?" Brad stood and got into his face. "Everyone knows what went on yesterday. Beginning with that so-called offering."

"Offering ... ?"

"Don't pretend you don't know!" Brad yelled. "Do you guys believe this? He's still trying to con us."

Martin pushed Brad aside. "If you can't control yourself, leave." The two men locked eyes. As Brad returned to the couch, he straightened his back. His lips formed a thin line of defiance as he crossed his arms.

Martin motioned to Dalton. "Take a seat."

Dalton's rubbery legs welcomed the easy chair by the T.V. while Martin dropped onto an ottoman. Martin shot Brad a look. "Apparently I need to remind everyone, that I'm the spokesperson for this meeting. Jeremy will take notes." Martin returned his attention to Dalton. "We hope you'll be forthcoming."

He'd been blind-sided. The realization stole his voice. Who ... how ...?

"We'll follow what's outlined in scripture regarding church discipline," Martin continued. "Do you have any questions before we begin?"

"H-how ... did you ... ?" Dalton stammered.

"Samantha followed you yesterday."

"Sammy?" There had to be some mistake. "Where is she?"

"At the bereavement meeting." Martin cleared his throat. We decided this will be easier coming from us. Normally it could be a private council matter, but since it involves church funds, we must inform the congregation."

Dalton balled his fists between his knees, sucked a deep breath.

"You're being placed on an unpaid leave of absence effective immediately. Your name will be removed from all church accounts and the locks on the buildings changed."

Good thing he'd taken a pill just before they arrived. A surge of confidence had him smiling and holding up a hand. He could nip this in the bud. "Hold on a minute. You can't do this. I'm the head pastor."

"Not anymore. Check our bylaws," Brad shouted, his face beaming with victory.

"We have a fifty-one percent ruling authority," Martin added. "Even if you'd been present for the council vote this afternoon, it wouldn't have mattered with our unanimous decision."

"Hey guys ... things have been hard for a few months since my accident. People do desperate things ... uh ... when they are in pain." Dalton pointed to his knee. "Who would be the pastor if I was laid up? Let's talk about this. I don't want to step down." *I can't be removed from ministry.* How would that look at his interview Thursday? *Oh, God, what have I done?*

"You should be fired *and* arrested," Brad said. "Unfortunately, I was overruled on that ... at least for today."

"Should you make a false insurance claim, more charges will be added to the ones you're already facing," Martin said.

"Charges?" Dalton's confidence deflated like a popped balloon.

"There's no other option but to tell the authorities the truth," Martin told him. "We hope you'll do the right thing."

"We're driving to Prescott tomorrow, to press charges," Harold said. "We're willing to take you if you'll turn yourself in."

"No!" Dalton's heart galloped through his chest. "You don't understand. I plan to pay it back. We can work this out."

Martin leaned toward him. "Look Past—I mean ... Dalton ... if there was a way we could do this within our church family for the sake of your wife and kids, we would. But you filed a false police report. If we collude with you in covering this up, we become accessories to a felony. For the sake of Saint Luke's, we have no alternative."

"Everything I borrowed is recorded. I can show you. It's in my desk." Anxiety lodged itself in his throat. "I just need my meds a few more weeks, that's all."

"Typical addict talk," Brad said. "Don't listen to him."

"How dare you, Sanders." Dalton glared at him. "I am *not* an addict."

Brad scoffed. "Denial. Another sign."

"The pain in my knee is excruciating." Dalton squirmed, looking at the other men. Everyone was silent. Why wasn't anyone coming to his defense?

"You're hooked, Baxter. Face it," Brad said.

"Look ... I ... I don't want to go to jail ... please..."

Jeremy stopped typing and gave him an empathetic look. "As your friend, I'm asking you to come with us. Things might go easier if you do."

Worry surged, drowning him in a pool of panic. This couldn't be real.

"The path to freedom is truth," Harold said. "Jesus told us that." The old man's tone brought Dalton's anxiety down a notch. His words and tone seemed void of condemnation.

Martin's voice softened. He gently placed a hand on Dalton's shoulder. "Maybe your lawyer can ask the judge for a drug treatment program instead of prison."

Prison? Lawyer? Treatment program? These were suggestions for a common criminal. Not him.

"Gene Snyder might help you," Martin continued. "Maybe he'd represent you for a lower fee."

"I don't think he will." Dalton gripped the arm of the wing chair and stared hard at the brown carpeting. In a very short time, Gene would learn about his mother's prized tea kettle. He'd probably file more charges.

Harold gave him a fatherly look. "We've decided to stand with you as you go through this legal process. But with one condition. We need the truth. Is there anything you'd like to tell us?"

Nothing he'd *like* to tell them. But yes, there was more. All written in the ledger in his desk.

"I ... borrowed funds from others." He moistened his lips.

"From who?" Martin asked.

"From congregants."

"You borrowed? Or you stole?" Brad's tone sharpened on the last word.

Dalton frowned. "None of them know how I used their money. I intend to pay them back with interest. Please believe me, I'm not a thief. They were loans."

"Who?" Martin repeated.

So he told them about Deidra loaning him four thousand dollars for the cooler repair. But it was hardly his fault that the repairs never happened. He'd needed the money for an emergency supply of pain pills. "The HVAC company couldn't come right away. And I was in agony. I had no choice!" They had to believe him.

"What else?" Martin asked, not blinking.

He swallowed and confessed hocking a priceless heirloom from Winnie Snyder. "She believed it was for the Sunday school improvement fund."

"I saw those cribs. They looked brand new," Jeremy said, giving him a quizzical look.

"Almost new," Dalton admitted. "I found them on Craig's List. I located some whiteboards and other supplies from a liquidation sale."

"So you bought used goods and passed them off as new?" Martin asked. "What'd you do with the rest of the money?"

"I needed to buy my meds."

"Why didn't you ask your doctor?"

"I did. He told me to take Tylenol even though I'm in agony."

"Are you guys even listening? Did you hear what he just said?" Brad scanned the room. "He took money from an old lady. Can you believe that?"

"That's enough, brother," Harold admonished.

"That's why I can't ask Gene," Dalton said. "Once he finds out about his mother's kettle, he won't want to help me."

"Anything else?" Harold asked.

Matt Connor? But no point dragging him into this. The man was living his own hell.

Dalton shook his head. "No. Nothing."

CHAPTER TWENTY-NINE

3:15 p.m.
Grams' cabin
Huckleberry, Arizona

THE SCREEN DOOR SQUEALED. GORDON entered the cabin.

"Grams?"

Plastic bins filled with corn covered the kitchen counters where he'd left them earlier. She hadn't done much while he'd been gone.

Where was she? No dinner scented the air and the oven was off.

"Grams ... ? Are you here?" Gordon hollered toward the hallway.

A door opened and footsteps approached. His grandmother plastered on a smile as she joined him in the living room. Her eyes looked swollen and red.

"I wondered where you were," Gordon said. "The sky is perfect for sun viewing right now. I rushed back so I could show you."

"Oh goodness ... is it past three? ... I haven't done a thing today."

"Is everything okay?"

She ignored his question and walked to the freezer where she took out a box of corndogs. "I bought these especially for you," she said as she opened it. "I'll make a salad. How about I whip up some brownies for dessert?"

"Sounds great," he said.

"While they're baking, you can give me that astronomy lesson."

He picked up his equipment and headed toward the door. "I'll set up. See you outside."

Once on the deck, he squinted at the afternoon sky. Dipping toward the horizon, the sun glared white. Excitement climbed. He opened the case and removed the telescope. From a side pocket, he retrieved a Pegasus H-Alpha filter.

He threaded it to the scope and positioned his eye over the viewer. The sun seemed much brighter than what he had witnessed at home in McCormick. He made adjustments to the lens. He focused on the center of the sun's pulsating surface.

"Grams! Come quick," he called.

Moments later his grandmother emerged and raced to his side, wiping floured hands against an old checkered apron.

"Take a look. The sun's having fits today." Gordon stepped back and made room for her, gesturing to the lens. He held the viewer still, resting his hand on her shoulder as she lowered her face. "Sunspots come in pairs. Do you see any?"

"Wow ... everything's blue."

"It's the filter. It does that." He grinned.

"Uh oh ... what was that?"

"What did you see?"

"A huge blast of white light." Her head bobbed up. "Look!"

His eye found the scope. "It's gone." He lifted his head. "Sometimes there are several at once. There might be another one soon. NASA reported an X-12 last week."

"X-12?"

"Solar flares have classifications," he explained. "The X ratings are the highest. Scientists don't worry much about them unless they're higher than ten."

"What happens then?"

"It depends. If we had a direct hit, satellites could be disrupted. Internet might go dark. That sort of thing."

"Sounds scary."

"Scientists have been warning about a super geomagnetic storm for years. They call it a Carrington Event."

"Why?"

"Named for an astronomer a long time ago. Richard Carrington observed massive fireballs exploding from the sun's surface. Within hours, telegraph equipment melted. Some all over the civilized world even caught on fire."

"Explain it to me in layman's terms."

"The sun belches." Gordon smiled, waiting for her reaction, but she only gave him a puzzled look. "The sun ejects out a massive amount of gas, Grams. If it hits earth, we might have problems."

"What kind of problems?"

"We could lose power for a long time. If that level of CME happens again, it could be devastating. People in 1859 were self-sufficient. Today, people would lose it."

Seeing concern in her eyes, he added, "Don't worry. The earth has its shields up ... Most CMEs are harmless."

"But you just said it could be bad."

He kept his gaze on the telescope so Grams couldn't read anything more into his words. He should've kept his mouth shut. Freaking out his grandmother right at the beginning of his vacation wasn't smart. "Sometimes I get carried away with my science hobby. I tend to exaggerate."

"Gordster ... don't do that." She poked him.

He looked through the telescope. "Nothing much going on now. Lots of sunspots though so there's a great potential for flares."

"Hey ... it's my turn. Move over, would you?" She laughed.

He lifted his face and stepped aside.

"I never imagined something so beautiful," she said. "The sun is alive." As she lingered at the scope, Gordon explained about the earth's closest star's many idiosyncrasies.

Grams raised her head. "Better get those brownies in the oven." She turned toward the cabin. "I'll call you when dinner's on."

ꕤ

Eighty-eight million miles out, barreling through frigid blackness, a blast of ionized plasma hurtled toward Earth. Only known to the powers-that-be and a handful of backyard astronomers, the massive blob of radioactive energy, one hundred thousand miles in diameter, careened toward the planet at five million miles per hour.

ꕤ

The sun left a magenta halo in its wake as it dipped below Mohon Peak about fifty miles west. The breathtaking panorama of colors poured through the cabin window. Gordon watched the sky wax deep purple in minutes.

"That type of sunset usually means bad weather," he told Grams. "The weatherman was right. There's a storm on its way."

Grams careened her neck upward as she held a salad bowl in her hands. "Hopefully no lightning. We sure could use the rain, though. Ready to eat?"

He followed her to the maple table off the kitchen area. They talked about Gordon's upcoming college plans.

"Dad and I are driving across the country," Gordon told her. "We planned the road trip as soon as I got my acceptance letter. We'll tour New Mexico, New Orleans, and some Civil War sites before we head north. We'll have a few days in D.C. checking out the museums. I can't wait."

She looked away and her voice quivered. "That's nice, Gordster."

"That's all you have to say, Grams? You've been everywhere in this country. I thought you'd give me a state by state itinerary."

"You and your dad will figure it out," she said. She walked to the kitchen. "Ready for me to whip you at Scrabble?" She found the box in the pantry and brought it to the table.

Twenty minutes into the game Gordon's stomach wrestled with his last corndog as he watched Grams ponder her next move. It figured, he had the valued "Q" but no vowels.

She fumbled with five remaining letters.

M ... A ... C ... A ... L

She switched them around on the game board in several positions.

"Ah ha!" She beamed.

She adjoined her remaining five letters crossways, spelling

CALAMITY

How did she do that? Gordon smiled.

Grams grinned back and headed to the kitchen. She returned with a plate of warm brownies and set them on the table. But their tantalizing aroma failed to distract him from the scrabble tiles. Had Grams' letters predicted something dire? The word calamity and sunny conjoined by the "y" sent a quiver of unease through his body.

CHAPTER THIRTY

9:35 p.m.
Gram's cabin

AFTER HE SHOWERED, GORDON PADDED downstairs to tell his grandmother goodnight. Grams sat at the table as the fire in the hearth snapped at the evening chill. Seeing him enter, her anxious eyes betrayed her smile. He could read her like a book. He drew a deep breath, bracing himself for bad news. "Something's wrong. What is it?"

Two mugs and a plate of leftover brownies waited on the table while a teapot steamed. "I wanted us to have a good evening like we always do your first day here," she said. "I need to talk to you. Please sit, Gordy." She retrieved the kettle and a box of cinnamon tea as he joined her.

"Your mother called earlier."

Mist wafted between them as Grams unraveled a story about his dad. Gordon's jaw dropped when she got to the part about Dad sinking the BMW and then hitting himself. With a *hammer*?

The brownie on the plate remained untouched.

"That's all I know," Grams finally said. "I'm sure your mother will have more to say when you call her."

Gordon lifted his tea, then gulped the spicy liquid, trying to drown the conflicting emotions crowding his throat. "What will happen to Dad?" His words cracked like a twelve year-old losing his voice.

She lifted her shoulders. "No one knows. Your mother hopes the authorities will agree to a substance abuse program instead of prison."

"Prison? You can't be serious." He stood. Paced. "What should I do?"

She gazed at him steadily. "I think you should go home tomorrow."

"Why?" This wasn't fair. He dropped into his chair.

"Your mom needs you."

"I can't believe Dad did this."

Grams gripped his hands. "Addiction changes people. I took drugs, I know."

Gordon's mouth gaped. "You took drugs?"

"Unfortunately, yes. Way before you were born. If your grandfather hadn't helped me, I could have been a full blown addict."

Gordon wasn't sure what surprised him more: the fact his father was addicted to pain medication or his grandmother's confession about her own lifestyle.

"You were a druggie?"

"I was a foolish teenager and didn't understand how blessed I was with the family I'd been given. Do you know what the Summer of Love was?"

"Some music festival in New York?"

She smiled. "No, that would be Woodstock. I missed that one." She sipped her tea. "The Summer of Love took place in San Francisco. Young people all over the nation congregated in Golden Gate Park to hear live bands and get high."

"Mom told me you were a hippie but not much else." Other than her long hair and Birkenstocks, his grandmother seemed pretty conservative. The image of her holding a joint, inhaling, holding her breath, then exhaling slowly—he coughed to cover his sudden laugh.

"At fifteen I ran away from home and hitchhiked to California," she continued. "I think I'd rather not tell you what I did in those days. Trust me, it wasn't good. That's where I met your grandfather. He helped me get my life together."

"Gee, Grams, I never knew you had a wild side."

"Wild it was. Before meeting Grandpa, I'd sleep in the park and dumpster-dive for food. It didn't take long for my California dream to become a nightmare. Like your dad, I couldn't get free. Apart from God sending your grandfather, I might have died from an overdose."

The thought of this sweet woman sprawled in a dirty alley, an empty syringe by her side, made him shudder.

He pushed the image from his mind and changed the subject. "You guys met on a street corner, right? He invited you to some church thing at a coffee house?"

She nodded, a faraway look in her eyes. "I didn't want to go. But I was hungry and out of money and they offered free food."

He remembered the story. His mother had often told him. "So grandpa missionary-dated you ..."

"What?"

"He dated you, hoping he could convert you."

Grams chuckled. "Well ... I guess it worked then. Grandpa was very patient and took care of me helping me through the worst of withdrawals. It was awful but he never gave up."

"So when you kicked your habit, he married you, right?"

"Not yet. I wasn't eighteen yet."

"Did you live together?"

She shook her head. "Grandpa had the purest of intentions. We never uh ..." She paused seeming to search for the right words. "We never consummated our union until our wedding night four years later."

A flash of heat traveled through his face. Considering who he was talking to, the conversation felt uncomfortable but he continued, "You held off that long? Why?"

"That was your grandfather's doing. His walk with his God dictated abstinence. Also he believed I should come to faith in Christ first. If I didn't, our marriage would never work."

"When did you come back to Arizona?"

"First, Grandpa got me situated at a drug rehab place in Palo Alto where I got clean. Then he drove me home in that old VW you love so much. The day we pulled up into my driveway was the hardest day of my life. My mother had aged ten years. I had literally broken my parent's hearts.

"They were so indebted to Grandpa, my father gave him a job and found him a place to live." Grams smiled, enjoying the memory. "It took me awhile but little by little, my faith grew. God does that."

Gordon knew where this conversation was headed and he didn't feel like talking about his own faith, or lack thereof. He was no longer sure what he believed. It was time to bring the conversation back to his father.

"Do you think my Dad could die?"

She squeezed his fingers. "I think your dad will be okay once he goes through rehab. He's a great father. And I couldn't ask for a better son-in-law. From what I heard, he sounds desperate. He doesn't want to go to jail."

"Does Grace know about this?" he asked.

"Your mother hasn't told her."

"I guess I should head home then." He shrugged. "I can keep Grace distracted before school starts. We'll sugarcoat it. She doesn't need to know everything."

"Your mom will figure it out." Grams looked at the wall clock. "I guess you should call her. It's getting late."

"I can do that later." Gordon got up. "Gotta get my stuff packed. I'd like to finish some of my chores tonight. It'll get my mind off this."

"That would be great, Gordy. I'll stay up and keep you company." She gestured toward the garden bins at the back of the kitchen. "I'll get the corn bagged so you can put it in the cellar freezer."

"Sure thing, Grams, as soon as I pack my gear."

"And Gordy ... you might want to change your ticket. Take a later bus. That way you can have a little fun in town tomorrow before you go."

Good idea. Might as well enjoy the last of his vacation before heading back to a desert of change and turmoil.

ꕥ

10:01 p.m.
McCormick, Arizona

Samantha's cell chimed. Dalton's smiling face appeared in the display. As much as she didn't want to talk to him, she accepted the call.

"Sammy?"

"Hello, Dalton."

"Why ... how could you ... go against me?" His voice, noticeably absent of anger, seemed laden with defeat.

She almost felt sorry for him. Almost. "How could you steal, Dalton? And from God's people, no less?"

"It was a loan, Sammy. I told the council I'd pay everyone back. I kept a tally in my desk with the amounts I borrowed."

"When you borrow something, the lender knows about it. These weren't loans." Her voice notched up. "They were thefts. Stop making excuses. Accept responsibility."

Dead air hung between them.

"I applied for a new job in Phoenix. It pays a lot more than I'm making now. I was doing this for us."

Anger climbed through her throat. A new job? What was he talking about?

"Sammy ... Can't you come home?"

"I need some space. I'm hurt too," she said. "But ... I'll pray for you, Dalton." She clicked off.

ꕥ

11:38 p.m.
Grams' cabin

Gordon finished most of the chores and felt drained. As he stared at the computer screen, his grandmother rubbed his shoulders. Changing the leaky pipe in her downstairs' bathroom hadn't been easy. He'd checked all the smoke alarms, replaced their batteries, tacked down some loose carpeting in the back hallway, and the squawking screen door was well-oiled and mute. Twenty freezer bags packed with fresh-picked corn were stacked like library books, waiting to be taken to the cellar.

"I've got to get to bed," Grams said. "You need your sleep too, Gordster."

He looked up at her and smiled. "In a little bit. I'm trying to get on the SDO site to check on that flare you saw this afternoon."

"A space website, right?"

"Solar Dynamics Observatory. Part of NASA. I'm about ready to give up. I've tried several astronomy sites, but they all seem to be down. Very strange."

"Something worrying you?"

"I found a screen shot of the flare. It was massive. Maybe greater than an X18."

"That's a bad one, huh?"

He nodded. "What bugs me is there are no live feeds tracking it."

"So you think someone has deliberately blocked the news about this?"

"At least here in the States. Australia has a government site up, but the traffic's too heavy. Probably every backyard scientist on the planet is trying to get on."

"You worry way too much for a kid." She tousled his hair. "What time's your bus?"

"Late afternoon. I'll get to the rest of your list in the morning." He smoothed his bangs back into place.

"Don't bother. Why not see a movie with Jerome? He's up here for several weeks with his aunt and uncle."

"I know. He finally emailed me," Gordon said. "I'd rather work. I need the money."

Hanging out with Jerome Williams would have been fun in normal circumstances but within a few hours, things had become strange. First the news about his dad. Now a potential kill shot from the sun, if directly aimed at earth, could cause major problems with the national power grids.

"I can loan you what you need. It isn't your fault you have to go home early. You can work it off next summer."

Gordon's eyes lit up. "That would be great. Thanks."

She smiled at him, fondness in her gaze. "You'll be facing hard stuff at home soon enough. Have some fun." She shuffled down the hallway and he returned to his screen.

There must be something somewhere about that flare.

Tuesday

For I hold you by your right hand— I, the Lord your God. And I say to you, 'Don't be afraid. I am here to help you. Isaiah 41:13

CHAPTER THIRTY-ONE

Tuesday, 12:11 a.m.
Grams' cabin

GRAMS, WAKE UP!" GORDON RAPPED on the cedar door a second time. He almost turned the knob, then stopped, hearing her clear her throat.

The door swung open and she stood, wide-eyed in the threshold. "Goodness ... it's past midnight. What is it?"

"Come here, let me show you." She followed him to the living room where he pointed at the computer. "That's the Australian site. See that spike. It's the initial flare." He swiped the image with his finger. "That's a CME. It's massive. It could be an X-28 or greater which is the highest on record! I've never seen anything like it."

"What are you saying?"

"I know lunatics on the 'net say ridiculous things, but this is an official site. This thing's on a collision course with Earth." He clicked another tab and pulled up Fox News. "See ... our media isn't reporting it." He clicked a third tab. "CNN ... again, nothing ... what's wrong with these people?"

"Did you try Drudge?"

He tapped in the URL for *Drudge Report* and a crimson headline scrolled across the top.

AUSTRALIAN GOVERNMENT
SAYS CIVILIZATION
EXTINCTION EVENT POSSIBLE!!

Drudge linked to the original Aussie site he'd been perusing which contained dire warnings advising people to stock food and water. Army reservists had been deployed to keep the peace and to prevent looting.

"You've got my attention," Grams said. "What will happen in the U.S.?"

"Best case scenario? We lose a few satellites."

"And the worst?"

"It hits our side of the planet and everything goes black."

"Even in America?"

"Especially here. The whole country is wired. Cell phones won't work, no Internet, buildings go dark."

"No Internet?"

"Not getting online is the least of our problems."

"How bad could it get?"

"No electricity would produce chaos. Think of Hurricane Harvey times ten. People get desperate when there's no food and water.

She folded her arms. "It's a good thing I'm stocked up."

"You and Mom, both. We've got a ton of saved water in our shed."

"Your grandfather always believed in prepping. Thank goodness he rubbed off on us."

"Something else is bothering me." Gordon returned his attention to the computer screen.

"What?"

"The media blackout." He clicked between several sites, usually reliable for breaking news. "Our government has the technology to pinpoint an accurate trajectory. Why is Australia warning their people and we aren't?"

"Good question," Grams said. "What do you think?"

He cocked his head and considered. "The Australian authorities probably know they're not in the direct line of fire. They're warning their people just in case the calculations are wrong. Our government probably knows something dire is headed our way. They don't want to panic the population."

"Then there's Drudge," Grams said. "That site always manages to cover uncovered news." She leaned over him and clicked back to the *Drudge Report*. The computer's operating system warned,

THE SERVER IS DOWN. PLEASE CHECK BACK LATER.

"Where'd it go?" Grams gasped.

"The powers-that-be must have killed it."

She sank into the chair next to him. "Can we pray?" she asked. "I'm scared."

Gordon wasn't sure he had the faith to believe God could do anything to stop impending doom. Not with hard empirical data staring him in the face. But his grandmother's worried expression prompted him to bow his head and clasp her trembling hands.

Grams prayed a lengthy appeal, begging God to intervene and have mercy. Gordon shifted impatiently. There was so much to do and so little time. Relief surged when she said "Amen."

"Okay, we've asked the Lord. Now, it's time to use the brains He gave us," Gordon said. "The CME could strike earth sometime after eleven a.m. tomorrow. I'll call Mom." He fished his phone from his pocket.

"What should I do?" Grams asked.

"Go pack. You need to come home with me."

"You want me to leave Huckleberry? You know I can't deal with your heat."

Gordon stifled a groan. She didn't get it. "You'll be safe with us. If nothing happens, we'll come back tomorrow night." He was surprised by his own forcefulness.

He clicked on a preparedness website. "I'll print you a list. Find everything you can while I'm on the phone. Then we'll load the car." He rubbed his eyes and yawned. "I need coffee."

Grams pulverized some espresso in a grinder, then started the coffee maker. She held up the jar of beans. "I may not be able to do this tomorrow. Maybe I should grind all of these."

"Good idea," he said, giving her a thumbs up. "Do you have more? Grind everything you have. Even in the 1800's they couldn't live without their coffee."

The crush of beans convinced him to retreat outside. He found a quiet place on Grams' deck and tapped his mother's cell number. She answered after two rings. "Mom? I ... uh ... sorry to call so late ..."

"That's okay, son. I can't sleep. I guess Grams told you. I'm sorry, honey."

"Yes, I know." She thought he was calling about Dad. His father's drug problems seemed small compared to what they now faced.

"Where's Dad?"

"At the house. Grace and I are staying at Laney's"

"Are you and dad getting a ...?" Why say it? After tomorrow would it matter?

"A divorce?" she finished for him, then promised him a secure family future he wasn't sure he believed in. Not tonight, when her assurances were eclipsed by the possibility of a solar death shot.

"Mom, I didn't call about Dad. There's something I need to tell you."

CHAPTER THIRTY-TWO

LANEY RAN THROUGH THE EMPTY streets of McCormick dressed in a summer nightgown. She crossed her bouncing breasts with her arms, hoping townspeople weren't watching. Blinking lights from a diner guided her way through the inky blackness. Someone in the restaurant would hopefully let her use the phone to call Martin. He'd come to her rescue.

Pink neon spelling "Gabby's" popped and crackled. One by one, each letter lost its light, surrendering to the darkness. The diner's inside lights flickered, giving up their ghosts as Laney knocked on the front door.

Tap, tap, tap.

No one answered. Where was Gabby?

Tap, tap, tap.

"Laney? It's me ..."

"Huh?" Laney's eye snapped opened and she shook herself, facing her cherry wood footboard. She swiveled around. Martin slept soundly.

"Laney?" the voice came again.

She climbed out of bed, grabbed a robe, and opened the door. Samantha, face written in worry, wore jeans and a t-shirt.

"Are you okay?" Laney squinted at the hall light. Losing sleep a second night was hard on a woman in her late sixties.

"Sorry to wake you. I need a favor."

"Let's go to the den. We won't disturb Martin." Laney guided her to a cozy room off the kitchen.

"I'm going home," Samantha said when they had taken seats on the couch. "There's something I should do before Dalton gets up. Can I leave Grace here?"

"Not a problem. What's going on?"

Samantha looked uncomfortable. "I'll tell you when I get back."

"Can't this wait? Do you really want to face Dalton right now?"

"He won't hear me. He's probably taken a sleeping pill." Samantha seemed resigned. Her eyes were framed by new lines. Lines of worry and anxiety she'd acquired in the last day. The past twenty-four hours wreaked havoc on so many. Barring a miracle, Dalton would be processed at the sheriff's office in a few hours.

Their pastor's dismal future combined with Charity Connor's funeral Saturday ... it all seemed too much. It *was* too much. How could they bear it? Her mind flew to Paul's words to the Corinthian church: *We were under great pressure, far beyond our ability to endure, so that we despaired of life itself.* Yet Paul and Timothy had survived. Persevered. Paul even claimed in 2 Corinthians 1:10 that God had delivered them, and continued to deliver them. She drew a deep breath. If God could sustain Paul and Timothy, He would surely show up for their church.

Laney focused again on her friend. "Have you found a lawyer? Will Dalton get bail?" she asked.

"I spoke with Gene Snyder. He said any bail offered would be very high."

"You spoke to Gene?" Laney couldn't keep her surprise from her voice.

Samantha met her gaze with a rueful smile. "I know. After what Dalton did to his mother, I couldn't believe I had the nerve to call him. Or he'd have the grace to answer." She twisted her t-shirt hem into a knot. "Believe me, if I could scrounge up the money, I'd get her tea kettle back."

"Martin knows the pawn shop owner. We'll see what we can do. You have enough on your mind. What else did Gene tell you?"

"Anything over a thousand dollars is considered grand theft and falls into the felony category. Dalton's bail could be as high as a hundred grand."

"Wow ... I didn't realize..."

"That means I'd have to come up with ten thousand dollars to get him released." She let go of her hold on her shirt before bunching it up again. "We don't have that kind of money."

"I'm certain the congregation won't press charges. Will that make a difference?"

Samantha shook her head. "Once he turns himself in tomorrow, it'll be in the hands of the District Attorney. If they add the intent to commit insurance fraud, most likely he'll be prosecuted."

"The congregation adores you, Samantha. I know they'll want to help. Maybe we could come up with the bail money. We could start one of those online fund-raiser things. Kick Raiser? Or is it Crowd Starter?"

Samantha finally smiled, but it was gone just as quickly. "Brad Sanders won't agree. He's furious. I can't say I blame him."

"Martin and the guys will have a word with him. He can be surly sometimes. Maybe they can change his mind." She grasped Samantha's hand. "Two things might work in Dalton's favor. He didn't file the insurance claim and he will voluntarily turn himself in."

Samantha stared at the carpeting. She carried a heavy load and it wasn't fair. Laney put an arm around her back. "Stop. You didn't cause this."

Tears streamed down her young friend's face. "But why didn't I see it? That day Dalton went ballistic about his refill, I should have known."

"Blaming yourself is futile. Dalton made his own choices."

Samantha chewed her bottom lip. "Confronting him sooner might have changed things."

"And it might not have. Addicts must hit bottom before they want help. Jail may be his bottom."

"I better get going." Samantha stood. "I have my cell if you need me."

Laney gave her a hug with a word of advice. "If Dalton wakes up, be careful what you say. Fatigue removes our speech filters. Things come out wrong."

ꕤ

2:12 a.m.
Grams' cabin

When Gordon entered the cabin, Grams had stacked emergency provisions on the kitchen table. Candles, flashlights, batteries, and three kerosene lamps stood in tidy rows along with match-boxes, twine and other supplies.

A pile of novels towered on one of her chairs. "Those will come in handy," she said. "Life will be boring without my computer Solitaire and Scrabble. I've got a bookcase of paperbacks in my room. Can I take a few more?"

"Sure, we can squeeze them in someplace."

"Do you think the power will really go off?" she asked. "What if we're overreacting?"

"I'd give anything if that was true." He rubbed his forehead, trying to think. "Do you have any gas cans?"

"There's one in the shed."

"I'll be right back." He sprinted outside to a wooden shack near the garden. He found a five-gallon red poly container, along with a cobweb-laden camp stove. He stacked them both on the redwood deck before returning to the kitchen.

"After we load up, we'll go into town for cash," he said. "We'll fill up your car and the gas can. Do you have any propane? I found Grandpa's old stove. It's outside. Mom will need it."

"I don't. There's a minimart in Kirkland that's open all night. They stock camping equipment for the hunters."

He scribbled *canned fuel* on the growing list, then trolled through a few more disaster websites. "I packed some food from your cellar. Can you check out these online supply lists and decide what else we need?"

Grams collapsed into the desk chair. She squinted at the computer screen. When he saw how her shoulders drooped, he changed his mind. "Why don't you lay down for awhile? I'll look at them later."

She shook her head. "Pour me a cup of coffee, I'll be fine."

He refilled her cup and doused it with cream, then handed it to her. "I'll be downstairs. We'll leave in thirty minutes." He smiled, realizing she was still in her p.j.'s. "Maybe you should change."

Her face remained stoic. "When I finish my list."

ཽ

Gordon emerged from the cellar, carrying the last box of canned goods. Grams huddled at the table again. She'd changed into denim overalls and a t-shirt. Her hair was tightly wound in a little grey bun on top of her head. She seemed intent, writing something on a piece of paper.

"You've been busy," he said, looking over her shoulder at the lengthy shopping list. More items had been added such as fishing tackle and kerosene wicks. She'd written a big note at the bottom, "BP meds."

"BP meds?" he asked.

"My blood pressure pills. What if I can't get them?"

"How many do you have?"

"About two weeks' worth."

"I'll call Mom," Gordon said. "A nurse at our church works at the hospital."

"Laney Fernández?"

"Do you know her?"

"She's an old friend from high school. We keep in touch. I'm sure she's got connections."

"Let's hope so. You ready?"

"Not really." Grams sighed, looking around the cabin.

Gordon wiped his sweaty palms on his thighs and drew a deep breath. "I know it's hard. But you can't stay here."

"You're right." She pushed against the table and stood. "I'll be okay."

After moving supplies to the porch, Gordon returned to the kitchen. Grams opened an upper cabinet, removed a ceramic jar, then unscrewed the lid. "We'll need this at some point when our debit cards stop working." She pulled out a wad of cash and divided it in half, then handed him a stack of bills. "There's about a thousand each. Some of that is what I owe you. We'll go to my bank's ATM to get more." She looked out her window at the nearby cabins. "Shouldn't we be warning my neighbors?"

"I wish we could but we can't take the time, Grams. And we don't want to start a panic."

She looked at him, eyes wide, and he held up a hand. "I get it. That's exactly what the government is doing. But we need to keep a low profile until we get to Mom's."

She crammed her money into her purse, loaded up her arms with boxes, then headed outside as he followed. After they packed the trunk and backseat with everything they could fit, Gordon secured the cabin's doors and windows, shut off the utilities, then drained the pipes and water heater. Moments later he joined his grandmother in the Olds and started the engine.

He studied the front of the cabin. Had he forgotten anything? How often he and Dad had shared this moment, tightening down Grams' hatches when she came for her annual visits. Everything he knew about mountain life, he owed to his father. Now Gordon had to step up. He'd be the man his father taught him to be. The man his father would hopefully become again.

CHAPTER THIRTY-THREE

2:35 a.m.
Baxter Home

STAIRS CREAKED AS SAMANTHA SKULKED upstairs. She stopped at the closed door of her master bedroom and listened. Dalton's snores filled the darkness. When she opened Gordy's door, she snapped on his light and closed the door behind herself.

She cringed. Laundry, dirty, indistinguishable from clean, was strewn everywhere. Socks and shoes cluttered the carpet along with scattered papers and magazines. On his desk by the window, she looked for a green binder and found it squished between two thick astronomy books.

She perched on her son's bed and opened the notebook. Its meticulous organization contradicted the pandemonium at her feet. Plastic tabs segmented sections representing a summer of research.

Solar Cycle 24 was written on the first tab. She skimmed through the material. Everything made little or no sense. When she got to the tab that read *Sun Observations*, her son's hand-written notations confused her as if he'd written in a foreign language.

He'd told her to study the middle section. "It'll explain what could happen after a CME," he'd said. She leafed through the section. Close to fifty typed pages. She scooted back on the pillow and began reading.

Pages later she was convinced. The planet might be facing what Gordy had called "a death shot." Her heart ramped and she regretted not telling Laney. If this really happened, the older couple would need to get ready too.

At the back of the binder she located the supply lists Gordy mentioned. They'd help her determine what else her family needed. If they had even half the stuff, where would she find the rest? Her sleepy little town never came to life before nine a.m. Purchasing whatever was left on the list within the waning hours was critical.

Samantha tucked the binder under her arm and walked to the door, nearly tripping over a bulging backpack.

An idea came to her as she descended the stairs. She plopped down the notebook and headed to the back yard, to the shed on the back of the property. Inside, a row of barrels lined one wall. It had been a smart move on Dalton's part, to store the emergency water after that storm that had knocked out the power last summer. She scrunched below the sink, reached behind the water barrels and pulled out the hidden gym bag. Her disaster preparation would have to wait a few minutes.

ဢဢ

A noise downstairs woke him. Dalton sat up in bed and listened.

There it was again. Running water? Who was in his house at three in the morning? He went to the closet and pulled out a baseball bat then took cautious steps down the stairs, gripping it over his shoulder.

He walked through the foyer. A light from the guest bathroom streamed across the laminate. He raised the bat above his head.

When he came to the door. Disbelief anchored his feet.

Sammy crouched at the toilet with an empty Ziploc bag in her hand.

Realization registered. "Are you crazy?" He tossed the bat aside, and charged toward her.

She looked up, eyes wide.

He plunged his hand into the spiraling water. All that remained was a tinge of yellow in the bottom of the bowl.

"My pills!" he yelled. He whirled to face her. "How could you?"

"I'm saving you from a longer prison sentence." Sammy slammed the lid shut and got to her feet.

He dashed to the staircase. Sammy had lost her mind. He had to hide the rest of his stash.

"Dalton, I need to speak to you," she shouted, climbing up after him.

He twisted around, glared. "And I need those pills."

"I did you a favor. It's the only way to help you." Hurt flickered across her face. "Don't you see, if they can't find them, your sentence might be lighter?"

"You don't know what I've gone through since my skiing accident. My meds help me function. Now what will I do?"

"You have a problem, Dalton." Her voice seemed to soften. "You're hooked."

Had she been talking to Brad? He pointed to his knee. "I'm in pain! You don't get it!"

"I get a lot more than you think." She folded her arms across her chest.

He leaned closer, narrowed his eyes. "What's that supposed to mean?"

"You're a troubled man dealing with much more than physical pain. You need to get your head on straight."

"Are you saying I need a shrink?" His leg buckled. He dropped to the stairs. She joined him.

"You've got issues, Dalton. You need to get some professional help. A counselor can help you. If you don't deal with this, those drugs will kill you."

He considered that. Could she be right? No. He shook his head. Regurgitating childhood memories wouldn't do any good. The past was the past and should stay in the past.

He suddenly wanted to wound her. First, tattling to the council, now flushing his pills?

"What will really help is to move away from this nosey little town and start over. Instead, I'm facing prison, thanks to the church council. And you."

Hurt flashed across her face but she spoke calmly. "The council had no choice. They could be charged as accessories."

He rattled off his spiel, in an exaggeratedly patient tone. "Like I told you on the phone, I have an associate pastor interview Thursday at New Generations Church in Phoenix. The starting pay is eight hundred dollars more a month than I'm making at Saint Luke's. Full benefits, a paid vacation, all the perks." He shrugged, watching her from the corner of his eye. "I guess that's over. They won't want a convicted felon on their payroll."

"You never discussed this with me." Sammy's brows drew down. "Did you think I would just pick up and move? I grew up in McCormick. What about what I want?"

"I didn't see a need to discuss it until I was offered the position."

"Dalton ..." Sammy's eyes pooled. His heart tugged, but he firmed his resolve. This was all her fault. Her voice dropped to a whisper. "Who are you?"

The pull on his heart grew stronger. How had he gotten here? "I just wanted ... a new start ... in a new town. I only need my meds for a few more weeks. Then I'll wean myself off and everything will go back to normal."

She looked at him a moment, her eyes glistening with sadness. "I'll be at Laney's." She got to her feet. "I'm tired, Dalton. Very tired."

She wasn't the only one. He watched her retreat, feeling spent. With a groan, he hobbled up the last few steps to the bedroom.

Those meddling jerks would be here soon to take him to Prescott. Before he could get back to sleep, he'd hide the last of his precious medicine. Who knew how hard the next few days would be?

CHAPTER THIRTY-FOUR

3:17 a.m.
Baxter Home

SITTING AT THE BREAKFAST TABLE, Samantha's eyes burned and she couldn't stop yawning. She tried to read Gordy's supply lists but kept wondering if getting rid of Dalton's drugs had been a smart move. Would law enforcement prosecute her for destroying evidence? She shuddered. That's all her kids needed. Two parents behind bars.

According to Gordy, the impending CME was hours away. If it obliterated the nation's power grids, the resulting domino-effect could destroy normalcy. Most likely civil unrest would ensue. Arresting a pastor's wife for flushing drugs probably wouldn't be high on the police's priority list.

Between sips of coffee, Samantha jotted down what she needed to purchase. McCormick wasn't a place to find hard winter wheat or long term survival food and Phoenix was well past an hour away.

But there was no time to talk herself out of it. She gathered her keys and purse and headed toward Gordy's VW parked by the side of the house.

Samantha cranked the ignition and the old van rumbled to life. Minutes later, she barreled through the blackness of Highway 89, formulating a plan.

The council guys were due to arrive at seven-thirty to escort Dalton to Prescott. She'd call Martin at daybreak and see if he'd delay the trip north a few hours. Even though it served him right, Dalton being stuck in some jail without power, without air conditioning—that was unthinkable.

If Gordy's predictions came true, a CME would change everything. Waiting until afternoon was just plain smart. By then, they would know if the planet had been spared.

ജ്യ

5:16 a.m.
24-Hour Wal-Mart
Phoenix, Arizona

Samantha loaded two Wal-Mart shopping carts and pushed them to a check-out stand. She stacked several batteries end to end then watched them teeter toward the checker who swiped each package across a glowing laser light, before bundling them into plastic bags.

"That's a lot of batteries," the young man with a nametag reading *Sean*, observed.

"I'm from the desert," Samantha explained. "The monsoons are coming. We have a lot of power outages."

Her words didn't explain the twenty cans of survival food rolling past. Vegetable seeds, gardening tools, and a copy of *The Ultimate Guide to Inside Seed Sprouting* followed. Mounds of camping equipment that included multiple canisters of propane, preceded several blankets.

"Going camping?"

"Are you familiar with a CME?" Samantha asked.

"A what?"

She spilled out a Reader's Digest version of what she knew. He looked at her skeptically and said, "Whatever ..." as he stuffed the kerosene wicks into a bag.

Once Samantha left the empty parking lot, she joined a sea of early morning commuters heading north through downtown Phoenix. She tapped Laney's number on her cell, but it went to voicemail, as did Martin's.

She sighed, tossed the phone onto the passenger seat, and whitened her knuckles on the steering wheel. She'd try their land-line once she got out of the city.

ꝏ

6:25 a.m.
Fernández Home
McCormick, Arizona

An olive green wall phone near the breakfast table rang and Martin answered it. "Hello?"

"It's me," Samantha said. "Sorry to call this early. I'm twenty minutes away. I need to tell you something."

Samantha explained about the geomagnetic storm headed their way. Martin listened intently, conveying tidbits to Laney, who stood nearby.

"I emailed you web links from my phone. Did you get them?"

"Check your email for links," Martin told Laney.

Laney tapped a sleeping laptop on the kitchen counter and checked her inbox. "Tell her we got them," Laney said.

"They're here," Martin said.

"They'll tell you what to expect and how to prepare. Stocking water is your number one priority. Warn the congregation with the phone chain.

Forward these links to each person on your list. We've only a few hours left."

"What about our trip north?" Martin asked. "We're picking up your husband in an hour. Laney can't do all this by herself."

"About that? Can you postpone that until this afternoon? By then we'll know what we're dealing with."

"I'll call the council but I can't promise anything." Martin stirred cream into his mug.

"Thank you. Things could get dangerous. If they say no, can you at least delay your trip for an hour? Grace should say goodbye to her father."

He told her they would. Laney grabbed the phone and said, "I'll see that Grace is dressed and ready when you get here."

"I honestly don't know what I'd do without you two."

Once they'd hung up Martin said, "We need lots of water. Where can we put it?"

Laney's eyes kindled. "We've got that inflatable ring pool for the grandkids. It holds thousands of gallons. Has a cover too."

"Grandchildren?" Martin's brows arched. "Rachel, Ben ... the kids! They need to get out of Phoenix. Get a hold of them while I call the council."

Laney wagged her head. "Rachel won't listen. I can hear her now. She'll think this is one of our conspiracy stories."

"Forward her the links. We'll pray God convinces her." Martin's apprehension climbed. Weariness nagged at his muscles. He hadn't had a good night's sleep in two days. He and Laney huddled at the breakfast table and poured out their hearts begging God's intervention. After they finished, he poured a second cup of coffee, then entered his office behind the kitchen as Laney tapped in their daughter's number.

CHAPTER THIRTY-FIVE

7:20 a.m.
Baxter Home

"DADDY!" GRACE BURST THROUGH THE bedroom door. Dalton jumped. He pitched the Oxy bottle into an open drawer near the bathroom sink and slammed it shut.

"Hi, Sweetie. Where's Mommy?" He held out his arms.

"She's in the garage putting stuff away. She told me to wake you up." Grace encircled his waist with her arms and squeezed. He hugged her back. "I've been awake for hours, Sugar."

Grace pointed to his cheek. "Does your face hurt?"

"Not too bad. The doctor gave me stitches. I'd show you but he doesn't want me to take the bandage off." He cupped his screaming flesh. The pill he'd just taken should kick in soon.

"Mommy says you're going away. Will you be gone long?"

"I'll be back this afternoon," he told her. "See ..." He pointed to himself in the mirror. "All dressed and ready for my appointment."

"You promise to be back before dinner?" Her worried eyes penetrated his.

He scrunched to her level. "I'll do better than that. I'll be home after lunch. Then we'll go to town for ice cream."

"Yay!" His daughter giggled and bounced on both feet.

"Grace, I need to talk to Daddy." Sammy stood in the doorway. "I put *Frozen* on downstairs. Your father will be with you in a minute."

Blond curls danced with excitement as she hugged Dalton's waist again. "Hurry, Daddy," she said as she raced out of the bedroom.

"Promising her ice cream? What's wrong with you?" Samantha shook her head. "You still don't get it."

"I'll be back in a few hours. You'll see." He stood up straight, gritting his teeth against the pain in his knee and face.

"Gene says that won't happen."

"What does he know? He's a small town lawyer in a cheap suit."

She leaned against the doorjamb. "Has it ever occurred to you that he shops at Suit World instead of Tom Ford because he's a good man? He doesn't gouge clients—or steal offerings—to get by." Sammy scowled then let out a long sigh. "No point in talking about this. I came home so you could spend some time with Grace before you leave."

Gee ... thanks for thinking of me. The simmering anger he'd nursed most of the morning came to a boil. She betrayed him. His wife. The one person in the world who was supposed to be on his side, no matter what. He pierced her with his gaze. "Sammy, how could you? ... Why didn't you come to me first? Why did you have to tell everyone? Get me into trouble?"

She shook her head. "You're blaming me? For what you've done? Unbelievable."

He gripped her arm. "I made mistakes. I realize that."

"Mistakes? Is that what you call them?" She grimaced, pulled her arm from his grasp, and left the room. Moments later she yelled from the foyer. "Dalton ... your daughter's waiting."

He checked himself a second time in the mirror. Other than his eye injury, he looked the role of a clean, upstanding clergyman, dressed in his best shirt. Made from fine cotton, it was a blue Armani.

As he hunted for a tie, a thought came to him. He went to the bedroom and foraged behind his socks in the dresser's top drawer where he located his collection of clerical collars. He grabbed one and returned to the bathroom, where he tucked it in around his neck. He breathed deeply through his nose and felt the Oxy hit. His confidence soared.

This meeting at the Sheriff's Department would be no big deal. The guys from the council might have scared the hell out of him yesterday but surely they'd overreacted. Once he was released on his own recognizance, he and Grace would be picking out their favorite flavors from Brewster's Ice Cream Shoppe.

He grabbed the prescription bottle he'd buried in the bathroom drawer and carried it to the walk-in closet. He flipped on a light and scoured the shelves for a hiding place. Behind some shoeboxes, a pair of dusty Tony Lama cowboy boots stood tall like grey tombstones. He'd worn them a couple of times since his father's funeral but his feet never felt comfortable. Fine crafted alligator skin, they reminded him too much of their previous owner, stiff and unyielding.

He pulled one down and dropped the bottle into the shaft, rolling the container to the toe, then placed the boot back on the shelf. No one would find his medicine. He'd reward himself with an Oxy once this horrible day was over.

ꕥ

"They didn't go for it?" Samantha asked Martin. She cradled her cell with her chin while she poured a third cup of coffee. After one too many sleepless nights, drinking the thick black brew helped her to stay upright.

"Brad objected and persuaded the others during my conference call. No one but Amanda would agree to a delay despite what I told them about the possible solar disaster. I managed to postpone the trip for an hour but that's it. I'm sorry, Samantha. I tried."

"That's better than nothing." Samantha's voice cracked and her legs felt like jelly. "You'll be here by eight-thirty, right?"

"Yes. Harold, Jeremy and me. Brad's busy."

"This is becoming more real by the minute. He'll be locked up, won't he, Martin?"

His voice gentled. "Barring a miracle."

"Part of me asks for divine intervention. But the angry part wants him to suffer. I feel like I'm going crazy."

She told Martin goodbye and headed to the den. Grace sat on Dalton's lap transfixed by the movie. Neither noticed her come in so she left the room. No point in interrupting. The doorbell would do that soon enough.

ꕥ

Grace was mesmerized by colorful cartoon fish so Dalton set her down on the carpet.

"I'll be right back, sweetie," he told her as he headed to the kitchen for a cup of coffee. When he entered the breakfast room, Sammy stood at the sink, staring out the window.

He paused. The last couple of days had been awful. His car was gone, the pain in his face, unbearable. And his priceless Oxy, sucked into oblivion.

He opened the cabinet and she jolted back as if he were an intruder. Her eyes narrowed. She pointed to his collar.

"Why are you wearing that?"

"I'm a minister, that's why," he bit out.

"So you haven't worn it in what?—three or so years and today you've decided to? That's rich."

He poured his coffee, then dumped in a heavy dose of sugar. He didn't answer her, but let his spoon do the talking, swirling the brew with a vengeance, striking the inside of the mug as he stirred.

"They're on their way." She let it go. "Martin says to leave your personal items with me."

"I need my license. I might have to drive myself up there."

"Why?"

"It's the 7th."

"Dalton, you can't be serious."

"I'm going. If those troublemakers refuse to make a quick stop then I'll meet them in Prescott." "What is this obsession with your dead mother?"

Sammy never understood. Visiting his mother's grave was nonnegotiable. The councilmen would make an allowance or he'd use Gordy's VW. "I'm making my visit."

Sammy shrugged. "At least leave your cash and credit cards."

He flipped open his wallet and pulled out a few twenties along with a Visa and Master Card. He slapped them on counter. "This isn't necessary, you'll see."

"If you explain you're an addict they might put you in a medical unit. That has to be better than jail."

"Addict? Why do people keep saying that? I take medication now and then, that's all."

"You're a junkie. And your habit is destroying our family."

"What don't you understand?" He slammed a hand on the counter. "I'm in pain."

Her eyes scowled like she wanted to say something. Instead, she whirled and left the kitchen. That was the second time she walked out on a conversation.

A cautious sip of hot coffee produced a lob of spit into the sink. He cupped his cheek as pain radiated. He added ice chips to the mug then scavenged the fridge for something to eat. His stomach yearned for sizzling steak but his mouth said no. He settled for buttered toast with jam. He chewed cautiously between sips of lukewarm coffee. He'd have to watch Grace eat her ice cream this afternoon. His mouth rejected extreme temperatures.

The three-man inquisition would arrive soon. He needed to hurry. He grabbed scissors from a kitchen drawer and headed outside to Sammy's garden.

After clipping an assortment of wild flowers, he examined them in the morning sun. They weren't the usual daisies Mama liked, but they'd have to do. He returned to the kitchen and rinsed the blossoms in water, then wrapped the stems in a wet paper towel. He set the flowers down and headed upstairs to take another Oxy. It might be too soon but so what? The morning's stress compounded by another argument with his wife meant he'd earned an extra.

When he entered the bedroom, Sammy sat on the bed, an opened Bible spread across her lap. Through bleary eyes she looked at him, swiping fingers across her wet face.

"Grace is asking for you," he lied. Samantha said nothing, but got up and left.

He walked to the closet and closed the door, then retrieved a couple of pills from their hiding place. After returning the boot to the shelf, the door opened.

"I had a feeling you were up to something." Sammy stood in the doorway. Her mouth formed a tight frown as she eyed his clenched fist. "I wouldn't take that if I were you."

"You're not me," he barked. He left the closet and went to the bathroom sink. He placed a tablet in his mouth, cupped some water, swallowed. He slipped the second tablet into his sock.

The front door bell chimed.

"Gotta go, they're here," he grumbled.

"Okay." Instead of the caustic tone she'd been using, she sounded almost kind. "I'll be praying."

"Don't bother. God's never been there for me." Dalton's stomps punctuated his anger as he descended the stairs.

CHAPTER THIRTY-SIX

8:45 a.m.
Desert Memorial Gardens
McCormick, Arizona

DALTON KNELT AT HIS MOTHER'S grave, grateful for the massive headstone. It cast a luminous shadow across his body. But even in its shade, scalding temperatures took their toll. He mopped his brow with his sleeve while sweat soaked through his shirt. The bouquet he'd brought from home felt clammy in his hands.

He snatched dead flowers from a plant well and tossed them aside. He inserted the wild flowers in their place.

"Let's wrap things up. We've got over an hour on the road," a voice told him. He turned to see Martin standing a few feet away. Harold and Jeremy, hands in their pockets, stood on each side.

"Martin's right," Jeremy said. "Let's go."

Dalton's throat tightened. "Give me five more minutes. Would you?"

Martin looked at him, then nodded once. "Okay Dalton, but only five minutes. We'll be in the car."

When the men had returned to the vehicle, Dalton drew his finger across the engraved "G" in the black granite. He read the inscription as he had done dozen times before.

GRACE ELLEN BAXTER
Born December 6, 1941 Died August 7, 2001
I Am the Resurrection and the Life ~ He who believes
in Me shall Live Even if he Dies ~ John 11:25

Tears escaped and he wiped them away. "You're the only one who understands me," he said. "I'm in trouble, Mom. Deep trouble." The rectangular burial plot became her kitchen table as he emptied his heart.

"Sammy warned me about the avalanche forecast but you know me, I've got Wallace Baxter's stubborn streak. What a legacy, huh?"

He scooted closer to the tombstone. "Things have gotten bad between Sammy and me. I messed up big time. I might lose her. I don't know what to do." He closed his eyes.

"You always said, 'The prayers of the righteous avail much.' I know I'm not righteous but you are, Mom. God listens to you. If you can hear me, please pray for me."

Dalton glanced at the men who stared through open windows in the car. He got to his feet, then looked at the grave next to hers. The dead flowers he'd tossed had landed below a row of block lettering that spelled his father's name.

How fitting. Everything you touched died. Especially Mom.

CHAPTER THIRTY-SEVEN

8:59 a.m.
Baxter Home

SAMANTHA SPREAD BUTTER ON TWO pieces of sourdough toast. It seemed surreal to be doing ordinary household tasks with Grace playing upstairs, while Dalton went to jail. The doorbell chimed. She wiped her hands on a paper towel and headed to the front door.

Brad Sanders, dressed in a linen designer shirt, stood on her front porch, his hands in his pockets. He furrowed his brow as he spoke. "I know I'm the last person you expected, Sam."

"What do you want, Brad?"

"To check on you. To see if you're okay. With Dalton on his way to ... uh ... Prescott ... this must be very hard on you."

And you're here to gloat? She frowned at him. "Since when have you cared?"

"I've always cared, Sam." He moved toward her. She took a step back. The tips of his boots now claimed her threshold.

She eyed his feet, then raked his body, meeting his gaze. "You sure have a great way of showing it."

"I admit I was harsh at the council meeting." He inched forward, his body now inside the house. "It pains me to see Dalton treat you this way. You deserve better. You've always deserved better." He ran a finger across her cheek.

She slapped his hand away. "Stop ... Brad." Her voice cracked. "You need to leave."

"I want to lend a hand. Can't we let the past go? We can be friends, can't we?"

"Friends?" She grimaced. "We haven't been friends in twenty years. And we won't be, ever again."

He moved into her space, his breath smelling of tobacco. "Dalton will go to jail, Sam. You'll need support. I'll be there for you. Unlike that ... that looser you married."

She gasped. "To think we were there for you when Maggie left. And against my better judgment you were appointed to the council. Now you act like this, how dare you!"

Brad leaned close. "My marriage was only an unfortunate detour." His barrel-like chests within inches of hers. "I had to do something while I waited for you to come to your senses about that creep you married."

"How dare you come here and insult Dalton!" Anger tightened the knot in her chest. She swung the door closed, forcing him to take a step back. But before she could latch it, he shoved his way through.

"Leave ... now ..." She pushed at the wood but it refused to budge.

"Calm down, Sammy. I mean no harm. I'm here to help."

"Help? All you do is cause problems. Why on earth you came back to Saint Luke's I'll never know. I feel like I'm being stalked." She glanced at the staircase. *Please God, let Grace stay up in her room.*

He snickered. "That's a bit over reactive on your part, isn't it?" He stroked her hair. She snapped her head back. "After all, Saint Luke's is my home church, too. It's not my fault our denomination only has one chapel in this God-forsaken town. What can I say?"

"Considering our history, I thought you would have gone elsewhere. Like back to Phoenix."

"I'm done with that fast life. Besides, I don't recall your husband objecting at the time."

Thanks to her. She'd been cautiously okay with Brad worshipping at Saint Luke's—five years ago. At the time she'd decided to extend him an olive branch, hoping Brad had changed. But unfortunately he was still the same man she'd dated in college. Obnoxious. A Jerk. And fixated. With her.

"Dalton approved my council appointment, didn't he?" A sneer spread across Brad's face . "That was just one of his many mistakes. And now ... well, he'll be in prison a long time. You're going to need help. A man around the house."

"That won't be you." Her voice clipped as she pushed against his snake-skin boots again. The door gave ever so slightly. Then he backed out to the porch.

"We'll see about that." He turned and strode toward his car.

Samantha slammed the door, her heart hammering. She twisted the deadbolt and rested against the wood, trying to catch her breath.

Brad Sanders. Why wouldn't he leave her alone?

With a pounding heart and shaking hands, she returned to the kitchen, finished scrambling the eggs, and called Grace to breakfast.

As she took her first bite, the sound of jostling locks made Samantha freeze for a moment. Brad wouldn't come back. He wouldn't dare. Would he?

She jolted up from the table, knocking over an empty coffee cup. It wobbled to the formica's edge and she caught it. Grace continued to pull off crusts from her toast, oblivious.

"Mom, we're home!" Gordy called through the hallway. Samantha breathed in relief. Her son appeared at the breakfast room entry, her mother Shirley, following.

"Grams!" Grace bounced from the table, skirted around her brother and hugged her grandmother tight.

"Thanks for coming, Mom," Samantha said.

"Gordy didn't give me a choice. He's convinced about this disaster. What do you think?"

"I'm in total agreement. I want you safe." Samantha eyed her mother's suitcase. "We've got the sofa bed ready for you in Dalton's office. I cleared a shelf in the downstairs bathroom."

"Hopefully I won't stay long. Maybe things won't be as bad as you think."

"If the power's still on at one o'clock, then I'd say we've dodged a bullet," Gordy said. "And you and I can head back to the mountains."

"Grace, can you help your grandmother put her things away?" Samantha asked.

"Come on, Grams." Grace grabbed her grandmother's hand.

"You just missed your father," Samantha told Gordy once they were alone. "He's on his way to Saguaro Junction with the council members. Grace doesn't know yet so could we keep things quiet when she's around?"

He shrugged. "Didn't you ask them to wait? If we lose electricity, things could get really bad."

"I tried, Gordy. Other than the Fernándezes, no one believes me. How about something to eat?"

"Grams and I ate on the way. But coffee would be good."

Samantha grabbed a carafe of hot brew and filled a cup as Grams reappeared in the doorway.

"You've trained your daughter well. She's a great hostess," Grams said. "She even gave me a fresh toothbrush."

"Sounds like Grace. Where is she?"

"Outside looking at the storm clouds. It's getting darker by the minute."

Samantha glanced out the window. The forecasted monsoon bore down on her little desert town and she hoped it wouldn't be brutal. They didn't need bad weather on top of everything else.

Samantha turned to her mother. "You look exhausted, Mom. Grab some sleep."

"I will once I empty the car. Gordy and I brought a ton of stuff. Where do you want it?"

"We'll take care of that," Gordy said. "Get some rest."

Her mother didn't argue again. She turned and disappeared down the hallway.

After several trips to the garage, Samantha and Gordy had emptied the Olds.

"I could use a nap too," she said, rubbing her eyes. "So could you, son."

"No time for that. Bee's on her way."

"How is she getting here?"

"Her mom's bringing her. I'll drive her home later."

"Have you told her about the CME?"

"I called her before we left the mountains. The Brewsters are well-supplied. I've seen their food storage." He hunched his shoulders. "I've got to tell Bee about Dad before she hears it from someone at church. This is so embarrassing."

"I know. I'm sorry." She kissed his cheek as she headed toward the stairs. "If I'm not back in thirty minutes, come wake me."

Samantha dragged her body upstairs. When she reached the landing, the front door chimed. She leaned an ear over the railing. Bethany Brewster's infatuation was apparent to everyone except Gordy. When would her son finally catch on? Although, it was kind of sweet that he didn't.

After detecting muted voices below, Samantha gave up trying to interpret what was being said. Fatigue pushed her to her bedroom where she collapsed on the king-size bed. Within minutes she fell asleep under a rattling fan.

ജ്യ

"That looks nasty." Bee pointed at the blackening clouds outside the breakfast window.

They talked about the different CME scenarios as lightening splintered dark clouds. The storm gathered speed.

Sipping drinks across from each other at the table, Gordy knew he should tell her about his dad. But how could he bring it up? How do you tell someone your dad was an addict and a thief?

"Gordster. Spill it." Bee's order broke the silence between them.

He shifted on his chair. "What?"

"You wanted to tell me something."

Gordon cleared his throat and looked down at the table. "My dad ...he's in major trouble. He broke the law."

"Pastor D?"

He listed his father's crimes. "He's ruined everything. He'll probably go to jail."

"Jail?" Bee's eyes formed large blue pools, her mouth fell open.

"We don't have bail money. Dad will have to stay put while he waits for trial. Mom called a lawyer who goes to Saint Luke's. He thinks Dad will be charged."

"I can't believe this. Pastor D baptized me ..." Bee's voice trailed off.

"I'm shocked, too. I never suspected my dad would do anything like this." Gordon exhaled, then took a sip of coffee. His best friend finally knew. He wasn't alone anymore.

She seemed to sense his relief because she segued to a lighter topic concerning the upcoming school year. "Can you believe classes start in two weeks? Well at least I hope so."

"I know. Me too." Would a high school education be part of a non-electric America? He kept that thought to himself.

"I'm supposed to lead the cheer squad this year." She winked at him.

Heat climb into his cheeks. "That doesn't surprise me. You're really good. When's practice?"

"Next week. Coach Jensen told us to bring our suits. They're letting us use the pool afterwards." She stared at the weather outside. "A storm like this would be nice. At least we'd be inside. I hate doing our routines in the heat."

Rain pelted the windows. Gordon stood. "Time to get you home before this gets really bad. Gotta wake my mom and then we'll leave."

CHAPTER THIRTY-EIGHT

9:45 a.m.
Near Saguaro Junction, Arizona

DALTON MASHED HIS FACE AGAINST the passenger window. He stared at the pines lining the road. One of Martin's windshield wipers scraped across the glass, grating on his last nerve. He needed more medicine. He still had a pill in his sock but couldn't be seen taking it. Not now. Not in front of Martin.

This couldn't be happening. Tears collected in the corners of his eyes. He used his shirt cuff to wipe them away. Rain sheeted the window as they neared the mountain town of Saguaro Junction.

"Not much further," Martin said.

Dalton twisted around. He could see buildings ahead. Regret roiled through his gut. Surrendering at this small sheriff's substation was the deal he'd made with the councilmen.

"If you turn yourself in at Saguaro Junction," Martin told him earlier, "we'll make the stop at the cemetery." Dalton agreed. Now he wondered if it had been such a good idea. If Sammy was right and he was arrested, Prescott's upscale jail had to be better than what this one-horse-town had to offer.

As they moved through the quiet community, hushed whispers came from the backseat. Were Harold and Jeremy debating whether he should be fired? Hadn't he worked at being an excellent pastor? Had they forgotten all the good things he had done? Couldn't they cut him some slack?

"According to the GPS, it's three blocks up," Martin said. Dalton looked at the digital display on the console. New knots formed in his stomach.

ЖOG

9:55 a.m.
Baxter Home

The rhythmic pelt of rain lulled Shirley Weston to sleep under a homemade quilt in Dalton's office. One of hers, in fact, a gift to Samantha for her wedding.

Dreaming, she saw her husband, Stephen. His waist-length hair whipped through the wind. They walked together through a park. He stopped suddenly and pointed to a bank of black clouds. "Hold on, sweetheart! Storm's coming."

Clap! Boom!

The thunder outside jarred Shirley awake. She sat up and scanned her surroundings. Stephen was gone and once again she was alone. Relief came, seeing the neon alarm clock on her son-in-law's desk. They still had power. She rubbed her eyes and thought about the vision. Her husband's ominous words seemed like a warning. She got up and headed to the kitchen to find Samantha.

ЖOG

10:15 a.m.
Saguaro Junction Sheriff's Office

"You have the right to remain silent and to refuse to answer questions. Anything you do say may be used against you in a court of law."

Miranda's famous words. Until now, Dalton had only heard them on cop shows. This all seemed surreal. When he had emptied his pockets on the counter, Sheriff Owen Winters, a short man with hairy arms, turned him toward a wall and cuffed him. "If you decide to answer questions now without an attorney present," Winters continued, "you still have the right to stop answering at any time until you talk to an attorney. Do you understand your rights, Reverend?"

"Yes," Dalton answered. Other than addressing him as "reverend", a lot of good the collar had done. When he searched the councilmen's faces, he saw widened eyes filled with worry.

The officer guided him toward an open doorway and Dalton heard Martin call out, "It'll be okay, brother. The church will be praying for you." If only God would hear their prayers.

ЖOG

10:20 a.m.

Sherriff Winters inked and pressed Dalton's fingers on a fingerprint chart then snapped two mug shots in front of a white wall. He hadn't been given a placard of numbers to hold against his chest. The technology of the modern world, he guessed. Even in the boonies, numerical assignments were issued from cyberspace.

He walked with Winters to a holding area. Dalton tried to give him eye contact. The man remained stoic.

"Everything off," the officer ordered."

"Everything?" Dalton swallowed hard as he took off his clerical collar.

"Standard protocol. We need to cavity search you."

Heat flushed through Dalton's face as he removed everything but his socks. He shivered on a steel bench, naked. A monster of a man entered the room. The giant smiled, revealing a gap between his two front teeth.

"This is Deputy Chachu but we call him Charlie." The Native American walked toward him, thick black hair tied behind his neck, the tail tucked into his collar. "Take those off." The deputy pointed to his socks. Dalton stifled a groan and carefully removed them, staring longingly at the little yellow pill that bounced and rolled across the floor, out of reach. The deputy failed to notice.

Chachu rummaged through a satchel he'd brought with him. He pulled out two LED flashlights, a tube of petroleum jelly and some rubber gloves. The sound of snapping plastic made Dalton's skin crawl. How had it come to this humiliation? An eternity passed while he gritted his teeth through the procedure.

"Here," Winters said when it was finally over. The officer handed him a stack of clothing. A Ziploc with toiletries, including a new rubber toothbrush had been placed on top. "Put these on."

Sandwiched between the plastic bag and a towel, was a bright orange jumpsuit, some tube socks and sneakers. Dalton winced.

"Wear your own skivvies. Get moving. We don't have all day."

He put on his underwear, then climbed into the carrot-colored garb. It was at least three sizes too big. He tugged at the gaping sides, questioning both men with raised eyebrows.

"It's all we have," Deputy Charlie said. "Once you're taken to the detention center, you'll get something that fits."

"Detention center?"

"Your new home if you can't make bail. It's in Prescott. Our facility only has holding tanks."

Goose flesh prickled his skin. He ground his teeth, tried to control the ensuing shaking in his arms. The thought of being locked up indefinitely caused ... panic to coil like a rattler about to strike.

He pulled on socks and sneakers while Winters stuffed his pricey duds into a blue plastic bag. After the officer crammed in the Italian leather shoes, he zip-tied it shut. He threw the bag over his shoulder, then left the room.

Dalton stared at the tiny tablet about four feet away.

"Let's go," the deputy said, interrupting his thoughts.

"Don't I get a phone call?"

"That comes next."

After being cuffed a second time, Dalton was led through a narrow hallway to a room with three pay phones.

"Make it collect. All calls are recorded." The officer removed Dalton's restraints.

Sweat beaded his forehead as he pressed zero for the operator.

Once Samantha accepted his call she asked, "You're in custody?"

"It's horrible. Can you post bail for me?"

"We don't have money for that or an attorney. Thanks to you, there's nothing in our bank accounts."

"Borrow it from your mother!" That come out harsher than he'd intended. "I mean, please ask your mother."

"She promised to help us with the mortgage so we won't lose our home. I can't ask for anything else."

His vision narrowed and he swayed, like he was going to pass out. He inhaled sharply. A doctor had once told him, "Take a deep breath and count to ten." It was supposed to ward off a panic attack. He felt calmer but the phone quivered in his fingers.

"Dalton ... are you there?"

"Isn't there anyone you can call?"

"No."

"I guess I'll figure things out on my own."

"Gene Snyder says you'll have to stay put until your arraignment."

"You talked to him?"

"This morning. And despite you hocking his mother's heirloom, he was very helpful over the phone. That teapot had been in his family for over two hundred years." Sammy's voice climbed. "How could you?"

He shook his head even though she couldn't see him. How could he do any of this? And lie to Winifred Snyder. She was one of the pillars in the church. What kind of man had he become?

"The pawn ticket's in my office at the church." He cleared his voice then spoke louder. "I can get it back, Sammy. I have thirty days."

"Gene picked it up a few hours ago." Her voice hardened again. "Thanks to you, I now have to come up with five hundred dollars to pay him back."

He let out a long sigh. "When do I go to court?"

"Gene said it could be three days to a week. He wasn't sure."

Three days? He'd never been that long without his medicine.

"There's one more thing I need to tell you," she said. "It's not good."

What could be worse? "You better hurry. They say I only have a few minutes."

"Gordy came home early. The sun's doing strange things. Are you familiar with a CME?"

"Some type of a solar flare?"

"One's headed toward Earth. It will hit some time in the next few hours. Gordy says it's massive. We could lose power for months. I want you to know in case something happens."

Dalton gripped the phone and shifted on his feet. She was freaking out about a few blackouts when his whole future was at stake?

"Time's up, Baxter." Dalton pivoted and glared at the gigantic Apache standing over him.

"They say I have to hang up ... Sammy ... I'm sorry. You don't deserve any of this ..."

Before she responded, the deputy took the phone and slammed it to the receiver. "Calls are restricted to five minutes. You got six. Let's go." The deputy replaced the handcuffs and led him back the way they came.

ഌ

Samantha yanked the cell away from her ear and looked at her mother. "He hung up on me!"

"I'm sorry dear," her mother said. "I couldn't help but overhear. I can loan you more money."

She shook her head. "You've done enough. Dalton's made his own bed."

The sound of an engine rumbled outside.

"Gordy's back." She wiped her eyes and squared her shoulders as the front door opened. Her son's rapid footsteps approached.

"Have you heard from Dad? Is he in jail?" Gordy asked when he joined them. He dropped his keys. They clattered across the counter. His hair was wet and disheveled, his t-shirt soaked.

"He's being processed." Samantha quickly changed the subject. "It must be bad out there." Darkness swallowed the mid-morning sky. "How'd it go with Bethany?"

"She couldn't believe it." He shrugged. "I hated her knowing."

"It's a hard thing to tell anyone." Samantha studied her son. Gordy's bleary eyes were circled in red. "Why don't you get some rest?" she asked.

"I can sleep later. Tell me about Dad."

"He's at Saguaro Junction Sheriff's Office."

"What happened to Prescott?"

"It's the 7th and you know your father rarely misses."

"Really? He went today?"

"Wouldn't turn himself in unless they agreed"

"This fixation with Grandma's grave is nutty. It's been ... what ... ten years since she died?"

"Nutty or not, he got his way. With the condition that they go to a closer town."

Gordy poured himself a glass of Mountain Dew, then tossed in three ice cubes. "I can't believe Dad's a druggie."

"I can't say I was surprised," Grams said. "That man has a lot of pain."

Samantha turned to her mother. "You're not excusing him, are you?"

"No, dear. But I do understand."

"Remember Trevor Johnson?" Gordy interjected. "He got hooked on meth last summer right after graduation. He's in rehab right now."

"The football star?" Samantha's eyes widened.

"Yep." Her son chugged a gulp of soda. "He blew a full ride at A.S.U."

"Bad choices can ruin our lives," Grams said.

"Dad's have ruined mine." Gordy set his soda down.

"Don't believe that for a minute," Grams said. "Your future's in God's hands, not your father's." She lifted Gordy's chin. A tear slipped from his eye. He quickly wiped it away, looking embarrassed.

"Things will be okay," Grams said. "Hold on to the Lord, Gordy."

Gordy wasn't the only one needing a faith boost. Samantha wished she could hold on to God. If only she could grab His hand and not let go until this whole mess was over. But right now He seemed a million miles away.

"The whole town will know about this," Gordy said. "How will I face my friends?"

"With your head held high," Grams said.

"If this thing hits earth, do you really think people will care about what your father did?" Samantha asked.

He shrugged at both of them, looking at the storm outside. "I guess you're right. If the grids go down, all hell will break loose."

"One thing's for sure. Your father needs treatment," Samantha told him. "Laney says coming off these drugs is excruciating. From how he sounded on the phone, I believe he's starting withdrawals." She flipped on the electric kettle. Her coffee cup needed filling.

Gordy responded with another shrug. He picked up his soda and walked toward the back door, then turned around. "I've got to check our supplies in the shed. Can you make me a sandwich?"

"Sure, hon. I got most of your check-list this morning. We can make a run into town if we need anything else. Thank goodness we have a pool."

"It's great we live in the boonies, too," he said. "We may need to hunker down a few weeks."

"Take down the umbrellas on your way to the storage unit. Put them in the back, near the Christmas boxes. The winds are raging out there."

"I will. Sure looks gloomy out. Sort of how I feel right now."

"Me too," Samantha said.

"Me three," her mother added as she sat in the breakfast booth.

Samantha watched Gordy leave the kitchen. He hurried through the rain toward the shed, a large umbrella tucked under each arm. Only three days had passed since he'd left for her mother's cabin, yet in her eyes, the boy who had left had become a man.

What awaited them today? Would her faith hold out long enough to get her through? Hopelessness crept up her bones like overgrown ivy swallowing a shack. Even if they were spared this CME catastrophe, Dalton's legal troubles and the family's public disgrace were too much to bear. She moved to the breakfast booth and collapsed with a thud across from her mother.

CHAPTER THIRTY-NINE

10:40 a.m.
McCormick, AZ

WIND ASSAULTED SAMANTHA'S FACE. SHE ran through the yard, cradling a plate of food. The black sky grew more ominous by the minute, a tell-tale sign of the impending monsoon.

She opened the shed's side door and found Gordy nestled among several boxes. He'd organized them, forming towers across the cement floor. Samantha offered him the plate which contained a chicken sandwich and his favorite chips, along with an apple. He took a seat on a heavy box of kerosene and dove in.

"I never found the heirloom vegetables you wanted." She pointed to a box of seeds near the lawn mower. "I think Jacobsen's Hardware has them. I can stop by on my way back from Laney's."

"Buy everything they have. GMO seeds are useless," Gordy said. "They don't reproduce. We can save what you bought for bartering."

"Bartering?"

"If this thing happens, paper money will be useless. Food stockpiles will be like gold. Especially seeds."

"How do you know so much?" She'd always known Gordy was smart, but pride in her son's knowledge swelled in her chest.

"I've done a lot of reading."

"That's for sure. You are miles ahead of the rest of us." She winked at him.

"And Mom ... just so you know, the internet is erratic right now."

"It's off?"

"No, it's still on. But the free flow of information seems to be restricted. Australia's government site is down. So is Drudge."

"What's going on?"

"Not sure. Governments might be killing the news. Fear of wide-spread panic."

"Including the folks in our little town if we can't get information," Samantha said as she headed to the door. "Got to get on the road. Keep an eye on your sister. She tends to freak out during thunderstorms."

"Grams and I can handle it. Don't worry."

ꕥ

11:03 a.m.
Martin and Laney's Garage

"This is wonderful." Samantha inspected Martin and Laney's stockpile in the back of their two-car garage. The older couple huddled nearby. Their red-rimmed eyes matched hers.

"You bought a lot," Samantha said.

Laney nodded. "Two car loads. I purchased the two-way radios you suggested." Laney pointed to some boxes covered with aluminum foil. "I wrapped them several times like Gordy instructed."

"How many did you buy?"

"Four sets. I emptied the shelf and even found the rechargeable batteries you told me about. The radios have an eighty mile range."

"Good. Perfect for our little town. I was able to pick up ten sets in Phoenix and some solar chargers so I think we're ready. At least I hope so." Samantha wiped her forehead with the back of her hand. Outside temperatures were already climbing. "Did Tom wonder what you were doing?"

"You know Tom. Once I told him about the CME, he thought I was nuts," Laney said. Everyone knew Tom and his sarcastic ways. If earth was spared a disaster, the Baxters and Fernándezes would be the butt of jokes for months. Tom would certainly lead the charge, gossiping to anyone who'd listen.

"I wish I would have been there. I would have let him have it," Martin said.

"I think you still should," Laney said. "We spent hundreds of dollars today."

"I might just do that later." Martin's brow arched as he took in a deep breath. "Right now there's too much to do and frankly, I don't care what anyone says. This could be devastating. We need to tell whoever will listen ... even the naysayers."

"We'll have their undivided attention if the lights go out," Laney said.

"I see you loaded up on long term survival food." Samantha eyed the containers of powdered eggs, cheese and oatmeal. "Not to worry you ... but this event might bring out the worst in folks. Shouldn't you hide this?"

"No need, Samantha. Laney and I would never turn away a hungry person. God will take care of us."

Samantha shrugged. "Wish I had your faith."

"After what you've gone through, that's understandable. In time you'll get your bearings back," Laney said. "I'll be praying for you."

"Thanks, dear friend." Samantha clung to Laney, then turned to Martin. "How was Dalton when you left him?" she asked.

"Very upset. He tried not to show it, but I could see the fear in his eyes. I hated leaving him there."

Samantha flinched, visualizing handcuffs on her husband now under arrest and facing numerous felony counts. She tried to push the thoughts from her mind. If she let her imagination go, she'd be a mess.

ꕥ

10:50 am
Saguaro Junction Sheriff's Office

The deputy removed Dalton's cuffs, then clicked a remote, opening a holding cell. Two prisoners looked up as Dalton entered. They straddled a long metal bench, facing one another, playing cards spread out between them. They wore jumpsuits like his.

"Meet your new cellie, boys. This is Dalton." The officer gestured toward the men. "That's Bulldog over there." He pointed to a tattooed prisoner with a mustache. "Next to him is T.T." An overweight man sat across Bulldog. Fatty folds of pink skin escaped through his uniform sleeves. The frowning men said nothing, only stared.

After Dalton entered the cell, the deputy pressed the remote. The door clanged shut. Dalton jumped, then drew a deep breath. He would not panic. He would not lose it. He would not appear weak to these men.

"This will be home for a few days until you're arraigned," the officer told him. "Meals are at 8:00 a.m., noon and 5:00 p.m. Sleeping cots will be brought in each evening. Any questions?"

Dalton's anxiety notched. "Can I talk to an attorney?" he asked.

"Your paperwork will be processed by tomorrow morning. Your public defender should follow sometime in the afternoon."

"How about water?" The roof of Dalton's mouth and the back of his throat felt clogged with cotton balls.

"Help yourself." He pointed to the sink fastened to the wall next to an exposed toilet in the corner. The deputy turned to the others. "No trouble in here. Understood?" It wasn't a question.

A sadistic smile drew across Bulldog's face. Dalton's stomach twisted. Trouble? As soon as the deputy left, he was toast.

The Apache started to walk away but then pivoted. "I mean it you two. No trouble."

"Sure, Chachu-man." Bulldog's grin revealed two missing teeth.

The officer disappeared into a hallway. Bulldog turned to the three-hundred-fifty pound man next to him. "Hey, T.T. What do you say? Wanna go easy on the new guy?"

"Why not?" T.T. chortled and his stomach bounced under the fan of cards he held in one hand.

Dalton watched them for a moment. Would all his gym workouts help if they tried to mess with him? He could box, and he always held his own against his trainer. When he didn't have a bum knee and a throbbing face. But street fighting? Against criminals? He sized them up. If he had to, he could probably take the fat man. He wasn't too sure about Bulldog though.

He took a seat at the far end of the bench. His legs twitched and a wave of nausea swallowed his insides. Circles of perspiration under his arms soaked through the jumpsuit. Sweat beaded his forehead. A thousand bugs seemed to crawl across his skin. Dalton swatted and scratched but at closer inspection, there was nothing there. He went to the sink and cupped water into his mouth. If only he could have his medicine. Why hadn't he taken that last pill in the car? He'd never get it back now.

When he had enough water, he sat and glanced at his cellmates. The plastic chips piled between them indicated poker. Dalton wondered how they paid up.

"Five-card stud?" T.T. asked.

"I ... uh ... don't have any chips," Dalton said.

"We can front you some, can't we, 'Dog?"

Bulldog pulled out five chips from the pile and extended them toward Dalton.

"I'll pass." He wasn't up to a card game. He felt dizzy. He tried to slow his breathing so he wouldn't pass out.

"So much for being nice," T.T. snarled.

"You think you're too good for us?" Bulldog growled.

Dalton pointed to the gauze on his face. "I had an accident. I'm not feeling well." He decided to change the subject. "What does T.T. stand for?" he asked the fat man.

"Tiny Tim."

Dalton had to look away and stifle a laugh. Despite his misery, that was funny.

"You're probably wondering why, huh?"

"Well ... uh ... no ..."

"I was born on Christmas Day. They named me after my uncle. My ma said I came early and was a scrawny little runt. For years the family called me Tiny Tim and it sort of stuck."

CHAPTER FORTY

11:53 a.m.
McCormick, Arizona

SAMANTHA GRIPPED THE STEERING WHEEL of her Camry. It kept jarring from her fingers, surrendering to the fifty-five mile per hour winds assaulting her car. She clenched with all her strength, forcing the car toward her desert home on the edge of town. Outside her windshield, inky-colored clouds shrouded the sun as ragged lightning stabbed the earth. Hail pelted, striking the glass so hard Samantha thought it might crack. She straightened her back and bit her lip. Grace wasn't the only one who hated these storms.

Thanks to Gordy, hidden inside a shoebox on the passenger seat, was her cell phone. The box, enshrouded in three layers of aluminum foil, would be protected from an electromagnetic pulse, should it happen. Well, that was what Gordy thought, anyway. She wondered if having the capability to turn on one's phone would even matter in the long run. An EMP would end their phone service and the cell would become nothing more than a high tech photo album and address book.

She was tempted to tear through the packaging and check for messages but could still hear her son's voice. "Open only if you have an emergency," he'd said when he handed it to her after breakfast. He'd placed a similar box in her mother's hands. "The foil acts like a Faraday cage."

"A what?" her mother had asked.

"How to construct one is really simple. The instructions are explained in those prepping links I emailed you last night. Did you forward them to the congregation?"

"Laney did. According to her, most people laughed."

"Too bad." Gordy frowned. "Those web sources were critical, Mom. The information provided could save lives."

"I know. I did my best in the short time I had. People sometimes find a state of denial more comfortable. Much like your father."

Gordy gestured with his hand. "Follow me." He led them to a large aluminum trashcan on the outside patio. He lifted the lid. It was crammed with electronic equipment.

"This is a Faraday cage. The experts don't all agree on this but the metal is supposed to protect the contents," he said. "I'm not sure it will work, but it can't hurt to try. I also loaded the microwave oven in the kitchen. It's filled to capacity with spare batteries, some old phones, Ipods, stuff like that."

"My microwave?"

"I sealed it with duct tape. Trust me, we won't be needing that oven if this thing hits earth. For now, it makes an excellent Faraday."

Samantha leaned over and looked in the trashcan. A small television, some laptops, radios and other stuff filled the container to the brim. "Why the cardboard?" She pointed at the thick brown paper, fastened to the metal sides with duct tape.

"It acts as an insulator against radiation."

Samantha pointed to her iPad. "Will my tablet work?"

"With the solar chargers we bought, yes. But the Internet will most likely be down."

"If we have no Internet and you can't make calls, why bother?" her mother asked.

"No one knows how the CME will affect us," he had told them. "A few transformers may survive. We might be able to get online within a few days. If that happens, we'll be glad we did this."

Gordy was right. If power was restored, being able to make a call might mean the difference between life and death.

Samantha turned on to Casa Blanca Road. Though the downpour had weakened to a sprinkle, the winds still raged. Grayish light peeked through billowy black clouds overhead.

As she drove through her neighborhood, an eerie crimson fog gathered and glowed over the mountains. Swaying curtains of reddish light moved above Prescott National Forest. Awestruck, Samantha swerved and slammed on her brakes. She pulled to the side of the road and stared. Like party streamers strung from heavenly ceilings, the lights shimmered and danced through the dark sky.

For several moments she drank in the wondrous beauty before pressing the gas pedal and easing back to the road. As much as she wanted to linger at the splendor, she couldn't waste any more time. Gordy had warned about the auroras. "If they're red, it's because we've had a CME," he said. Thank goodness her car still worked. Maybe the electricity hadn't been affected after all. She flipped on the radio and pressed programmed stations. Each one emitted crackly static. Samantha swallowed hard, the beat from her heart graduated to her ears.

ꟷ

"Grace ... would you look at that?" Shirley pointed outside the window. Rosy light invaded the breakfast room. Grace stopped drawing, flung down a colored pencil and ran to the glass.

"Wow, Grams! They look like Christmas lights."

"They're called auroras." Shirley joined her, placing her hands on her granddaughter's shoulders. "Gordy told us we'd see them."

"They're beautiful," Grace exclaimed.

Aurora borealis. Shirley had seen them once when she and Stephen had taken that cruise to Alaska.

After a few minutes, the growing fatigue in her legs convinced Shirley to return to the breakfast table where she could enjoy the light show sitting down. That brief nap she'd taken hadn't done much good. Her legs felt wobbly. She sipped green tea while Grace remained at the window. Who could blame the child? The lights rippled, then folded and unfolded, to suddenly disappear, then morph into new shapes moments later. It was breathtaking.

A vintage wall sconce above the breakfast booth flickered off. The florescent light over the kitchen sink sputtered, before going dark as well. Shirley slipped into her Birkenstocks and padded to the pantry. "Do you have any candles?" she asked Grace.

Her granddaughter appeared at the pantry door and pointed to the top shelf. "Mommy keeps a box up there."

Shirley pulled down a container labeled "emergency supplies" where she located six white candles and some holders.

ꟷ

Gordon should have checked on Grams and Grace but he was frozen, unable to move. With his green notebook tucked under his arm, he could do nothing but stare at the sky. The oxygen-rich auroras were deep red which could only mean one thing. Earth had been struck by a mega flare.

Why hadn't he brought a pen? He was seeing history. He should be taking notes. Like Richard Carrington over a hundred years ago, these events should be recorded for posterity.

He dropped his notebook on a wrought iron table and rushed to the trash can. He'd left his Canon Rebel inside. By now it should be safe to open. He yanked off the duct tape and raised the lid. He grabbed his camera, then quickly put the top back on.

"It's remarkable, isn't it?" someone asked.

Gordon spun around. His mother walked toward him clutching her keys.

"There isn't a sound anywhere," she said. "Not even a bird chirping."

"It's amazing, Mom." Gordon aimed the camera at the sky.

"How long do they last?"

"If they were normal auroras, ten ... maybe fifteen minutes." He fired his camera in rapid succession. "But today nothing is normal."

"Thank goodness my car still drives," she said. "My car radio doesn't work. Only static."

Gordon lowered his camera. "We had a CME. See the reds ..." He pointed. "Those are very rare. The ionosphere is super-charged. Electrons and atoms are colliding.

"The ejection had to be enormous," he explained. "This could be the worst case scenario we talked about yesterday." He gestured toward the trashcan. "The Faraday cage was a success. My camera still works."

"Have you checked on your grandmother and Grace?" his mother asked.

"Not yet. I have to document this. We'll never see this again in our lifetimes."

"That's for sure," she said as she went inside.

ജ്ജ

12:01 p.m.
Saguaro Junction Sheriff's Office

Dalton huddled on the floor, shaking in one of the cell's corners, near a barred window. An eerie light leaked into the room. Slivers of red streaked across his feet. Bulldog and T.T. slept across the bench, oblivious, sawing logs.

He managed to stand and look out the glass. A few people in the parking lot outside stared heavenward at the pulsating auroras. This must be what Gordy warned about. Something about the sun ... a flare up? He'd been too caught in his own problems to listen.

Two ceiling lights flickered, then gave up their spirits, leaving the room full of shadows. Dalton went to the bench and sat, rubbed the goose flesh covering his arms. After several requests, the deputy had finally brought him a blanket. He wrapped himself in the black scratchy fabric, laid down on his side, using his elbow for a pillow. Flu-like aches invaded his muscles while his stomach tossed and turned. He'd felt this way one time before when he'd tried to stop using his medicine. He'd lasted only two days.

He closed his eyes and swallowed. An agonizing afternoon and never-ending night awaited.

ജ്ജ

12:05 p.m.
Baxter Home

Samantha entered the dimly lit breakfast room. Her mother and Grace nestled together, reading a book. An enormous three-wicked candle produced golden streaks across the table. They looked up and smiled. The homey atmosphere defied the reality of their situation. A wall clock behind them confirmed Gordy's prediction. Its frozen time of 11:59 seemed ominous.

Samantha tipped the book to see its title. *The Lion, The Witch and The Wardrobe*. "I loved this story when I was your age."

"We're taking turns reading," Mom said. "Grace's language abilities are impressive."

Grace's eyes lit up over a happy smile. She hugged the hardback to her chest. "I can't wait for second grade." Samantha wondered if attending second grade at Pueblo Elementary would even be possible. Homeschooling might be in her daughter's near future.

"Let's go outside and see if there's any storm damage," Samantha told her mother. "You stay here, sweetheart."

The girl nodded and opened the book again as they left through the side door.

"How'd she do during the monsoon?" Samantha asked when they'd joined Gordy outside.

"The thunder made her nervous but once the lights appeared she forgot about the storm."

Samantha looked at Gordy. "No lights on inside, son. What should we do now?"

"You're having that church meeting, right?"

"Yes. Martin wants to get together in the annex on Thursday. We'll see where the needs are, so we can help one another."

"How will people know about the meeting?" he asked.

"Laney and Martin printed a flyer at the church office early this morning. The plan was to assemble a team and distribute them door-to-door this afternoon."

"Will everyone be there ... uh ... or ... is it just for the adults?" Gordy asked. Samantha noticed the worry in his eyes. Enduring two long days before seeing Bethany again would be difficult.

"Anyone can attend. You too, Mom." She looked at her mother, raising her brows.

Mom smiled. "Really? I'll go. It's been years since I've seen Laney."

Samantha forced herself not to stare at the shimmering auroras over the horizon. "We've got to get some news," she said. "We need to know how bad this thing is."

"Maybe someone in the church has a short-wave radio. People on the other side of the globe might have power," Gordy said. When he twisted a faucet, the water dribbled.

"Uh oh. That's not good." He dropped the hose.

Samantha shook her head. "I didn't think about that," she said. "The well's powered by electricity."

"Do you have a hand pump?" Gordy asked.

"I'm not sure. I'll check the garage."

"I'll go," Grams said. "I have one at the cabin. I know what they look like."

"I'll go with you, Grams," Gordy said.

"I don't know what I'd do if you weren't here." Samantha smiled at her son. "You've become a man overnight."

"I don't feel very brave, Mom. I'm sort of freaked out." His eyes seemed to search hers. "After we get back, can we talk? I have an idea."

Samantha agreed and watched them walk toward the shed. "Look behind the blue storage tubs," she called. "There's stuff stashed there from when we first moved here. You might find a pump."

Gordy shuffled behind his grandmother. The lack of sleep seemed to be taking its toll. From the back, his wide shoulders and brown spiky hair mirrored Dalton's.

But today, that was where their resemblance ended. Dalton was in jail because of his selfishness and his addiction. While their son was growing into a man—a good and caring man—right before her eyes.

CHAPTER FORTY-ONE

12:20 p.m.
Saguaro Junction Sheriff's Office

THE DEPUTY APPEARED AT THE bars carrying small paper sacks. "You guys ready for lunch?" he asked. Dalton dragged himself to a sitting position. The Apache pressed the remote several times. Nothing happened. The deputy slapped his forehead and chuckled to himself. "I keep forgetting." He set down the food, then pulled a massive ring of keys from his pocket. He set the lunches on the floor. "Eat up," he said. He secured the jail and left.

Bulldog lunged at the food like a ravenous wolf and tossed one of the bags to T.T. Dalton picked his up and looked inside. There was a sandwich, an apple, and a pint of milk. He debated with himself. He'd need to eat to keep up his strength but surging nausea seemed to be winning the hunger game.

But he had to eat. He'd become weaker if he didn't. He opened the sandwich and scowled. Bologna and processed cheese between white bread. He took a cautious bite, chewing on the good side of his mouth. It was dry, no mayonnaise or mustard.

Hot needles stabbed through his cheek so he rewrapped the sandwich and set it aside. He'd save it for later. He opened the milk and took several gulps, washing away the remnants of bread that clung to the roof of his mouth. He refilled the milk container with water a few times, enjoying long drinks. He dropped the apple into his pocket.

"I'll take that if you don't want it." T.T. pointed to the bulge. Bread crumbs clung to the fat man's face. He licked his lips. "How about the rest of my sandwich?" Dalton offered.

"Give me both."

Dalton decided this would not be the hill he would die on. He had no energy to argue. He handed T.T. his food.

"Thanks, man." T.T. chomped into the red skin.

"I wonder how long the lights will be off." Bulldog looked up at the darkened lights.

"It could be a long time," Dalton said. "My son believes the outage is from a CME."

Bulldog cursed. "That isn't good."

"What's a CME?" T.T. asked.

"A plasma ejection from the sun that zaps the planet's electricity," Bulldog told him.

Dalton stared at Bulldog. T.T. stopped chewing.

"What are you sayin'?" T.T. asked through a mouthful of food.

"We might not have power for months," Bulldog added.

"How'd you know that?"

"High school, man. I paid attention in some of my classes."

Bulldog took over the conversation and Dalton leaned back and closed his eyes. Misery climbed through his gut and talking was difficult. His stomach agitated like an old washing machine. He felt like regurgitating the milk he just drank.

"For months?" T.T. asked, then shrugged. "As long as I get my bail hearing, I don't care."

Dalton wondered about his court appearance too. If everyone was worried about the CME, he might be stuck here a long time. He shut his eyes and stretched across the bench. It might help if he dozed off. But his body shivered and his skin crawled, preventing any sleep.

ᘓᘐ

12:59 p.m.
Connor Home

Matt Connor looked out his daughter's window. The waning auroras had been eclipsed by grey, gloomy clouds, matching his mood. Carla was in the kitchen, mere feet away yet the distance between them felt like miles.

The electricity had been off for an hour. Just what he needed on top of everything else. He dreaded the funeral home appointment. It solidified his nightmare. This wasn't just a bad dream. His little girl lay on a slab of metal, her cold cheeks waited in the darkness for his final kiss.

The church council had voted to help. Money trickled in from the congregation, giving them enough to bury their daughter. Laney and Martin offered to join them at the mortuary, but Matt told them no. He and Carla would handle it themselves. As much as he liked Carla's church friends, seeing them reminded him too much of their pastor.

Minutes ticked by. He stared at nothing in particular. The lack of electronic noise grated his nerves. A blaring television might have helped silence the voices in his head. The atmosphere seemed laden with accusation.

He'd been a terrible father and a failure as a husband and he still hadn't told Carla the truth. What would she do once she found he was dealing again? Would she believe that her own pastor was his biggest client? He doubted it. She thought the world of that so-called minister.

Matt ground his teeth. Baxter would pay. But not in dollars. That would be too easy. Baxter must suffer like Matt had suffered. Now the only problem was how to do it.

ꕥ

"We found it." Gordy clutched a water pump and some papers when he and Grams joined his mom inside. He grinned. "Brand new in the box ... with instructions."

"Are you ready to tell us what's on your mind?" she asked, cradling a steamy cup.

"I am. Can we sit down?" He slid across the vinyl seat. Samantha scooted next to him as Grams pulled up a chair. "Where did you get the hot water?" he asked, pointing to his mother's coffee.

"I boiled it outside." She nodded to the kitchen window. A kettle steamed on the Coleman he and Grams had brought from the mountains. "Thanks for bringing Grandpa's camp stove. It works fine." She gestured to an assortment of Starbucks Via boxes and teabags. "Choose your pleasure. I'll get the water."

When his mom returned, Gordon drowned two instant coffee packs with water.

"Whoa ... that's a lot of caffeine," his mom said.

"I need the extra shot," he said, stirring the brew.

"Gordy ... tell your mom your idea," Grams said.

"As soon as I get some cream." He exited the booth and opened the fridge, then retrieved some half and half from the top shelf. He slammed the door shut and spun around. "We're going to lose most of this food."

"I've been thinking about that," his mother said. "We'll move everything to the garage freezer. It's caked with ice and should give us a few days if we don't open it much. I can grill the meat and make sandwiches for the church meeting."

"You won't need to do any of that once you hear my idea," he said.

"Tell me. I'm too tired for suspense right now." She grinned, giving him a curious look.

"Let's load up the cars and head back to Grams. It'll be safer in the mountains."

"Gordster and I talked about this," Grams interjected. "The whole family can come. I've got plenty of room."

His mom shook her head. "It would be nice, but we can't. What about our friends? What about the congregation? Then ... there's your dad. I need to go to his hearing."

"Why should we care about him?" Gordon bit out. "He didn't think of us when he took those drugs and stole that money."

"You have every right to be angry, Gordy," his mom said. "But we need to put those feelings aside, just for now. If the power doesn't come on, something horrible could happen to him."

"Dad's locked up and being taken care of," Gordon said. "I'm sure he's okay."

"He needs medical attention. The withdrawals have probably started and if civil unrest becomes a reality, law enforcement will have their hands full. Your dad's condition won't be very high on their priority list." She took a sip of coffee and studied her steaming mug. "Don't get me wrong. I'm still angry, too. This has hurt me in ways I ... I never imagined. In ways I can't tell you. I've even considered divorce." She looked up finally, met his gaze. "But the more I pray, the more I feel sorry for him. God must be changing my heart."

"I agree with your mom." Grams grabbed his hand and squeezed. "This type of addiction is similar to what I went through. It took a miracle to kick heroin. I wish your grandpa was here. He'd tell you."

Seriously, Grams? Gordon stifled a groan. There was no comparison. His grandparents had been hippies. No one understood the implications of drug use back then. Not like today. His dad knew better. Gordon shrugged. He wouldn't argue but rage continued to simmer inside.

He drained his mug and grabbed another package of Via. Hopefully the coffee would revive him. A looming list of chores competed for his attention but the fatigue that had stolen his energy seemed to be winning. Figuring out how to hook up the water pump might take hours so that would be first.

He tapped in the powdery coffee and stared at the empty packet. He held it up. "This could come in handy."

"How?" his mom asked.

"Can you imagine what people would do to have a cup of Starbucks if the lights stay off? How many of these do you have?"

"About twenty boxes. Got them on sale in Phoenix last month."

"Hold on to them. They're gold." Gordon refilled his mug from the kettle, then picked up the pump and placed it on the table. He spread out the two page instruction booklet. "I'll do this first. Then we'll transfer the food."

"Grams and I will do that. Grace's old wagon is perfect for hauling."

"I'll get Grace," Grams said. "She'll love to help."

His grandmother hurried from the room toward the den. Good thing she'd agreed to leave her mountain home and come with him to McCormick. He might be "the man of the house," but having Grams here somehow made him feel everything would be okay.

CHAPTER FORTY-TWO

1:55 p.m.
Grace Park Funeral Parlor
McCormick, Arizona

"THIS IS RIDICULOUS. HOW CAN they be closed?" Matt pounded on the door. Ironically, like its patrons, McCormick's only funeral home was deathly quiet.

"Shouldn't we call?" Carla asked. "Maybe we got the time wrong."

"My phone's not working. What about yours?"

"Mine's off, too. It's weird, monsoons never do this."

"Let's go around back." Matt suggested. They crossed the manicured lawn to a side gate.

Matt fingered the top and found a latch. He pulled the gate open and they hurried through a narrow walkway. Metal shelving laden with grave stones leaned against the building. Matt looked away and hurried to catch up with Carla. She'd already disappeared around the corner. The sight of the headstones must have gotten to her. Him too.

They reached the back door and banged simultaneously.

Moments later Mr. Copeland, the undertaker, opened it.

"You must be the Connors." He stepped back, gesturing them in. "Please come to my office. I wanted to call you but the phones are out." They followed him into a small room with an oak desk and two chairs. A thin candle flickered near a desk phone, barely lighting the room. "Please have a seat." Matt collapsed into one of the chairs but his wife remained standing.

"I want to see my daughter," she demanded.

"She's not ready." The mortician's brows knitted and his eyes glistened with sympathy. "Please ... Mrs. Connor ... give me some time." He seemed to struggle for words. "The little one will look like an angel when you see her. For some strange reason, I can't get my generator to start but I'm sure the power will be on soon. Let's reschedule for tomorrow. Will morning work for you?"

Carla bolted toward the door. "I want to see her now!"

Matt jumped to his feet and followed. “Mr. Copeland’s right, honey.” He gently turned her to face him. “We’ll return in the morning.” He pulled her close. She bristled.

“I don’t care what you say.” She wiggled free, her eyes shot bullets. “No one’s going to stop me from seeing my baby.” She walked to the hallway, then turned to Mr. Copeland who stood next to Matt. “Where can I find her?”

The mortician wagged his head. He walked around Carla and spread his hands to each wall, blocking the narrow hallway. “I can’t let you do that, Mrs. Connor. It’s against regulation. Besides, during a power outage, the vault remains sealed.”

“Just try and stop me!” She pushed at his shoulder but he didn’t budge. His exasperated expression begged Matt to do something.

“Mr. Copeland, seeing that it’s monsoon season, the power might be off for days,” Matt said. “If that’s true, wouldn’t it be better to let Carla see her now ... uh ... before ... she begins to ... uh ... look worse?” Matt hoped his attempt at negotiation would prevail. He could tell Carla was close to her breaking point, close to exploding.

Mr. Copeland sighed deeply. “I’ll make an exception just this once.” He dropped his arms to his sides. “Only five minutes, Mrs. Connor. We must keep the body preserved as long as possible. Do you understand?”

Carla nodded and he let her pass.

“This is a mistake,” Mr. Copeland mumbled loud enough for Matt to hear.

Yeah, it probably was.

CHAPTER FORTY-THREE

3:12 p.m.
Downtown McCormick

MATT GRIPPED THE STEERING WHEEL. If only he could do something to help make this nightmare go away.

Carla dabbed her eyes with a crumpled tissue while she sobbed in the passenger seat. Lifeless stoplights slowed the afternoon traffic while tensions mounted on Main Street. Driving through the sluggish street, he searched for an open restaurant. Carla hadn't eaten a decent meal since Sunday morning. But everything looked closed. No power, no cooking, no food. He wondered how long this could last. Had the monsoons done permanent damage to the grid?

"Are you hungry?" Matt touched her hand.

"No." She jerked away and turned toward the window. A painful lump lodged in his throat. May as well head home. He turned down a side alley and took an alternate detour to their neighborhood.

When they entered the house, Carla rushed to the bedroom, slamming the door behind her. He hesitated in the hallway, wanting to twist the doorknob while horrific memories from the funeral home replayed in his mind.

Their precious baby lay naked on the mortician's slab. Her eyes were sealed and her blue lips sagged over ghostly white skin. Carla screamed. Matt would never forget the image of his wife clutching their daughter's body to her chest.

Did she blame him for Charity's death? Hadn't he done all he could to keep a roof over their heads during the treatments? So what if he'd chosen the life of dark alley deals and low-lifes. What else could he do? Though government assistance helped, Charity's outpatient care took everything they had. If Carla was this broken now, what would happen once she found out he'd gotten back into the drug trade?

Matt went to the garage to find his camping stove. He hunted through some shelves until he located his four-burner Coleman. Inside a metal cabinet he found some lanterns and a short-wave radio. Near one of the walls, he collected some fuel containers. He piled everything on the patio table and attached a canister to the stove.

A hot cup of coffee sounded good right now, but he'd make Carla some tea first. He filled a pot with water and lit the burner. While the water heated, he flipped on the radio's toggle switch. Hearing the crackly air, he smiled. The short-wave worked. That was a relief. With everything else out, Matt was surprised. He scanned the channels. The little unit emitted foreign broadcasts. After several attempts at positioning the antenna, Matt finally heard English. A British broadcaster announced, "America seems to be affected most," he said. "Our contacts in Washington report most of the nation has no power. Officials agree this could last for months. Already our Prime Minister has deployed troops as requested by President Turner. Most members of NATO are sending aid."

Months with no power? What was going on? What had happened? Had the country been hit by a terrorist group?

"NASA is sure the worst is over," the broadcaster continued. "Scientists around the world agree this was the worst CME on record."

CME? That had something to do with a solar flare, Matt remembered, recalling a documentary he watched about a year ago.

Matt hung his head. With all that he'd gone through the past two days, now this. This couldn't be happening. What would he and Carla do if there was no power for months?

Matt counted four fuel canisters. Not enough for a few weeks, let alone a few months. He must get to town. Maybe he could beat the panic and hoard a supply before his neighbors realized the urgency. He clicked off the gas, drenched a Chai bag with water, then returned to an empty kitchen. He opened the fridge and he pulled out an egg sandwich from a container one of the church ladies had left. He placed it and the steamy mug on a plate, then headed toward the bedroom.

When Matt entered the room, Carla's back was to him. She lay on her side.

Matt carried the plate to the bed and sat. "You need to eat."

"I'm not hungry, Matt. Please go."

The lump in his throat grew larger. "Don't shut me out, Carla. Not now."

She twisted to her back and leaned on a pillow. "I'm not trying to hurt you. I need to be alone." Her eyes filled. He yearned to hold her but she wasn't ready.

"All right. We'll talk later."

"Thanks." She offered a weak smile. "It was nice of you to bring me tea."

Matt set the plate next to her. "I'll leave the sandwich. Take a few bites. You'll feel better."

He left the room quickly, gently closing the door behind him.

A knock at the front door startled him. What now? He wasn't in the mood for company.

When he opened it, Amanda Benson, one of Carla's church friends, extended a shopping bag.

"It's not much," she said. "With the power out, I couldn't cook so I put together some sandwiches from last night's barbecue. Keep them in your freezer until you're ready to eat them."

"That was kind of you," Matt said, taking the bag. "I'd invite you in but Carla is resting."

"That's okay. Is there anything else I can do?"

Make my wife better. Give me my child back.

"No, you've done more than enough, thank you," Matt said. "I would like to know one thing, though. Do you have any information about what is going on? I heard we might lose power for months. Is that true?"

"I thought you knew," Amanda said. "We've been hit by some type of solar flare. It's really bad. We're having a meeting at the church on Thursday with more information. Everyone's invited."

Though he said he'd try to be there, he lied. He'd never set foot on that church property again. He'd have to find out about the catastrophe from someone else.

"I'm sure you've heard about Pastor Dalton," she said.

"Pastor Dalton?" The sound of the creep's name notched his anxiety.

"He was arrested for embezzlement. He stole over four thousand dollars from the church and used the money to buy illegal drugs."

Heat warmed Matt's face. Why hadn't he been arrested too? Surely Baxter had ratted him out by now.

"He turned himself in a few hours ago," she said. "I'm a council member, that's why I know. I still can't believe it."

Matt was surprised too. Baxter had quite a con going.

"You and Carla don't need to worry. Martin Fernández will figure things out."

"Worry?"

"About Charity's service," she said. "The church will take care of everything."

Not on his life. He'd handle his daughter's burial himself.

"I'll stop by tomorrow." Amanda interrupted his thoughts. She flipped up a kickstand from her bicycle and climbed on. "The solar flare zapped my car but a little exercise never hurt anyone. See you soon."

ꕥ

Dalton struggled to breathe, coiled on the cement floor. His heart ramped and he trembled. Temperatures inside the dank cell had to be close to one hundred degrees. It didn't matter. Dalton felt cold.

His cellmates had made their disgust known hours ago. They lobbed expletives his way each time Dalton let his insides explode in the toilet. He didn't care if they pounded him. Death would be better than this. No intestinal flu ever felt so bad.

"Help me, Deputy," Dalton shouted. "I need a doctor!"

"What's wrong with you, dude?" T.T. asked, leaning over him. "Are you contagious?"

Dalton vomited his answer, projecting dry heaves over T.T.'s feet. The fat man backed away, cursing at him. Dalton hugged his knees tight, hoping to stop the shivering. He yearned for the blanket wadded in the corner.

When Dalton heard the jangle of keys, he lifted his face. Deputy Chachu appeared at the jail door. He unlocked it, slid in a water bucket, then relocked the cell. "You'll need this," he told them. "Pour in some water when you flush or else things will back up." He covered his nose. "By the smell of things in here, I couldn't have come sooner."

"Something's wrong with that guy," Bulldog said.

"Hey Baxter ... what's wrong with you?" the deputy asked.

"I'm sick." Dalton twisted his face and begged, "Get me to a hospital ..."

"Sorry. We can't. Due to the outage, we're short-handed. You'll need to stay put for a few more hours."

Dalton rolled over and looked at the barred window in back. Waning light formed crosses over his knees. Would he even last a few hours in here?

ᘓᘒ

After Amanda left, Matt went to the kitchen. He wrapped his legs around a barstool and sipped whiskey from a paper cup. He stared into the cup, then swirled the magic gold. He tipped the Dixie, taking a generous sip. The alcohol heated his throat, calmed his anxiety.

Why hadn't the police come? Were they too busy with the power outages to bother with him? Had the dots between him and Baxter remained unconnected? Time was running out. Carla was at a breaking point. The alcohol helped him to make a decision. He'd put his plan into motion. He'd act now, before Charity's funeral on Saturday. Leaving McCormick with all its memories was the only way forward.

Hopefully someone would bail the preacher out. Then Baxter would have to come face to face with what he did. They'd share a lifetime of sorrows once Matt followed through on his plan.

Wednesday

"There is no pit so deep, that He is not deeper still·" Corrie ten Boom

CHAPTER FORTY-FOUR

Wednesday, 1 a.m.
Baxter Home

HUMIDITY WRAPPED THE DESERT IN a wet blanket. The night seemed to swallow Samantha, drowning her in misery. Her arms ached. Her wrists were sore. From Gordy's green notebook she'd learned how to keep the toilets flushing. Thank goodness they didn't have horrible plumbing problems like other folks on the city water system. Like their well, the septic tank had been a God-send. The only drawback was the endless chore of pumping water and lugging it upstairs. The family soon learned it was better to use the downstairs bathroom when nature called. Hauling water at ground level was easier. Carrying heavy buckets upstairs was tiresome. Suddenly back-breaking work went hand and hand with the simple things she'd once taken for granted.

As hard as she tried, sleep refused to come. Moonlight silhouetted the shape of an alarm clock on her bed stand. The glow of florescent digits was gone. Not seeing their greenish glow left her distraught and full of worry. She rolled over, burrowing her face into a pillow. She felt lost. The dawn's early light couldn't come soon enough.

Though the temperatures outside dropped to ninety-two degrees, the stifling air felt unbearable. If this was the new normal, she'd have a hard time getting used to it. She threw off the sheets and stared at her ceiling fan. It mocked her with its lifelessness. Funny, how the paddles' spinning noise had once annoyed her. She'd give anything to hear them again.

If only she could take a dip in the pool, now tightly protected with a cover. Gordy had seen to that. He warned them that the water was to be only used for drinking and necessary cleaning of dishes and clothes. Nothing else. The way he took charge reminded her of Dalton, once upon a time. Gordy assumed command of their listing ship, the SS Baxter, determined to get them righted again. Come hell or high water, he took the helm and forged ahead into an unknown future. For that she was incredibly proud. How she and Dalton had managed to raise such an amazing young man was beyond her.

Hours later when sunlight finally streaked over her mattress, Samantha stirred awake. She looked at the 1968 Timex watch loosely strapped to her wrist. "Thanks, Daddy," she said as she kissed its glass.

Seven-thirty. Samantha couldn't remember when she'd fallen asleep.

She studied the frayed leather band strapped to her wrist.

She'd been at her wit's end with insomnia when she remembered the watch. She'd ravaged through her drawers with a flashlight locating the Timex behind her socks. Seeing it woke up many memories. Her dad's favorite time piece, a gift from her mother—became a gift her mom gave Samantha the day her daddy died. Upon finding it, she put it on, guessed the time and wound it tight. After climbing back into bed, she laid her wrist near her ear. The rapid ticking quieted her soul and lulled her to sleep.

She'd need to synchronize it with Gordy's atomic watch later. One of Gordy's most prized possessions, the fancy watch had been on the top of his Christmas list last year. When he pulled it from the make-shift Faraday cage after the EMP, he lit up like a Christmas tree. It worked fine.

Samantha entered the breakfast room. Gordy, dressed in boxers and a t-shirt, sat at the table. He pushed the remains of a peanut butter and jelly sandwich into his mouth and drained a glass of milk. He got up, gave her a hug before picking up the milk carton and walked to the kitchen where he quickly stuffed it inside the freezer.

"We've got a lot to do today," he told her. "I better get dressed."

"Wait, Gordy," she said. "I've been thinking about your dad. He's got to be having terrible withdrawals by now. What if he can't get help?"

"Not our problem." Gordy frowned, wagging his head. "He brought this on himself."

"No argument there but he needs medical attention. Martin and Jeremy told me last night, they'd drive up there to check on him. I was hoping you'd go with them."

Gordy let out a long sigh. "I guess. I just can't promise I won't lose it when I see him." As he walked to the foyer he called out, "Let me know when they're here."

ജ

Loud banging jarred Dalton awake. He lifted his head and squinted against the morning sunlight. He clutched his knees, pressing against the pain that tormented his gut.

Bulldog shouted obscenities and T.T. bashed the plastic bucket against the metal. No one came.

"Stop that! My head hurts," Dalton yelled. The noise was too much. If he could, he would climb out of his own skin and run away.

"Oh ... you're finally awake." Bulldog crouched in front of Dalton. "Are you a priest?" he asked.

Where'd he get that idea? Dalton shook his head.

"You were talkin' in your sleep last night. Something about absolving sins."

Dalton's stomach twisted. He hadn't recited the Confession in three years, the same weekend he'd abandoned his clergy shirt.

"Reminded me of my church days as a kid," Bulldog continued. "My ma made me go to confession every Saturday."

Dalton tried to remember. Bits and pieces of dreams floated to the surface. He'd been serving the communion, wearing the chasuble. The voluminous outer garment hadn't been a part of his service in a long time. Why would he dream about it?

"What gives you the right to forgive sins? I thought only priests did that?"

"I ... uh ... I-I don't know ..." Dalton stammered. A wave of nausea assaulted him but he had no strength to run to the toilet.

"Well ... are you a priest or not?" Bulldog demanded.

"I'm a pastor ..." Dalton managed. "We're not Catholic ... uh ... but we use the liturgy. At least we used to."

"Liturgy? What's that?" T.T. asked.

He had no energy to explain but eked out a few words. "It's ... a type of ... uh ... formal ... church service."

A type of service he'd abandoned over three years ago, along with the stiff white collars, black shirts, and long embroidered stoles. They were casualties of modernization, replaced with fancy Brooks Brother suits and Florsheim wing tips. The ancient attire, seething with moth balls, hung in a rickety armoire deep within the church's basement.

What a joke. To think that he could absolve anyone of anything.

"I've got no room for the likes of you," Bulldog continued. "How about we have a little fun with this preacher man, T.T.?"

Dalton no longer cared. Anything inflicted upon him by these two would be nothing compared to the agony wrenching his body.

A pair of sneakers stood in front of his face. Dalton looked up. T.T. stood over him.

"He smells like puke," T.T. said. "Leave him alone."

"I can't stand preachers," Bulldog growled. "They're phonies. They think they're better than everyone else. I wanna teach this guy a lesson."

"He's got the shakes," T.T. said. "He's coming off something. Give him a break."

Dalton peeked through steepled fingers. Maybe he'd been spared.

"He's coming off Oxy." Bulldog sneered.

"How do you know?"

A blanket was dropped over him. Dalton opened his eyes and mouthed a "Thank you" to T.T.

"I'm a dealer, remember? Got busted yesterday," Bulldog said. "Did a drop with one of my best customers in Prescott. He got all whiney on me. Said his kid was dying and could he pay me after the score. Never saw him again. That's what I get for trusting people. Somebody must have seen the drop and snitched. The cops came to my house right after that."

Bulldog was Matt's supplier. How in the world had they ended up in the same cell? Talk about crazy. Dalton frowned.

"What *you* lookin' at? Are you judging me?" Bulldog's knotted fist was inches from Dalton's face.

Dalton braced himself to be hit.

"I said, leave him alone!" T.T. shouted.

"What gives?" Bulldog scowled. "You going soft on me?"

"I'm a PK."

"A what?"

"Preacher's kid. My dad still has a church in the Midwest."

Bulldog laughed. "That's too funny. You must be one helluva disappointment to your folks."

"Probably. I ain't been home in years." T.T. sat on the bench behind Dalton. "They don't even know they have a grandson."

"That's a bummer, man. What are you in for this time?"

"Petty theft. I'm lookin' at a felony since it's my third offense."

"What'd you steal?"

"Same thing I always steal. Food and a little booze from some liquor stores around town."

"Haven't you heard of food stamps?"

"I'm not a charity case. I can do for myself and my family."

"Tell him what the good book says, Preacher Man." Bulldog glared at Dalton. "Pride goeth before a fall, don't it?"

Dalton nodded. Even in this desperate dungeon, the scripture pierced him like a sharp knife. The avalanche accident eight months ago on the backside of Agassiz Mountain had only been the beginning of a long and prideful descent.

Had he finally hit bottom? Dear Lord, he hoped so.

God, please help me, he prayed. *I can't go any lower than this.*

ꕥ

Wednesday, 1:00 p.m.
McCormick, AZ

Time to get on the road.

Jeremy climbed into the back of the old VW while Martin took shotgun. Gordon eased the clutch, pressed the gas pedal and the van rumbled to life. It bounced and jostled over the rocky driveway before Gordon turned onto Casa Blanca Road. The 1966 van seemed like a good alternative since Martin's Fusion, though operable, was running low on fuel. Besides, it offered more room. They were hauling some equipment they might need.

The gas tank had been filled the previous morning so if they were careful, it would get them back and forth to Saguaro Junction at least twice. Hopefully, due to the power outages, the cops would release his dad into his family's care, making any future trips north unnecessary.

"My mom made us some grub. It's in the back." Gordon pointed to an Igloo chest on the bench seat.

"Not hungry. Maybe later." Martin said.

"I ate with my family an hour ago," Jeremy added. "Natalie's pushing the fridge food before it spoils."

When the VW reached Kaibab Road, Gordon noticed a few cars heading toward the freeway.

"I wonder why some cars work and some don't?" Jeremy asked.

"It depends on the year and if the car has electronic components," Gordon answered. "Those with electric or hybrid engines seemed to be the ones affected, especially if they were charging during the CME. Fortunately for me, any car manufactured before 1973 will drive." Gordon patted his dashboard affectionately. "My grandfather left me this baby. It runs on pure gas, nothing else."

"My wife's going a little nuts right now," Jeremy said. "She didn't want me to come. The kids are climbing the walls and have been banned from our pool."

"We covered ours," Gordon said. "Anyone with a pool should do that. Water will be like gold, eventually."

"I've got to locate our cover when I get back," Jeremy said. "How are you and Laney doing, Martin?"

"Since we got the heads up from Samantha yesterday, we got what we could and filled up the inflatable swimming pool. Got close to three thousand gallons of water in it right now. It came with a cover to keep the critters out. Not quite sure how we're gonna get bath water out of there."

"You're not on a well?" Gordon asked.

"Unfortunately, no. I picked up a siphon at Jacobsen's and it seems to work with the pool water, though it's a slow process. Laney and I already washed a load of dishes."

“We have a well,” Gordon said. “I found a hand pump and was able to prime a steady supply of water last night. It made our morning coffee possible.”

“You’ve really stepped up in your dad’s absence,” Martin told him. “Your mother must be proud.”

Gordon wondered if that was true. Right now anger boiled beneath the surface. When he saw his dad today, he might explode. He’d been ruminating all morning on how to tell him off. What his dad had done to the family was unforgivable, especially to Grace. Yesterday all she talked about was ice cream and why her daddy hadn’t come back. How any decent person could do that to a kid was beyond him.

CHAPTER FORTY-FIVE

DALTON HELD HIS HAND IN front of his face, the silhouettes of his fingers duplicating the cell bars. He strained to see past the shadows, then let his hand drop and crawled to the bench. He pulled himself up, sat on the steel and scanned the cell. A voluminous orange shape came into focus. He squinted, adjusting to the sliver of sunlight penetrating the window. A large Black man with peppery hair stared back, wearing a jumpsuit, a twin to his in color, but three sizes larger. The inmate's mouth drew a broad grin, revealing a row of alabaster teeth.

The older prisoner walked toward him. He shook Dalton's hand, then sat next to him. "I'm Moses. My friends call me Mo."

"Dalton. When did you get here?"

"A few hours ago. You were sleeping."

The man's warm smile disarmed Dalton and a sense of peace wrapped him as snug as one of his mother's quilts on a winter night.

"I'm surprised they brought in anyone new with the power off." Dalton leaned past the man and stared. Bulldog and T.T. dozed in the corner.

"I'm not afraid of the dark." Mo chuckled, then eyed Dalton, his gaze raking from his toes to the top of his head. "Did they give you something for those?"

"For what?"

"You're having withdrawals, right?"

Dalton's eyes widened. "N—no. I'm not going through withdrawals ... I—I have the flu."

"You don't say?" The man's brows knitted together.

"Yes, I do say," Dalton snapped. He wasn't about to admit anything to this stranger. Though truth was, the pain he'd felt hours ago had certainly waned. Maybe the worst was over. His gut let out a rumble and his stomach cried for food. That was a switch.

Mo handed Dalton a paper sack. "Here's your supper, brother."

"Gee ... thanks ... I'm starved!" Dalton ripped it open. Yesterday's bologna had been replaced with roast beef on rye. There was a pint of milk, some vanilla pudding, and a banana. Someone had gone to a lot of trouble making this stuff in the dark. Must be leftovers from the staff refrigerator. Better give it to the prisoners since it might spoil anyway.

Dalton devoured half the sandwich. His stomach received the nutrition without complaint. Though his facial injury still felt stretched and uncomfortable, the pain was nothing to yesterday's. He probed the bandage with his fingertips. His cheek had deflated to half its previous size.

Mo bowed his head silently for several seconds, then dove into his own meal.

A believer? In jail? How did *he* end up here? Dalton shook his head. *How did I end up here?*

"Where are you from?" the older man asked, through a mouthful of food.

"A town called McCormick. About an hour south." Dalton took a long sip of milk. The coldness surprised him. With the power off, everything should be lukewarm.

"Your people there?"

"My wife, Sammy. I have two kids.

"How large is your church?"

"Huh?" Dalton's eyes narrowed. "I never mentioned church."

"Many folks go to church." Mo stuffed in the last of his sandwich, then opened the pudding.

"Well ... uh ... I actually pastor a church."

"You do?"

Dalton's shoulders sagged. "I used to anyway. Might lose my job." What was he saying? *Stop talking, stupid!*

"We all have our share of troubles," Mo said. "You can tell me 'bout it if you want." The big man wadded up his empty lunch sack, set it aside, knotted his burly hands between his knees, giving Dalton his full attention.

Dalton thought for a second. "Not sure I want to."

"I get that." Mo cocked his head. "Just sometimes it's easier to talk to a stranger. I've got all night to listen. Gettin' out tomorrow."

He was getting out of here? This guy must have a good attorney. If only Dalton hadn't cashed out his stocks, he wouldn't be stuck with a public defender. And maybe he'd get released too.

Dalton leaned back, crossed his ankles in front of him. This man would be gone in a few hours. What harm could it do to tell someone what was going on? With Bulldog and T.T. asleep, now might be the best time.

"You were right about the withdrawals," Dalton admitted. Once he loosened his tongue, his words tumbled out. "They started yesterday. I've never been as miserable in my life. They seem better now, but honestly, if they come back, I don't know what I'll do. It's excruciating."

"From what I see, you're probably getting better," Mo said. "What are you coming off of?"

Coming off of? Did this guy think Dalton was a common drug addict? He stalled for a moment, rubbing his temple. "Legal drugs. Prescription painkillers I needed." Dalton tried to control the edge in his voice and couldn't resist the urge to explain himself even though he didn't know Mo from Adam. "I was injured."

"It's the legal types that are more dangerous."

"What do you mean?"

"Prescribed pills can be slippery. They sucker folks," Mo said. "Because they're legal, people get fooled, making it easy to overdose. They've been okayed by a doctor, right? Why would they hurt us? That's the lie that gets us in trouble."

Dalton stared into Mo's eyes, then furrowed his brow. Mo said *us*. Dalton relaxed against the wall.

"Why did the doctor give them to you?"

"It began with a back country ski trip," Dalton explained. "I should have listened to my wife, Samantha, that morning, but I didn't." He described being buried chest-high in snow at the base of Doyle's Saddle. He told Mo about the knee surgery and agonizing recovery. "I wouldn't have been able to cope without those pills," he said. "The pain was too much." He paused.

Should he tell the rest of the story?

As he recounted the events from Sunday, the realization of what he'd done hit him with a clenched gut. "My car ... is at the bottom of Copper Lake." His cheek muscles tightened, bringing a tinge of pain as he spoke, realizing his own life had hit bottom, too.

"Look here." Dalton pointed to his face. "I did that. To myself. With a hammer."

Had Sammy really watched him the whole time? He stared at his feet. How could he have traumatized her like that? What kind of husband was he?

Mo's eyes misted. "As the adage goes, 'desperate times call for desperate measures.'"

Dalton had been desperate. But had it been worth it? The unbearable agony that had radiated through his flesh had driven him close to madness these past few hours.

"I've ruined everything with my family," Dalton said. "I don't know if they'll ever forgive me. I'm not even sure God will forgive me."

"You know the Good Book says, 'ask and you will receive' ... have you asked?"

"Huh?"

"The Father. Have you asked Him?"

No, he hadn't thought to pray. The distance between God and him seemed impossible to close.

"I know He loves me," Mo asserted, then smiled, looking longingly at the cement ceiling overhead. "He loves you too, brother. He forgives when we ask. You, being a minister, must know this."

Dalton shrugged. He *was* a minister. He'd been to seminary. Had letters after his name. But did he really know the love and forgiveness Mo talked about so easily? What he preached on Sunday mornings was for others—those searching for hope, for an anchor—not for him. He knew that love from a far-away God was as unreachable as his dead mother's arms.

"Something much more painful than a torn-up knee caused your addiction." Mo interrupted his thoughts.

"Everyone keeps saying that," Dalton snapped.

"What?"

"That I have an addiction." The man had crossed the line and it stung. "I have a problem, that's all. A problem that I'm dealing with."

A pregnant pause hovered between them as Mo's chocolate eyes bore through him. "Problems don't torment a person's body with an appetite that can't be appeased," Mo said with certainty. "Problems don't shackle folks like handcuffs, making them feel it's impossible to change."

Dalton twisted his wedding ring.

"Father-wounds choke us, leaving a strangled soul," Mo continued. "Addiction can be the result."

Dalton's scalp tingled. He hadn't mentioned anything about his dad, so how had Mo nailed it? It was bad enough that his memories stabbed him at the most inopportune times. Like during a worship song at church or at his mother's graveside. Subduing them with Oxy was the only thing that ever worked.

The older man scratched his chin stubble. "Opiates numb a deeper pain."

Mo saw through him. And he was right. No matter how hard Dalton tried to kick the drugs, he'd failed.

He nodded and considered the black man. "I couldn't get free." The words tumbled out. "I craved more. And more. And then even more."

"Your soul hunger is insatiable. Nothing in the physical realm can feed its craving."

Mo was filled with wisdom, even greater than Dalton's own mother. "I noticed you praying earlier," Dalton said. "Are you a Christian?"

Mo smiled and nodded. "Yes, I believe. Do you?"

Dalton studied the iron bars a few feet away. "It wouldn't matter if I did. God's done with me. I really messed up."

"It's actually quite the contrary," Mo said. "The broken have a special place in His heart. *The bruised reeds, the smoldering wicks*."

"Bruised reeds?"

"A great verse. You oughta' read it sometime."

"In the Old Testament?"

Mo nodded. "A gold nugget for sure. It's tucked away in the book of *Isaiah*. Unless you're looking for it, you might miss it."

"I've heard it before. Never gave it much thought."

"Not surprised. Can I be honest with you, brother?"

"I guess." Dalton's lips formed a straight line. His clenched teeth prepared him for the criticism. It usually came after a question like that.

"You've spent your whole life trying to get a smile from God, haven't you?"

A smile from God? I don't think so. Being tolerated and put up with was more like it. Eating the meager scraps under God's table, absolutely. But an affectionate beam? He couldn't imagine God smiling at him.

"Rigid obedience is nothing more than a patch kit for a leaky boat. Eventually you run out of epoxy and begin to go under. None have what it takes to make it across this angry sea, called *life*. Eventually folks flounder. They mess up and lose their will to perform. Their boats start sinking."

Dalton's chin collided with his chest. "I lost my will last year." He remembered when he'd finally stopped obeying "the rules."

After his skiing accident.

Dalton looked up. "Where's that verse? I don't have a Bible with me."

"Chapter forty-two, verse three. *What is bruised and bent, He will not break; He will not blow out a smoldering candle.*" Everyone ... even those guys ..." Mo waved his hand toward the sleeping cellmates a few feet away. "... are 'the bruised and bent, the smoldering candles.' Unfortunately, most people fail to see their need for God. They miss out in realizing they have a Father in heaven who loves them and wants to show them the way." The fire in Mo's eyes pierced Dalton's heart. "There's a flickering wick inside of you, brother. God wants to reignite your passion. Here ... in this darkness, you could be a light to others."

Was the man crazy? Look at where I am!

"How old are you, brother?"

"Forty-five. Why?"

Mo chuckled. "I'm surprised it took you so long."

"Huh?"

"This is your Jacob moment. A place where most believers end up at some point.

"I don't get it." Dalton's gut clenched as the sandwich hit.

"In the Bible, come on, man ... you're a minister, for heaven's sake."

"Oh ... that Jacob." He forced a grin. "Genesis, right?"

"Jacob wrestled with God at the Jabbok River, remember?" Mo asked. "He was at the end of himself. Sort of like you." Mo leaned in and lowered his voice. "Tonight, right in this cell, could be a turning point. If you're willing, here is where you will wrestle with God."

"Wrestle? I'm exhausted. I have nothing left." Dalton stared at the concrete, picturing Jacob struggling against God, begging to be blessed. He'd taught that passage a few times through the years. It seemed to comfort and reassure parishioners who'd grown weary of persevering, who felt God was against them. He never applied it to himself.

"The fight won't be one of self-effort, brother. Your boat-patching days are over."

That's a relief. The thought of wrestling drained him.

"You are exactly where you're supposed to be."

Dalton's head snapped to the side. "What? Here? In a jail cell?"

"Yes, here! Give it up, brother. He never asked you to save yourself. Your fight will be against the lies you've believed all your life. This war cannot be waged apart from trusting in a Father who deeply loves you."

Dalton shot a look at their cell mates but T.T. and Bulldog slept on. He turned to Mo. So far, the guy had described his whole situation. And now he knew Dalton's deepest insecurities about God. Until this moment, only Sammy had seen his vulnerability, the anxiety lurking beneath the layer of pomp that undergirded his Sunday show. He'd always been jealous of her friendship with God. But he'd long since given up trying to get into God's good favor. Mo was right. He didn't trust God. Not in the least little bit.

Mo's eyes glistened and his enormous black hand gripped Dalton's shoulder. "You may know His book, brother ... and God might even be an acquaintance. But you don't know His love. If you did, you would have run to Him instead of those drugs."

Mo was right. How could he trust a God who seemed like his own father. Cold. Distant. Harsh.

"The only path up is down."

"What?"

Mo smiled. "On the floor, brother."

"There?" Dalton pointed to the cement. His wadded blanket lay crumpled in a corner near the remnants of dried vomit.

Mo joined his gaze with a knowing look. "I speak of a lower place. It's your bottom. Only you know when you've reached it."

Dalton looked around the shadowy room. His cellies snored loudly, oblivious to the surreal world around them. Could he really go lower than this? He couldn't imagine anything worse. *God ... if You're still listening ... please help me. I'm lost, Father. I need You.* His preconceived scale of righteousness had been drastically tipped and Dalton knew he could never even it out again. He looked at Mo.

"How do I find this lower place?"

"You'll recognize it. It's a dark and slimy with no way out. A place where only God can rescue you, not yourself."

"I must be there." Dalton shook his head and sighed. "I'm desperate."

Mo's eyes lit up and he smiled, revealing perfectly chiseled teeth. "You're getting it, Dalton. He waits for you to cry out." Mo slapped his knees and his eyes widened. "You will have the fight of your life against the lies you've believed since childhood. Embrace the truth, brother. Your Father will help you to wage this war. He meets you in your pain. Otherwise, He remains a two-dimensional Sunday school picture hanging on a wall."

Dalton turned to the bar-embedded window. Sunlight penetrated the cell, casting checkers of white light across his sneakers. The shaft seemed much brighter, as did his spirit. Could God really rescue him after all he had done? For the first time in a long time, hope surged. Maybe Mo was right. Maybe God was smiling at him, despite his blatant failures that magnified a bruised soul.

Dalton's eyes burned and felt heavy. He dragged in a deep breath and yawned. Suddenly he felt very sleepy.

"Looks like you're ready for a nap. Can I bless you first?" Mo's eyes glistened.

Dalton eyes snapped open and his heart leaped. "Really? Would you?" The last time he'd been blessed was his ordination.

With a chunky index finger, Mo touched Dalton's forehead, made the sign of the cross between his brows. "In the Name of the Father, of the Son and of the Holy Spirit, I bless you."

Mo dropped his hand to his lap and smiled. "Your Father waits for you, Dalton. He's waiting for you to come home. Cling to Him and don't let go."

ꕥ

Bang! Bang! Bang!

Dalton's eyes snapped open. His body had a tinge of achiness, but nothing like the agonizing pain earlier. T.T. once again bashed the plastic bucket against the bars.

"Is anyone out there?" Bulldog shouted.

"Face it. They're not coming," T.T. said.

Dalton lay on the bench under his blanket. He lifted his face and scanned the cell. Mo was gone. "What happened to the other prisoner?" he asked.

"What other prisoner?" T.T. asked. "Are you trippin' man? No one's come to this cell since Charlie brought our food last night."

Had the sheriff removed the man while they slept? Or had the encounter been a dream or worse yet, a hallucination? Was he losing his mind?

"He waits for you, Dalton." The familiar words flooded his soul.

Waiting for me? Lord, whether this was a dream or not, please let it be true.

Moments ticked by. He drifted back to sleep.

CHAPTER FORTY-SIX

Wednesday, 2:30 p.m.
Saguaro Junction, AZ

PULL INTO THAT PARKING LOT, son." Martin pointed to Foley's Chicken Plant ahead.

Gordon blew out a sigh of relief. The trip had taken three times longer than usual. A roadblock on the highway with cops directing traffic to turn around had them scrambling for an alternate route. After a missed turn, they ended up on a muddy track, but it got them here. No telling what that so-called road did to his van's suspension.

"Right here." Martin gestured to empty tarmac, glistening under the afternoon sun, next to a huge commercial building. Overhead, voluminous industrial windows emitted no light.

Gordon stopped next to a dark blue trash container. He left the van idling. "Where's the sheriff's office?" he asked.

"Nothing looks familiar," Jeremy said.

"Let's follow that rail line." Martin pointed to a loading dock. "Train tracks lead to the older parts of the city. The jail was downtown."

Gordon throttled the engine, then put the van into first gear.

Crash!

Gordon jumped, his heart racing. What happened?.

A toothless man shouted obscenities from outside the passenger door. He proceeded to bash the van's window with an empty liquor bottle. Gordon gunned the engine and followed a frontage road near the railroad track. He inspected the rearview mirror. The vagrant gave him a single digit hand sign.

"That was close," Gordon said. "People are nuts right now."

"Let's be hyper-vigilant, men. At least until we get back to McCormick," Martin said.

Minutes later they reached a major intersection. People scattered in all directions, some carrying what looked like new merchandise from stores. Police appeared to be outnumbered.

"This isn't safe. We need to get out of here," Martin shouted. "Drive on the tracks, Gordy, quick!"

Gordon wedged the VW between two train gates that must have dropped during the outage. He pressed the gas and straddled the iron rails. The van agitated like an old washing machine. After traveling a mile or so, modern structures surrendered to 1860's brick and mortar. They'd arrived at the town's historic district.

Martin gestured to a water tower ahead. "Hey Jer', didn't we see that yesterday?"

"We sure did." Jeremy perched on the edge of the back seat, leaning forward between Gordon and Martin. "I think the jail is south of the tower."

"Get off the tracks, son," Martin said, pointing. "Drive to that old bank building."

With a jerk of the wheels, the van clattered off the tracks. Gordon drove to a dilapidated three-story building.

Painted across red brick in white paint, high up on the top floor, were the faded words *Colonial Savings Bank*. Gordon careened around the bank's corner into an alley free of looters and potential carjackers. When he'd gone through several passageways, he ended up facing a busy avenue, teeming with people, rushing in all directions. Across the street was an old park.

"Where do I go now?" he asked.

"Back up!" Martin ordered. "I remember that park. We're close to the jail."

Gordon slammed into reverse and hit the gas. When they reached a crossway, he did a turnabout, then followed some side streets until the van ended up in the jail house's parking lot.

"We're too exposed here," Martin said pointing to another alley. "Park over there."

Gordon squeezed the van between towering red brick walls, probably built in the early 1900's. The tight space had most likely accommodated horse carriages at one-time. He turned off the engine and looked at his companions.

"I'll get my tanks. Can you unlock the hatch?" Martin asked. Gordon climbed out and met him at the back window, then twisted his key. Two metal canisters strapped to a dolly had been laid on their side. Martin carefully unloaded the contraption to the ground. "This thing's a fuel cutter," he said. "Even your grandmother can use it. Let's see if the cops will let us in. If not, we'll use this puppy to get your father out the old-fashioned way."

Gordon's heart skipped a beat. "What are you talking about? We're just here to check on Dad, right? Because of the power outage and his withdrawals."

Martin patted his shoulder. “Yes, that’s the plan. This is just in case. If the deputies are off trying to keep order, and your father needs medical attention, we can get to him.”

“We’d be breaking the law, gentlemen.” Jeremy suddenly appeared, shaking his head.

“By the looks of things, law enforcement can’t keep up.” Martin handed Jeremy a tool bag. “Like I said, this is for a worst-case scenario, only if we have to. Then later, if the power comes back on, we’ll return Pas ... uh ... Dalton and face the music.”

Gordon shrugged. “Okay. No argument from me. I’m a minor.” He forced a chuckle. “I was unduly influenced by my father’s friends.” A judge *might* believe that.

Martin led them through the narrow passageway, lugging the equipment while Gordon followed. Jeremy brought up the rear. When they arrived at the sidewalk, Martin leaned the dolly against the wall. “Hopefully, we won’t need this.” When he took the tool bag from Jeremy, they followed him around the corner. Under an old awning, they huddled near the building, trying not to draw attention. The sheriff's office lobby was dark.

They peered through the double glassed doors, pounding in unison for several moments. Gordon spun around and looked behind. People hurried past but so far, not a cop in sight. “We need to break the glass, Martin,” Gordon said. It was obvious no one was coming. They shouldn’t waste any more time.

Martin removed his shirt and wadded it up. “Stand back, guys,” he said. He positioned the balled shirt against the glass door, then struck it with a mallet. The glass shattered, expelling shards in all directions. After widening the entry with the hammer, Martin guided Jeremy and Gordon through to the lobby, then returned to the sidewalk. Within moments he reappeared, lugging the dolly.

Once they carried the dolly across the floor, crunching broken glass as they walked, Jeremy pointed toward an entrance behind the counter. "They took your father through that door.”

Gordon heard a noise. He waved the men silent. “What’s that? Someone’s banging.”

ꙮ

Another round of bucket bashing woke Dalton. When he sat up, he felt surprisingly better. He’d expected to be suffering for at least a week. It had only been one day. Fresh hunger settled in his stomach.

Afternoon light penetrated through the cell’s only window. From the shadow’s direction and length, Dalton guessed it must be close to three p.m.

He scanned the small cell. Mo was definitely gone. Had he been released early?

"Guard!" Bulldog shouted. "We're starving back here. Is anyone there?" He cursed. Then cursed again, louder. "What's wrong with these people?

Dalton got to his feet and stood on wobbly legs. "We're probably stuck here, guys. The cops are dealing with civil unrest."

Bulldog glared. "What are you sayin' Preacher Man?'

"We talked about this earlier, remember?" Dalton asked. "We have no power. A solar flare caused this."

T.T. frowned. "What about my wife and kid? I got to get out of here!"

"We're in God's hands," Dalton told them. Had he really said that? Did he finally believe it?

"Hey, what's that?" T.T. pointed to Dalton's forehead.

"What?" Dalton asked.

"You've got a black cross on your face," Bulldog said.

"Really? You see a cross?" Tears collected in Dalton's eyes.

Bulldog stared. "How'd you do that, Preacher Man?"

Dalton said nothing. He sat down and covered his face with his hands. Sobs wrenched from his chest. "It wasn't a dream, was it, God?" Had Dalton received a heavenly visitor? Was Mo an angel? He leaned his head back and studied the cinder blocks. But angels were supposed to be fierce and frightening. Mo ... Mo comforted him, left him feeling better. Dalton rubbed his eyes. He noticed the wadded lunch sack on the bench. Just where Mo left it.

"Who you talkin' to?" T.T. asked.

Dalton ignored him and continued whispering a prayer. "Thank you, God. For sending Mo. For reminding me I'm not alone. For waiting for me. I'll do whatever You say. Just help me to change."

Instead of the fear that tormented him hours before, he felt ... peace. Instead of the aches and nausea, he felt ... calm. Instead of anger and betrayal, he felt ... acceptance. He didn't know what would happen next, but he'd be okay. He'd had his Jacob moment and was tired of fighting. He lightly touched his forehead. When he removed his finger, black ash coated its tip. He'd been blessed by God.

ഇൾ

Someone yelled through the darkness. Dalton sat up straight. The voice sounded familiar. Like Gordon's? But it couldn't be.

"Dad? Are you here?"

Dalton leapt to his feet. "Gordy? In here!"

Moments later, three shadowy figures converged in front of the holding cell.

"Gordy!" Dalton raced to the bars. "How did you get in here?"

"Mr. Fernández bashed in the front door."

"We've broken more laws than we can count," Jeremy said, waving a flashlight. "We're here to rescue you. If you need it."

"Of course, they need it." Martin shouldered his way to the door. "You saw what's going on out there. And no deputies around. They left these men to starve. Or get heat stroke."

"I never took you for having friends who could spring us outta here, Preacher Man," Bulldog said. "I might have to go back to church."

Martin measured the gap between the bars with his fingers. "This is going to be tricky. Bring your light over here." Martin directed Jeremy as he crouched in front of a dolly loaded with what looked gas cans. He appeared to be making connections with the tanks, turning on valves.

Dalton heard the hiss of escaping gas.

Martin lifted a large welder's torch. "Let's hope my readings are correct." He pulled on thick gloves, then positioned gigantic goggles over his eyes. "Get back. Sparks will fly."

Dalton and his cellmates moved to the cement wall. Gordon and Jeremy retreated to the hallway.

Martin struck the torch. A yellow flame blazed like midday sun.

Now for the oxygen," Martin said. "Say a little prayer." He twisted a knob. The golden flame transformed to a streak of white light, reminding Dalton of Luke Skywalker's light saber.

Martin sliced the first bar of reinforced steel as if it were butter. He cut through six more, creating a two-foot slit at the top. He then severed a cross bar in the middle. All that was left was the bottom row of bars and then the cell's occupants would be home free.

"This could get loud," Martin said. He made a slice three-feet below the first cut. The steel rod toppled, bouncing against the cement with earsplitting clunks. The same thing happened with the remaining bars until all that was left was a large two by three-foot hole, shrouded in smoke.

Bulldog charged to the opening like a hungry dog, but Martin stopped him. "Wait! You'll burn yourself. Is there any water in here?" he asked, looking at Dalton.

"The sink's not working," Dalton answered. "We used up what the deputy gave us to flush the toilet."

Martin scanned the room. "Grab that blanket." He pointed to the grey wad on the floor. "Soak it in the toilet."

"No way. It's disgusting," Bulldog said.

"It's either that or you'll have to wait forty minutes for the metal to cool," Martin said.

"I'll do it," Dalton said. He went to the commode and stuffed in the fabric. He extended each end of the fabric with both hands. When he reached the cell door, he threw it over the smoky bars. Steam and sizzling sounds rewarded his efforts.

The men carefully climbed through the opening while Martin packed away his gear.

Dalton hung back and came through last. Gordy waited at the jail entrance, his expression, unreadable. Once he'd climbed out, Dalton reached for his son and pulled him close. He felt Gordy stiffen and let him go.

"Sorry about that, son," Dalton said weakly. "I must really stink." He wiped his hands against his jumpsuit.

Dalton could tell Gordy wanted to say something but held back. Maybe now wasn't the best time. Hopefully they could have a talk on the ride back to McCormick.

"Let's get out of here," Martin said, leading the way through the dark jail house. Dalton picked up one of the flashlights and brought up the rear, lighting their way.

CHAPTER FORTY-SEVEN

Wednesday, 4:20 p.m.
Connor Home
McCormick, AZ

MATT FOUND CARLA IN THE kitchen seated next to the granite island. A single candle flickered in the corner. Something simmered on the camp stove outside the kitchen window.

"What's for dinner?" he asked.

"Laney's stew. It's for you. I'm not hungry."

"Neither am I." He touched his wife's back. "But we have to eat. How are you doing?"

Outlined in red skin, her brown eyes pooled. Seeing her like this broke his heart. His eyes filled too. He planted his hands on the counter and took a bar stool next to her.

"I scared you at the funeral home, didn't I?" she asked. "Everyone must think I'm crazy." She leaned her head against his chest. "I can't believe she's gone."

His throat tightened, a tear escaped. "I keep seeing her run through the house, asking me to take her to the park. Why didn't I get her that puppy last month?"

She looked up at him. "We were exhausted, Matt, remember? Housebreaking a dog is a lot of work."

He shook his head. "That's no excuse. My baby wanted a puppy. I should have gotten her a squirmy, fat-bellied, bundle of fur. She would have loved playing with it, laughing, and cuddling. Her last days could've been happy."

Carla put a hand on his arm. "We didn't know she had so little time left. It's not your fault."

Her touch seared his flesh. He reached for an apple from the fruit bowl. "I let her down. Then. And Sunday. I should have been there all day. I feel awful about leaving."

"You never told me what happened." Carla raised her head. "Why were you late?"

He let a silent curse word fly. Why did he say that out loud? Sharing their grief ... he'd let down his guard.

Should he tell her the truth? Would she forgive him?

He couldn't take that chance. Not now.

"It's not important. I'll tell you later. We should plan the service." A service they wouldn't attend. But Carla didn't know that.

"What if Amanda's right and the power doesn't come on? How will we conduct a funeral in the dark?" she asked.

"Let's wait another day before we jump to that conclusion." Matt pulled her close and kissed her forehead. "I'll head to the mortuary tomorrow and talk with Mr. Copeland about his plans." There wouldn't be time to talk to Copeland, but he'd already told Carla so many lies, one more didn't matter.

"Amanda says we could have the service this Saturday," Carla said. "She assured me the sanctuary will be available whenever we need it."

"Not at your church, Carla. I can't do that." His clipped tone sounded angrier than he intended.

Her brow furrowed. "Why?"

Because he'd promised himself he'd never enter that building again. Now he wouldn't have to. There'd be a funeral service all right, but without them. They'd be long gone before Saturday. Others would have to bury their daughter. That would be hard, yes, but staying in McCormick would be harder. They needed to follow Matt's plan and leave the desert town for good.

"Did you hear me, Matt? Why can't we have the service at Saint Luke's?"

He'd wanted to wait. But her penetrating gaze and wobbly voice demanded an answer.

He sighed. "I have something to tell you."

The silence grew while he gathered his courage. The image of Charity struggling to breathe in that hospital room swam in front of him. If his baby could face dying, he could tell the truth.

"Matt? What?"

"I ... I've been dealing again." He wanted to close his eyes, brace himself for her reaction, but he forced himself to keep talking. "I had to, babe. I did it for you and Charity."

Carla's eyes grew large as she shook her head and inhaled sharply. "Am I hearing this right? After all we've been through ... what are you saying?"

He interrupted. "The bills were mounting, more than I could ever pay working that crummy job. I didn't know what else to do." He reached for her hand, but she yanked it away.

Carla moved away and shook her head. "I can't believe this."

"I'm sorry, honey. I was desperate."

"No more excuses, Matt! How could you do this?"

"We could have lost our home." He reached for her, but she pulled back.

"Don't touch me! You promised, Matt." Her face twisted with pain. "So when you were delivering a package for your boss, you sold drugs?"

"Yes ... to your minister."

"Pastor Dalton?" Her face emptied of all color. "You're lying."

"He's a junkie. He's my biggest client."

"This can't be true."

"He got arrested yesterday. Ask his wife, she'll tell you."

"If that's true then why haven't *you* been arrested?"

Good question. "I don't know." Matt tried to connect with her eyes, but she looked away. "Please believe me, Carla. I'll never do it again."

"I've heard that before." She folded her arms across her chest.

"Let me make it up to you." He may as well move forward with his plan. "Let's sell this place and get out of McCormick."

"Move? I can't move. This is where Charity is." She climbed down from the stool and left, slamming their bedroom door.

Okay, so he'd need to convince her. There was no way they could stay in this horrible town. They would move far, far away and have a new start.

An hour passed. Matt pondered, ruminating through his plan. He drained the last dregs of his cold coffee. Carla would forgive him. Especially when she had another chance at being a mom.

He heard the bedroom door open. Finally. Now he could talk to her rationally, help her see moving, a fresh start, was for the best.

Matt turned to face her. She carried a small suitcase. He frowned.

"I need some space." The coldness in her voice rattled him.

"I'll be gone awhile," she said. "I need to think."

An unbearable cocktail of fear and desperation mingled in his chest. "Don't go." His eyes welled. How could she leave him like this, with his heart in pieces? He needed her. He jumped from the stool and went to her. "Can't we talk this out?"

An open hand stopped him. "You broke your word. Don't follow me." She left through the kitchen door. The rumble of her classic Ford Mustang as she drove away spurred his already racing emotions.

He slammed balled fists on the counter and clenched his teeth. Fresh rage fueled his determination.

This was the preacher's fault.

Matt fought the urge to scream his charge at the top of his lungs. But he forced deep and even breaths instead.

It wasn't time yet.

But soon.
Yes, soon.

CHAPTER FORTY-EIGHT

Saguaro Junction, AZ
Wednesday, 5:30 p.m.

WHEN THE GROUP CONGREGATED AT the street, relief eased Gordon's tight shoulders. He watched his dad's cell mates high tail it to an alley and disappear. Good. He, Martin, and Jeremy had done what they needed to do, bust his dad from jail and now could get back to McCormick as soon as possible. Joining up with criminals wasn't part of their plan.

As they made their way to the alley, a forest fire of rage kindled inside his gut. Gordon hung his head, refusing to look at his father. If he did, he might say something he'd regret. Sunlight pierced the dark clouds, splashing through a long, narrow passageway. He followed Martin and Jeremy as his dad trudged beside him. With a sideways glance he noticed his father wore a big grin.

"What gives, Dad?" Gordy frowned. "Why are you smiling?"

"I still can't believe I'm free. Thanks for coming, son."

Truth was, he'd come for his mother. For Grace, too. Not for his dad. Letting his father stew in his own mess for a few days would serve him right.

Anger boiled inside. He'd better talk about something else. He tempered his tone best he could and asked, "What's with that black stuff on your forehead?"

"A cross, I think." The smile returned to his father's face. "Someone put it there this morning."

"One of your cell mates?"

"No. Someone else."

"Who?"

"I'll tell you later. It's a cool story."

Another one of your stories. I can't wait. Seeing the Volkswagen parked at the end of the alley, everyone heightened their pace.

Once they'd climbed in, Gordon cranked the engine and ground the gears into reverse, then backed to a wide opening where he could turn around.

He suddenly applied the brakes, then looked at his father. He had to get it out. If he didn't, he might drive off a cliff. He narrowed his eyes. "I want you to know, Dad, I only came today because Mom was worried about you. It may be months before the power comes back on."

His dad looked surprised. Were those tears in his eyes? No way!

"I'm very grateful to all of you, I really am."

Gordon jerked toward the windshield and stared at the road. He pulled the van to an abandoned parking lot, then slammed on the brakes a second time. He turned to his dad and scowled. "You've ruined everything."

"You're correct and I'm sorry, son. There's no excuse for what I've done."

"You got that right." Gordon yanked the clutch into first gear. With each shift, new anger raged. "My life's over, Dad. How could you do this to me? To any of us?" He listed the offenses, then asked, "How could you steal from an old lady? Who does that?"

Martin and Jeremy were mute in the backseat. His father too.

"Why, Dad, why?" Gordon pounded the dashboard.

His father shook his head. "Gordy, I wish I had a reason. Something that made sense. The past eight months I've lived a lie. The drugs .... I did whatever I could to get them."

Gordon straightened his spine and clenched his jaw.

"If it takes me a lifetime, I will pay everyone back," his dad continued. "If there's jail time, I'll serve it."

How can I believe anything you say?

"Gordon ... please ... look at me."

Gordon gritted his teeth and twisted his face toward his father. "What?" he snapped.

"I have no right to ask you," he said. "Could you ... could you forgive me?"

Gordon glared for a moment, then wagged his head. "I don't know ... I need time, Dad. I'm really angry at you."

ꕥ

Wednesday evening, 5:50 p.m.
Baxter Home

Matt hid behind a Palo Verde tree. It was one of many that lined the opposite side of Casa Blanca Road. His eyes lingered at the Baxter's front windows. The sun draped the horizon, casting an orange silhouette around the home. Sunsets like this usually calmed him. Tonight, the orange and red hues magnified his simmering rage.

Lights flickered through the windows. Probably candles. Like his family, the Baxters must have found rudimentary light sources wherever they could. He'd been in their home a few times before, for some church gatherings with Carla. He thought he remembered the layout. He'd never been upstairs though. That could be a problem.

It was good he came early, while it was still light out. He'd gotten the lay of the land. He'd return later. After midnight, when darkness would be his best friend.

Matt climbed into the old station wagon and cranked it to life. He'd always been ashamed of driving this bucket of bolts, but now he was glad he had a car that ran. Many didn't. When he drove through the empty street, headlights approached. An aging Volkswagen van rumbled past. Matt looked at its driver. Baxter's son, Gordy. Matt's eyes swept to the man sitting next to Gordy, and he stilled. Dalton Baxter sat shotgun.

You got out of jail, you S.O.B.! Matt steamed. Your day of reckoning will come. He smiled. So this was what revenge felt like.

It *was* sweet.

He pondered his plans while he drove toward McCormick to look for Carla. She often liked to take walks to clear her head. Maybe he could find her. She might even be with Laney. He wasn't sure. Wait until she saw what he brought her tomorrow. She would forgive him and then they'd have a fresh start, far away from this place of misery.

ꕥ

"That was Matt Connor," Dalton said, watching the tail lights of the old brown Buick disappear around a corner. "I wonder if he's looking for me."

"Why would he need to find you?" Martin asked.

Dalton shifted nervously. He was tempted to lie. But he wouldn't. The old Dalton must be kept at bay. No matter what.

"Matt was my dealer. He's the one I met in Prescott on Sunday. I've been buying from him for months." Seeing their shocked faces, he quickly added, "I forced him to meet me, threatening to tell Carla he was dealing again."

Gordy's face filled with revulsion. "Are you kidding me? His little girl died on Sunday."

"I know, son." Dalton ran a hand over his face. "I'll do whatever I can to make that up to the Connors."

"You can't—" Gordy stopped, drew a breath.

"You can't give Matt more time with his daughter, Dalton." Martin spoke quietly from the back seat. "Those minutes are gone forever."

Dalton sensed the fog of disappointment filling the van. He gulped down the unwelcome truth. Some things couldn't be made right, no matter what.

CHAPTER FORTY-NINE

Wednesday evening, 6:30 p.m.
Baxter Home

DUSK SETTLED OVER THE BAXTER home depositing rosy splashes of light throughout the den. Grace's golden curls reflected candlelight. Dalton snuggled close and they took turns reading *Little House on the Prairie*. How appropriate. They were now 21st century pioneers existing in an 1860 reality. Maybe he could learn something from the classic story.

"Your cross is still there." Grace pointed to his face.

"I know it's getting lighter but I don't want to wash it off," he said.

"Why, Daddy?"

He looked into her curious eyes and thought about his answer. He had carefully washed around the ash mark earlier. From its faded appearance, it was only a matter of time and it would be gone forever. Yet soap and water could never remove its impact from his life.

"It means a lot to me. A friend put it there."

That seemed to satisfy her, so he read another paragraph.

"What about my ice cream?" Grace nudged his arm.

Dalton looked up from the book and smiled. "I'm never going to finish this chapter, Grace."

"It's been two days, Daddy." She frowned, crossing her arms. "Two days since you promised. And you got home this afternoon. It's time for ice cream."

"I did, didn't I?" He set the book on the coffee table. "Let's go to town, kiddo. Maybe we can find something open."

"Yay!" She jumped up and found her sneakers.

It would be nice to get Grace out of the house, even if the stores were closed. Sammy had said barely a word to him since arriving home. There was still some time before the family meeting he'd requested for that evening at nine. He and Grace might as well enjoy what was left of the day.

Grace trailed him as Dalton entered the kitchen. He grabbed Gordy's keys from a wall hook. Shirley smiled, but Sammy said nothing.

"Grace and I are going to town. Be back in a bit," he said, walking through the breakfast room.

Small town McCormick with its quaint Mom and Pop stores resembled the renowned Mayberry from the sitcom reruns his mother let him watch as a child. But the shopkeepers who boarded their windows on Main Street disrupted that image of old time Americana. The homey 1950's atmosphere had surrendered to a 21st century panic.

He turned left on Lincoln hoping Brewster's Ice Cream Shoppe might be open. If the power stayed off, they'd be trying to get rid of their premium ice cream before it spoiled. He pulled to the corner and parked near the building. Grace exited the passenger seat and ran to the front door. Her face was mashed against the glass when he caught up with her.

He joined her and looked inside. "I don't see anyone. They must be closed." He rattled the brass bell, then knocked. No one came. He waited a few seconds and tried again, then wrapped an arm around her back. "Let's go. Maybe the market's open." Bailey's Supermarket was likely closed too, but spending time with Grace would be worth the ten or so minutes it would take to walk there.

"Sure, Dad," she said as they rounded the corner to Jefferson. An older man with a paunch walked toward them, yielding a large mallet.

Dalton stopped and tugged Grace behind.

"Reverend Baxter, could I have a word with you?" the man asked.

Dalton squinted through waning sunlight. At a closer look, it was Larry Woodbury, from Woody's Toy Store.

He relaxed. "Sure Larry, what's up?" Grace resumed her place at Dalton's side.

"Have you talked with the mayor? Does he know how long the power will be out?"

"I haven't heard anything," Dalton said. "If I do, I'll let you know." Apparently, Woodbury was in the dark in more ways than one. Larry wasn't aware of his arrest and that Dalton been too busy vomiting on a jail floor to check in with the mayor.

ꕥ

Matt trolled another empty street hoping to see Carla. He'd have to implement his plan before she came home, but still he yearned to see her, just to make sure she was okay. But she was nowhere in sight. As the sun was quick to set, McCormick bustled with foot traffic amidst a stream of bicycles that seemed to be the new mode of travel.

He'd passed a few blocks on Jefferson when he saw them. The preacher was talking to old man Woodbury. The girl stood near, while Baxter wrapped an arm around her back. Matt looked longingly at her.

Fresh anger surged.

How dare he pretend to love her? He wasn't fit to be a father. Especially not to a beautiful and innocent daughter.

He eased on the pedal and crawled past. Baxter didn't notice him but the girl did. She looked up and smiled, then waved. He could almost see Charity's eyes in hers. As he drove past, he returned the gesture, then watched her through the rearview mirror.

This was the final sign he needed. God was showing him His favor. The girl obviously recognized his car. Probably because he'd taken Charity and her to the movies last month. He looked at the empty passenger seat, remembering. Charity should be there.

She would be soon.

CHAPTER FIFTY

Wednesday, 8:15 p.m.
Baxter Home

SAMMY AND SHIRLEY WERE CANNING in the kitchen when Dalton and Grace returned home. They'd been preserving butter in mason jars using a pressure cooker. The boxes of frozen butter they'd stocked up on a few months ago at Costco were being transformed into a much-needed staple. Shirley insisted the final product would keep for twenty-five years.

Dalton wondered if they'd need to cope that long but was grateful for his mother-in-law's expertise. Still ... all the propane needed to complete such a task would drain their fuel resources. He shrugged. Oh well. Better not argue. Tonight, Sammy clearly called the shots. He'd stay out of her way until tonight's family meeting.

He looped Gordy's keys on the hook and asked, "What can I do to help?"

Sammy's face remained void of emotion. "You can keep Grace entertained," she said coolly.

"Not a problem. I'd love to. In fact, she keeps me entertained," Dalton said.

Shirley chuckled and nodded. "Me too, son. She's got so many questions these days."

Questions he'd always shoved off on Sammy. Not any longer. He'd take time with his daughter. No more distractions from the important things in life. T.V. shows and texting had been eliminated. Hours pondering his future, gone. *Ask all the questions you want, Grace.* Though he felt like an open book, ready to be read, only Grace dared to lift his cover.

He joined her in the den and picked up the *Little House* classic when she announced, "I really want ice cream, Daddy."

"You know we tried. This is out of my control."

"It's not fair." Her lower lip quivered. "I waited for you to come back. You promised."

Yes, he had. He'd also promised God he'd live in truth. Confessing to Grace could be his dress rehearsal for when he talked to the rest of the family in a bit.

"I have something to tell you, Grace." He set the book down. "Remember my skiing accident last year?"

She nodded.

"Because I was in a lot of pain, the doctor gave me pills. Unfortunately, I kept taking them when I no longer needed them."

A puzzled look filled her eyes. "Why, Daddy?"

"Sometimes grownups do things that don't make sense. I couldn't seem to stop."

"You got hooked on drugs?"

As usual, she surprised him. "Where'd you learn that?"

"Red ribbon week at school," she said matter-of-factly. "Drugs are bad. Didn't you learn that when you were a kid?"

"I forgot those lessons. I made some really bad choices." He shared briefly about his activities on Sunday. He confessed his theft and about hurting himself. "What I've done is horrible, Grace. I hope you can forgive me."

Her eyes offered adoration. Her words seemed effortless. "I will, Daddy. I do."

"It's my job to help people," he explained. "I've let everyone down, especially God."

Grace looked up at the ceiling. "Is God angry at you?"

The old Dalton would have thought so. For the first time in his life, he felt cherished by the Lord, not kicked aside. Not like a dog eating scraps at the table.

"I hurt Him, Grace. It must have broken His heart to watch me go my own way. He's our Father, after all. There's nothing that hurts a parent more than to see one of our kids make bad choices. I hope you never experience that when you become a mom. Years ago, God called me to be a pastor. I should have been at the hospital helping the Connors."

"I slept in Charity's bed," Grace said.

Dalton wasn't sure where this was going. "I know you and Charity were close. How are you feeling?"

Tears filled her eyes. Dalton pulled her close. She laid her head against his chest.

She raised her face and her misty eyes seemed to plead. "I'm scared, Daddy. I don't want to die. What if I get sick?"

"We all will die someday, darling. If you know Jesus, there's nothing to fear." Dalton's confidence rang true. These weren't just platitudes. He really believed what he said. "God helps us to die when it's our time."

"Did He help Charity?"

"I know He did. His Word tells us children are special to Jesus. Unless we become like children, we will never enter heaven. I forgot that. I hope you never do."

"Sometimes I forget Charity's gone. She was my best friend. We both got Mrs. Franklin this year. Now her desk will be empty."

Dalton doubted McCormick's only elementary school would open in two weeks. Grace had talked about second grade all summer.

"Charity's parents are going through a rough time," he said, turning the conversation elsewhere. "They'll need our help."

"I want to help."

"The service is on Saturday. Mr. and Mrs. Connor are really sad. Since you were Charity's best friend, maybe you could give them some extra hugs."

"I will, Daddy." Grace snuggled near. He picked up the book and opened it to where they'd left off. He continued reading about Ma and Pa and life on a primitive prairie.

The family meeting was set for nine p.m. Grace should be sound asleep by then. She'd be spared the onslaught of anger headed his way. Once she was out, it was hard to wake her up. It was good that the day's craziness exhausted her.

Thirty minutes later, Dalton tucked her into bed. He clicked on her nightlight a couple of times before he remembered. She suddenly sprang up and threw back the covers, her wide eyes reflecting the moonlight.

"Daddy ... I can't sleep in the dark. Mommy gives me her flashlight."

"It's okay honey. I'll leave mine." Dalton placed his flashlight on the floor. White light sprayed across her carpet. Batteries would be dead by morning. He must come up with something to help Grace break her nightlight dependency. She'd need to grow up a little and learn to face the new realities of a powerless world. But not tonight. Maybe not even this week.

He left her door wide open and headed downstairs where the inquisition waited. He squared his shoulders. Whatever his family had to say, he deserved.

When he entered the den, kerosene lamps glowed at each end of the mantle. A flickering candle from last Christmas infused the room with cinnamon. Sammy and her mother sat on the sofa while Gordy straddled a footstool. Dalton collapsed into the same easy chair where three days before, the church council had tried and convicted him. Now, Gordy and Sammy seemed ready to do the same. His mother-in-law, Shirley, offered him a compassionate smile.

When he turned to face them, Sammy crossed her arms and glared. Dalton searched for one of his trusty anecdotes but stopped himself. None seemed fitting now.

He looked at each family member. They didn't deserve the hell he'd put them through. Though God had miraculously changed him hours earlier in a dark jail cell, it would take a while for any of them to see it. It was easy to understand why.

"Not sure what to say ..." he began. "Saying 'I'm sorry' seems inadequate."

"You've got that right," Sammy snapped. "Truth is you're sorry you got caught."

He bowed his head, unable to meet her cold gaze. "I know I deserve your anger. Please forgive me."

"I find it hard to believe anything you have to say," Sammy said.

Shirley squeezed Sammy's arm. "Listen, Samantha. Hear him out."

He'd always put up with Shirley. She embarrassed him with her hippie-like attire and long hair. Through the years she'd stuck her nose in where it didn't belong, and he'd been glad when she moved to her cabin, far away from McCormick. But now he saw a different woman. Someone who was genuine, kind, and wanting to help.

"Thank you, Shirley." Dalton smiled.

"Call me 'Mom,'" she reminded him for the umpteenth time. He usually shrugged her off. No one could take his mother's place, but ... things were different now. He needed a mom.

His eyes watered. "Uh ... okay ... Mom ... thank you." Had her own struggle with drugs enabled her to give him the greatest gift of all? Grace in his shadows.

"There's no easy way to say this," Dalton said, turning to his wife. "You were right about everything, honey." He dragged in a deep breath. "I need help. I'm a drug addict." Admitting this seemed to loosen the knots in his clenched stomach. He suddenly felt different ... almost lighter. Jesus was right. The truth did set you free.

Sammy frowned beneath narrowed eyes. Her arms remained crossed. She wasn't budging, not even a millimeter in his direction. His admission meant nothing and he couldn't blame her one bit.

His eyes met hers. "Had you not followed me Sunday, I'd still be lying to myself, in search of my next high and willing to do anything to get it. Who knows where I would have ended up. I know I blamed you for speaking to the council ... but Sammy ... what you did, saved my life."

Sammy still said nothing, but dropped her hands to her lap. The bitterness in her face, softened. She bit her lip, as if she wanted to say something but stopped herself.

He stared at his son. Gordy looked like he was about to explode. He caught a glimpse of Shirley. She gave him an assuring nod and he continued.

"I ended up in a place I never thought I would be. Jail ... it was horrible. It broke me. I still can't believe I was arrested."

"You deserved to be there, Dad," Gordy said. His son's eyes pooled and he quickly wiped them. "How could you do this? You're so selfish!"

Sadness constricted Dalton's throat. He looked down at the carpet trying to think of something to say. Gordon's disappointment weighted him down. His accusations stabbed at his heart.

Dalton looked up. "Gordy, you're right. I hurt you in ways I'm ashamed to admit. I know I can't change what I did."

Please Father ... can't You fix this?

"I promise you son ... in fact I promise all of you ... I'll face my pain ... I'll let God do what He needs to do in my life."

He turned back to Sammy. "I hurt you the most." His fingernails indented chair's leather, resisting the urge to get up and hold her. "I love you so much. What can I do?"

"I need some time, Dalton," Sammy said. She shook her head and looked at her mother. "Mom ... please don't say anything. I need time to process."

Shirley reached over and squeezed Sammy's arm, but said nothing.

Dalton turned back to Gordy. "Everything your mother told the council is true. Even the part about my car at the bottom of Copper Lake."

"Why would you do that?" Gordy's face contorted with anguish.

"For the insurance settlement. The BMW was a collectible. Once they reimbursed me, I planned to buy a cheaper model, then use the extra cash to buy more drugs."

"I'm not just talking about the car," Gordy said. "All the other stuff. You stole from a lot of people. I'll be humiliated. McCormick's a small town, Dad."

Dalton forced his hands to stay put on the chair's armrests, instead of curling over his chest, a protective barrier. He had to stay open to his family, open to their anger and condemnation. "Again son, you're right." He nodded. "I've been a thief. Once I started using, I couldn't seem to stop. They numbed the pain inside. That's what I need to deal with now. My childhood demons."

"Don't start that again," Sammy interrupted. "We all had things happen to us as kids. I am sick to death of your lame excuses about how horrible your father was."

The tightening of his jaw produced pain under his stitches. "Sammy ... how can you say that? You, of all people, know he was a monster."

"Grandpa?" Gordy asked. "Grandpa was a bad man?"

He'd answer Gordy later. Sammy's comments didn't make sense. He connected with her eyes and spoke deliberately. "You saw my mother's bruises, Sammy. You begged me to call the police, remember? I refused, and you grabbed the phone. Are you telling me you forgot how horrible he was?"

She looked down and wagged her head. "I remember every moment. You wouldn't let me call. We made—no, *I* made a mistake that day. I should've called anyway, put a stop to it."

"She begged us not to. He would have hurt her more."

"Back up the truck." Gordy's voice broke through. He waved his hand. "Grandpa hit Grandma?"

"Your grandmother wasn't the only one," Dalton said. "There were days I couldn't go to school because of the bruising." He detected a tinge of sympathy in Sammy's face—the first hint that maybe she heard him, maybe she could believe him—while Gordy's eyes widened.

"The drugs numbed the memories. As time went by, the pain seemed greater, so I took more. Before I knew it, I was addicted."

"You took them every day? Gordy asked.

"I couldn't stop."

"What about Sundays?" Gordy's expression filled with shock. "Were you on drugs during church?"

"I couldn't preach without them."

Gordy swung around and faced his mother and grandmother. "Are you hearing this? Unbelievable!"

"I'd snort Oxy thirty minutes before the service started," Dalton continued. "I lied to myself a lot, Gordy. I thought they empowered me to deliver spell-binding messages to the congregation."

"They weren't spell-binding, Dalton," Sammy said. "Most of the time you seemed rattled and on edge. There were days you couldn't string two thoughts together."

"Really?" Dalton shook his head and looked at the floor. "Why didn't you say something? No wonder you think I'm pathetic."

"I tried. You wouldn't listen. Not to me, not to your friends, not even your doctor."

He rubbed his jaw. "I got pretty good at lying, I guess."

"That's one thing we agree on," Sammy said.

He refocused on his son. "Gordy ... after my mother died, I went on auto-pilot. My appointment at Saint Luke's became nothing more than a boring job. I lost my passion. Then when my dad died, I came into a windfall. I bought the Beamer and started spending like crazy. I took up skiing and ... well ... you know the rest. My accident, followed by knee surgery ... and ... then the drugs."

"Didn't you think about us, Dad?" Gordy's eyes glistened. "Didn't you think about what you were doing to us?" His son looked down. "I never realized how self-centered you are. I thought you were tougher than that."

Dalton's chest tightened, and he swallowed the sudden lump in his throat. "I have been, yes. I hope I can be different. I want to try anyway.

"Chemical abuse captures the strongest people. You tell yourself you can quit. That was the biggest lie I told myself. I was in a deep hole and couldn't get out. I thought a new job would be my answer. If I made more money, I could pay everyone back and kick the drugs. I know now, moving to Phoenix wouldn't solve anything. I still need to face my past and not run from it." He drew a deep breath. "The truth is, I don't ever want to leave McCormick. I see things differently. What I believed about God was not Who He really is."

"What did you believe?" Shirley leaned forward, tucking a fist under her chin.

He met her steady gaze. "That He was unpredictable and full of anger, just like my dad. I have been so wrong about Him. He picked me up when I was at my lowest point. He pulled me in to His family. I'm no longer a cast out. In fact, I never was. I get it now."

"I'm glad you've had your epiphany, Dalton," Sammy bit out. "But the truth is, it's going to take more than your new relationship with God to fix anything."

She was right. He'd hurt so many. "I know it'll take time."

"What you did to Matt on Sunday ... I still can't believe it," Sammy said.

"I can't believe it either. Every time I look at Grace, I hate myself. You can't imagine how many times I've begged God to show me how to repair this."

"Some things can never be fixed." The way Sammy knotted her fists on her knees, he knew he'd been tried and convicted. He was powerless to bring Charity back to her grieving parents. If only he could hit the reset button. How would he face Matt at Charity's service? Maybe it would be better if he didn't go.

"I saw him driving through our neighborhood when we got home today. I wondered if he was looking for me."

"He never came to the house," Sammy said. "I'm grateful for that. I would have cringed seeing him after what you did. It's bad enough I have to face Carla tomorrow."

"Tomorrow?"

"At the church meeting."

"What meeting?"

"Not now Samantha," Shirley interrupted.

"He might as well know."

"I might as well know what?" Dalton asked.

"The council is having a congregational meeting and potluck dinner in the annex. Emergency preparation and checking on our elderly will be the main topic. Then they will take a vote on whether to dismiss you."

Gordy jumped to his feet. "You'll be voted out in front of the whole church. How will I ever live this down?"

"They can't have a felon running the church, Gordy" Sammy said.

Felon? The word seemed a badge of horror. He hadn't been arraigned yet but that was only a matter of time. But what surprised him was the sense of calm he felt. Instead of fear, the peace he'd felt in the jail cell settled in his heart.

"Once the meeting's over, the bereavement committee will meet with the Connors to discuss Charity's service on Saturday," Sammy said.

"I should be there," Dalton said. "I need to talk to the congregation."

"It won't be a friendly crowd once they find out," she warned. "Not at all like you're used to."

"I need to do this. I'm going."

He knew what he'd face tomorrow would be not be easy but at the same time, he trusted ... perhaps for the first time in his life ... in a Father who would take his hand and walk him through. Just like this moment. In time, God would speak to his family. Dalton was certain of it. "I know none of you see it now and I don't blame you, but I want to show you I'm different. I'll do whatever I can to help the Connors. If I can alleviate their suffering, I will."

"You *caused* a lot of their suffering," Sammy said. "I'm not sure you can do anything to change that." She seemed determined to rub salt into his still-raw wounds. Wait till she found out about Deidra. Would he lose her forever?

"I'm going to the kitchen," Shirley said. "Tea anyone?"

"Yes, please, Mom," Sammy said. "Make the herbal type. I need to sleep tonight."

"None for me," Gordy said. "I need some air. I'm going outside." His son twisted around and stalked toward the front door. Shirley left for the kitchen.

Dalton fixed his gaze on Sammy. "Could we go to my office? I need to tell you something."

"You can tell me here. No more secrets, Baxter."

He dragged in a lengthy breath, searching for the right words. He needed to get it out before Shirley returned.

"What is it?" Sammy's back stiffened, her jaw seemed to clench. "What could be worse than this?"

"Something happened at the Storm's ... three weeks ago."

Her mouth dropped. "I knew it! What's going on with that woman?"

"I went to ask for a furnace donation and she came on to me. She kissed me. Not just once. Twice." There, he said it. He finally exhaled.

Tears collected in the corners of her eyes. "I can't believe this. What is she? ... fifteen years older than you?"

"I left before she tried anything else."

Sammy seemed to cave in on herself. She shuddered on the couch, shoulders hunched.

If only he could hold her. But her coldness dictated distance. He looked at her with a deep longing. How could he have been such an idiot? Most men would have cherished such a beautiful woman, yet he had shredded her heart. He wanted nothing more than to start over, to regain her trust. Her mouth was taut and impenetrable. *Lord, how about a miracle?*

Her head bobbed up. "Are you attracted to her?"

"You're joking, right?"

"No!" Sammy's voice notched. "I found her asleep here, in our *home*, when I got back from the hospital. She was wearing my slippers! What went on here?"

"She spent the night? I didn't know, Sammy, I swear." With the drugs, Sunday had been a blur. "I thought she left when I went to bed.

Sammy brought a shaky hand to her forehead. "I can't tell if you're lying again." Her voice choked. "Am I supposed to believe you didn't sleep with her?"

He raised both hands in surrender. "I didn't, Sammy. You've got to believe me."

Her eyes cast doubt; her lips formed a tight thin line.

Despair lodged in his throat.

She slammed her empty cup on the end table and got to her feet. "I can't do this right now."

"Give me a chance—" Dalton stood to follow her.

As he left the den, the downstairs bathroom door slammed shut. He grabbed the nearest flashlight.

He tapped lightly and heard sniffling.

"What do you want?" she asked.

"I brought you a light."

She cracked open the door and peeked through. The flashlight revealed a trail of new tears across her cheeks. Now, as he'd done with her on Sunday, she barred his entrance to her sanctuary. Turnabout was fair play. But unlike him, nothing nefarious was going on in Sammy's darkness. He guessed the bathroom had suddenly become her prayer closet.

Shutting him out of her life was well-warranted. Turnabout was indeed fair play.

He handed her the light.

She gently closed the door. If only she didn't close her heart along with it.

Thursday

The Lord says, "I will rescue those who love Me. I will protect those who trust in My name. When they call on Me, I will answer; I will be with them in trouble. I will rescue and honor them.
Psalm 91:14-15

CHAPTER FIFTY-ONE

McCormick, AZ
Thursday, 1 a.m.

NO SURPRISE THE WINDOW WAS open. Insufferable temperatures clung to the upper desert like a coat of wet paint.

Matt ground a cigarette into the dirt, then gulped a swig of Durum whiskey. He refastened the cap and stuffed the bottle down his back pocket. He needed just enough to take the edge off.

He straightened his shoulders and walked to the window, adjusting the straps of his camo backpack.

He could do this. He had to. For Carla's sake.

God was giving him a second chance to be a dad. And the girl who lived here needed a real father. Not some drug addict faking it.

He peered through the window. Good thing the Baxters didn't have dogs. At least as far as he remembered. Matt clamped his mini flashlight between his teeth and aimed it at the window. After prying open the screen, he lifted it out of the frame and leaned it against a honeysuckle bush.

He snapped off the flashlight and stuffed it into his pocket before climbing inside. Oh yeah. The living room. Nothing much had changed since he'd been here once with Carla. After his eyes adjusted, he navigated around the furniture to a wide foyer with ceilings tall enough for the kind of Christmas tree Carla always wanted.

He lifted his face toward the wood beams and listened. Nothing. Just like home, no mechanical noises.

To his right was the staircase, his destiny. To the left, the front entrance, his escape.

He padded across laminate flooring to the massive front door, unlocked and opened it, letting in a foot of night sky. Ready for his getaway.

The staircase stretched upwards. He took a cautious step, gripping the railing. Then another. And another. His reward waited at the top. As he took the last step, he paused. Three bedrooms connected with the landing. The first door was slightly ajar. The center room, closed.

The last room's entrance stood open. Moonlight outlined a large stuffed animal. Bingo. This was the girl's room. His girl.

He balled his fists and clenched his jaw as he peeked into the master bedroom. He listened for snoring. Was the preacher asleep? Matt could slip into the room, put his hands around the man's neck ... increase the pressure until Baxter's eyes flew open, knowing what was happening, seeing who was taking his life.

Matt's heart hammered.

Wake up, stupid!

He eased the door shut. His plan was sweeter than any slugfest with Baxter. He'd serve the preacher a three-course meal of terror, misery, and hopelessness. With a dessert of revenge.

He crept across the landing and entered the girl's room. She lay on her stomach, clutching a tiny doll. A small flashlight on the floor directed a beam of light toward the bed showing the bedcover had been thrown back.

He had to move quickly and keep her quiet. If he startled her awake and she cried out or screamed and woke her family ...

He tugged gently at the bedspread, but it was tangled between her legs. She rolled over, pulling her knees to her chest. His breath caught in his chest and he stepped back into the shadows, staring at her breathing form. She was so much like Charity. The way she slept, curled on her side, in her cotton pajamas. How often had he gone into Charity's room in the dead of night just to hear her breathe? And now, he'd never be able to do that again. Except he would.

He dragged in a deep breath, leaned over the girl and shook her shoulder. "Charity ... I mean ... Grace," he whispered close. "Wake up, Grace." She stirred, but her eyes stayed shut.

He jiggled her arm . Grace's eyes fluttered open. She blinked several times, then her eyes widened.

He leaned close and whispered. "It's me, Grace, Mr. Connor ... Charity's daddy."

"Mr. Connor?" She sat up and rubbed her eyes. He shined the flashlight on his face.

"See? It's me." He knitted his brows, forging concern. "There's been an emergency. Your family asked me to get you. You're staying with us a few days."

"Where's Mommy and Daddy?" The girl wrapped her arms around herself and stared at the doorway. "Where's Gordy?" Her voice cracked, like she was about to burst into tears.

He held up a shushing hand. "Don't cry, sweetie. Everything is fine. They asked me to help. That's all."

"Are they okay?"

"They're just great. We'll call them tomorrow. You'll see." He waved the flashlight around. "Ah ha ... here are your shoes," he said in a low voice as he picked them up. "Put them on. Hurry!"

She swung her feet to the floor and climbed into the sneakers, then fastened the Velcro straps.

"I'll get you some clothes for a few days." He went to her dresser and grabbed some underwear, a few pairs of shorts, some t-shirts, and socks. Maybe seeing him stuff them in his backpack would calm her. She wouldn't need much. Charity's closet was full of clothes and it looked like they wore the same size. Or close enough.

"Mrs. Connor is waiting," he lied. "She'll make you some hot chocolate in the morning." He stuffed the clothes into his backpack, then slipped the straps over his shoulders. "You and Charity loved her cocoa, remember?"

Grace nodded. In the shadowy darkness he couldn't tell if she was still scared. She finally spoke. "Mrs. Connor made it on our camping trip." Grace's voice was soft but calm.

He smothered a grin. This was really going to work. "That's right," he said. "When we went to the Grand Canyon last summer."

"Charity and I climbed rocks. It was fun. I miss her so much."

His heart stumbled. Everything inside ached when he thought about his little girl. He missed her happy brown eyes and infectious smile. Tears threatened. He wiped his eyes.

"We miss her too, Grace. When you come over tonight, it will make Charity's mommy so happy."

"My daddy asked me to help you." She stood and smiled. "He wants me to give you hugs."

Using the kid to make amends, huh, Baxter? It wouldn't work. He was such a phony.

Aiming the flashlight, he walked behind Grace as they headed to the stairway. The girl clutched the Barbie doll, grabbed the railing, took cautious steps downward.

When they got to the bottom, she pointed to the open door. "Did Mommy forget to close the door?"

"Probably. They left in a hurry. I'll lock it. Don't worry."

She walked across the outside porch to a stone pathway. When he followed close behind, he heard the clatter of glass against pavement. He stopped and looked, felt his pocket. His whiskey.

Grace turned and stared at him. "What was that?"

"I dropped something," he told her. "It's okay ... we need to hurry."

They shuffled to the station wagon where he opened the passenger door. The girl climbed in and fastened her belt.

Matt hurried around to the driver's seat and slid inside. He cranked the engine and jerked the car into drive, then flattened the gas pedal. The crunch of gravel sounded behind. About fifty yards further ahead, he turned on the headlights.

The girl squirmed in her seat, looking around the car for something.

"What are you looking for, Char ... uh ... Grace?" he asked.

"I dropped my Barbie." She furrowed her brows. "Can we go back, Mr. Connor?"

"You can play with Charity's doll when we get to my house."

Tears escaped from her eyes and she bit her lip.

"Please don't cry. Is it the doll? I'll buy you a new one."

"I miss Charity. Why did she die?"

"I don't know." He steeled his voice, trying to hide his anger. "Life isn't fair sometimes." This crap shoot they called *life* didn't make sense at all.

He studied her profile, outlined by the moonlight. His breath hitched and his gut twisted. She looked so much like Charity. Until tonight, he'd never noticed the resemblance. If not for the difference in hair color, they could have passed for sisters.

A lump gathered in his throat. He'd failed as a father. He'd been such a coward, agreeing to meet the preacher. So what if he tattled to Carla? She knew now, and all that happened was that he'd lost precious minutes with his baby before she died.

He glanced at the girl again. Grace leaned her head back, nearly asleep again. He smiled. God was giving him a second chance.

That monster shouldn't be her dad! Matt was rescuing her. He was the hero in this. He pressed his lips together and tightened his grip on the steering wheel, focusing on the roadway stripes as they disappeared under the car.

Tomorrow would be a good day. He just had to find Carla, and then they could leave this place forever. Leave the memories. Leave the stench of chemo and death. Leave everything.

Yes, tomorrow would be a good day.

At the end of Desert View Road, Matt turned into his neighborhood. In the short trip from the Baxters, the girl had become his daughter. He loved her and he'd never let anyone hurt her or take her from him.

Carla would be so happy to have a child around again. She'd always liked the Baxter kid. Sure, it might take a bit of convincing to get her to agree to an overnight camping trip. Especially with Charity's funeral on Saturday. But if he couldn't convince her himself, he'd enlist the girl's help. Who could turn down Charity's best friend?

Carla would go ballistic once she realized they weren't coming home on Friday. They would inconveniently run out of gas—but it wouldn't be his fault since the gas gauge was faulty—and, since there were no stations open, what could they do but camp out a few weeks by the gorge? Eventually Carla would settle in and enjoy mothering Grace.

He turned on Desperado Lane. The gravel road that carved through his neighborhood had been aptly named, at least for tonight. There was so much to do before morning and convincing Carla he had done a good thing would be hard. As the old wagon wrestled with pebbles, an idea came to him.

"Would it be okay if we call you Charity for awhile? You look just like her. It would mean so much to Mrs. Connor."

"Charity?" The girl looked puzzled.

"Just for a few days. And when we get home, you can sleep in her room."

"No, Mr. Connor. I can't sleep there. You can call me Charity, but please don't make me sleep in her bed."

"Okay Charity-bug. You can sleep in the den."

"Can I call my mommy? I need to remind her about Boris."

"Boris?"

"My hamster. She might forget to feed him."

"None of our phones work," he said. "We'll try to find one in the morning. Then you can call her."

She nodded as Matt pulled into his driveway. He parked near the side of the house so they could enter through the back door. Less noisy, away from prying neighbors.

When he'd settled her with a blanket and pillow on the couch, he returned to the carport to stock supplies for their trip. They'd need several weeks of food and water while they camped at the canyon's edge.

He hooked up the tent trailer to the tow hitch on the wagon, than began loading supplies and camping gear as his mind returned to Carla. Where was she staying?

He shoved a case of bottled water into the back of the car. Probably with Laney. Their ranch home in the country had spare bedrooms. And Laney was the type who took people in. He also knew for certain she was one of the religious types who didn't believe in divorce.

That would work in his favor. When he showed up on Laney's doorstep, he'd plead with Carla to go on a brief camping trip. Laney would probably be on board. Getting away for a night would do Carla and him some good.

Maybe with enough time enjoying the outdoors as a family, Carla would begin to see the girl as her own. Just like him.

CHAPTER FIFTY-TWO

Thursday, 1:40 a.m.
McCormick, AZ

SCREECH!

Dalton jolted from a sound sleep. Not sure what he'd heard, he sat up on the couch and listened.

There it went again. What was that? He rubbed his eyes as they adjusted to the den's darkness.

Dalton stood and walked toward the foyer where he flipped a dead switch.

Blast! He kept forgetting.

He felt his way to the breakfast room, found a flashlight and snapped it on. Grace's hamster Boris ran like a scared rat over his metal wheel. Dalton aimed the light at the cage. When Boris tried to exit from the wheel, he squealed.

"What's wrong, little buddy?" The hamster shook. Dalton leaned close. Boris's tiny paw had gotten wedged between the platform's narrow bars.

Dalton unlatched the cage, stuck his hand inside and carefully pulled at the hamster's foot. Boris rewarded his efforts with a sharp bite.

"Ouch!" Dalton yanked his hand from the cage and examined the blood dripping from his finger. "I was trying to help you, buddy."

He wrapped his finger with a paper towel and pressed, then turned back to the hamster cage. Boris shivered and glared at him. "It's gonna be okay." Dalton reinserted his hand and cautiously stroked the animal's back. "Let's try again." Dalton collared the hamster's neck with his right hand while firmly holding the back leg between his left thumb and finger.

"Hold on." Dalton tipped the little foot forward and then extricated the limb from its wire manacle, setting the hamster free. Boris darted to the edge of the cage, shaking, his fur puffed like a round fuzzy ball.

Dalton extended his hand to the animal's face. "You had quite a scare, didn't you?"

Boris relaxed and sniffed Dalton's finger. All was forgiven.

Dalton picked Boris up and cupped him with his hands. A lump climbed into this throat and his eyes filled.

Like this helpless creature, he, too, was safe in God's mighty hand. Even when he howled in pain, afraid and angry, God always had his back. Dalton had been just too blind to see it.

I deserve to be cast away, he prayed as he stroked the animal's head. *Yet Father, You love me.*

When Dalton set him down Boris darted to his Popsicle stick hideaway shelter. Dalton tossed in a handful of gerbil pellets, hoping Boris would emerge. The hamster remained sequestered as Dalton closed the cage, then refilled the water bottle.

"Thanks for the object lesson, Boris. Now stay off your exercise wheel for a while. I need some shut eye."

When Dalton returned to the couch, he peered at the wind-up alarm clock he'd found in his office.

1:56 a.m.

His body ached with fatigue but his mind raced with energy. How could he make things right with Sammy and Gordy? That seemed as insurmountable as his nemesis, Agassiz Mountain. Now though, no longer his enemy, the rugged side of Agassiz proved to be his friend. It was that plunge to its base that had led him straight to God.

"*The only path up is down,*" Mo had told him.

He cradled his head in his hands. "Father, please give me my family back. Most of all, Sammy, Lord. Help her to forgive me."

Sammy never deserved the misery he'd put her through.

Why didn't he appreciate her? She'd left her teaching career, the passion of her life, and settled for the mundane duties of a pastor's wife. Yet she never complained.

Why had she sacrificed so much?

Because she loved you, you idiot. She would have gone to the moon for him. And look what he did. Allowed that Deidra to kiss him. Not once. But twice.

What kind of man was he?

Drugs ruined him. But was he still addicted? He had no desire to take them again. It had been two days since his last dose. He held out a hand, looked at it. Rock steady. Not a tremor or quiver to be seen. It had to be a miracle. There was no other way to explain it.

Wide awake, Dalton felt a tug in his spirit to pray for each family member. He got to his feet and headed to the staircase. When he reached the landing, he entered the master bedroom. Curled up in a sleeveless nightie, Sammy had her back to him. Without touching her, he positioned his hand over her head and prayed silently. *Give her back to me, Father. Show me what to do.* He prayed another ten minutes then left the room.

No surprise his son's door was locked. Dalton pressed his hand against the wood and whispered, "Thank You for Gordy. I don't deserve such a son." He confessed his inadequacy as a father. He admitted again that his addiction had blinded him to the most formative years of his son's life. "Time is short, Father. Restore what the locusts have eaten."

Grace's door was wide open. Dalton couldn't wait to plant kisses on her cheeks.

He entered her room, and stopped.

Her bed was empty.

What ...?

He looked around, making sure. Oh! ... the flashlight he'd left for a nightlight. It was gone. Where could she be? Where would Grace go in the middle of the night, with a flashlight that had to be dimming with low batteries?

Maybe to see her grandmother? He hurried down the stairs and tapped lightly on the office door.

It took two raps before she stirred.

"Just a minute," Shirley said. The door creaked open. She'd thrown on her robe and carried a LED lantern. Her hair was chaotic and her eyes barely open.

"Sorry, Shirl ... uh ... Mom. Is Grace with you?"

"No, son." The wave of the light affirmed what Dalton didn't want to see. The other side of the hide-a-bed was empty. Shirley strode to the kitchen and he followed.

"I just came from there," Dalton called after her. "She's not downstairs."

"Look on the patio. She loves looking at the moon."

They both searched the backyard without success.

"I'll check the garage," he said. "Would you look in the living room?"

"I'm on it." His mother-in-law headed inside.

Dalton shone a light around the stacked boxes that nearly reached the garage ceiling as he called Grace's name. When he got back to the patio, he heard Shirley call him.

He found her peering through the double-door entryway.

"It was open," she said.

They followed the walkway, aiming their lights. Grace's Barbie doll lay face-down on the cement.

He picked it up.

A chill chased up his spine and air stalled in his lungs.

"Sammy! Wake up. Grace is missing!" Dalton shook his wife's shoulders. He couldn't believe the words even as he said them. Where could their little girl be?

"Grace? What do you mean she's missing?" Sammy leaped out of bed and hurried to the landing, shouting the girl's name as she ran. After she inspected the empty bedroom, Sammy knocked on their son's door.

"Gordy?" She pounded louder. "Gordy, open up!"

The door opened. Gordy rubbed his eyes as Sammy pushed past. Dalton followed. She grabbed his flashlight and scanned the carpeted room, strewn with books and dirty clothes.

"Where could she be?" Sammy flew down the stairs. Dalton followed. Gordy and Shirley behind, Gordy shouting, "What's going on?"

At the bottom of the stairs, Sammy called their daughter as she ran from the living room to the kitchen to the den.

"Listen to me, Sam!" Dalton hollered. But she was a whirlwind, blowing in and out of every room, every corner of the house, intent on rousting out a small girl.

Sammy emerged from the den and dashed to the breakfast room, shouting, "She's not here!"

"Slow down, Sammy!" Dalton reached for her arm.

She stopped. Twisted around, glared at him. "What?"

"Mom and I think she went outside." He pointed to the open entryway, then handed her the Barbie. "I found this on the pavement."

"Why didn't you say something?" Sammy grabbed the doll and blew past him. He and the others ran after her.

When he got outside, Sammy was frantically waving a flashlight near the paloverde trees on the edge of the driveway. "Grace!" she screamed. "Grace ... where are you?" Her mother headed toward her.

Dalton wheeled around to check the opposite side of the house. He turned to Gordy. "Let's search around your mom's cactus garden."

They sprinted through the dark, jumping over shrubs to an eclectic collection of cactus planted near living room windows. "Gordy. Look." Dalton stooped and shined his flashlight to be sure. Yes. Adult-size footprints marked a muddy trail that looped through his wife's prized Century plants.

They followed the prints through the prickly plants. "Watch out, Dad," Gordy said, pointing to a jumping Cholla. They carefully navigated around the deadly bush.

Dalton froze. His heart hammered. "Oh, no." He pointed to the screen leaning against a shrub. Dalton swept the area with his flashlight. A cigarette butt poked out of a cakey footprint. Someone had been here, peering through his window. Standing ... watching ... long enough to finish a cigarette.

"Go get Mom and your grandmother, quick!" he ordered his son.

Gordy took off running, yelling, "Mom ... Grams ... over here!"

Realization walloped him. The window was wide open and his daughter was missing.

Oh Lord! Where's Grace? Help us, God. The nightmare he had in the E.R. flashed through his mind. "God ... please ... let her be okay."

This couldn't be happening. Not to Grace. Not to Sammy.

Was this his punishment? Would—he gulped—Grace die? Was this what he got for depriving Matt of his last hours with Charity? Was this divine retribution? Would Grace pay for her father's sins?

Words echoed through his head.

You deserve this.

You earned this.

This will end badly.

He shook himself. He had to stop it, pull himself together.

Stop listening to that voice. It wasn't God's voice. It was the enemy.

He pushed away all the thoughts, all the voices. He looked up at the starry sky. "I refuse to think that way. I know You've forgiven me," he said. "Please, Father. Please. Help me find her."

Moments later his family joined him, their frenzied light beams scoping the ground.

When Sammy saw the screen and open window, she pressed the Barbie to her chest and fell to the ground, screaming at the heavens. "Gra a a a c e! Dalton ... someone took my baby!"

Dalton ran to her, caught her arms and pulled her up. For a moment, she let him hold her. But only a moment. She wiggled free.

"Dad ... Mom ... what happened to Grace?" Gordy's voice cracked.

"This can't be," Shirley said.

"What, Grams?" Gordy asked again. "What can't be?"

"Grace's gone, son." Dalton pointed. "The window's wide open and there are footprints here."

Gordy stuck his face through the opening and looked, then twisted around. "We've got to call the cops, Dad. Now!"

"The phones don't work," Sammy said. "We'll drive into town."

Shirley emerged from the darkness, handing Dalton a bottle. "I found it over there." She pointed to a barberry bush.

Dalton held it up and read the label. Desert Durum. The same kind he'd swigged in the mountains. From the bottle he'd taken from Matt.

His mind raced, connecting dots. Matt in the neighborhood earlier that day. The muddy footprints. The cigarette butt. Now, the liquor bottle. The knowledge firmed in his gut like concrete setting on a July day.

"Remember that fight I had with Matt Connor at the bus stop?" he asked. "He hit me with a whiskey bottle. This is the same brand."

"So?" Sammy asked.

She didn't see it. But he did. He knew the truth as well as he knew how undeserving he was of God's forgiveness. "Matt took Grace."

"That can't be ..." Sammy's head shook.

"He told me he'd get even." Dalton never imagined it would be something like this. "The man's crazy. Come on, Gordy. Let's go."

"Not without me," Sammy said.

Dalton shook his head. "It's too dangerous."

"You don't get a vote. I'm going." She strode away, her back stiff with resolve.

"Take her with you, Dalton," Shirley said. "Gordy and I will go to the police station."

Within minutes his family had dressed, and collected car keys.

By the time Dalton opened the VW's passenger door and tucked his loaded Ruger into his pocket, Sammy had started the engine. He hopped into the seat as she revved the motor before slamming it into first gear and barreling through the rocky gravel.

"We'll find her, honey." Dalton touched her arm. She didn't react, but shifted to second, leaving a wake of flying rock behind them. Dalton looked out the back window. Gordy and his grandmother kept a safe distance from airborne stones as they followed in the Olds.

ଇଓ

Samantha squinted through the windshield. The streets of McCormick were dark and ominous, the perfect mirror to her mood.

Good thing Dalton hadn't spoken since they'd left the house. They'd had a tender moment back there when he'd held her, but as she drove through the blackened town, she ruminated through the past few days, becoming more and more angry. The man beside her had destroyed their marriage and now their daughter might be in the hands of a mad man.

"You haven't missed the turn, have you?" Dalton interrupted her thoughts.

"I know where I'm going." She spoke through a clenched jaw.

"Left on Jefferson. Two intersections, then left again."

"I *know*. I've been there a hundred times." She bit her lip and tried to quell her emotions but finally let go. She turned to him and ground out, "If anything happens to Grace, I'll never forgive you."

He didn't look at her but hung his head.

"You've destroyed everything, Dalton. I'm not sure I even love you anymore."

There. She said it out loud. He needed to hurt the way she hurt.

Silence ensued and she scrubbed a hand over her face. Why had she said that now? *Please don't hold this against me, Lord,* she prayed. *Find Grace. Please!*

Dalton twisted toward her. His expression was clouded with sadness. "I get your feelings, Sammy. I only hope that's not true."

"If you hadn't ripped people off and hurt that grieving father, God wouldn't be punishing me."

"That's what you think?"

"Of course." She pressed the brake as they approached Caliente Drive.

"He's not punishing you."

"Sure feels like it." Sammy stopped, scanned both sides of the intersection before easing the Volkswagen through. "Our family's lost everything. And now ... Grace ... I don't want to think what could happen to her. God must have turned His back or this wouldn't—" She swallowed the threatening sob.

"God loves you, Sammy."

"I don't feel loved." *By you or God.* But she didn't say the last part out loud.

"He's not to blame for what I did. He gave us free will. I abused it."

She lifted a hand to stop him. "Don't, Dalton. Just don't."

Life made no sense.

She stopped at Desperado and turned left.

Hadn't she been faithful? Hadn't she served other people? Hadn't she given to the needy? And what was her reward? An addict and a thief for a husband and now her innocent daughter in the hands of a lunatic. How was that fair? How was that deserved? How was that just?

CHAPTER FIFTY-THREE

Thursday, 2:35 a.m.
Connor Home

"PARK THERE." DALTON POINTED to the ranch-style home next to the Connor's. Sammy pulled the VW along a stone wall that hugged the circular driveway. The stretch of desert separating the residences would hopefully conceal their approach. Dalton patted the gun in his pocket, grabbed a flashlight from the floor, then faced his wife.

"Would you pray with me?" he asked.

"Of course." Her tone, while more conciliatory than earlier, was hardly inviting. But she agreed. He'd take it.

He took her hands in his and pleaded for help from on High.

Once he was done, Sammy snapped her hands back and climbed out of the van. Dalton followed her through the field using the flashlight to navigate around the cactus. When they reached the Connor's driveway, he turned off the light.

"Stay here," he said in the calmest voice he could manage.

"Don't tell me what to do."

He let out a heavy sigh. He deserved this, but could she put it on hold? At least for the time being. "Can you *please* keep watch over there?" Dalton gestured toward a stone wall sandwiched between the front window and the entryway.

She walked to the wall and leaned against it. She stared at him with her best fight face, but her trembling betrayed her. "I feel useless here. I need to find her."

"I know, hon. But having a second set of eyes will help," he encouraged.

Dalton crept through the carport. He recognized Matt's old Buick with a tent trailer hitched behind. He took guarded steps as sweat dribbled inside his t-shirt. Seeing a beam from a flashlight, Dalton dove in front of the wagon's front bumper.

Peering past the headlight, he saw Matt coming his way. Dalton twisted around, rushed to the car's opposite side and crouched in some weeds near a fence. He crawled toward the back. The tent camper leaned to one side.

Creak! The sound of a door opening startled him. He popped his head up and peeked. Matt disappeared into a shed behind the camper. Dalton flicked on his light and looked through the trailer's window. Several boxes towered to the canvas ceiling. From the black letter labeling they contained food and camping supplies. The one that said "Charity's clothes" filled him with dread. What was this man up to? Goose flesh spread across his arms. His fingers tingled as he gripped the gun and switched off the light.

When Matt appeared at the camper's door, Dalton ducked, gripping the Ruger.

ഇരു

Dread crawled up Samantha's arms and snaked around her chest. She was wasting time out here doing nothing. She had to find Grace. She peered around the corner into a long driveway. Matt's station wagon was parked near the back. Dalton was nowhere in sight.

She stood a moment in indecision, then hurried around to the opposite side of the house. Yes, just as she'd hoped. A wooden gate led to the backyard. Except when she fished for a latch, she found a padlock.

Samantha sucked in a deep breath and hoisted herself, only to fall backwards, landing in a muddy puddle. She got up, wiped away the sludge on her backside, then took a running leap. She pulled herself to the top, scraping her stomach. She gritted her teeth, toppled over, slammed her sore knee against pavement.

Samantha smothered her cry of pain, got to her feet, and hobbled toward the backyard.

Rounding a corner, she scanned the yard. She'd been here often, including several of Charity's too few birthday parties. Samantha swallowed the knot in her throat. She'd grieve Charity again when Grace was safe.

A sliding glass door near the patio framed one side of the Connors's family room. She tugged at the locked screen, then meshed her face against it and peered through. Nothing moved inside.

She turned to the yard again, searching for another option. The bright red Dutch door caught her eye. The back door that led to the kitchen. Relief swept over her. She skirted a patio table, then twisted the doorknob. Unlocked. Relief and elation flooded her in equal measure as she slipped into the laundry room.

ഇരു

What was that? Matt turned his head toward a scraping noise near the Buick. Probably a cat but he couldn't take any chances. Not with his precious girl asleep inside. He returned to the shed and once inside, got to his knees, then slithered on the ground like a rattler ready to strike. He used the camper as a shield.

Glancing past the trailer hitch, he could make out a man's shadow. A man who seemed to hold something in his hands. A gun?

Matt needed a weapon. A stack of used brick, remains from an old bar-b-que pit, was piled near the fence. Thank God he hadn't caved to Carla's pleas about dumping it. He grabbed a brick, studied his target, and heaved it at the stranger's head.

Crack! The intruder toppled over, a deep groan oozed from his lips. Served him right.

Matt straddled the man's body and seized the gun from his limp hand. He tipped the man's face into the moonlight.

Baxter!

He pushed the unconscious minister's head into the dirt. Should he press the man's nose and mouth into the ground, smothering him? Let his lungs fill with dirt, like Charity's filled with fluid as she died? Matt closed his eyes for a moment, imagining the feeling, the power, the revenge.

Too bad there was no time. If Baxter knew his plans there was a good chance others did too. Waiting till morning was no longer an option. He had to find Carla and leave before sunup.

ꕥ

Moonlight spilled through the kitchen window. Samantha inched her way forward, crouching across ceramic tile. When she reached the end of the granite island, she peered into the family room. A small form, covered with a quilt, slept on the Connor's sofa. Slivers of moonlight splashed over the patchwork. Long golden curls glistened in the light.

Grace!

She hurried to the sleeping child and placed a hand on her arm. "Grace!" She spoke softly but with urgency. "Honey, wake up!"

"Mommy?" Grace rubbed her eyes. Samantha scooped her baby into her arms and hugged her tight. "Come on, we have to hurry." She took her daughter's hand, pulled her to her feet, toward the sliding glass window.

"Be very quiet, Grace," Samantha whispered.

"Stop!"

Samantha spun around. Matt loomed in the shadows, pointing a gun at them. Samantha shoved Grace behind her.

"Give me my daughter!" he commanded. "Now!"

His daughter? The man had gone over the edge, delusional in his grief. "Matt ..." She'd have to tread lightly. Where was Dalton? Was that Dalton's gun Matt waved toward her? *Oh, God, help us!*

"Matt. This isn't Charity. This is Grace. *My* daughter."

Matt moved closer, aiming the pistol. Yes, Dalton's Ruger.

Terror tightened her throat, strangling her breath. "What have you done with Dalton?"

He ignored her. He leaned to the side, looking for Grace still behind Samantha. "Come to Daddy, Charity-bug."

"No!" Grace's nails clawed through the skin on Samantha's arms. "Don't let him take me! Please, Mommy!"

Samantha kept Grace behind her and took a step back. Steeling her voice, she said, "Matt ... this is Grace, *my* little girl. Charity ... your Charity ... I'm so s-sorry, s-she ... passed away. On Sunday. She was so sick, and then she couldn't fight any longer. Do you remember Sunday?"

His blinking eyes darted back and forth, wild and lined with red circles.

"Where's Dalton?" Samantha gentled her voice and asked again.

Matt shook his head as if shaking off her words. "Give her to me and I won't hurt you."

"No, Matt." She straightened her shoulders and braced herself.

"Let her go!" He leaped at her, reaching for Grace's arm. Grace shrieked and slapped his hands.

Dalton suddenly appeared behind him, blood leaking from his scalp. He dived forward, looped a cord around Matt's neck, then wrenched him to the floor. The Ruger flew toward the kitchen. Dalton cinched the rope. Matt coughed and clawed at his windpipe.

"Get Grace out of here, Sammy. Fine the gun," Dalton yelled.

Samantha tugged Grace's hand and dashed to the kitchen. "Quick! Go to the laundry room and stay!." Her daughter obediently hurried to the smaller room and slammed the door.

Crawling on the floor, trying to see in the dark room, Samantha frantically scavenged the floor with her hands. She patted the area, her injured knee protesting. "I can't find it."

"Here." Dalton rolled her his flashlight. Matt moaned, clutching his neck, writhing on the floor.

Seconds ticked by as she swept the light around. Finally, there, under one of the stools at the counter. She grabbed it, thrust it at Dalton.

Matt wheezed for air.

"He can't breathe," she said. "We don't want him to die. Not like this."

Dalton eased the tension. Matt gasped, tugging the cord.

"What should I do?" Samantha asked.

"Check the trailer outside for something to tie him up with," Dalton said.

Samantha joined Grace in the laundry room and opened the back door. "Wait here on the patio."

"No, Mommy, don't leave me, I'm scared."

Samantha's heart broke at the fear in her little girl's voice. She crouched before Grace. "I know, sweetie. I'm scared, too. But I need you to be brave for just another minute. You'll be safe, I promise. I'll be right back. Okay?"

Grace met her gaze then nodded. "Okay."

Samantha hugged Grace for a quick moment, then released her and hurried toward the camper.

When she made it to the driveway, she heard Gordy calling.

"Dad? Mom? Where are you?"

"Over here," Samantha answered.

Moments later Gordy and his grandmother arrived near the camper, brandishing flashlights.

"Gordy, Dad's got Matt inside but he needs rope. Can you find some?" Samantha pointed to the tent trailer.

Gordy opened the camper and disappeared inside.

"What happened? Where's Grace?" Shirley asked.

"She's safe. Follow me." Samantha led the way to the patio. When her mother saw Grace, she ran to her, planted kisses on her face. "Are you okay, sweetheart?"

"No ..." Grace's voice trembled and Shirley pulled her close.

"Dalton needs me." Samantha took the car keys from her pocket and handed them to her mother. "Take Grace to the van. Lock it. We'll be there as soon as we can."

Shirley took Grace's hand and disappeared around the corner.

ຣ໑ଊ

Inside, Dalton clenched the gun, pointing it at Matt's back. Crumpled on the floor, the man groped at his throat. Dalton had loosened the noose, so Matt wouldn't asphyxiate, but refused to set him free.

Sammy strode to Dalton's side. She gaped at his head. "Are you okay?" she asked.

"Just a flesh wound, I'll be fine. Did you find any rope?" Dalton asked.

"Gordy's looking for it."

"Where's your mom?"

"She took Grace to the van."

"Good move," Dalton said.

Seconds later Gordy joined them with some coiled parachute cord.

Dalton transferred the gun Gordy. "Watch him."

Matt's breathing seemed steady, though shallow. Dalton turned Matt face down, straddled his legs and sat on the backs of his knees. He grabbed his wrists and bound them, then removed the garrote from his neck. He helped Matt to his feet, then guided him to the couch, where he pushed him into the cushions.

"Where's Carla?" Dalton demanded.

Matt glared, hatred oozing from his eyes and his sneer. "She left. Yesterday. Thanks to you."

"Where?"

"I don't know." Matt shook his head. "One of her church friends, I guess."

"Why did you take our daughter?"

"Your daughter?" Puzzlement flashed across his face. "I didn't take your daughter."

"Yes, Matt," Sammy spoke up. "You kidnapped Grace. Don't you remember?"

"Grace?" Matt looked from Dalton to Sammy, then to Gordy, as if wanting them each to argue the point. "Are you sure?"

"Of course we're sure." Gordy scowled, waving the firearm. "You better not have hurt my sister!"

"Calm down, son," Dalton said. "She's okay."

"When we couldn't find her, we were terrified." Sammy's voiced hitched.

Dalton got to within a foot of Matt's face and glared. Matt stared back with unblinking eyes. Something must be wrong with him. Normal, sane men don't kidnap little girls, then not remember it.

"Why did you take her?" Dalton asked again.

It was as if Matt suddenly recognized who spoke to him. A sadistic smile twisted his lips. "I wanted you to suffer."

"By stealing my daughter?" Heat climbed into his cheeks.

"You stole mine!" Matt shouted. "You took the last hours I would ever have with her! You deserve to suffer. You deserve to lose your daughter!"

Dalton's mouth dropped open. This whole horrible night was his fault. The reality of what he had done came crashing down on him. His own selfishness, destroyed his family, hurt his friends, but most of all it had robbed a father something incalculable. Time.

"Matt ... you're right." Dalton's voice cracked. "I'm so sorry." He shook his head as tears threatened. He collapsed next to Matt on the couch and wrapped his arms around him. Matt's body stiffened. Dalton let Matt go and wiped his face with the back of his hand.

He searched Matt's eyes. "You must be in hell right now. I can't begin to imagine your pain."

How could he undo the havoc he'd created?

What can I do, Lord?

I give grace to the humble.

Dalton fell to his knees. Matt's eye's shot daggers.

"Can you forgive me, Matt? I was wrong and I'm so sorry."

Matt's face ever so slightly shifted, his brows relaxed, taut lips loosened. "I ... uh ... don't know," Matt said.

"I understand, Matt. You need time." Dalton got to his feet and turned to Sammy, her eyes wide. "Is it okay if we don't press charges?"

"What? No!" She shook her head. "He took our child, Dalton!"

"This will kill Carla, Sammy. She's suffered enough."

Her gaze softened. "I guess we could take him to the police station. If they decide to charge him, that will be their call." She walked to the couch and stood in front of Matt. "Okay, Matt. We won't press charges but we can't leave you free, able to try again."

"Grams and I just came from there," Gordy said. "It's locked and dark. No cops anywhere."

Dalton considered a moment, then decided. "We'll take him home. I'll figure out what to do in the morning."

Sammy spun around. "He's not coming to our house near my daughter!"

"I'll guard him all night. I'll lock him in the pool house." He gave Sammy his most encouraging look. "I won't let anything happen."

"It'll take two of us to watch him, Dad. I'll help," Gordy said.

"Thanks, son." Dalton retrieved the gun from Gordy, then fastened the safety before jamming it into his back pocket. They led Matt to the kitchen, then filed outside.

Gordy illumined a path through the dark carport as everyone followed. Dalton brought up the rear, behind Matt. After they reached the van, he used the lap belt to secure Matt in the front seat.

"I'll take Grace and ride with Mom," Sammy said. She took Grace's hand and followed her mom to the Olds.

When Gordy scrambled to the back seat, Dalton started the engine, wedging the Ruger between his thighs. Matt hung his head and leaned against the window. Dalton's breathing eased. Matt no longer seemed threatening.

His headlamps pierced the darkness of Desperado Lane. Dalton followed Shirley's car thinking of the irony of the moment. He'd never felt less desperate, more free, lighter. The lack of electricity or even a job, no longer mattered. He had his daughter back.

CHAPTER FIFTY-FOUR

3:27 a.m.
Baxter Home

DALTON ENTERED THE KITCHEN, TOED off his sneakers. Of all the things he'd thought he may do in his lifetime, tying up his former drug dealer would not have made it to the list.

"Where's Mr. Connor?" Gordy asked as Dalton washed his hands.

"In the pool house. He's secure." Dalton looked at Sammy who stirred a cup of tea. "It's past three. I thought you'd be asleep by now."

"I'm too wired to sleep. Having Matt here makes me nervous. Do you really think this is a good idea?" she asked.

Her gaze met his and his heart skipped a beat. Please don't let him imagine it. She almost looked like she wanted to rely on him. Depend on his strength to keep them safe. She looked ... hopeful.

He spoke softly. "We talked it out. He'll be fine, trust me."

"Trust you?" Her voice notched. Her gentle expression turned skeptical. "Trust you that the delusional man who just kidnapped our daughter is now thinking rationally? Trust you that your drug dealer is sorry for terrifying a seven-year-old girl? Are you kidding?"

Any defensive response on his part wouldn't serve him well. He deserved no one's trust, least of all hers. "Sammy ... I plan to watch him all night."

Sammy shrugged and turned to face the sink, then began scrubbing a dirty pot. Angry strikes against metal spoke volumes.

"Find some pillows and blankets," Dalton told Gordy.

When his son left, he scrounged through the pantry, retrieving a six-pack of water and some energy bars.

"Not those." Sammy pointed to the bars.

"Why not?"

"Perishable food only."

That made sense. "What do you have?"

She opened the freezer and rummaged through ice cube maker. She handed him a package of cheddar cheese and a container of juice. She topped the cheese with two ripe bananas.

Gordy returned, carrying the bedding.

Father and son took the supplies and left through the patio door.

Dalton paused by the pool. “Get some sleep, Gordy. I can handle this.”

“Don’t you need my help?”

“I’ll take it from here.” He took the bedding from Gordy, tucked it under his arm and made his way to the pool house. He untied Matt’s wrist rope, releasing him from the steel rack that held pool equipment. “Sorry I had to do that. Sammy’s freaked out.” He handed Matt a blanket and a pillow, then stuffed the rope into his pocket. “I’ll be right outside if you need anything.”

Matt nodded but didn’t say anything. Dalton closed the door behind him.

Gordy had apparently ignored his suggestion about going to bed. He found him sitting on a lawn chair gesturing proudly to the chaise lounge nearby. He’d made it into a bed, covering it with one of Gram’s quilts. A pillow was perched at one end.

“Thanks.” Dalton adjusted the chair to a sitting position, then sat down. “Get some shut-eye,” he told him again. “I need you awake tomorrow.”

Gordy reached for Dalton’s hand and dropped something hard into it. “If something happens, blow this and I’ll be right down. I’ve got your back, Dad,” he said as he stood. Gordy turned and walked to the house.

Dalton held up the metal object and smiled. Attached to a nylon lanyard was Gordy’s scout whistle from the time he’d been a Cub. A lump climbed into his throat. Those days of father and son innocence seemed so long ago. He remembered his prayer, asking God to restore their relationship. Gordy seemed different tonight. Helpful. No longer angry.

Maybe this was the beginning.

CHAPTER FIFTY-FIVE

4:15 a.m.
Baxter Home

SAMANTHA SWIPED SWEAT FROM HER forehead, then adjusted a pillow behind her neck. August temperatures smothered their ranch home with suffocating misery as a layer of hot air clung to the second floor.

Sleep escaped. Her muscles screamed for relief.

Gracie, sprawled on top of the sheets, slept next to her. Samantha watched her child's chest rise and fall in the shadows.

She redirected her attention to a motionless ceiling fan. Her mind whirled with scattered thoughts about what had happened during the last two days.

It seemed like a blur of unbelievable events.

Dalton's betrayal. Followed by horrific events that had stolen both their 21st century existence and their precious daughter. Then the miracle of finding her unharmed!

A sliver of morning broke through the window stirring Samantha from a deep sleep. The old Timex on her wrist told her it was almost seven. She'd slept about three hours. Not wonderful but enough to enable her to function.

Gracie, curled up, her knees to her stomach had nestled close to her side. Samantha kissed her cheek and got out of bed. Her daughter should be out for hours. The child must be exhausted.

She went to the bathroom, pulled off her tee shirt and grabbed a wet sponge from plastic bucket. She squeezed it out and wiped her body, then wash her face and brushed her teeth, before climbing into some Capri's and a tank top. She padded down the staircase to the kitchen to begin breakfast.

Melting ice from the freezer preserved a mixture of meat that included bacon, steak, and hamburger patties. Samantha grabbed the grub, then quickly shut the door. She doubted what was left would be any good tomorrow so cooking the remaining chicken drumsticks and thighs should be done today before the church meeting. Sharing the remaining perishables with congregants would be better than tossing them in the trash.

Samantha stacked the meat on a cookie sheet and retrieved a box of pancake mix from the pantry. She measured the flour mixture into a glass bowl, then grabbed the last two eggs from the freezer. When she cracked them open, the yellow yokes stopped her. Such ordinary ingredients would be hard to find from now on. She whirled the batter with a metal whisk, collected her cooking utensils and a potholder and headed outside.

Twenty minutes later a pot of coffee steamed on the Coleman next to a pan of sizzling meat. The back two burners contained the batch of pancakes cooking on a long griddle.

Samantha checked her watch.

Nine a.m. Her morning routine certainly slowed due to the lack of power.

She turned at the sound at someone coughing. His back to her, Dalton sat on a chaise lounge near the pool. Samantha plopped down the spatula and headed his way. As she came up behind him, she paused. His Bible lay open on his lap.

The memory of him weeping in Matt's arms filled her thoughts. Dalton now seemed lost in thought, guarding the pool house. Just as he promised.

"Breakfast is ready," she announced.

He startled, looked up at her and smiled. "Good morning, Sammy."

"I hope it will be good. Have you checked on Matt?"

"I loaned him some clothes. He's getting dressed. I'll bring him inside." Dalton set the Bible down and headed to the pool house door. He cracked it open stuck his head in.

She picked up the Bible and flipped it over.

Psalm 51. One of her favorites.

A smile tugged at her lips. She shouldn't be surprised Dalton had gleaned strength from the Psalm's author. King David had done some horrible things and this particular psalm memorialized one of his greatest failures. Yet God forgave David fully and completely and restored David to his position of honor and even called him a *"man after My own heart."* If God forgave her husband, could she? She shoved away the thought. *I'm not ready.*

She placed the Bible on the lounger, then hurried to the make-shift kitchen. She stacked the cooked food on a cookie sheet. When she looked up, Dalton had an arm draped over Matt's shoulder and both headed her way. Whatever they'd talked about during the night had closed the gap between hatred and forgiveness. She shook her head, unsure if she could excuse either of the men who would sit at her table.

The last time she'd checked, Samantha found Gracie playing in the den with her rescued Barbie. It was like last night hadn't even happened. Gracie, lost in play seemed she hadn't a care in the world. She dressed the doll in beach attire and placed it in a pink car. Its tiny vinyl hands, perched on the steering wheel while Barbie's boyfriend, Ken, sat in the passenger seat. Their plastic smiles seemed to mock what was going on in the real world.

"What's cookin', Mom?"

Startled, Samantha looked up. Gordy appeared on the patio.

"Hopefully a good breakfast that'll keep you all satisfied for awhile."

He looked around the backyard.

"Matt's at the breakfast table. Where's Dad?"

"Probably upstairs getting dressed." Samantha's throat tightened. Hearing Matt was alone downstairs only feet away from Grace, the cause.

"Help me, would you?" She handed Gordy the trays of meat and pancakes, then grabbed her supplies and a pot of coffee before hurrying inside.

When they arrived in the kitchen, Matt and Dalton were seated at a long folding table Gordy had dragged in from the garage. She gave Dalton a questioning stare. Was it really a good idea to eat with Matt? Dalton returned a silent *it'll be okay* look before she left to find her mother and Grace. *Please God, let him be right.*

ജ്യ

Window light splashed across the honey-colored walls and Dalton's heart warmed as he studied his family enjoying pancakes and hot coffee as they had often done after church on Sundays. Other than being Thursday and having no electricity, the morning felt normal. Sammy seemed like her old self. She'd even offered Matt more coffee and filled his cup for him. Hope tinged his spirit for the first time in a long while. Maybe God was answering his prayers. Was Sammy beginning to forgive him?

An unexplainable joy surged through his insides as Dalton listened to the interchanges between family members. It was like the old days. Before his selfish actions had almost ruined everything he treasured the most.

Gordy dialoged Matt, explaining the CME. Sammy, hands propped beneath her chin, seemed awestruck with Gordy's intelligence. The kid had an amazing mind and it was shame that not only his college education but his whole future was suddenly up in the air.

"Do you think our power will come on, Gordster?" Shirley asked.

"It's hard to say, Grams," Gordy answered. "It depends if the authorities can get the transformers online."

"I hate not having T.V.," Grace said. "Everything is boring."

"Reading is fun." Dalton winked at her. Grace crinkled her nose and grinned.

"I heard about this from an overseas broadcast on a short wave radio," Matt said. "Then Amanda Benson stopped by and confirmed it. Carla and I were out of our minds with Charity's death so I didn't give it much thought. I wish my phone worked. I'd give anything to talk to my wife."

"Do you know where she might be?" Sammy asked.

"One of her church friends told her Sunday that if she ever needed anything, to come over so I'm thinking it might be her."

"Laney?" Samantha hazarded a guess. Matt nodded. "She stayed with Carla at the hospital most of Sunday while I was in Prescott."

"Thanks to me," Dalton said. He checked Matt's expression. It was absent of anger.

"We've both made some huge mistakes, Dalton," Matt said. "We've decided to put this behind us, remember?"

Dalton hoped that was really true.

"I'll drive over to Laney's and see if she's there," Sammy said. "Maybe she'll come back with me."

"Really?" Matt asked, hope in his eyes. "You'd help me? Aft—after what I did?"

"It'll take awhile to trust you, Matt. But I talked to Grace. She told me you were very kind. That helps a lot."

"Thank you, Samantha. I don't deserve any of this." Matt gestured at the food. He scanned the table, looking at each person, his eyes flled. "I don't deserve your kindness." Everyone nodded. Dalton noticed Grace offering a big smile. Sammy's lips curved up slightly as she grabbed her purse and keys. It was a start.

"Gordy, go with Mom," Dalton said. "Stop by Matt's. Maybe Carla's come home."

ꙮ

Carla wasn't home. Samantha was grateful Gordy was with her as they searched through the Connor home. It was eerie and full of reminders of how close they'd come to disaster hours before.

They retrieved some of the boxed food that sat in the tent trailer. After all, they were feeding another mouth and he was no small eater. Matt had told them where to find the radio. Gordy packed it in the back of the van.

Samantha drove on Kaibab Road, looking for the Spring View exit. Laney and Martin would be surprised to see them. Hopefully Carla would be there.

She eased through the circular driveway and turned off the engine. Gordy followed her to the front door. She pressed the dead doorbell, then let out a long sigh. "Will I ever get used to this?" Gordy chuckled and knocked.

Laney swung the door open and smiled. "Samantha, Gordon ... good to see you. Is Dalton okay? Those drugs are some of the hardest to kick."

"He's better than expected, Laney." It had been a long couple of days. She had much to tell her friend. "Is Carla here?"

Laney motioned them in and said in a hushed tone, "She's outside. Been here since yesterday. Hasn't said much. Only that she needed some space from Matt."

"He's with us. I need to tell you something before I talk with Carla. Is there some place we can go?"

Laney looked at Gordy. "There's some lemonade in the kitchen, dear." Laney waved him to the next room. "Serve yourself. We'll be right back."

Samantha told Laney about Grace's abduction and the nightmare that occurred hours ago in Matt's family room.

Laney gasped. "Is Grace okay?"

"Surprisingly, she's doing well. Better than the rest of us, I'd say." Samantha smiled.

"Thank the Lord." Laney touched Samantha's arm, giving it a squeeze. "I'll stop by this afternoon. The welt on Dalton's head should be looked at. Being hit by a brick could cause some damage."

The women went to the kitchen. Gordy sat on a bar stool enjoying a tall glass of lemony brew.

"Sorry it's warm, son," Laney told him. "Our ice is gone. But the lemons are fresh squeezed from our backyard tree."

Gordy grinned and took another sip while Laney retrieved three glasses from her cupboard. "Carla's on the porch swing. Go talk to her and I'll bring the drinks," Laney said.

Outside, Samantha walked through a long, covered breezeway. Carla gently rocked, staring at a blue sky dotted with puffy clouds.

"Hi," Samantha said. Carla looked up but didn't smile.

Samantha sat next to her. "Are you okay? Matt said you might be here."

Carla glared. "Is it true, Samantha? Is Pastor D a drug addict?"

Samantha's heart stumbled. She had to admit the Dalton she'd been with these past few hours seemed different.

"I'm sorry, Carla." Her voice cracked. "I didn't know anything about this. My husband made some horrible choices and—and he's so sorry. He knows he's hurt many people."

"Matt hurt me." Carla's voice quivered. "He promised me. He betrayed me. How can I ever trust him again?"

Samantha understood. Trust commodities in her heart had gone negative last Sunday.

"We've both been through hard things." She reached for Carla's hand, gave it a squeeze. "You most of all. We can get through this together."

Carla's eyes filled. "I don't know what to do."

"You have many friends. There's a congregational meeting this evening. People want to help with the service on Saturday."

Carla nodded. "The church did so much already. They bought Charity's coffin."

Samantha knew that. She'd been the one to suggest it at the bereavement meeting.

Carla's eyes filled. "My little girl lays inside a box at the funeral hall. We've made no arrangements for the burial."

Laney appeared with three full glasses of lemonade on a serving tray. After handing them each one, she pulled up a lawn chair.

"I couldn't help but overhear," Laney said. "Martin and I discussed this last night. Charity can be buried in the church's graveyard."

"In the church yard?" Samantha had always been drawn to the little burial area behind the sanctuary. It contained about seventy plots from many of the church's founders and their respective families. Surely they could find room for a small child.

Peace fell over Carla's face. "That would be perfect. I'd love to think of Charity there, close to the church where she accepted Jesus and sang worship songs to Him."

"I'll send one of the men over to the funeral home today. We'll make the arrangements. You don't have to worry about anything," Samantha said.

"Can I see her before ..." Carla couldn't seem to get the words out.

"We'll settle that with Mr. Copeland," Laney said. "I'm sure it won't be a problem."

Carla seemed better, less agitated, under a slim smile when she took a sip of lemonade.

"Matt is with us, Carla. He would like to see you."

She stared at her glass. "I'm not sure I can right now."

Samantha gulped her drink. "He's hurting too. He needs you."

"May I say something?" Laney asked.

Carla shrugged. "Okay."

Laney leaned forward, placed a hand on Carla's knee. "What you and Matt have shouldered these past few days is impossible. The shock and grief would do anyone in. Adding anger to that mix will could devastate even the strongest marriage." She paused and searched Carla's expression. "Can you put aside your emotions? At least for the next few days. You and Matt need each other desperately."

Carla sighed deeply. “I already miss him. Even if I’m mad at him.” She slowly got to her feet. “Let me get my things and I’ll follow you, Samantha.”

After thanking Laney, Samantha remembered to ask her something. “Today’s meeting’s at the church is at five-thirty. How are people finding out?”

“I’ve got a team gathering in an hour. We’re going door to door, letting congregants know.”

“Great,” Samantha said. “Tell everyone it’s potluck and to bring perishable food only.”

Laney assured Samantha she would and gave her a hug.

“See you soon,” Samantha said. She called Gordy from the kitchen and they followed Carla out the front door. Relief washed over her as they got in their respective cars. Carla seemed a lot more open to reconciliation than Samantha had imagined. But Matt had yet to tell her about what he’d done last night, how he’d kidnapped Grace. That might change everything.

Samantha put the car in gear and backed out of the Fernández’s driveway wondering if Matt would truly take responsibility for his actions. And how would Carla respond to another betrayal and possibly another felony?

God, we need you. Please go before us.

CHAPTER FIFTY-SIX

11:00 a.m.
Baxter Home

Matt washed his hair in a plastic tub filled with pool water, then rubbed his chest with a sponge. Once he'd eliminated the grime and sweat from the day before, pulled back his hair into a pony tail and slipped on the same shirt Dalton had given him earlier. He tugged on some jeans that were too long so he rolled up the cuffs. No matter how much he cleaned up, he felt blemished and unacceptable. He couldn't erase what he'd done and how close he'd come to doing the unthinkable. What kind of maniac takes another man's child?

If Carla came, he'd be ready.

Samantha had made it quite clear before she left that he was to tell Carla about the kidnapping. He would do his best but as much as he rehearsed it over and over in his mind, nothing he came up with would ever convince Carla to forgive him. How could she when he couldn't even forgive himself?

ꕥ

"Matt's on the patio," Dalton said as Sammy, Carla, and Gordy walked through the front door. Carla looked down at the floor as she passed him. Dalton didn't blame her one bit.

Samantha suddenly stopped and turned to face Carla, "Before you see him you should know something. What happened these past twenty-four hours is over. Dalton and I have put this behind us. Please hear him out."

Sammy had put it behind her? Dalton hadn't heard her say it until now.

"What did he do?" Carla's brows furrowed.

"He'll explain." Samantha gave her a quick hug. "We'll talk later."

Looking over her shoulder at them, Carla left through the sliding glass door.

"After I'm done filling buckets for the toilets, can I go to the Brewster's?" Gordy's voice broke through the silence. "I can tell them about the meeting."

"Be sure to take water upstairs," Dalton said. "I don't want your mom doing that."

"Okay, I'm on it."

"Also, check the pool cover, then you can go," Dalton said.

Gordy didn't waste any time retrieving his keys from the kitchen hook. He sprinted past them both toward the outside well.

"I need you and your van here by three," Dalton called as Gordy opened the front door. "We've got to load extra chairs for tonight's meeting."

"Sure, Dad," Gordy said.

"He seems anxious to do his chores," Dalton said.

"Hormones do that." Sammy smiled.

"Huh?"

"Are you blind, Dalton?"

"Well ... yeah ... lately I have been. Did I miss something?"

"Bethany Brewster. Haven't you seen what is going on between she and our son?"

"No, not really. What's up?"

Sammy rolled her eyes. "Men. You're clueless."

"Gordy ... Bethany? They're good friends, right?"

"Bethany isn't just Gordy's childhood buddy. She's grown into quite a young woman this past year and I think your son is love-struck."

Gordy was finally looking at girls? Dalton had often wondered if his son could ever get his nose out of a book long enough to do so.

Dalton had been so wrapped up in his own problems, this bit of news hadn't been on his radar. Though he'd missed the budding romance, his son's maturity was certainly apparent. Gordy became a man in a matter of days.

ജ്ഷ

Carla sat under the pool umbrella in shorts and a t-shirt, looking nervous. Matt studied her knotted hands she tried to hide between her knees as they sipped lukewarm tea. Though he'd apologized again for lying to her about dealing, he still hadn't told her what else he had done.

"There's something more," he finally said.

"I thought so." She inhaled deeply. "What did you do?"

He described the kidnapping and all that went on in her home. Her eyes got as big as saucers and she scooted forward on her chair, like she was a bird about to take flight.

"I hit Dalton with a brick. I'm surprised he doesn't have a concussion."

"I can't believe this," she said. She wagged her head and just stared at him.

"I lost it. After losing Charity, I needed someone to blame. Dalton was a good target. I wanted to drive a knife into his heart."

Her mouth dropped open.

"When he jumped me and nearly strangled me, I came to my senses."

"He strangled you?"

"That guy's pretty good with a lasso. It's obvious he grew up on a horse ranch." He pointed to the rope burn across his neck.

"I couldn't bear seeing your broken heart," Matt continued. "I thought I would be a better dad to Grace than he could ever be, so I took her. I know this sounds insane. It does to me, too. I still can't believe I did this." Tears channeled down his cheeks. He shook between sobs.

Carla got up, but instead of running away, she approached him, pulled his face to her chest. "It's okay, Matt. Let it out, honey."

Matt convulsed several moments, trying to swallow, then he heard the steady thump-thump of Carla's heart. He pulled back to meet her gaze. "Grace is such a sweet girl ... but she could never replace Charity ... I know that. Now." His eyes locked with hers. "I miss my baby, Car. How can we go on?"

Carla's eyes filled with tears, too. "I don't know. I wish I did. I wish I had some answers." She ran a thumb down his cheek. "But Laney convinced me about something. I can't add my anger to the mix. The grief is too heavy. I can't carry anything else right now."

Matt looked at the ground as shame covered him like a hot blanket. "I hate myself right now."

"Shhh, baby. Don't say that." Carla pulled up his face, cupping his chin with her hand. "We're going to make it, Matt. God brought us friends. The real kind. They don't walk away when you're in trouble. They'll help us through this."

She tipped his chin. "I forgive you. So have the Baxters. You need to forgive yourself."

Matt hung his head. Was she right? Dalton and he had come to terms, but had Samantha really forgiven him?

"I'm going inside to see if Samantha needs any help," she said. "Are you coming?"

"I need another minute," he said.

Matt watched her walk away as Gordy entered the patio.

Gordy scrunched down near one end of the pool, finagling with the nylon ties.

Matt stared longingly at the pool. Temperatures had climbed to 106 degrees. He wished he could swim a few laps. But Gordy protected the water like a bank guard. Which made sense. The Olympic size concrete receptacle had become a Fort Knox of sorts, containing liquid gold.

Dalton and Samantha had raised a fine boy. Matt eyed the teenager. He hadn't stopped working since breakfast and never once complained. From the way they'd interacted at the table it seemed the boy had forgiven him for taking his sister. At least he hoped so.

CHAPTER FIFTY-SEVEN

12:21 p.m.
Brewster Home

SITTING CROSS-LEGGED ON BEE'S bedroom floor, Gordon wrestled with a yo-yo. "I can't do this." He slung it to the floor, but the string refused to coil. "How does your dad make it look so easy?"

"He was the national champion in the eighties," Bee said. "He's got about a hundred of 'em in his study. Some are from the 50's."

"That's really old. Wonder if they're valuable."

"They are. My mom checked them out on Ebay once and told my dad he could make hundreds of dollars on each one. He told her, 'no way'."

Gordon laughed. "My mom's got a wind-up watch my grandfather gave her. She's really glad she kept it. Especially now."

"We've got a wind up alarm clock downstairs. It's the only thing that works. All of our phones are fried. Wish we would have known about that Friday cage."

"Friday cage?" Gordy grinned. "Faraday cage."

"Friday's my new name for it. Sounds really cool, doesn't it?"

"Sounds good to me. I ran around like crazy trying to prep my family." "I should have called you about your electronics. Sorry, Bee."

"That's okay, Gordster. My phone was on its way out. Dad was going to get me a new one next year."

Gordon rewound the yo-yo's string and placed the toy on the bed. "These might become popular again if the power stays off."

"What's the deal with that?" she asked. "When will the electricity come on?" She pulled up her knees and hugged them.

"I'm not sure. That's why they're having the meeting. Things could get bad." He stood. "I better go."

"So soon? You just got here." She got to her feet, encircled his shoulders with her arms and gave him a hug. One that seemed to last longer than usual. A gentle scent of some kind of flower tickled his nose as she stepped back.

The look in her eyes created warm tingles in his body. She quickly reclaimed the distance between them.

What was she doing?

Her soft, moist lips found his. Unfamiliar—but not unwelcome—sensations surged.

He looked down at her, surprised. "I didn't expect that."

She kissed him again. This time longer.

His first *and* second kiss. More fantastic than he ever imagined.

His black and white world changed to Technicolor. He'd just stepped into Oz.

She let go. "I'll see you at the meeting."

He walked to her door and spun around. "Uh ... Bee ...?"

"Yes?"

"Uh ..." The words stuck in his mouth. Finally a moronic utterance tumbled out. "Wanna come over? We could use some help ... uh ... packing stuff for the meeting."

"My mom might need me. I'll find out and meet you downstairs." After she disappeared into her parent's room, his feet seemed to tap down the stairs, matching the rhythm of a dancing heart.

When she joined him in the living room, she flashed a broad smile. "She said yes."

They climbed into the old van and Gordon cranked it to life. Between first and second gear, he clumsily tried to hold her hand. It felt like velvet in his. A large grin spread through her freckles setting off a swarm of butterflies in his stomach. If he was trapped in a primitive world, who better to spend it with than Bethany Brewster?

CHAPTER FIFTY-EIGHT

Thursday, 3:14 p.m.
Brewster's Ice Cream Shoppe

SHIRLEY RELAXED IN THE PASSENGER seat of the Olds while Gordy drove through McCormick's downtown. Bethany sat in the back. Dalton and Samantha, with Grace in tow, had gone to Saint Luke's to deliver chairs. She felt like a chaperone, watching the teenagers. Something had changed between them. She felt it as surely as she felt the desert heat pressing her into the sticky car seat.

They were headed to the Brewster's business. Milkshakes were on tonight's menu, courtesy of the EMP. The hand-mixed treats in all sorts of flavors would certainly be a hit with the church members after dinner. It was either that or tossing tons of thawed ice cream down the drain.

The sidewalks of Jefferson Street, framed with quaint boutiques, were crowded with walkers hurrying to get somewhere. Cast iron street lamps stood guard like ramrod sentries between the town's residents and the dangers of the darkness. They'd held torches high with pride on nights past. Now they were lightless and dead. Would they ever brighten the town again?

"Your dad is meeting us at the store, right?" Gordy asked Bethany as he turned on Main Street.

"He said he'd be there by three-thirty. He had to ride his bike. Both our cars are dead."

"It's strange how some of the newer cars start yet yours don't," Gordy said.

"Other than fewer cars, the town seems normal," Shirley said as she scanned the crowded sidewalk.

"That will most likely change tomorrow," Gordy said.

"What do you mean?" Bethany asked.

"It's known as a normalcy bias. For the first seventy-two hours, people assume everything will return to the way it was before. They think the government's got it covered. They don't have a clue that the government can't fix everything. Especially something like this."

"It's good we're having the meeting," Shirley said. "Members should be warned. This thing could get worse. I'm glad we have you, Gordster, to keep us in the know." She patted her grandson's arm. He flushed and glanced in the rearview mirror at Bethany. Shirley smiled and settled back into her seat.

Main Street bustled with activity. Bicyclists streamed through the intersections between a trickle of traffic. Brewster's was less than a block away.

"People might seem okay," Gordy cautioned, "but if anyone acts weird, let's get back in the car and go to your house."

Shirley and Bethany both agreed. It had been two and a half days since the CME. Another night without power would heighten panic, Shirley was sure.

Gordy turned into an alley that edged the back of the business. He parked near a massive steel door. They piled out just as Alan Brewster appeared in the doorway.

"How have you been, Shirley?" Alan asked. "It's good to see you."

"Better than I thought, considering all that's happened," she said as the group entered the store.

Alan led them to the deep freeze. Once inside, the windowless room felt crypt-like and chilly. Shirley shivered, wishing she'd worn a sweater.

Stacks of five-gallon drums containing ice cream in assorted flavors lined the walls. The Brewster financial loss would be overwhelming.

"Load up whatever you want," Alan said. "It'll end up spoiling anyway."

"Thanks, Mr. Brewster," Gordy said.

"Our contribution to the meeting. Shakes for everyone." He gave a rueful grin, ran a hand over his face. "It's better than letting it go to waste."

They loaded the trunk of the car then returned to the front of the store. Alan told them he'd need a few minutes to note his inventory for tax purposes. He pressed the button on his desktop computer and groaned. "I keep forgetting." He grabbed a notepad and pencil and began writing.

"Dad ... there's still a lot of cartons in the back," Bethany said. "How 'bout we put the rest on the outside bench by the front window. People passing by can take them home."

"Go for it," he agreed.

"I'll make a sign," Shirley said as Gordy and Bethany headed back to the freezer. Alan found a marker and piece of paper. Shirley wrote,

FREE MILKSHAKES AND ICE

CREAM SOUP - HELP YOURSELF

Alan and Gordy stacked the cartons on the wooden seat next to the front entrance. Bethany found a prominent place for Shirley's sign.

Shirley stared at the display. A milk shake night for the entire town might be kind of fun during normal times. The iconic treat represented old-fashioned American comfort food. The kind you offer folks during hard times like a funeral or a crisis. Maybe it would help to cool inflamed tempers and the dread that boiled beneath the surface.

Alan made sure all the doors and windows were secure, dragged his bicycle from a storage room, then led the group outside.

"No need to ride your bike home." Shirley pointed to the Oldsmobile. "Do you have some of those stretchy things? We can tie your bike down and give you a ride home."

"Thanks, I appreciate it." Alan located two bungee cords and with Gordy's help, anchored the Schwinn. Everyone climbed inside.

As they pulled out of the alley, Shirley glanced back at the store front. Two men had a grip on the last container and each seemed determined to keep it. They glared at each other. One of them squared up, like he was about to throw a punch.

Gordy hit the gas and they sped away.

༄༅

Thursday, 3:40 p.m.
Saint Luke's Community Church annex

"Park there, son." Mr. Brewster gestured to the church annex. Gordon eased the car over the gravel and stopped in front of a chain-link fence. He shut off the engine and they climbed out. Still high above the western hills, the sun had begun its descent. Though darkness was several hours away, Gordon knew everyone would be hurrying, setting up for the meeting. Daylight was a commodity that couldn't be wasted.

Lugging containers of ice cream, the group headed to a side door.

When they entered the rear of the annex where they found Mrs. Brewster setting out paper goods on folding tables. She looked up and smiled. "I was beginning to worry."

"It took longer than we thought," Mr. Brewster said.

"Hello, Shirley. It's been a long time." Mrs. Brewster attempted a hug but multiple ice cream cartons got in the way.

"Too long, Barb," Grams agreed.

"Where do you want this ice cream, dear?" Mr. Brewster asked.

"In the kitchen. Put as many as you can in the chest freezers. With the ice in there, it might not melt as quickly."

Gordon and Grams followed Bee and her dad to the kitchen where they unloaded before heading to the Olds for a second haul. After emptying the car they clustered around Mrs. Brewster who arranged rows of sandwiches on trays.

"Your family just left," she told Gordon. "They went to get another load of chairs."

Bee tugged at his elbow. Gordon smiled at her, a question in his eyes.

"Gordster and I will be back in a few, Mom," Bethany said. She led him outside.

ဢ

"What can I do to help?" Shirley asked. Those two couldn't get into any trouble at the church. She hoped.

"Amanda dropped off some cooked meat. It's in one of the freezer's. You can help me make more sandwiches."

"I'll get right on it."

When Shirley entered the expansive kitchen, waning sun streamed through windows above the stainless-steel double sinks. Two chest freezers and two refrigerators, their electric life blood now gone, stood like vertical corpses. Notably absent were the hum of motors and the buzz from florescent bulbs. A couple of large coffee urns, surrounded by boxes containing sugar and creamer powder, wouldn't perk for a long time. Maybe ever.

To think this commercial kitchen had been the hub of church fellowship, bought and paid for by the generous givers of bygone eras. Now it contained a lot of useless equipment.

Shirley twisted a faucet to wash her hands but nothing came out. She sighed and echoed Alan's comment from the shop: *I keep forgetting*. A small plastic bowl in the sink was filled with water. She dipped in a paper towel and cleaned her hands before setting to work on tonight's dinner.

ဢ

Bee tugged on Gordon's hand, pulling him toward the back side of the annex which juxtaposed a wooden fence. "Where are we going?" Gordon asked.

She spun around and stopped, then pressed him against a concrete wall. She planted a long kiss on his mouth.

The moments there, his lips against hers, were like heaven. It took everything in him to pull away. Gordon looked toward the parking lot. "Bee ... your dad could be anywhere."

"That's why we're being sneaky!" Her lips found his again. Her mouth was like honey.

"Let me talk with him first." Gordon wriggled free. Though he was larger and stronger, suddenly his body felt like Jell-O.

She looked at him curiously. "You're not handsy like those Falcon guys, Gordster."

"Is that a bad thing?"

"No." She snuggled close and gazed up at him. "It's exactly why I like you."

He'd seen those football jocks leering at her while she did her cheers. He'd wanted to punch them out. He almost did one time when one of them made an off-color joke about her cheerleading skirt. But Bee had laughed them off and walked away. He'd stuffed his hands in his pockets and given them a hard stare, before following her into the gym.

"What about your dad's no-dating-till-sixteen rule?" he asked.

"Are we dating?"

"I ... uh ... I don't know. Are we?"

He hoped so.

He'd never gone on a date. With anyone, much less one of the most popular cheerleaders in the whole school.

Although one time his mother made him take his cousin Jeanine to a 6th grade dance at school. That had been the "date" from hell. Jeanine, a self-proclaimed trend setter from Los Angles bragged too much and loved attention. About thirty minutes into the dance she'd abandoned him to a wallflower existence while she wiggled and synced with other kids doing the Macarena across the gymnasium floor. He didn't count that as a date. It was a favor for his mom that still haunted him.

When Bee raised her lips to his, he turned his face. "I need to talk to your dad."

"My dad's stuck in the last century. He won't understand."

"I still need to talk to him."

"My birthday's only three months away."

It would require enormous strength to avoid those lips for three months. But silencing his mother's voice would be harder. She'd taught him something that wasn't found in any science book. To always be a gentleman and to respect the girl's father.

"You're worth the wait, Bee. I'll talk to him right now. Before my parents get here."

She drew back and pouted. "Do you think that's a good idea?"

"I hope so," he said. "I better go before I chicken out."

She pecked his cheek, then opened the door to the kitchen. "See you soon. Let me know what he says." Bee disappeared inside.

ꕥ

In the back of the annex, Gordon shifted nervously in a folding chair next to Bee's father. He could see Grams and Mrs. Brewster working in the kitchen, putting together sandwiches, drinking iceless iced tea.

Mr. Brewster's eyes bored into his. "How long have you had these feelings?" he asked.

"To be honest, I've liked her for months now. I didn't know until today that she felt the same."

"Hmmm ..." Mr. Brewster's eyes narrowed.

"I know you have rules so I want to ask you ..." He cleared his throat. He could do this. If he was man enough to date and kiss a girl, he was man enough to talk to her father. "So ... do you think I could spend some time with her as ... well ... as more than a friend?"

Mr. Brewster stared at him without blinking. Torturous moments ticked by. Gordy finally had to look away. Grams had a knife and seemed to be slicing sandwiches.

"I hope I can trust you, son," Mr. Brewster finally said. "You practically grew up at my house. As long as there's no kissing."

"Kissing?" Gordon's voice cracked, climbing part of an octave on the second syllable. Heat flooded his cheeks. Maybe Bee's father wouldn't notice.

The older man folded his arms. "You've already kissed her, haven't you?"

Gordy rubbed the back of his neck. "Only today, I swear. I know we broke your rules. That's why I'm here."

"That was the first good decision you made today," Mr. Brewster said. A frown formed under his glare. "Mrs. Brewster and I will talk about this. In the meantime, you need to use some self-control. No more kissing. You may hold her hand in public. That's it. Do you understand?"

"Yes, sir."

"We'll talk some more after I discuss this with her mother. "

Gordon took a deep breath as he headed toward an exit. He could almost sense Mr. Brewster's eyes watching his every move as he walked across the long, empty room.

ꕤ

Thursday, 4:45 p.m.
Saint Luke's Community Church

Gordon watched as Bee and her parents approached, carrying folding chairs across the parking lot. He and Grams waited in a little patio near the sanctuary. They decided to have a quick meeting out of the earshot of church members who arrived early to help.

Bee smiled. Her father wore a poker face. Gordon shifted, unable to keep still, sitting between Grams and Mrs. Brewster.

After they unfolded their chairs, Bee sat down. Mr. Brewster remained standing. His arms were folded across his chest like a drill sergeant.

"I gave your grandmother and Mrs. Brewster a short version of what's going on with you two."

"I must say ..." Mrs. Brewster chuckled. "I expected this much sooner." She smiled at Gordon, ignoring her husband's scowl.

Bee's father plunged into what seemed like a prepared speech about the dangers of young people with too much time alone.

"Bedroom visits at either house are no longer acceptable," he said "Public displays of affection should be on the conservative side," he told them. "Hand holding okay. Long hugs out. No kissing. Not now. Maybe not until the wedding day."

"Daddy!" Bethany flushed pink.

"I'm sure your father's kidding," Mrs. Brewster said.

"He better be," Bee said. "When do we?"

"What?" Mr. Brewster asked.

"When do we get to kiss?"

"I'll let you know. Gordon needs to re-earn my trust."

Gordon kept quiet about who kissed who first. No sense in jeopardizing the trust issue between father and daughter. He'd take the blame.

"I will not kiss your daughter sir, I promise. At least not unless I have your permission."

Now ... if only Bee kept her lips to herself.

ഗ്ദ

Close to five-thirty, church members trickled in. Gordon's stomach grumbled, seeing people carry dishes and drinks to share. Dad and the rest of the family had arrived. Dad enlisted him and Bee to unload more chairs from the VW.

After walking across the parking lot, Bee dumped her chairs and grabbed his face, drawing him close.

"Didn't you hear your father?" He pulled away and stared into her sparking blue eyes. Gordon pressed a finger to her lips. "We've got to keep your dad's rules. If we want to keep seeing each other."

"Gordy. How will he know?"

"I'll know. And I gave my word."

She pouted again and he had to fight the urge to press his lips to hers. With a flounce, she turned away, picked up the chairs again, and led the way to the annex. A Sunday school lesson popped in his brain as he followed her. He might have to be like Joseph and make a run for it. She was one temptation he didn't think he could resist.

CHAPTER FIFTY-NINE

Thursday, 5:25 p.m.
Saint Luke's Community Church Annex

DALTON LEANED AGAINST THE CHURCH BULLETIN board and pain pierced his arm. "Ouch!" He twisted around. An offending push pin had lost its plastic cap. He perused the barrage of announcements attached to a cork wall.

Some were so faded, they were hard to read. The hodgepodge of hand-written and printed notices stirred the pot of guilt stewing in his gut.

"Job needed ... please call ..."

It was one of many. Others said things like, "Desperate for work ... I have skills in ..."

"Yard Sale ... this Saturday ... Everything Must Go!"

"Home for sale ... lost my job ..."

His people were hurting. He'd never paid attention to the bulletin board before. He'd supposed it held only notices of teenagers offering babysitting and lawn mowing services. Maybe not reading the announcements helped him stay in denial that anyone had a need more urgent than upgrading their cars from last year's model. Maybe it helped him think it was okay to badger congregants for money. Maybe it helped him keep his distance from hurting people.

He sighed, leaned his forehead against the wall. If remorse could fix anything, he'd gladly handle each of these pleas personally.

He deserved whatever they had to dish out today.

His family would experience real poverty soon. Gordy's prediction of a life without electricity would equalize everyone.

Dalton turned and watched church members stream in. He returned smiles as he jingled his keys in his pocket. People hurried past, forging toward the front seats. Some waved as they passed. Many more hurried by, not meeting his eyes.

Winifred Snyder shuffled toward him, dressed in a floral print dress, poking at the linoleum with her cane. He glanced at his dusty sneakers and polo shirt. He should have changed. At least worn a tie with a white shirt.

He pasted on a smile and prepared himself. Being chewed out by one of the congregation's matriarchs in front of everyone wouldn't be fun.

She leaned close. Her grey eyes searched his.

"Pastor Dalton ... my son insists I move in with him. What should I do?"

"I ... uh..." Dalton stammered, surprised. "Things might get bad, Winnie. You're staying at his place?"

"Since the power went off. I've been prayin' something fierce and I'm sure the Lord will bring back the lights." Tears filled her eyes, her cold hand squeezed his. "Mitzie and I will be fine. I don't want to leave my home, Pastor. Can you talk some sense into Gene?" Mitzie, the woman's scraggly terrier, was hardly a watch dog. It made sense her son wanted his mother under his roof.

"He's looking out for you, Winnie," Dalton said. "I'd do the same for my mother."

"Please talk to him, Pastor."

"I will but ... uh ... Winnie, there's something you should know."

"'Though you fall, you shall not be utterly cast down,'" she interrupted. "'For the Lord upholds you with His righteous right hand.'"

His eyes welled. "Thank you, Winnie." He hugged her. "That means a lot to me. I'll see what I can do."

She headed toward Gene who held a seat. Gene wouldn't take kindly to his interference. Not after hocking the poor woman's heirloom. But he'd made a promise and would keep it.

Maybe if he assured Gene he'd check on his mother a few times a week, he'd agree to let her stay in her home.

He held back a chuckle. Not likely. Gene would suspect he'd stop by to pilfer more heirlooms. He'd probably have to promise not to stop by.

ഈ

Samantha sat near a back wall, three rows from a make-shift stage in the sunlit annex. Gordy and Bethany snuggled close, holding hands next to her. Lost in each other's eyes, the teenagers provided a tinge of sweetness to the dismal atmosphere. Why Alan's concern and rules? This was Gordy, for heaven's sake. Her smart, geeky son, more interested in his telescope than girls. They had nothing to worry about. Right?

Thankful for her obscurity, she leaned against the chair's metal back. It offered some anonymity from incoming congregants who would ask questions about the meeting and why her husband hadn't taken the stage.

Her mother had gone home to be with Grace. Her daughter didn't need to hear any of this. Adults wrangling about whether or not to keep her father as a pastor would be hard enough. But to add to that the discussions about a powerless reality might frighten a child.

Saturday's memorial service for Charity Connor loomed. Thinking about it nudged her melancholy into full-blown sadness.

Matt and Carla seemed to be holding it together. At least for now. They sat a few rows ahead of Samantha. Matt kept his arm around Carla's shoulders, protective and caring.

The reality of their daughter's death would hit again like a tidal wave. Seeing their sorrow would be hard. Especially for Grace. Samantha questioned her decision again. Should she allow her daughter to attend the service? Grace would be upset if she couldn't go. She wanted to say goodbye to her best friend. But exposing her to the kind of raw grief sure to be displayed ... Maybe ... maybe she should talk about this with Dalton.

She sighed. How had that happened? In the space of a day, she'd gone from never wanting to see him again to discussing parenting decisions.

Thinking of Dalton ... she saw him lingering near the kitchen. He gazed over the congregation, seeming to be looking for someone. Her? She signaled him with her hand and their eyes met.

He mouthed again, "I'm sorry."

Today his words landed differently in her heart.

She mouthed back, "It's okay," then smiled.

This evening, the rest of his future would be determined by a room full of angry parishioners. Yet between him and her, his apology had finally take root someplace deep in her soul. Instead of judgment, she wanted grace. Instead of punishment, she craved mercy. The anger that had suffocated her spirit had quelled. Though her heart was bruised, it wanted to love again.

A strong scent drifted by. Samantha turned. Deidra and Drake Storm took seats behind her. Deidra's eyes fired hate. Then, as if to convey a message only for her, Deidra scooted close to Drake and leaned her head on his shoulder. Which seemed to say, *I have my husband, where's yours?*

Samantha faced forward. Nice try, Deidra. Why Deidra came to the meeting in the first place escaped her. The playwright's renowned quote, *"Hell hath no fury like a woman scorned,"* popped into her brain.

Oh. Of course. Deidra came to punish both Dalton, who had rejected her advances, and Samantha who had called her out on it. She sat up straight and firmed her shoulders. Deidra Storm would no longer occupy space in her head.

Church members found folding chairs as the time for beginning the meeting approached. Like a courtroom jury, twelve empty seats for the council members and their spouses formed two rows on an elevated platform that faced the congregation. Laney and Martin ascended, with the other church leadership trailing behind. Absent was the chair Dalton would normally take.

Laney Fernández tapped an empty glass with a teaspoon to get everyone's attention while Martin took the podium. Loud chatters tapered to whispers and stragglers quickly found seats.

"Thanks for coming, everyone," Martin said. "Can you all hear me?"

A chatter of yeses filled the room.

"Would you join me in prayer?"

The group obediently bowed their heads. A few clasped hands with their neighbors. Samantha whispered a silent thanks, grateful Martin was leading tonight.

"Lord ... there are many challenges ahead," Martin began. "We need Your help, Father..." He prayed for several minutes, then said, "Amen."

He picked up a sheaf of notes and read. Rita Clemmons scribbled minutes on a yellow legal pad.

"It's been three days since the solar flare," he said. "Fortunately we've got a science wiz among us who might be able to shed some light—pardon my pun—on what happened. Gordy, would you join us on the platform and explain?"

Gordy described an electric magnetic pulse and what that would mean for planet Earth. "I researched this all summer," he continued. "My grandmother witnessed the explosion from the sun. If she was here, she'd tell you herself."

Samantha swelled with pride hearing Gordy qualify his theories with what he'd read on an Australian government website that night.

"Unlike us, the Australians were warned."

Several churchgoers raised hands.

"Yes?" Martin pointed to Amanda.

"How long will this last?"

"No one really knows," Gordy said. "Congress was warned about it years ago but didn't do anything. Our transformers were never hardened."

"Hardened?" asked Charlotte Sims who sat in the front row.

"Protected," Gordy continued. "The government fixed their own stuff like military hardware and satellites, but never got around to shielding the transformers in every American city."

"So there's no way to get them up and running?" Martin asked.

"I doubt it. They're old. They need to be rebuilt. That will take months, if not years."

"Years? Are you kidding me?" Brad Sanders yelled from his seat with the council members behind Gordy. Samantha thought the council members knew how dire the situation was.

Seated next to Brad, Harold Roark raised his hand. "We who sit on this platform, including *you*, Brad ..." he said, "were alerted by Martin Tuesday morning. Laney emailed everyone on the church roster instructions on how to prepare. If you recall, at the time we thought

Martin was crazy. Had we heeded his warning, we'd all be in a better place. Those precious hours were needed to gather supplies and store water."

"We were dealing with other stuff," Brad bit out. He frowned at Dalton who waited in the back like a lamb to be slaughtered. Samantha shot up a quick prayer. *Help my husband, Lord.*

"Even with Gordon's expertise, people wondered if this could happen, so I don't blame anyone for not listening," Martin said.

Thank you, Father, for this humble man who leads our council, Samantha prayed.

When Gordy returned to his seat, Samantha hugged him while she whispered in his ear, "You did great, son." He smiled at her, then turned to Bethany, who reached for his hand.

"We must help each other," Martin continued. "Especially those among us who are shut-ins or elderly. You might have noticed several tables in the back. We'll have sign-ups after dinner.

"That is our visitation table." He pointed to the first table closest to the front. "It's the most important task we have before us. We need volunteers to check on parishioners who aren't here. Jeremy Andrews is heading up this team.

"If you notice someone absent, please go to the back and add their name. These homes will be visited this evening, even if it takes all night."

"The next station is labeled, *Practical Help* and will be manned by Gordon Baxter," Martin said. "Head over there for useful information about sanitation and water preservation.

"My wife, Laney, will be at the *Wellness* table. If you have any medical knowledge or expertise, we need you." Martin seemed to survey the crowd. "Is James Collins here? Dr. Jim, where are you?"

"Over here, Martin." The doctor signaled with his hand.

"Dr. Jim and Laney will co-lead this team."

Martin explained about another table labeled *Transportation* where people with working cars could sign up to transport folks. Those with extra bikes were asked to stop by.

"We also need a group of people to help with Charity Connor's ... uh ... service. Samantha will oversee that," Martin stammered. Samantha glanced again at the Connors, huddled together like a pair of penguins cradling their precious baby. Except Matt and Carla's baby was beyond their warmth, beyond their help, beyond their care. Samantha's heart broke all over again, seeing their helplessness in their hunched shoulders.

Martin paused, staring at Dalton who still hung back near the bulletin board.

Samantha's stomach lurched and she darted a glance at the nearest exit. If only she could leave.

Gordy gently squeezed her hand, his action producing fresh tears in her eyes. Thank God for this young man who had shown bounds of maturity these past few days. She leaned her head against his shoulder.

ℰℑℭℜ

Dalton twisted his wedding band, his heart raced as a new wave of apprehension assaulted him. Martin's stare cut right through him. He drew a breath, held it, and braced himself for Martin's next topic. Not since a doctor pronounced a death sentence over his mother had he felt so helpless. They planned for him to remain silent while Martin revealed his sins. Then a vote would be taken to have him removed.

Dalton readied himself, looking down at his sneakers. All eyes would shift to him once the truth became evident. If only he could run and escape the disappointment in their faces.

A week ago, he wouldn't have thought twice about slipping out the door and leaving Sammy to mop up his mess.

But healing began in his jail cell. If he had to return there, it was because God could use him on the inside. His days of running were over.

Lord Jesus, help me.

Martin finally spoke. "Our pastor ... is in a very hard trial right now ..."

Had Martin called him their pastor? Dalton glanced up. Martin's glistening eyes connected with his.

"I know we didn't discuss this, brother. But I think it best if everyone hears this from you. Is that okay?"

Dalton stilled. He knew what a deer felt, frozen in the path of a car. *Lord, I'm not prepared, help me!* Anxiety surged through him. There was no oxy to lean on or give confidence. All the words in his head lacked any power, any presence, any persuasiveness.

I give grace to the humble, son.

He walked toward the invisible altar through a room where no one let out a sound. Even the kids seemed to be still. Tears collected in his eyes.

When he joined Martin, he whispered, "Are you sure about this?"

"I prayed all morning, Dalton. I'm sure."

Martin took his seat as Dalton stood in front of the wooden lectern, gripping its sides. At least it shielded some of his shame. A room of puzzled faces held questions in their eyes. He looked at Sammy, who smiled and nodded. Seeing her ignited his courage.

"There's no easy way to say this. The truth is, I'm a drug addict."

Hushed murmurs could be heard. Eyebrows arched. No one spoke.

"I used the offering you so generously gave to the Yavapai Mission on Sunday to buy drugs." Dalton paused, as if he were back in the pulpit, gauging the crowd's temperature.

Audible buzzing, louder now.

"If that wasn't enough, what I tell you next will shock you. This injury ..." Dalton pointed, then gingerly touched the bandage beneath his left eye. " ... was self-induced."

A loud chatter filled the auditorium. He pushed through, describing his crimes. "I sank my own car in Copper Lake." People shook their heads, some covered their mouths while Helen Crawford clutched her pearls—he'd chuckle at the cliché, if it wasn't his real life here. "I intended to convince law enforcement I'd been carjacked. I hoped my insurance company would replace my car. Yes, I committed insurance fraud."

Dalton glanced at the council members who sat behind him. Brad scowled, but the others' faces offered sympathy.

"Remember my skiing accident last year?" he asked. "My doctor gave me pain meds. I abused them. I became addicted. I wronged many people ..."

His tears freely fell, tracking the top of the podium he clutched with his hand.

"I've hurt you ..." Dalton heaved a deep breath and wiped his eyes. "I've stolen your hard-earned money and more importantly, I've squandered your trust.

"My actions brought devastation to my family ..." He stopped in mid-sentence and looked at Sammy. His eyes held hers despite his blurry vision.

"Sammy ... I love you so much ... Please forgive me for the hell I put you through."

All day he'd imagined this moment in a private setting, just the two of them. But like their wedding day, he now made a public vow. "Before all these witnesses I promise to love you the way God wants me to. That is ... if you'll have me after what I have done." She nodded with a slight smile.

Did that mean she would? His heart leaped with hope.

"As far as the funds I embezzled, I'll do my best to make full restitution. If that means doing hard labor for congregants and at the church facility, I will. Gladly."

"What about *our* money?" A voice shouted from the hall. "You stole four thousand dollars from Drake and me for that phony furnace repair!" Deidra Storm stood, venom in her eyes.

Dalton's hand shook. His speech stalled. Deidra had come? How was Sammy? His eyes met hers and she nodded again.

“Sit down, Deidra,” Martin said. “Now’s not the time. We’ll decide later how everyone will be recompensed. You and Drake will be on that list, so please take a seat.”

Eyes still glowering, she sat.

Dalton found his voice. “It’s not necessary to take a vote. I am stepping down as your pastor immediately.”

“Hold on, brother.” Martin joined him at the podium. “The decision won’t be made today. We need time to pray about this,” Martin said, scanning the room. “Do that, folks. Pray. Consult the Lord. Follow His leading. Anonymous ballots will be handed out on Sunday. We’ll vote then.”

Dalton let loose of the lectern. So ... he was still their pastor?

Weren’t they just delaying the inevitable?

He cocked his head as realization struck. He no longer felt the need to demand things he thought he deserved. Like a second chance or the opportunity to make restitution. In fact, he didn’t even care about a second chance. God had his back. And maybe—just maybe—he had Sammy back.

Everything was a gift. Even the three days of reprieve he’d just been given.

ꕥ

Samantha glanced at the kitchen windows in the annex. Dusk cast an orange glow across the linoleum. Dinner was over and a few ladies were still cleaning up. She hated leaving them but she had one more meeting to attend.

One she dreaded.

Planning Charity Connor’s funeral Saturday.

She made her way to a long table with fifteen people seated around it. The flame from a kerosene lamp flickered nearby. They were already in deep discussion about the little girl’s service. Samantha was encouraged by the caring faces gathered here. They loved Charity and the Connors and wanted to see that everything was the best it could be, given the current situation. These were good people. She’d always believed that, even when Dalton used to talk about St. Luke’s and McCormick as being backwoods. The way Dalton accepted Martin’s grace and hug, along with so many of the other congregants, after his confession, it seemed he now believed it too. Her heart warmed with gratitude for her church family.

When Matt and Carla joined them, taking seats near Dalton, their eyes were red-rimmed and puffy. The chatter around the table dropped to a hush.

This would be hard. Really hard with Charity's parents here. The service would break their hearts again. *How will we get through this?* their eyes seemed to ask.

It felt odd leading the meeting, one normally Dalton would have commanded. Yet here she was in charge, with all eyes upon her.

"The bereavement committee was so kind to make copies," she said as she held up a stack of papers. "I only have eight so please share with your neighbor." When she passed them out, couples scooted close, huddling over hand-written notes containing the meeting's agenda.

"We're still looking for someone to conduct the service." She looked at the Connors. "Martin has offered if that's okay with you." Samantha hoped for a nod from Matt but instead he shook his head.

"No," he said. "Carla and I want Dalton to do it."

"I ... uh ... I can't," Dalton stammered. "It wouldn't be right."

"You're still our pastor. It's what we want," Carla said.

"What do you think, honey?" Samantha asked Dalton.

"You're sure?" He turned to the Connors.

Matt clutched Carla's hand and they both nodded. "We're sure."

Saturday

"Let not your hearts be troubled. Believe in God; believe also in Me. In My Father's house are many rooms. If it were not so, would I have told you that I go to prepare a place for you? And if I go and prepare a place for you, I will come again and will take you to Myself, that where I am you may be also ..." John 14:1-3

CHAPTER SIXTY

Saturday, 10:30 a.m.
Saint Luke's Community Church

MORNING SUN STREAMED THROUGH A stained window above the baptismal font. The light magnified a depiction of Christ carrying a baby ewe, producing rainbows throughout the nave. *Such a striking paradox,* Dalton thought. The same sun that blessed them with beauty today, just days ago had mercilessly cursed the planet.

Federal authorities said it would take weeks until they'd be able to assess the EMP's devastation. McCormick's residents were meeting this afternoon at City Hall with the mayor and the town council for a local assessment. Most of his flock would probably be there too. Hopefully, the cooler heads in city leadership would help panicked citizens with what they faced.

He hadn't thought much about the catastrophe until now. Finding Grace and putting his family back together took priority. As the community endured a fifth powerless day though, reality set in. Unless the government managed to get the lights back on, things would only get harder.

Dalton sat in his favorite chair on the platform, reading Charity Connor's memorial program. The service would begin in thirty minutes. Manually typed, he hoped the message about her brief earthly life would bless her family.

"I found some old typewriters in the basement," Sammy had told everyone at Thursday's meeting. "We'll create programs the old fashioned way. Do I have any volunteers?"

He'd enthusiastically raised his hand. After all, he was pretty adept on a computer. Surely he could type out a few programs. After a few minutes engaging the mechanical dinosaur, striking the wrong letters, he shoved it away and asked for a different job from Sammy. Besides, the church office no longer stocked Wite-Out, an ingredient he'd definitely need.

Soon he'd been relegated with a team of nimble-fingered men folding handouts at the back of the table, before passing them to Dot Wigglesworth and some ladies, who sketched a flower on each cover.

They'd chosen the American Daisy, Charity's favorite. Several teens from Gordy's youth group added colored-pencil embellishments. The finished products looked amazing. The Connors would be touched by the church family's love.

Though the nave gleamed from natural lighting, oil candles had been positioned throughout the sanctuary, casting golden glows, reminding him of the church's rich liturgical heritage. A container of fuel oil, discovered in the basement, resurrected dead wicks from the 1980s. Some ladies from the Tuesday morning Bible group felt that adding the glowing aesthetics would soften the sorrow.

Dalton studied the Paschal light, flickering white orbs across the little casket. Traditionally lit at Easter, it welcomed Christ's presence. A wave of warm comfort flooded his heart. *You are with us, Lord ... Your light still shines in the darkest places ...*

Today, lighting the Paschal seemed appropriate, even in August.

Congregants filed in, finding seats. Keeping the coffin closed had been decided by Matt. He and Carla should not have to bear an entire service with the face of their little angel "sleeping" near the altar.

Amanda Benson laid pink roses over the casket, then paused, her face contorted with grief. Behind her a few parishioners trickled in, waiting to pay their respects.

Dalton set aside the program and lowered his face into his hands. He steepled his fingers over his nose and prayed a few moments before standing.

He walked down a side aisle to the vestibule where he found Sammy waiting. Her beauty brightened the dark room as she clutched a stack of pamphlets.

"How can I help?" he asked.

She shook her head. "I'm feeling anxious."

"About the service?" His brow furrowed. "You've taken care of everything."

"It's not that," she said. "I'm scared, Dalton. We're well past the seventy-two hour mark that Gordy warned us about. It didn't hit me until we arrived this morning and I began lighting candles. Gordy believes people will go crazy. A mob mentality will form and there will be looting. Do you think he's right?"

"Hopefully not in a small town like ours. I think we'll be okay, Sammy." It's the outsiders he worried about but decided not to voice that.

Her eyes searched his. "Why are you so calm?"

Calm? He wasn't calm. Maybe God was helping him stay composed. "I'm trying to hold it together, for all of our sakes."

"I'm praying this will be a day of comfort for the Connors." She gazed at the anteroom's vaulted ceiling. "Let this be a good day, God."

He yearned to tug her close but reached for her hand instead.

She didn't pull away, but instead gathered into his arms. "Hold me, Dalton."

He held her to his chest and kissed the top of her head. "Sammy ... I love you. I'm so sor..."

"Shhh ... darling." She touched his lips with her finger.

Darling? She hadn't said that in months.

"No need to tell me again," she said. "I forgave you, remember?" She lingered in his arms, staring into his eyes. She lifted her face and covered his lips with hers. After a few moments, she pulled away, looking a little embarrassed.

"I don't think we've ever kissed in the vestibule." She smiled, looking around the paneled room. "Sort of feels wrong on a day like this."

He shook his head. "I think this is what God wants on a day like this. I'd kiss you anywhere, Sammy." He tugged her lips to his.

After a few passionate moments, they broke apart, her face, flushed. *I wonder what I look like,* Dalton thought. He felt as giddy as a teenager on prom night.

She pointed to the entrance. "Better use our heads, sweetheart. Congregants will be here soon."

Dalton gave her a long hug and turned to the nave, exiting with straightened shoulders and a spring in his step. Sammy's unexpected kiss had pushed him into the clouds. He could endure the gravity of the hour now. She'd given him more than he could have hoped for. Her love.

ꟷ

Seated again on the platform, Dalton stared as congregants gathered. He glanced at Matt and Carla in the front row, clinging to one another. Carla stared at the casket while Matt looked away.

Members of Matt and Carla's family were noticeably absent though Carla's sister, Jan, had managed to come in from Phoenix. She'd taken back roads as all major highways were shut down, due to looting in the city.

Dalton caressed his mother's name imprinted on her Bible. Would the passage he'd chosen offer some comfort? If Grace was in that box, would a Bible verse help him? He wasn't sure it would.

An a cappella group finished singing the Sunday-school favorite, *Jesus Loves Me,* then took seats on the platform. That was Dalton's cue. He hugged the Bible like an old friend and walked to the pulpit.

Those sitting in the pews gave him their full attention. Some smiled, others nodded their heads. A few more wiped stray tears.

With no microphone, he spoke loudly. "Let me begin by telling you something about Charity Connor." Dalton's voice boomed, then echoed.

He glanced up, surprised. How like God to provide the cavernous ceiling that amplified his words.

He looked at the small casket. “Though barely seven years old, she loved Jesus with all her heart. She suffered terribly in this life yet never stopped believing. We could learn a lot from this little girl.

“I once saw her gazing at that window.” Dalton pointed to the stained glass near the piano depicting Jesus blessing the children. “She seemed awestruck by it. Something about that artwork imprinted on her heart.”

Dalton opened the Bible. “Let’s read a passage in Romans,” he said. “It’s been typed on your program.” Though some rustled through paper pamphlets, most opened their Bibles. Even the younger folks.

“The Spirit helps us in our weaknesses,” he read. “For we do not know what to pray, but the Spirit, Himself, intercedes for us with groanings too deep for words ...” Dalton looked up, scanned the room. Everyone seemed to be listening intently. “Sometimes when our prayers feel inadequate, the Spirit of God can groan our agonies to the Father. This is one of those times.”

Dalton caught Matt’s gaze and paused. Sorrow warped Matt’s face.

“We don’t know how to pray, let alone what to say.” Dalton cleared his throat, then looked at the congregation. “Some of us may ask, ‘Why would God allow this? Why would He take this precious child?’”

He looked at Sammy who huddled with Grace, holding her hand. Their eyes met and she nodded, gifting him encouragement as she had done minutes before in the vestibule, as she had done for almost two decades.

“On this side of heaven, there is no answer to a question like this,” he continued. “There never will be. It’s best not to offer a mourning family answers as to why. They never help.

“But there is something we *can* do. God makes it clear we are to come alongside the broken-hearted. The Lord reminded me this morning of a verse in Ecclesiastes. Please turn to chapter four.” Once again the sanctuary filled with the sound of rustling paper.

“As a minister, I have used this portion of scripture for weddings. This is the first time I’ve chosen it for a funeral.

“‘Two people are better off than one,’” Dalton read. “‘If one falls, the other can reach out and help. But someone who falls alone is in real trouble.’

“What is Solomon saying? Does anyone know?” The pews remained silent, his question rhetorical. “The passage is obvious. We need each other.

“Look at this, brothers and sisters.” Dalton’s voice notched. “‘Three are even better--a triple-braided cord is not easily broken.’”

Dalton closed the Bible and looked at the crowd with affection. This might be the last time he'd speak to them as their pastor. He'd been unsure about conducting this service. But now he was thankful Matt insisted he officiate. He needed to see his flock as people and not numbers in an attendance log. Or dollars in an accounting report. Today, they had become precious to him. The physical lights had shut off but a new light inside could not be snuffed out. Like Mo had reminded him from the scriptures, God would not crush the weakest reed or put out a flickering candle. Dalton gazed at his people then looked up into the vast ceiling. *I don't know how you did it Father, but you've restored my passion!* Whether in an official capacity or not, it didn't matter, he loved his flock.

He turned to the Connors. "Today we grieve with you," he told them. "Tomorrow we walk with you. You will not be alone. That cord I just read about is knotted with the love of God's people."

He descended the steps around Charity's casket, and stood in front of Matt and Carla.

He took their hands. "We ... all of us here..." Dalton paused and looked up at the congregation. "Are so deeply sorry for your loss." Tears gathered. His eyes locked with Matt's. "I ... am so sorry. No matter what happens, brother, I'm here for you."

Still gripping their hands, Dalton looked at the parishioners. "In fact, we're all here for you, aren't we?" Heads nodded. Some people called out promises. Matt and Carla wept.

Dalton hugged them each a long time.

He returned to the pulpit. "Please join us outside for the committal rite. Ushers will be at the exits with the flowers so many of you donated. Take a few for the next part of the service."

ꕥ

Dalton surveyed the crowd. Mourners, holding hundreds of blooms, huddled around the heartbroken family. A myriad of colors, washed in resplendent glory, the historic graveyard resembled Monet's Giverny Garden in springtime. The floral fragrance permeated the air, filling the cemetery with what was surely the scent of heaven.

People stood behind the family who sat on folding chairs in front of the coffin. Grace clutched a white daisy with one hand and squeezed Dalton's hand with the other. Four pallbearers, including Gordy, lowered Charity into a six-foot grave. Once the coffin reached the ground, the ropes were removed and tossed aside.

Dalton attempted to hand off Grace to Samantha.

"No, Daddy!" she shouted. The crowd glanced their way.

Sammy bent over to whisper. “Gracie, it’ll be okay. Daddy needs to speak to the people.”

“No! I want to be with Daddy.” Grace’s face reflected an unusual stubbornness. She was usually so compliant. Dalton gave Sammy a puzzled look.

She shrugged. “She’s missing her friend. Let her stand with you, honey.”

With his seven-year-old clinging to his side, Dalton faced the congregation. “We are all made from dust, and to dust we all return,” he said, looking down into the deep hole.“Like this precious little girl, each of us here will someday make our own journey to God.” He looked into Matt’s and Carla’s eyes, searching their faces. “This is your hope. You will see her again.”

He invited everyone to drop their flowers onto Charity’s casket. The crowd formed a line winding through hundred-year-old tombstones. One by one, they filed past, dropping blossoms onto the coffin.

Plop ... plop ... Each flower echoed sadness. As the line dwindled, the sounds were muffled by the growing mountain of blossoms below.

Betty Roark began singing *My Hope is Built on Nothing Less*. When she launched into the chorus, the congregation joined her. “On Christ, the Solid Rock, I stand, all other ground is sinking sand. All other ground is sinking sand.”

Dalton closed his eyes, remembering his own mother singing the classic hymn. She played it and others on their Steinway during the rare times when his father was away. Songs like this always brought peace to his heart.

When darkness veils His lovely face,
I rest on His unchanging grace;
In every high and stormy gale,
My anchor holds within the veil.
On Christ, the solid Rock, I stand;
all other ground is sinking sand.

More often than Dalton liked to admit, darkness had shrouded God’s face. Especially during the last eight months of his drug addiction. But in one moment, in a dank cell, God rent the curtain, allowing Dalton to enter boldly to the throne room and find a Father who truly loved him. Then today, just as quickly, that same Father used an old hymn to show him his future.

He gazed at the clouds above. The song’s profound words stirred him with purpose. In the days and weeks ahead, people would need an anchor. A raging storm bore upon them that would leave a wake of chaos and terror. Friendship with the Father and believing He loved each of them would help quell its vicious path of destruction. All would need a loving Father waiting behind the veil.

The congregation had coalesced into a cohesive hum, while Betty, who knew every word from every hymn, continued to sing. Dalton smiled, his eyes misted, observing the people, and compassion flowed. These dear ones, especially these grief-stricken parents, would need his help, even if that meant as a layperson and not a minister. Without an anchored faith within the veil, they'd go under, helpless and floundering, swallowed by fear.

He perused the crowd and noticed Deidra, her face nodding toward him, tears falling into her clutched hankie.

He looked for Brad Sanders, hoping for a similar response. When their eyes met, Sanders returned a scowl.

Dalton smiled back, rejecting the man's disdain. The same God who had softened Dalton's stony heart, just days before, could do the same for anyone. Even Brad. Only God's light could penetrate man's deepest darkness. He was living proof of that. Dalton had found grace in the shadows.

The End

I appreciate your help... Since I am new author, getting the word out about *Grace In The Shadows* has been a bit of a challenge. If you enjoyed the book, would you mind leaving a review on Amazon? I would really appreciate it. Be sure to enter my name in the search engine as there are two books by this title. Thank you!

WHAT I LEARNED WRITING THIS BOOK

GRACE IN THE SHADOWS is my first work of fiction. I chose a church setting to display the theme of brokenness but actually brokenness can be found wherever there are human beings.

This story could be anyone's story, especially those who struggle with childhood wounds. They usually show up when we become adults and especially when we attempt to get close to God. The Lord has an amazing way of shining His light on our cuts and bruises.

Similar to Dalton Baxter, who as a pastor never understood the father heart of God, many of us, likewise, fail to appreciate this amazing reality. Instead, as new Christians, we hop on the performance treadmill, thinking we can earn His approval. Unfortunately, many injured kids in grown up bodies are still trying to figure out why our earthly dads never doted on us, held us on their laps, or gave us butterfly kisses. It is within that prism that we often see God. So we work harder. God seems like the dad who raised us. Unpredictable. Angry. With high expectations we will never meet no matter how hard we try.

Then when life becomes too difficult (as it does for everyone), we seek comfort from drugs, food, workaholism, pornography, alcohol, and even religion. And then after engaging in such behaviors, we are slammed with guilt. It's then we become desperate, making promises we will never be able to keep. If we abuse these passing pleasures long enough, undesirable patterns can be carved into our brains, forming pathways of thinking that are hard to change. Breaking addictive thinking and behavior is as hard as redirecting the mighty Colorado River that serpentines through the Grand Canyon.

Is there hope? Are we destined to stay stuck?

No. Jesus emptied Himself of His deity and came and dwelt among us. The key to "unstuckness" is to surrender to His love. Completely. Realizing that you have absolutely NOTHING to bring to the table except belief in what He has done for us. Giving up on self effort and our striving to pull-ourselves-up-by-our-bootstraps is not easy. For many of us, God is a last resort, when we find ourselves in trouble.

In 1995, songwriter Eric Bazilian, wrote a pop tune called, *One Of Us*. The lyrics were a bit odd, describing God as "one of us" and how He rides a bus and is a slob like us. You might think the words even border on blasphemy, but actually they are quite profound.

God did become one of us. The songwriter threads this theme throughout his song. It tells a story of God's friendship with ordinary men and women, who travel in buses instead of Jaguars.

In 2014 my family went through a very hard trial. There were days I wasn't sure I'd make it. During that time, I found this verse to be so comforting: *What is bruised and bent, He will not break; He will not blow out a smoldering candle.* Isaiah 42:3. God never beats us down when we are low. In fact, He meets us on the floor. It is here we discover a deeper grace than we ever imagined. It is here we find grace in the shadows.

Karon Ruiz
www.graceintheshadows.com

ACKNOWLEDGMENTS

To my husband and best friend, Armando. We've walk through the fire together and survived. Only because of Jesus. We held on to the hand that would not let us go. Thank you for choosing me to walk with you through this wild adventure called, "life". Thank you for your love and support as I devoted hours to writing this book. I love you.

To my children: Natalie Meyer, Bethany Nasont, Amanda D'Amico, and Luke Ruiz. I am blessed to be your mother. Each of you holds a piece of my heart. There are no words adequate to describe how you have enriched my life.

To my sister, Elizabeth Conkle (Beth), who walked my husband and myself through the hardest season of our lives. We love you, Sis!

To the A-Team: Alan Meyer, Adam Nasont and Andrew D'Amico. I could have not have asked for better husbands for my girls. I thank God for each of you.

To my grandchildren, eight little reasons I enjoy life more these days: from the Meyer family: Elijah, David, Matthew and Emma Grace.* From the Nasont family: Daisy, Pearl and Charity. Our latest little addition from the D'Amico family, is Andrew Michael III, due in April, 2022. The best part of getting old are grandchildren!

*To Emma Grace: As you get older, you might wonder why your Mimi was the only one in the family who called you "Grace." Besides one of the character's names, an amazing theme of Grace is woven throughout this book. When you learn a life of Grace, your life will never be the same.

To my sisters in Christ: Jenny Vanderhoof, Mary Siemens, Cathy Crumley, Nancy Breckenridge, Barbara Mertz, Rocky Cleary, Ralaine Fagone, Margaret Licon and Jan Coyne. Thank you for letting me laugh with you, cry with you, and pray with you. You are kindred spirits and true friends.

To ten dear writers: Susie Bessinger, Toni Weymouth, Carrie Padgett, Terell Byrd, Ralaine Fagone, Twyla Smith, Elizabeth Hiett, Sheri Humphreys, Phyllis Brown, and Bethany Paige. Week after week, I developed my craft in this safe and accepting environment. I couldn't have done this without you!

I wish to acknowledge my pastor, Father Carlos Raines, who gave me a wealth of knowledge about the liturgical style of worship. Father Carlos was my go-to guy for High Church. Thank you, Father Carlos, for your love and support through a very dark, yet redemptive time in my life. Thank you--Emmanuel Anglican Church family for being a "safe" place to heal.

I am grateful for the "grace" writings of Wayne Jacobsen, Dr. Andy Woods, Henri Nouwen, Andrew Farley and others who have been traveling companions along my journey of grace. Similar to Dalton Baxter, I too, struggle with a performance-based life. These authors have given me great insight into the truth of the Gospel. During the Covid shutdown I discovered some amazing online video friends: Barry Scarbrough, Gregg Jackson, Pastor Tim Henderson, Lisa Boyce (Watchwoman 65), Pastor J. D. Farag, Pastor Jack Hibbs, Pastor Tom Hughes, Dr. Andy Woods and others who taught me that **Jesus + Nothing = Salvation**.

Thank you Bethany Shumate, a writer in her own right, my neighbor and dear friend of over thirty years, who muddled through my first drafts with red pen in hand. You encouraged me to keep going when I wanted to quit.

I cannot forget Alisha Lamp, a recovering addict, who helped me to understand opiate addiction, especially with OxyContin. God has done an amazing redemptive work in her life. She is currently helping other addicts as a substance abuse counselor as she earns a Bachelors Degree in Social Work at Fresno Pacific University.

Made in the USA
Monee, IL
17 January 2023